Blood of the Reich

ALSO BY WILLIAM DIETRICH

FICTION

The Barbary Pirates

The Dakota Cipher

The Rosetta Key

Napoleon's Pyramids

The Scourge of God

Hadrian's Wall

Dark Winter

Getting Back

Ice Reich

FONFICTION

On Puget Sound

Natural Grace

Northwest Passage

The Final Forest

Blood of the Reich

A Novel

William Dietrich

An Imprint of HarperCollinsPublishers

HarperCollins books may be purchased for educational, business, or sales promotional use. For information please write: Special Markets Department, HarperCollins Publishers, 10 East 53rd Street, New York, NY 10022.

FIRST HARPERLUXE EDITION

HarperLuxe™ is a trademark of HarperCollins Publishers

Library of Congress Cataloging-in-Publication Data is available upon request.

ISBN: 978-0-06-201796-3

11 12 13 14 ID/OPM 10 9 8 7 6 5 4 3 2 1

To Holly, once more

The chief task of the Tibet expedition was political and military, not scientific. Details may not be revealed.

—REICH PROPAGANDA MINISTER JOSEPH GOEBBELS, IN A MEMO TO GERMAN NEWSPAPERS, 1940

My ambition is to see all of physics reduced to a formula so elegant and simple that it will easily fit on the front of a T-shirt.

—PHYSICIST LEON LEDERMAN, 1993

Author's Note

This novel is inspired by a 1938 Nazi expedition to Tibet, its purpose debated to this day. The story is also based on a real quest. The complex philosophic tradition that gave rise to the Nazi Party included a speculative Vril Society and, in the 1930s, reports of a Wahrheitsgesellschaft, or Society for Truth, which sought Vril to power new machines. Heinrich Himmler's Ahnenerbe, an SS research organization, existed as described. Himmler's castle at Wewelsburg can be visited. The Tibetan legend of Shambhala is real. String theory, dark matter, and dark energy are all part of the theoretical framework of modern physics.

Blood of the Reich

1

Firirst day of spring, and pregnant with the same expectancy that gripped Kurt Raeder at his unexpected summons from Reichsführer-SS Heinrich Himmler. The Prussian sky was cold, ragged sunlight dappling the German capital with that glitter atop iron that promised an end to winter. So might Himmler be the pagan sun to part the clouds of Raeder's stalled career. So might Raeder win his own expedition.

"We have read with interest your books on Tibet," the summons stated. With that simple missive the explorer had been yanked out of the ennui of his university teaching and the gloom of his wife's death, the opportunity like the twin lightning bolts of the SS Rune.

As Raeder walked from the U-Bahn into the heart of Nazi power, Berlin seemed to share his anticipation. The city was its habitual gray, buds swollen but little green on the trees yet. The paving was bright from a night's rain, however, and the capital seemed poised, purposeful, like one of the new steel tanks that had waited on the border for the *Anschluss* with Austria just nine days before. Now the two nations were united in a single German Reich, and once more public apprehension about a Nazi gamble had turned to excitement bright as the red swastika banners, vivid as a wound. All the world was waiting to see what Germany would do next. All Germany was waiting to see what *Hitler* would do next. His New Order was improbably succeeding, and on Wilhelm-Strasse, marble blocks and columns were stacked to the sky where the *Führer*'s imposing Chancellery was rising. Speer had promised completion in less than a year, and workers scrambled across the pile like frenzied ants. People watched, with pride.

Raeder secretly liked the theatricality of his black SS uniform and the medieval ritual of SS indoctrination. It meant brotherhood, the satisfaction of being one of the chosen. Entry into the new German knighthood in 1933, suggested by a politician friend, had been a way to establish Aryan ancestry and win a measure of grudging deference in a university system glacial in its advancements. But while appointments had come quicker with the exodus of the Jews, Raeder's brief fame had not solidified into promotion.

University intellectuals were snobbish toward the Nazis. At school, Raeder had mostly avoided the costume, preferring to blend in with high starched collar and restricting tie through years of brief celebrity, dull instruction, and finally private tragedy.

But now the *Reichsführer SS* had somehow taken notice. Here was the hinge of Raeder's life. So the young professor had put on the *Schutzstaffel* uniform with its runic insignia, both proud and self-conscious. When his faculty colleague Gosling spied him from a café and joked about it, the zoologist managed the good humor to shrug.

"Even scholars have to eat."

Life, the Nazis preached, was struggle.

Raeder knew he cut a fine SS figure. Brown hair a shade too dark to be ideal, perhaps, but handsome and fit from his explorations: erect, wiry, what a German youth might wish to be, the new man, the Aryan prototype. Crack shot, alpinist, university scholar, hunter, author, and scientist for the Third Reich. Lotte's death had not been publicized, out of deference to his achievements. His self-doubt he kept to himself.

Almost unconsciously, Berliners swerved around his uniform on the crowded Wilhelm-Strasse, a caution he accepted as normal. The SS was not to be loved, Himmler had preached. But Untersturmführer Kurt Raeder, adventurer! His resolute gaze had been in magazines. Women swept by him and peeked.

Pedestrians thinned as he walked past the sterile, massive headquarters of Göring's new Air Ministry, the power of the Luftwaffe implied by its modernist bulk. And then thinned still more as he turned left onto Prinz-Albrecht-Strasse and arrived at Number 8, the most notorious address in Nazi Germany. Here was the home of the Reich Security Ministry, which included the SS and Gestapo. Next door was Number 9, the Prinz-Albrecht-Palais Hotel, also subsumed by the growing security bureaucracy. To Raeder's eye the home of the police was a more inviting structure than the plain severity of Göring's headquarters. With classical arched entry and Renaissance styling, the SS buildings harkened back to the more refined nineteenth century. Only the black-clad sentries who flanked the door hinted at its new purpose.

There were rumors of Gestapo cells in the basement. There were always rumors, everywhere, of the very worst things. This was good, Raeder believed. Menace promised security to those who followed the rules. None could deny the Nazis had brought order out of chaos. While the democracies were flailing, the totalitarian models—Germany, Italy, Spain, Japan—were on the rise.

This building was the fist of the future. Raeder's future.

There was a hush inside, like a church. A grand stairway with thick balustrade, steps carpeted in red plush like a movie palace, led up a flight to a vaulted entry hall. The only decorations were three hanging swastika flags and busts of Hitler and Göring. Public depictions of Himmler were rare; his power was his air of mystery. Bare wooden benches as uncomfortable as pews lined one side of the waiting area, glacial light filtering in from arched, frosted windows. At the far end three steps led to another entry (like an altar, Raeder thought, continuing the church analogy) with black-clad guards presiding instead of black-robed priests. Himmler had modeled his elite on the Jesuits, and SS zeal on the discipline of the Inquisition.

Raeder's credentials were checked and he was admitted to a more private reception area, the offices beyond barricaded by a massive counter of dark-stained oak, stout as a dam. Now a more thorough check, this time by a blond-headed Nordic guard of the type the SS put on its posters. The officer scrutinized his insignia skeptically.

"An *Untersturmführer* to see the *Reichsführer?*"

Raeder showed the letter that had summoned the SS lieutenant from his residence in the respectable Wilmersdorf district, the apartment haunted now since Lotte's death. "The *Reichsführer* expects all ranks to serve."

The comment drew no reaction from a man with the expressiveness of a robot. "Wait."

The explorer stood stiffly as the orderly spoke into a telephone and then returned it to its cradle. The guard didn't bother to look at Raeder again.

Long minutes passed. Raeder could hear the faint clack of heels on tile, the cricket-murmur of typewriter keys and code machines, the rumble of wooden file drawers sliding out and slamming home. Each muffled ring of distant phone was answered before it could jangle a second time. All was whispered, as if the ministry building had been selected to absorb sound. Was noise from the basement muted, too? The colors were institutional green and cream, the lights a somber yellow.

"This way, Professor Raeder."

Another SS officer, a *Sturmbanführer*, thicker and pinker, briskly led him into the maze of corridors beyond. They wound one way and another, climbed a flight of stairs, and wound again. Raeder was (perhaps deliberately) lost. The office doors they passed were shut, shapes moving behind obscured glass. The few people in the hallways were male, hurried, boots drumming, conversation a murmur. The walls were blank. Floors gleamed. The calm efficiency, the monkish concentration, the paper-and-glue smell of a library . . . it was admirable and disquieting.

Then more SS guards as strapping as Vikings snapped to attention, a double door swung open, and they came to a high-ceilinged anteroom paneled in beech. Sentries checked Raeder for weapons and scrutinized his identification once again. No one smiled or spoke more than the minimum. It was a wordless play, the anteroom dim, windowless. He was in the middle of a vast hive.

A knock on a side door, an answering buzz, and he was ushered through.

Raeder expected another corridor, but instead found himself in a modest painted office, with a lower ceiling than in the anteroom outside. A single window looked out on a courtyard, the wall it faced blank stone. No one from outside could look in. There was a large but plain desk, left over from some Prussian ministry, and three leather chairs in front of it. Behind sat the second most powerful man in Germany.

Himmler looked up from a manila file and gave Raeder an owlish blink. With round spectacles, receding chin, and narrow shoulders, the *Reichsführer* SS was nothing like his praetorians outside. In fact, he resembled a bank clerk or schoolmaster. He had a thin mustache, pale skin, and white, fastidious, womanly hands. His hair was shaved close to the skull above his ears in the dull helmet shape of Prussian fashion.

A much fiercer portrait of the *Führer* looked down on them with burning zeal: that shock of black hair, that punctuating mustache.

The office was otherwise absent of decoration. There were no personal pictures or mementos, just a wall of books, many of them old, leather-bound, and cracked. Raeder couldn't read the faded titles. The *Reichsführer's* desk was as neat as that of an accountant, stacks of files with colored tabs precisely squared and ranked. Either this was not Himmler's regular office or the *Reichsführer* had no need of the baronial opulence of a Hermann Göring. The abstention was eerie.

Himmler closed the folder and turned it so Raeder could discern his own name and picture.

"Sit."

The zoologist did so, sinking into a chair. Its legs had been trimmed so that he almost squatted, looking up at Himmler. The *Reichsführer* smiled thinly, as if to relax his guest, but the chilliness simply reinforced the man's power. There was something oddly vacant about the personality he projected, as if Raeder were meeting with a facade.

Then Himmler abruptly leaned forward in a disconcertingly intense way, with a predatory glare like an insect, eyes obscured behind the reflection of the glasses, purpose ignited as if with a match.

"*Untersturmführer*," the security minister began without preamble, folding his hands on Raeder's folder, "do you believe in the importance of blood?"

2

Seattle, United States
September 4, Present Day

H e was cute, he was checking her out, and he was
a frozen foods guy.

Rominy Pickett believed a man's character could be
divined by his location in the supermarket, a method at
least as reliable as the signs of the zodiac. She usually
dismissed males spotted in the beer-and-chips aisle,
on the theory they might represent the man-child-slob
archetype in need of too much reform. Those in stock
foods she suspected to be conservative and dull: only a
Republican would buy canned peas. The wine section
was more promising (she supposed that marked her a
bit of a snob, favoring wine over beer), and fruits and
vegetables were also possible. She didn't need a veg-
etarian, but a man who thought about his greens and

took time to cook them might be thoughtful and slow about other things as well.

The bread aisle was a place to find solid whole-wheat types, but too many already wore wedding rings. Picnic supplies suggested an outdoorsman, while intellect could be gauged by where a guy planted himself on the magazine aisle: Was he browsing *The Economist* or *Truck Trend*?

But spices, condiments, and wine were best, Rominy believed, suggesting a fellow open to detail, experimentation, and taste.

Admittedly, this screening was far from perfect, given the tendency of grocery hunks to move from one aisle to another. But then the zodiac was open to interpretation, too. Her criterion was at least as reliable, she maintained to her friends, as the arch fiction encountered on Internet dating sites.

Frozen food was a problem. The likelihood of meeting bachelors rose here, given the stacks of entrees aimed at singles. But the freezer cases also implied haste, microwaving, even (could you read this much into a grocery cart?) a certain lack of ambition. Defrosting was too easy.

True, *she* was in the frozen foods aisle, too, with Lean Cuisine Cheddar Potatoes and Broccoli and a pint of Häagen-Dazs. But this was about prospective life partners, not Rominy's own singleton existence as software publicist. She'd achieved a bachelor's in communication, a gray forty-square-foot cubicle with industrial carpet and underpowered PC, two longish relationships broken off well short of real commitment, and personal resolve not to settle for competent mediocrity. Yet nothing ever *happened*. Grim global news, limping economy, girlfriends who only quipped, men who only wanted to hang out.

And shopping at Safeway. For one.

She was almost *thirty*.

Not that old, she reminded herself. Not nowadays. She was due for promotion soon. She was due for things to happen.

And yes, cute frozen foods guy was glancing again. Rominy caught herself instinctively and embarrassingly flipping her brunette hair as she imagined a thousand things about him: that his lingering by the pizza case made him interested in Italian food and Renaissance art, that the way his left foot with trail shoes rested on the shopping cart gave him the athletic stance of a mountain biker or rugby player, that the pen in his shirt pocket announced not nerd-with-grocery-list but poet prepared for spontaneous inspiration. Unruly surfer blond hair, icy blue eyes, an intriguing scar on the chin: how delicious if it had been from reckless danger! (Probably a juvenile skateboard accident.) And there was a hint of a muscular physique under the denim shirt. Yes, Rominy was a regular Sherlock in the way she could scope out the human male at a glance. Too bad if the scrutiny took them aback—and damn them if they did too much of the same to her.

What *she* wanted was to undress their souls.

He wasn't approaching, however, just looking. Too much looking, in fact. Evaluating her with a curious, hesitant stare that was anything but coy, flirtatious, or even leering. He simply regarded her like a curious specimen. Creepy, Mr. Frozen Foods Guy. Or boring. Get a life.

On to the condiments! Rominy pushed her cart two aisles down and pondered the advance in civilization represented by squeeze bottles of ketchup. Her ambition was to invent something simple and practical, like the paper clip, retire to the beach, and try Proust or Pynchon again. Master Sudoku. Train for the Iron Man. Open an animal shelter. Build a kayak. Figure out her camera.

But then Frosty the Snowman idled into view, leaning on his own cart like a handsome cowboy over a saddle horn, oblivious to whatever might be melting on his metal mesh. Still looking but not doing. Shy or stalker? Not worth it to find out. Maybe she read too much chick lit, but she wanted a man who showed confident initiative. Who came up and said something funny.

So she wheeled around and took a quick dash to the feminine products aisle, territory guaranteed to ward off unwanted males the way garlic and crucifix could deter vampires. Rominy should never have returned his glance in the first place, but how could you know? She'd camp here until the lurker had time to move away.

But no, he'd peeked down the aisles from the broad corridor at the back of the store and tracked her to this new refuge. Now he turned his cart into terra incognita and, looking questioningly at her, mouth opening like a fish, hopelessly uncertain what his first line should be. Next to the tampons? Did she know this dude? No. Why was he trailing her? Why hadn't he said anything? He wasn't just checking her out. He was *watching*.

So she pivoted and squeezed behind a middle-aged shopper who had her cart nearly athwart the aisle in that worst-of-Safeway rudeness. Now Mrs. Dumbo could unintentionally run interference while Rominy headed for the cash register. The fast-checkout lane, eight-item limit be damned.

Escape! But, no, Mr. Frosty appeared again, the front of his cart cutting in her direction like the prow of a battleship, his look anxious and his pace quicker. Would he make a scene? Where was pepper spray, or self-defense kickboxing training, when she needed it? Or was this klutz just socially inept, like so many men?

Calm, Rominy. Just another of your countless admirers.

As if.

But then his jacket opened slightly and she gave a start. There was something black on his hip.

Let the ice cream melt. She abandoned her cart, squeezed by the rump of another overfed matron tapping password numbers into a debit card reader, and headed for the door. Sorry, Safeway. No sale.

Rominy's experience (which included more than a few dead-end dates as excruciating as an IRS audit) was that intriguingly eccentric men turned out to be . . . weird. Politeness only encouraged them. Avoidance was a mercy.

Nor could she call for help.

Please, a man with a grocery cart is looking at me.

But instinct screamed that something was wrong.

Rominy had dropped some overdue bills in the mailbox at the lot's outer limits, so her car was parked a good fifty yards away. The vehicle was her pride and joy, a silver 2011 MINI Cooper scrubbed bright as a new quarter, suddenly as distant as a football goalpost.

It had taken the trade of her ancient Nissan, a diversion of funds that should have gone into her 401(k), and the commitment to four years of monthly payments to buy the runabout, but my, how she loved its cuteness and handling. Now it represented refuge. She knew she was probably hyperventilating about Abominable Snowman, but she'd never had a grocery guy track her relentlessly as a cruise missile without first attempting a friendly hi.

"Miss!"

He'd come out of the store after her. Rominy quickened her pace toward her car. This clumsy come-on would make a snarky text message for her girlfriends.

"Wait!" Footsteps. He was starting to run, fast.

Okay. Get in the car, lock the doors, start the engine, engage the transmission, crack the window, and *then* see who this lunatic was. If harmless, it would be a story to tell the grandchildren.

So she ran, too, purse banging on her hip, low heels hobbling her speed.

"Hey!"

His footsteps were accelerating like a sprinter. Wasn't there anyone in the lot who would interfere? Run, Rominy, run!

Her MINI Cooper beckoned like a castle keep.

And then without warning the creep hit her from behind, sending her sprawling. Pavement scraped on hands and knees. Pain lanced, and she opened her mouth to scream. Then his weight crashed fully on top of her, a body slam that knocked out her wind, and the bastard clamped his hand over her mouth.

This is it, she thought. She was going to be raped, suffocated, and murdered in the broad daylight of a Safeway parking lot. Frozen food guys, it seemed, were psychopaths.

But then there was a boom, the ground heaved, and a pulse of heat rolled over them. Her eardrums felt punched. She lay pinned, in shock. A cloud of smoke puffed out, shrouding them in fog, and then there was the faint rattle of metal pieces clanging down all around them.

Her beloved MINI Cooper had blown up. She still had thirty-nine months of payments, and its shredded remains were bonging down around her like the debris of some overextended Wall Street bank.

Her assailant put his mouth to her ringing ear and she winced at what he might do.

But he only whispered.

"I just saved your life."

3

ational Socialism is based, Herr Raeder, on the inevitable conclusion one must take from modern biological science: we are locked in Darwinian evolutionary struggle." Himmler took the tone of pedantic lecturer adopted by men who have risen so high that none dare disagree. "Just as species vie with one another in nature, and individuals struggle within those species, so are the human races locked in eternal conflict. This is the lesson of all history, is it not?"

Raeder knew this interview could be a path to promotion. "So the *Führer* teaches, *Reichsführer.*" He felt like he was squatting, looking up at the big desk.

"The Aryan race has continually been in competition with the Slavic, the Asiatic, and the Negroid,"

Himmler said. "Rome was invincible until it allowed itself to be polluted by the inferiors it conquered, and then was defeated by our ancestor Arminius in ancient Germany. And the Germanic tribes were invincible as long as they kept to themselves behind the Rhine, and vulnerable once they became mongrelized. Ultimately, there can only be one evolutionary winner, and the Aryan can win only through purity of blood. It is about breeding, *Untersturmführer*—breeding. Take it from a chicken farmer."

The dogma was nothing Raeder hadn't heard in the tedious SS classes that half the membership skipped—the men wanted action, not eccentric pedantry—but the reference to chicken farming startled the explorer. There were jokes about Himmler's brief unhappy experiments with animal husbandry, but he'd never dreamed the *Reichsführer* would bring up this past. "Your scholarship is reflected in the teachings of the *Schutzstaffel*," he managed.

Himmler's smile was thin as a razor. "You think I don't know the disparagement of my agricultural background? I know everything, about everyone." He tapped the files. For a horrible moment Raeder thought the reference was directly to him, and he furiously wracked his brain for when he might have mocked the head of the SS. Was this meeting a prelude to a concentration camp?

"I hear all the jokes," Himmler went on. "About our *Führer*, about me, about Göring, about the lot. Do you think this makes me angry?"

Raeder was beginning to sweat. "I swear I've never . . ."

"Listen to me, *Untersturmführer*. The powerful act, and the powerless make jokes about them. Better to be the superior who is the butt of a joke than its minion teller, trust me. This is how society functions. This is how *life* functions. Struggle." He held Raeder's gaze. "Yes, I raised chickens and learned life is breed against breed, and the holy mission of the SS is to purify our race and raise mankind to a new level. Our mission is scientific. It is mystical. It is evolutionary. And when we're done, the planet will be a utopia unknown since the ancient days of Ultima Thule when our ancestors came down from the stars." He nodded, as if affirming the point often enough would ensure its truth.

Raeder finally managed a shaky breath. "Why are you telling me this, *Reichsführer*?"

"Because you've been called to duty by God as I have," Himmler said calmly. "I, to purify. You, to apply your expertise in Tibet toward the National Socialist cause. You've been there twice, have you not?"

"Yes." He exhaled, realizing he was here for his experience, not some indiscreet remark. "Two exploratory zoological and anthropological missions."

"Hunting. With a rifle."

"To collect specimens."

"A Mauser M98, .375 Magnum, on expeditions with American funding and led by Dr. Benjamin Hood of the American Museum of Natural History in New York." Himmler was reading from the folder. "Four months from Nepal to the Himalayas in 1930, and six from China to eastern Tibet in 1934. You wrote a book, *High Himalaya*, and used classification and preparation of the bird and animal skins to win your doctorate from the Berlin Academy. Adventure combined with science, and notoriety before you were twenty-five. An alpinist as well, with some notable first ascents. An exemplar, one might say, of the new Germany."

"I had some good fortune."

"And the swastika is an ancient symbol of good fortune in Tibet, is it not?"

"Yes, *Reichsführer*. You see it everywhere."

"Have you ever wondered why?"

"An Eastern invention, I suppose."

"Or an Aryan invention, and a connection between our Aryan ancestors and the inhabitants of Tibet. It is a symbol of the god Thor. Fifty years ago Guido von List made it a symbol of the Thule Society's neopagan movement. A key to our racial past in the high Himalayas, we could speculate."

"You think the Tibetans are Aryans?"

"Their royalty, perhaps, are our cousins. There are theories." Himmler bent to the folder and summarized its contents. "Invited to hunt with Air Minister Göring, lectures in London and Heidelberg, a lovely young wife"—the *Reichsführer* paused, looking at Raeder over the rim of his glasses—"who you killed."

Now the sweat again. "Accidentally." He felt continually off-balance in this interview. Was that purposeful?

"Bitter tragedy. Hunting, was it not?"

"I was swinging a shotgun on a flight of ducks and stumbled on another loaded weapon on the bottom of our boat. It went off. Lotte died instantly." That was the official story. His tone was hollow, remembering the horror, guilt, and relief. Her blood had pooled to the floorboards. Her brains had spattered the water. He'd felt trapped by Lotte's family, which had grown suspicious of his needs. And now? "It was inexcusably clumsy."

No, it wasn't. Did the Kripo, the criminal police, suspect?

"The kind of cruel memory that can only be expunged by new experience," Himmler said briskly, flipping a page. "By returning, perhaps, to Tibet, but this time without the Americans. Returning with men from my organization's Ancestral Heritage Research and Teaching Society, the Ahnenerbe, which studies our Aryan past. Are you hard enough, committed enough, to lead an SS team there, Raeder?"

The zoologist swallowed. Here was what he'd hoped for, dreamed of, now offered despite—or was it because of?—the bitter memory of Lotte's death. "If called on by the Fatherland, *Reichsführer*."

Himmler snapped the folder shut. "You have ample reason to desire a change of pace, to forget the past, to put all your energies into a mission for the Reich. Germany has a bright future, Raeder. If you succeed, it will make any lingering questions about the end of your marriage irrelevant. If you fail . . ."

He swallowed. "I understand." His heart was pounding, which annoyed him. Control.

"Did you have apprehension about today's visit, *Untersturmführer*?"

"Any man would be nervous at meeting so august a personality . . ."

"Any man would be frightened." Himmler waved his hand to acknowledge the obvious. He enjoyed the fear, Raeder realized. He drew strength from it. He reveled in the black uniforms. Himmler had longed to serve in World War I, missing by a year. "And yet tell me, Raeder, am I really that intimidating? I, a man who only wants to secure the future of the German Reich?"

"I appreciate . . ."

"I am direct because I have to be. I mentioned the unfortunate death of your wife because I don't like things unsaid, sticking to the corners of normal conversation. I do unpleasant things for our *Führer*, blunt things, direct things, so that he can fulfill his destiny without their burden. He sees what ordinary men cannot. He leads our purification."

"The *Führer* is a remarkable man." He felt like Hitler's picture was looking down on them.

"'Why Tibet?' you wonder. Does the chicken farmer Himmler want more bird skins from Asia?" He gave that thin smile. "No, more than that. Much more, Raeder, more than you've ever dreamed in your life. So I want you to visit me in my SS headquarters near Padenborn, the new center of the world."

"Center of the world?"

"I'm inviting you to be my guest at Wewelsburg Castle. I want you to understand the full meaning of your mission in the place I'm making the true heart of our organization. Bring your maps of Tibet, Raeder."

"And my goal, *Reichsführer*?"

"To help conquer the world. Bring your maps, in one week's time."

4

Seattle, United States
September 4, Present Day

Frozen foods guy rolled off Rominy and hauled her upward with arms around her rib cage, breasts lifted, delicacy ignored. "I tried to warn you but you kept moving away," he said. "I feared they'd try this."

"What happened?"

"You almost died."

A contact had popped out. People were beginning to shout and run. In the distance she could hear sirens. Christ, it was downtown Baghdad. Her head, hands, and knees hurt and the bastard had just about crushed her torso. Her purse had spilled. "Who are you?" Rominy's voice was thick.

"At the moment, the only friend you have." He pulled on her arm. "Come on."

She shook loose. "Let go of me!"

He grabbed her again, persistent and impatient. His fingers hurt as they clamped. "Come *on*, if you don't want us both to die!"

"My purse."

Holding her by one arm with an iron grip, he stooped to scoop things into her handbag and brought it up, tucking it under his arm. "Good catch. We don't want to give them more information than they already have." Then, dragged by his pull, she began to stagger away from the wreckage of her car. People hung back, bewildered. Someone's cart had spilled and bright oranges spotted the pavement. The air didn't just have a smoky smell, it had a chemical *taste*, and she realized her teeth ached from clenching. Her assailant, or savior, was pushing her toward a banged-up Ford pickup that was nothing like her late, lamented dream mobile. She clutched her arms to her aching torso. All her energy had been sapped by the shock of the explosion.

"Are you abducting me?" she asked dully.

"I told you, I'm *rescuing* you." He shoved her into the cab, pushing on her butt without apology, and the door slammed shut. She looked at it foggily, trying to decide if she should flee. Her body felt sluggish.

"Rescuing me from what?" she asked as he climbed in the driver's side.

He threw her purse into her lap. "Don't you mean from whom?" He started the engine. The pickup was a stick shift like her MINI Cooper. Everything was a dream.

"Wait." She looked outside. Blue lights were coming fast. "Police!"

He pulled away from the curb. "They can't help." He sounded grim.

The pickup swerved to let a fire truck pass and then accelerated. It was old enough to have locking knobs on the door by the window, but hers was missing. Had he locked her in? She tried the door handle and her heart sank. The lever jiggled uselessly. This was her worst nightmare. She was an idiot, a victim.

"Listen, I know you're freaked out," Frozen Foods said. "I am, too. I didn't know they'd go this far. This whole thing is a royal mess. I just want to give us a little space in case the skinheads are hanging. Look behind. Are we being followed?"

Rominy looked out the dirty rear cab window. There was a gun rack behind: classic rural Washington. Was her rescuer, or kidnapper, from some gawd-awful backwoods *Deliverance* den like Twisp or Mossyrock? There was a chrome toolbox that spanned the width of the pickup bed, and surely there'd be a chain saw inside. Or maybe Leatherface here kept it back home in his creepy cabin.

"How would I know?" She had a headache.

"Any tough-looking guys with shaved heads?"

She looked. Following windshields seemed opaque. No, there was a driver . . . but with big hair, as puffed as a TV anchoress doing a storm report.

"No."

Her head was beginning to clear, and she was in the one place she'd vowed never to be, locked in a vehicle with a stranger hurtling toward god-knew-where. She had no weapon, no clue, no . . . wait.

She *did* have her purse again. Frozen Foods guy had made a mistake. Hallelujah. Cell phone, car keys— now useless, she realized with sorrow—Tic-Tacs, a tissue packet, lipstick she rarely used, ChapStick she did, compact with mirror, business cards of her own, business cards of boring software clients she'd immediately forgotten and had failed to file, a packaged condom with an embarrassingly old shelf date, a wallet with thirty-two dollars (she had been going to get twenty more on her debit card at Safeway), forgotten souvenir wristband from a Dave Matthews concert, glasses . . .

She popped out her other contact and put on the spectacles. Her sight hadn't been lost after all. Somewhere in there was a comb with a wicked pointed handle. Nail clippers. Loose earrings with a tip; she had inserted studs for shopping and brought along the others in case Erica texted about Happy Hour.

A veritable arsenal.

Frozen Foods glanced at her. "You wear glasses."

"Duh."

"They look nice."

She regarded him with disbelief. "You've got to be kidding me."

"No, I mean . . ." He looked impatient but also somewhat intriguingly frustrated. Was he frightened, too? "Look, we're going to be friends, okay?"

"The pickup door won't open."

"It's an old truck."

"Stop and let me out."

"It's not safe."

"I can't even roll down the window."

"Give me a chance, Rominy." It was a plea, not a threat.

She took a breath. "Tell it to the cops." She pulled out her cell phone. How did he know her name?

"If you dial that, they'll track us."

"*Who* will track us?"

"The guys who blew up your car."

"And who are they?" Her finger was poised.

"Men who are looking into your past like I have."

"I don't have a past worth looking into."

"I'm afraid you do. I'm an investigator."

"Is *that* why you have a gun?"

"What? I don't have a gun. Wish I did, right now."

"I saw it on your waist. In the grocery store."

"This?" He pulled his jacket aside. "It's my cell phone. What, you think I'm a dick? A private eye?"

"More along the lines of a serial killer. And where's the twelve-gauge to fit into the gun rack here?"

"I'm a reporter for the *Seattle Times*. Investigative journalist with low pay, stingy budget, and an eye for a Ford pickup deal when he sees one. She's a beast when I punch the gas, though I pay for her eight cylinders at the pump. The environmental writer gives me hell." He held out his hand. "Jake Barrow. Harmless, when I'm not behind a typewriter. Or, well, terminal."

She didn't shake his hand but set her phone in her lap, still gripping it. "You tackled me like a linebacker."

"You're not the first girl to complain about my lack of finesse. Look, I'm new at this, too."

"New at what?"

"Hiding from the bad guys."

"*What* bad guys? And why are you looking into my past?" Her fist curled around her comb. How could she get out? Stab and climb over him at a stoplight, maybe. Make a scene. Holler. Anything but wait like a nitwit. Did she have the courage? Did he deserve her doubt?

He glanced, as if to seek alliance.

But then he accelerated up an on-ramp, merging into crowded Interstate 5 heading north, and took a breath, hesitating. She glanced back. The Space Needle was receding like some signpost to reality, Lake Union shimmering like a mirage.

"Because you're not really Rominy Pickett."

5

Wewelsburg Castle, Germany
March 30, 1938

Two hundred miles west of Berlin, in the Westpha-lian countryside not far from where Arminius had destroyed Varus's Roman legions in A.D. 9, a triangular sixteenth-century castle crowned a rocky outcrop above the village of Wewelsburg. The triangle's apex pointed, with less deviation than a compass needle, to true north.

"The *Reichsführer*'s Camelot," said the SS pilot who'd flown Raeder from Berlin. Bruno Halder banked the light civilian Messerschmitt and circled to give the zoologist a view. "Its reconstruction is far from complete, but there are plans the castle will be the tip of a spear-shaped complex of modern buildings. A ceremonial avenue will provide the lance's shaft. The

Spear of Destiny, inspired by the legendary lance that pierced Christ. The village will have to be relocated, of course."

"I'd not heard of this."

"The *Reichsführer* is not a show-off like Göring." Halder made the disparagement casually, secure in his own SS rank, and aimed for a nearby airfield as they dropped steeply. "Himmler's mission is veiled. No air shows, no medals. But he's far more visionary. A romantic, actually. Below you, Raeder, is the place that will someday be known as the birthplace of modern man."

"What does that mean?"

"Its Aryan future. And a crypt for its leaders. Camelot, as I said."

"Beautiful," Raeder said politely, confused but still flattered to be flying—a first—and enjoying the vista over the greening countryside. "Almost too beautiful for the *Schutzstaffel*."

"It has its own austerity, as you'll see. The castle even has a *Hexenkeller*, a witches' cellar. They burned more than fifty witches down there in the seventeenth century. Not so long ago, really." He cut the power and the plane bounced as it landed.

It was dusk when a staff car delivered them to the castle gate. The village of Wewelsburg was subdued, its streets empty, house lights veiled behind lace curtains. Raeder sensed people peeking at them as they drove past. When they got out of the auto at the ramp across a dry moat, the only sound was of jackdaws crowing. Then German shepherd guard dogs on chains sent up cacophonous barking, their teeth phosphorescent in the gloom.

The gate wood was blond, varnished, and obviously new, carved with swastikas and the twin lightning-bolt runes of the SS. Sentries stood like statues and torches burned like a medieval dream. It was a Renaissance castle, meaning broad glass windows instead of narrow arrow slits, but most were dark. There were towers at the three corners, the southern ones domed with roofs like a homburg hat. After scrutiny by the guards, Raeder and Halder were ushered inside.

The courtyard was curiously claustrophobic, a narrow triangle with walls as sheer inside as out. At the northern apex, a fat round tower with flat roof was surrounded by scaffolding. There were lumber, planks, piles of stones, and bags of mortar.

"Modernized?" Raeder asked.

"Reimagined. The *Reichsführer* has selected it as a spiritual home for our order. A labor camp is being constructed to implement his visionary plan. Slaves have been screened to find the best craftsmen. Wewelsburg will be a capital, a Vatican, for the SS. This will be a center of scholarship for inquiries into the origins of the Germanic people and the Aryan race. There will be a planetarium at the crown of the North Tower and a crypt for Reich leadership in its cellar. Reichsführer Himmler sees across centuries, Raeder. He's a prophet."

"It is our *Führer*, Adolf Hitler, who is the prophet."

The correction was mild, professorial, but spoken with authority. They snapped to attention and wheeled. There was Himmler studying his own creation, dressed in military greatcoat, jodhpurs, and boots. He stood very straight. Since the interview in Berlin, Raeder had read about his superior. At Hitler's failed 1923 putsch, Himmler had carried the staff of the Imperial Eagle as proudly as a schoolboy.

"And I am the mystic scholar, the Merlin, of my brotherhood of knights," Himmler went on. "Our *Führer* does not share all my intellectual interests; he is a politician, a man who must wrestle with the practical and immediate. But he allows me the indulgence, the luxury, of exploring the distant past and possible future. I'm fortunate to have such a patron, am I not, Professor Raeder?"

"As are we all, *Reichsführer*."

Himmler nodded. "We live in the presence of a great man. A very great man." The spectacles caught the dim light so that Raeder once again couldn't see the *Reichsführer*'s eyes, but only hear his tone of worship. The fervor, of one powerful man for another, surprised him. He'd expect more jealousy, more doubt, but no. The zoologist was silent, not knowing what to say.

"Well," Himmler finally went on. "Thank you for visiting me in my castle."

"The honor is of course mine."

"I do not invite everyone—this is a quiet place, a secret place, until I finish it—but I'm intrigued by Tibet, *Untersturmführer*. Intrigued by what such a mysterious country might tell us. Will you join me in my study?"

"*Reichsführer*, I am bewildered by your hospitality."

Himmler smiled at the confession. "I look for men who can serve. Men who have a *need* to serve." Once more his gaze was intense, and Raeder felt it probing the recesses of his soul. The zoologist hoped his life was about to be given meaning. And, with it, salvation.

"Halder, thank you for bringing my guest. They are expecting you in the dining room." The dismissal of the pilot was plain. Halder betrayed a flicker of disappointment, clicked his heels, and left.

Then the *Reichsführer* became a temporary tour guide as he led the way, explaining how a wreck of a castle was being transformed into a showcase of

German craftsmanship. "There's been a fort on this outcrop for eons, but the present castle was built between 1603 and 1609. It was bombarded in the Thirty Years War."

"And witches in the cellar?"

"Ah, your pilot shared the folklore. Don't worry, they don't haunt the place. No more than any other vermin that is eradicated."

There was an exquisite spiral staircase, a reference library, dining rooms and canteens, and carvings that included runes and swastika-centered sun wheels, all of it a display of Teutonic carpentry. "The North Tower will have a shamanic sun wheel inlaid into its floor, and a roundtable for the twelve primary leaders of our order," the *Reichsführer* said. "My architects joke with me about King Arthur, but I am not joking. I think the modern world would benefit from some of the ceremonies of the past. In the East they believe in reincarnation, do they not, Raeder?"

"Most certainly, *Reichsführer*. Life in Tibet revolves around the next life."

"I believe it, too. I believe I'm the reincarnation of King Henry the Fowler, who fought the invading Magyars from the East a thousand years ago. Does that strike you as odd?"

"It would not surprise a Buddhist."

Himmler gave a glance to show he'd not missed that Raeder had swerved from the question. "But I believe in focusing on *this* life. We're reincarnated to fulfill a purpose. Come to my study where we can speak alone."

That room was in the West Tower and thus circular, and had a stone fireplace, bearskin rug, and wooden furniture. The walls were mostly bare, showing the same austerity that had been present in Himmler's office in Berlin. Despite his rehearsed warmth and nostalgic architecture, there was a vacuum to the man's surroundings. Lending the only color was a bowl of fruit.

The *Reichsführer* invited his guest to sit and took a chair opposite. Both seats were high-backed, straight, and rather uncomfortable. SS lightning bolts had been stamped into the leather.

"Now, Raeder, you're familiar with the Ahnenerbe?"

"The SS research division."

"I'm sending missions all over the globe to investigate intriguing theories about the origins of our race. Iceland. Peru. National Socialism believes in drawing logical conclusions from modern science, as I told you—even if the conclusions are uncomfortable. We do not fear the truth. But we believe the German people are descended from a root, master race and that these

Aryans—us, Raeder—represent the best hope of the future evolution of humankind. Do you agree?"

"So teaches the SS."

"So teaches common sense. Do you know where mankind went wrong, *Untersturmführer*?"

Raeder was laboring again not to say the wrong thing. "Well, the Bible suggests Eve's apple." He meant it as a joke.

But Himmler remained deadly serious. He took from his belt an SS dagger, gleaming in the candlelight. The edge was feathered from repeated sharpening, and it glinted in the light. The *Reichsführer* took an apple from the bowl of fruit and sliced it neatly in two, but instead of cutting from top to bottom, he cut horizontally. When the apple was opened, each face had a pattern around the core that made a star. "Yes, the apple. Do you know what it represents?"

Raeder was silent, baffled by what he was supposed to see.

"It's the five-pointed Aryan star, the pentagram, Lucifer's star that traces the path of Venus. Not the six-pointed star of Jewish corruption. And so the apple represents knowledge. The secret powers that unify the universe. Here we see the celestial in lowly fruit. All is one." His head bobbed to confirm his own statement.

"The Jews don't want us to know. That's why they wrote that fairy story about Eden."

"Know what?"

"It wasn't Eve who led us astray, Raeder. It was, and is, the Jew. They invented a monstrous idea that goes against all natural law and reason. Do you know how they confused the world and distorted civilization?"

Raeder tried to remember if SS lectures had covered this. "By usury?"

"They invented meekness!" Himmler's voice crackled with scorn. "Here is Moses coming down from the mountain, and what does he proclaim? Thou shalt not kill? Raeder, killing is the most fundamental truth of our planet! Everything kills everything, to survive, as the strong get stronger. Struggle, ceaseless struggle. Thou shalt not steal? Nonsense. So the weak can hold on to resources they make no use of? Thou shalt not covet thy neighbor's wife? Bah. So the strong are limited in how they breed? The Jew invented a coda to weaken our species. And then the worst Jew, Jesus, took it a step further and preached that the meek shall inherit the earth. What a perversion of everyday experience. Why is this, Raeder? Why would the Jew tell such lies?"

"To preserve order?"

"No!" Himmler's palm slammed down on the fruit table, the apple halves jumping. "To weaken everyone who believed them. To weaken *us*, the Aryan, so that Jewry can control the world. Lies to blind and bind us, Raeder. Lies to make us forget the power that our Aryan ancestors once had. But now we are awakening from our long sleep. Now we are shaking off the Jewish hypnosis. We are remembering that strength by right should triumph, and that our ancestors had powers we can scarcely dream. What if such powers could be discovered? What if they have been buried in the most secret place in the world?"

"You mean Tibet."

"When a race becomes diluted, when it becomes *polluted* with miscegenation with the Jew or the Negro or the Asiatic or the feebleminded or the crippled, it weakens and devolves. It begins to slip into primitivism. But when the Aryan becomes purified, when the very best of the best breed with each other . . . well. Evolution goes in the other direction, led by what Nietzsche called the Superman. That is what Nazism is all about, Raeder. This will be our gift to our descendants. It is this, not war and monuments, that will make us immortal to history."

"But how, *Reichsführer*?"

"By expelling the Jew, of course. By sterilizing the feeble. By annihilating the deviants. By segregating the races. By encouraging the best stock to bear children. By seizing what the strong deserve, be it land or women. It's no different from weeding and breeding on the farm."

"The work of centuries."

"Perhaps the work can be accelerated." Himmler's expression was opaque.

Raeder decided not to know too much. "But what has this to do with Tibet?"

"Our ancient ancestors wandered widely. The high Tibetans have some of our noble bone structure, and there are theories that they are direct descendants— our natural cousins, if you will. Yet how to establish this? They forbid visits to their capital. The selfish British have a small mission, forced on Tibet by invasion in 1904, but otherwise that country is the most secret place in the world. It's a theocracy, ruled by a god-king lama and his temporary regent, with authority more absolute than any pope. There men live for their next life, not this one. And yet not all men, perhaps. There are legends of earlier Aryans who discovered powers since entirely forgotten— powers that could decide the fate of the world in any coming war."

"Powers in Tibet? Its wilderness seemed a backward place, *Reichsführer*. They hardly use the wheel. Only the monks are literate."

Himmler stood and restlessly moved to the fireplace. It was old, carved with Christian allegories, including one that looked like Cain smiting Abel.

"Powers that could make us gods in our own time. Herr Raeder, have you ever heard of Vril?"

"No, *Reichsführer.*"

"I'm going to tell you a secret story. And then you're going to tell your men."

"My men?"

"I'm sending knights-errant with you." He ran his hand over the carvings on the mantel. "You know of Frederick Barbarossa, unifier of Germany, Holy Roman Emperor, hero of the Crusades?"

"Every German schoolboy admires Barbarossa and his wife, Beatrix."

"He was charismatic, brave, visionary, and scholarly. A tragedy that he drowned during the Third Crusade when he was at the height of his powers. His army crumbled at his death, in 1190."

"He was buried in the Middle East, was he not?"

"*Someone* was buried there. Legends surround Barbarossa. That he sought the legendary kingdom of Prester John somewhere in the East. That he sleeps, undead, in a mountain in Germany and will emerge to restore the Fatherland to its former greatness. Some have even whispered our *Führer* is his reincarnation.

History records that the body of a man of Frederick's age was found in his armor after being swept away in a river. But what if Barbarossa did not die, but escaped?"

"I don't understand."

"What if he set out alone to seek Prester John? And what if the legend of that mythical Christian kingdom was confused and combined with one about the ancient Tibetan kingdom of Shambhala? What if, Raeder, Barbarossa found Tibet?"

"Surely that's impossible. Tibet is difficult enough to reach today. In the twelfth century, all of Islam barred the way. Deserts, mountains, wild animals, savage tribes . . ."

"Since our *Führer* became chancellor of Germany, the Nazi Party has gained access to historical records and artifacts we've sought since our beginning. We've become students of legend. We're privy to medieval secrets kept by the Catholic Church. I've become a scholar of possibility."

"You really believe Frederick Barbarossa reached Tibet?"

"I do not *believe* anything, but one thing I know. In the cathedral of Aachen, ancient seat of German emperors, was stored a curious relic. Church records show it came into the cathedral's possession some years after Frederick's death." Himmler reached inside his tunic and drew out a sealed silver tube about the size of a rifle shell. It hung from a silver chain. "This is reputed to be the blood of Barbarossa, one of the most priceless relics of German history. Hold it, Raeder."

"I hardly dare, *Reichsführer*," he said, taking the vial gingerly. "This is a great honor." *Do religious relics have any foundation in fact?* He looked at it. "Sealed since medieval times?"

Himmler was watching him gravely. "Yes."

"I'd not heard of this blood vial."

"No, it's been a closely guarded secret."

Raeder held it out. "Please take it back before I drop it."

"On the contrary, *Untersturmführer*, you're about to wear it across the most difficult terrain on earth. It's a very sturdy container, and you'll wear it on that chain, next to your heart."

Raeder stared at the vial. "Why?"

"Because the name of that artifact, for more than seven hundred years, has been 'The Shambhala Key.' By legend, it is the vital blood needed to open the gates of the secret city of Shambhala. It is the blood of the worthy, to inherit the terrible powers that lie within. And it is *that* power that would mark the real return of the spirit of Frederick Barbarossa."

6

North of Seattle, United States
September 4, Present Day

Y"ou don't think I'm Rominy Pickett?"

"I'm sorry, I don't want to shock you. But I *know* you're not."

"Then either you've kidnapped the wrong woman or you're even loonier than I thought."

Jake Barrow looked straight ahead, both hands on the wheel at ten and two, like a driving student, the pickup a careful six mph above the speed limit, just enough not to risk a ticket. He seemed to have a clear idea where he was going. The freeway north of Seattle was an artery, its cars corpuscles, the vessel walls dark evergreens. Broken overcast kept everything the habitual Northwest gray. "Look, I realize I should have broached this subject a little less dramatically," he said. "Car bombings are not the way I usually meet my sources."

"I'm not your source, Mister Investigative Reporter, if that's what you really are. I'm your victim, and you've probably committed about eighteen felonies to get me to this point. Do your editors approve your tactics?"

His lips were tight. "My editors advised me to drop the whole thing."

"Touché."

"But they're wrong."

"The lunatic creed."

"You're the biggest story of my life, and I never dreamed it would play out this way. A skinhead wannabe spilled something about a car bomb. I realized I couldn't just research any longer and had to check you out in person. Then I saw their Explorer across the parking lot near your vehicle and didn't know what else to do. It was tackle or watch you blow up." He sounded more embarrassed than triumphant. And less like a serial killer than she'd have expected. Was there a chance, however slight, that this guy wasn't totally full of bullshit and homicidal intention? If he was behind the bomb, why tackle her?

"But why would anyone—what, skinheads?—want to kill *me*?"

"Because they're Nazi knotheads who think you know a lot more than you do."

"About what?"

"A seventy-year-old secret, a fairy story, about strange powers and a lost city."

"Jake—if that's really what your name is—"

"I have a press card . . ."

"Whoopee. I'm sorry, but you're not proving your sanity here. I mean, you're getting goofier by the minute, I can't open my truck door, your own editors don't believe you, and we're almost to Everett." She held up her cell phone. "Sounds like it's time for 911."

"Wait." His look was pleading. "If the cops come and my editors get wind of this fiasco, I'm probably finished, I know it. No story, I'm trying to give answers I don't have, and you still don't know who you really are. I *will* look like a criminal, or a nut job. But if you give me a day—two days, at most, on *your* turf—you might get something that will turn your life around, I get the big scoop, and maybe the good guys even win. Maybe. But I need you to give me a chance to explain without holding that cell phone like it's another bomb. And I'm serious, the skinheads can track us with that thing."

"Why do you keep saying I don't know who I really am?"

"Have you ever heard of a man named Benjamin Hood?"

"No."

"Well, you're his heir."

"I'm *what*?" Rominy glanced at her cell phone and noticed there were no bars. In fact, there was no display at all. Of all the times to have it off. She pushed the power button. She needed a backup plan instead of trusting Mr. Jake Barrow, and it involved the Washington State Patrol.

She pushed and pushed.

Nothing happened.

"My cell won't work."

Barrow looked relieved. "A sign from God, don't you think?" He glanced in the rearview mirror. "Shit!" He slammed the accelerator and the pickup rocketed and swerved, throwing her against the door that wouldn't open. "Shit, shit, shit!" They lurched across two lanes and back, cars honking, and then hung on the rear quarter of a tanker truck, its warnings of explosive cargo spattered with mud.

"What, what!"

"Get down, it's them!" Another burst of speed and they shot ahead, pulling narrowly in front of the truck, its horn blaring. Barrow's hand, wide and powerful, grabbed Rominy's head and shoved it down on the bench seat so hard that her cheek bounced against the old vinyl, her only view his blue-jean thigh and the dirty floor of the pickup. "Stay down, they might shoot!"

She didn't dare look, imagining bullets puncturing the old truck as if it were aluminum foil. They were weaving like Road Warrior lunatics, and all Rominy's attentions were focused on trying to recall half-forgotten Hail Marys for what she was convinced were the last seconds of her life. The nuns were right, she should have gone to Confession.

"They're coming . . ."

She squeezed her eyes shut. She could hear the full-throated roar of a heavy SUV or truck and the answering whine of the old pickup. Then a pop, and a whistle of wind.

"Damn." He seemed resigned. "They're shooting."

"Please, please, stop this thing . . ."

"Cops!" He sounded exultant and their speed abruptly slackened. "They tried to keep up and the Patrol nailed them!" They swerved a final time and steadily decelerated. "Hallelujah yes, the cops are stopping them! Oh boy, they'd better get rid of that gun."

"Are the police following us, too?" she asked with hope.

"No, thank God. They're busy with skinheads." The truck's sound changed, and she sensed they'd taken an off-ramp. She was shaking in fear and confusion, humiliated at having her head almost in this bastard's lap. Then they coasted to a stop.

He put his hand on her head again. "Stay down, for a light or two."

Of course, *maybe* he'd saved her life once more. Or he was a complete schizoid. Hail Mary, what in heaven is going on? "Where are we?"

"Everett. We'll go through town to make sure we've shaken them before getting back on the freeway."

"*Please* go to the authorities." She felt defeated, exhausted, hopeless.

"I told you, the police can't help us, not yet. Though I gotta say, three cheers for the Washington State Patrol. They nailed those bastards. That's a big ticket, driving like we were. They'll have to breathalyze, the whole nine yards. I think we're safe, Rominy. At least for the next five minutes."

"I don't feel safe. I thought we were going to crash."

"I'm a better driver than that."

"It felt like Mister Toad's Wild Ride in Disneyland."

"I've done some amateur stock car." He gently touched her shoulder. "You can sit up now."

They were on an avenue that ran by Puget Sound, still heading north, a bluff with houses to their right. Rominy felt sick, and light-headed from fear. Her cheeks were wet from tears, and she was ashamed of them. Shouldn't she be braver?

"I just want it to end."

"Sorry, it's just beginning." He gave her a sympathetic look, his features strong but not unkind. "But we'll make it, you'll see. It's important, or I never would have involved you."

She groaned and noticed a draft of cool air by her neck and a thin whistling. She turned.

There was a bullet hole in the pickup's rear window and a web of radiating cracks.

7

New York, United States
September 10, 1938

The American Museum of Natural History was a castle of curiosities bordering New York's Central Park, a national junk drawer of the sensational and the educational. Depression crowds still paid their quarter to see bone hunter Barnum Brown's Tyrannosaur in the Jurassic Hall, the reconstructed Pueblo Indian village in the anthropological wing, or the speculative trip to the moon at Hayden Planetarium. There was a diorama of mountain gorillas against the volcanoes of the Belgian Congo, painted to re-create the spot where the museum's Carl Akeley had succumbed to tropical disease. In adjacent halls were Carter's mounted animals from the upper Zambezi, Inca relics from Bennett's explorations of Peruvian ruins, and stuffed birds from Burma's

Irawadi River. And there was the magnificent *bharal*, or blue sheep, brought back and mounted by the Benjamin Hood Expedition of 1934. The horned male looked eternally over a high, rolling plateau toward the distant snowy crests of the painted Himalayas, school children viewing the Roof of the World through glass.

Hood's office was in the prestigious southeast tower overlooking Central Park, just one floor below the museum's mercurial director, famed Gobi Desert explorer Roy Chapman Andrews. Hood's family had the money to finance his explorations and contribute to museum coffers, meaning that he'd been given a higher ceiling and better view. Less favored (or less rich) curators sweated in tighter, darker rooms. The favoritism made Hood feel guilty, but not enough to give the office up.

The flamboyantly self-promoting Andrews perched above them all. The museum director had led the first Dodge trucks into Mongolia and protected his dinosaur bones in shoot-outs with bandits. Since those cowboy days he'd proven to be as bad an administrator as he was good at finding bones and attracting publicity. He was erratic, demanding, and forgetful. It was no surprise, then, that Hood reacted with distrust when his boss telephoned to say he was sending down some government functionary to confer. The director had wasted Hood's time before with political errands and donor meetings that came to nothing.

"Can't see him," Hood lied. "I've got a meeting with a Rockefeller Foundation man on that Hudson Bay expedition I proposed."

"Forget Hudson Bay," Chapman said in his brusque manner. "Hudson Bay isn't happening. Even if you can afford it the rest of us can't. The Depression won't let up and our budget is bleeding. We need to gear up for next year's world's fair here in New York. You know that."

"Roy, I'm not a world's fair type of guy."

"Which is why you need to speak with Mr. Duncan Hale. Don't close doors just when they're opening for you, Ben. This one will get your blood up, I promise."

Hood remained suspicious. "Then why'd you send him to me?"

"Because it's *Agent* Hale and you're the expert he wants on loan. Oh, and by the way: we don't have a choice." Andrews hung up.

The director asserted his authority over Hood because in truth he had little leverage; the millionaire had no need for a curator's job. Hood's family was rich from lumber, paper, and real estate. Ben could have been like a thousand wealthy sons, rampaging his way through private schools and plowing nubile debutantes before marrying the proper pedigree and managing an empire he'd not created.

But Hood was different. He stayed outside even in foul weather while growing up at Palisade, the family estate in the Hudson Valley. He was fascinated by the natural world. His father taught him to hunt and fish—they'd hiked the Rockies and gone on safari in Africa—and he climbed and hiked on his own. Rich people were boring, he decided, knowing nothing but money, while scientists, who worked for pennies, were pursuing the secrets of the universe. The least rewarded had the most fascinating jobs.

There's snobbery in the sciences, as in all professions, and it was a reverse snobbery that would have discriminated against a rich man like Ben. But Hood bludgeoned his way into their fraternity by contributing to others' causes and financing his own expeditions to unknown Tibet. He took along British, German, and Swiss companions and bore hunger, thirst, and insects without complaint.

Like Andrews, he was featured in *National Geographic*, and it was quietly let known that the Hood family might make a donation to the hard-pressed New York museum if a permanent position could be made on its staff. The fact that Dr. Hood had published in the best peer-reviewed journals made such an appointment defensible to the museum employees he vaulted ahead of. So he'd been given the second-best office, a starving wage, and periodic reminders from Andrews that he must answer to the museum hierarchy. The subordination grated, but it also gave him something in common with the other curators. He'd become, through routine slights from his boss and quiet contributions to his rival's projects—he was buying friendship, Hood knew—one of them.

Too bad it didn't satisfy.

Hood led a double life. He was handsome, single, and circuited the New York clubs to bring home to Park Avenue the carefully coiffed women who were curious about his eccentricity. Everyone was betting on when he'd tire of the museum charade and buckle down to the family business. Women gambled on when he'd settle into domesticity, sleeping with him in hopes of timing his change of heart.

But he didn't buckle down. Hood's scientific travels were the one place he could escape his birthright and reinvent himself as scientist, scholar, and explorer.

So he met whomever Chapman told him to.

Agent Hale reminded Hood of a dark lamp pole: a narrow, ink-haired man with a bulb-pale face who was dressed in that kind of cheap, somber suit that was the uniform of civil servants everywhere. The visitor let Hood study his credentials—Army Corps of Intelligence Police—while the agent examined the animal heads and Asian maps that decorated Hood's office. There were Chinese flintlock firearms, Afghan scimitars, polished fossils of ancient ammonite shells, Persian pikes, and Victorian-era paintings of wilderness panoramas and women bathing naked in a stream. There were photographs of Hood with shahs, lamas, and movie stars.

"You got more stuff than Woolworth's," Hale said, his flat tone making it unclear if he meant it as a criticism or a compliment.

"It's a curator's office. We're collectors."

Hale took in the view across Central Park, Manhattan's towers rising like Oz. "I don't even have a window."

"Yes, your agency," Hood said, holding Hale's identification card. "I'm afraid I've never heard of it."

"That's the way we like it," the agent replied. "Active in the Great War, and then down to as few as twenty officers this decade. However, with the Japanese at war in China, Italy in Abyssinia, and Hitler into Austria and hot for the Sudetenland, we're back in fashion. Now we need your help with the Germans."

"You're spies? And Hale, is that really your name? Like Nathan Hale, 'I have but one life to give for my country'?"

"It's my name to you."

This was just the kind of cowboy intrigue that thrilled the flamboyant Andrews. They'd probably been comparing decoder rings upstairs. "And you're here to see a museum employee, a curator of stuffed animals, because of Hitler?"

Hale plopped into a fat leather chair without being invited. "I'm here to see an employee who has the means to get himself what he wants, including a trip back to Asia." He took out a cigarette and lit it, without offering one to Hood. "The museum director agreed that you're the one to help us."

"I'm an expert on Tibet, not Germany."

"You're about to become an expert on both." Hale took a drag and let out a long plume of silver smoke. "We understand you know a German explorer named Kurt Raeder."

Hood started. He thought he'd put that mess behind him. Best to be careful here. "*Knowing* Raeder might be an overstatement. He keeps his own counsel, and he's an odd duck. But, yes, we journeyed together to Tibet four years ago, as I'm sure you're aware. Difficult man to deal with, but a great hunter. He brought down a magnificent ibex for the Berlin collection at four hundred yards. Crack shot."

"Do you know he's returning to Tibet?"

"No, we don't correspond. We had a falling-out."

"Over a woman."

Hood frowned. "How do you know that?"

"You saved her."

The zoologist looked uncomfortable. "It's complicated."

"I'll bet." Hale took a puff again. "A new SS expedition left Genoa in mid-April. Passed through Suez, Colombo, and on to Calcutta. The British tried to hold them up in India but they couldn't come up with a good enough reason, and now the Nazis have pushed ahead for the Himalayas. Trying to reach the Tibetan capital at Lhasa, from all reports. Why do you think the SS is sending men to Tibet?"

"I have no idea."

"Did you know Raeder was a Nazi?"

"He wasn't overtly. Politics rarely came up."

Hale puffed again, considering. "Just the pair of happy hunters, were you?"

"It was a scientific expedition, sponsored by this museum. Raeder had been to the Himalayas once before and was recommended. We didn't always get along, but that's normal among scientists. Why this interest in a German zoologist? Nazi or not, he's hardly a prominent figure of Hitler's regime."

Hale nodded, as if this was an entirely reasonable assessment. "Not yet."

"What does that mean?"

"Hood, we have information that Raeder is being sent back to Tibet by none other than Heinrich Himmler himself, director of the German secret police. Exactly why is unclear. Hunting for Shangri-la, for all we know."

The mythical utopia, invented by the British author James Hilton, had become a popular Hollywood movie the year before—a nice antidote to the Depression.

"Which is fantasy. Hilton's never even been to Asia."

"So were El Dorado and the Fountain of Youth, but the Spanish still looked for them. The krauts are up to *something*, and my office thinks war is on the horizon. If it comes, we think the United States will be dragged into it, and not on Hitler's side. We can't allow the Nazis any advantages."

"Tibet is not a strategic power, Agent Hale."

"The hell it isn't. It squats between India, China, and the Soviet Union. It's more inscrutable than Fu Manchu. It's the high ground of any Asian contest. And Himmler is sending Raeder there for a purpose."

"What purpose?"

"That's what we want you to find out."

"And how am I to do that?"

"Roy Chapman Andrews tells me you like the outdoors as much as he does, and you're about as content in this curio closet as a ferret in a bag. Said he had to give you this grand chamber here to keep you from wandering off to the Smithsonian or Philly."

How had Andrews known that? Hood *had* talked with rival museums but thought he'd kept it a secret.

"The United States government, Mr. Hood, is offering to give you the necessary paperwork and introductions for your next trip to Tibet, including a reserved flight on the *China Clipper*, a genuine government-issue Colt .45 automatic, and letters of introduction to the Chinese government, such as it is. We're giving you diplomatic status to go to Lhasa and, if possible, see this Buddhist pope I understand is cooped up there. Lama, they call him. I thought that was some goat in South America."

"The current lama is just a child. There's a regent, the Reting Rinpoche, or the regent from the Rinpoche monastery."

"So we'll help you see this Reting."

"*If* I track down Raeder and find out what he's up to."

Hale nodded and stubbed out his cigarette on a side table. There was no ashtray; Hood didn't smoke. "Exactly. Find him, learn what he's after, and get it first for Uncle Sam. You get an excuse to get out of this mausoleum and serve your country."

"At Uncle Sam's expense?"

"Actually, we need you to help out with that, given your personal resources and presumed patriotism. America's wallet is tight. You've heard of the Great Depression?"

"Why, I think that's the thing that cost my family millions. You want me to spy for you *and* pay my own way?"

"I've looked at your tax return, Hood. You can afford it. If *Vanity Fair* was still on the newsstand, you'd be on the cover."

The magazine had suspended publication in the depth of the downturn, but Hood got the point. His London coat and tie cost several times that of Hale's suit, his shoes were Italian, and the dark hair and strong chin gave him, women said, the dash of a matinee idol. He enjoyed looking good. He enjoyed spending money on travel and research. He enjoyed sleeping on the ground while knowing he didn't have to.

"You've got nerve, Mr. Hale."

"I just got a hunch that you'll jump at a chance to go back to Tibet. Because it's there, and all that mountaineering crap."

Hood was annoyed this obnoxious bureaucrat knew anything about him, but such was the modern world. Privacy eroded, the income tax a plague, gangsters glorified. "What if Raeder's purpose is innocent? Scientific and cultural?"

"Put it in your report. But if it isn't . . ."

"What?"

"Then hunt him down. It's imperative that Germany not win any advantage over there. Kill him, if necessary."

"Kill him!"

Hale stood and brushed ashes from his lap. "We understand that might not be as difficult for you as it sounds."

8

On board the Trieste, *Mediterranean Sea*
June 25, 1938

More than two months before Hood's meeting with Hale, the Italian liner *Trieste* had cut across a Mediterranean placid as a pond, an avenue of silver leading away from the starboard side to a fat full moon. The air was as warm as a mother's breath. Now that they were safely away from land, Raeder had invited the men whom Himmler had recruited to share some schnapps by the anchor capstans. The German quintet was deliberately out of earshot of the other passengers, or any chance a steward might overhear.

The ship was steaming for Suez, and then beyond to the Red Sea, Indian Ocean, and Calcutta. British India, unfortunately, was the quickest doorway to the forbidden palaces of Tibet. They'd have to bluff and bargain their way through it.

Raeder's "knights" were professionals like himself, SS officers who were newly named members of Himmler's Ahnenerbe, the *Reichsführer*'s research bureau. They were veterans of expeditions like this one, and experienced mountaineers. While they had packed their black uniforms away until ceremony demanded in Lhasa, they were soldiers, too. The expedition's crates in the hold included rifles, pistols, and even a new submachine gun called the Erma MP-38, much smaller and lighter than the Thompsons that gangsters used in American movies. There were daggers, explosives, fuses, detonators, and telescopic sights. There were pitons, climbing ropes, and crampons. There were field stoves, scientific instruments, and film cameras. The Germans were ready for partnership, or for war.

Julius Muller was their geophysicist, whose job was measuring magnetic variations in the earth. The work might be scientifically useful in understanding the earth's interior because it would be the first time such readings would be taken on the world's highest plateau. Muller had also used explosives in his research and could be counted on to use his expertise in demolition. The Rhinelander had a skeptic's instincts, however—he was the kind who reflexively questions authority—so his SS superiors had been happy to let him go. Raeder was determined to keep an eye on the maverick. When the time came, Muller must exhibit complete fealty and obedience.

Wilhelm Kranz was their anthropologist. One way to tell Aryan from Jew was to measure face and head, giving authorities an objective way of segregating the races. Kranz planned to use his calipers and plastic casts on the Tibetan aristocracy to establish whether they were indeed ancestral cousins of the German race. Kranz was Nazi by creed and need, a devoted reader of race theory. "Maybe I will find an Aryan princess to seduce, eh?" he added with his sense of humor. He was also an expert with the garrote and knife.

Hans Diels was their archaeologist and historian, the man who'd absorbed what was known about the past of Tibet and who could be called upon to interpret the remains of any lost civilizations they might find. He had a crate of books from Tibetan explorers like Sven Hedin, Nicholas Roerich, and Alexandra David-Neel. Diels had served in the Great War and knew what it was like to fight and kill. "It's not like the movies. It's murder. You try to murder them before they can murder you. Pow, from two hundred yards away. And if the artillery can do it for you, so much the better."

He'd been gassed, like Hitler, and at forty-three he was the Old Man of the group.

Franz Eckells was their cameraman. He'd worked with the celebrated woman director Leni Riefenstahl and photographed for the SS magazine *Germanische Leithefte*. He was the expedition's political officer, present to ensure there was no deviation from SS orthodoxy. His superb eyesight had helped win awards for marksmanship. In the Winter Olympics in Bavaria two years before, Eckells had narrowly missed winning a medal in Military Patrol, a skiing and shooting event. He carried himself with catlike grace and confidence, and Raeder looked forward to shooting against him.

The zoologist liked his comrades' combination of brains and brawn, curiosity and courage. They were prototypes of the new Germany. The men had signed on for adventure without being exactly certain where they were going or what they were to risk, trusting Himmler. Now Raeder would tell them. The Germans were all a little drunk, and mellow because of it. It was a perfect night, the air silken, music playing from the salon, the ship throbbing purposely. Their wake ran back toward the Fatherland.

So far the expedition was like a holiday.

Raeder had taken a whore in Genoa to feed his cravings, and by the time she could report his savagery they were far at sea. He felt satiated and anticipatory.

"Gentlemen," he began, raising his glass, "we are carrying the swastika to Lhasa, the capital of Tibet."

They nodded, having guessed as much.

"The British may try to impede us, but we'll not be deterred. There's ample reason to believe that the goals of the Tibetan government should coincide with our own."

"Which goals?" Diels asked.

"I'll get to that. While none of what I'm about to relate is secret, nonetheless Germany is alone in acting on it. Accordingly, what you're about to hear is for your ears only. It must not be repeated to anyone on this ship or anyone we meet until we are deep in Tibet. Our success depends on our ability to surprise the world. If we succeed, all of you will be heroes to a greater extent than you can possibly imagine."

"Is it dangerous?" asked Kranz. The possibility did not necessarily displease him.

"Our goal is not to provoke danger, Wilhelm. But, yes, enjoy this leisurely night. Be prepared for hard times once we reach the Himalayas."

They nodded again.

Raeder took a breath. "As you know, except for the polar regions, central Asia is the most remote and mysterious place on earth. It's also one of the most strategic, the birthplace of empires for the Mongols, Tatars, and Turks. It's the high ground between Soviets, Chinese, and the British Raj. It has the highest mountains, the driest deserts, and is the source of great rivers like the Indus, Mekong, Yellow, and Ganges. Its inhabitants are trapped in religious superstition, ruled by monks, and yet Tibet is rumored to be a land of astonishing magical powers. Tibet's technology is primitive, its history is poorly understood, but its religious and mental magic is intriguing."

"We're going to make names for ourselves as scholars," Diels predicted. "We're going to learn what they know."

"Over the centuries, few Europeans have penetrated this region. I myself have been on its edges with two expeditions, one financed by an American millionaire named Benjamin Hood. The Russian monk Agvan Dorjiev studied in Lhasa. Germany's Baron von Ungern-Sternberg fought the Communists for the White Russians in Mongolia, and heard tales there. The Pole Ferdinand Ossendowski served with the baron and wrote of wonders he'd seen. Nicholas Roerich led an expedition through Tibet a decade ago, bearing a wish-granting gem entrusted to him by the League of Nations. He hoped to return it to a secret underground kingdom called Shambhala, but never found it. All these explorers brought back curious legends of fabulous ancient kingdoms that were repositories of wisdom and power, ruled by a King of the World, or Dark Lord. Tibetan tradition holds that the armies of secret Shambhala shall someday ride forth to redeem the world. Some Westerners believe that the Shambhalans were refugees from Atlantis and built a hidden city to preserve ancient knowledge."

"Does your old friend Hood know all this?" asked Eckells. "Do we have to worry about the American?"

"He's not my friend. He's a playboy, looking for things to occupy his time in New York. Don't worry about Hood." There was an edge to Raeder's voice, but the others had already taken note of his moodiness and temper. They knew better than to ask more.

"David-Neel saw monks levitate and move from place to place at supernatural speeds," Hans Diels volunteered instead. "Roerich saw a mysterious oval spheroid speeding across the Asian skies in 1927. It was immense and instantly changed direction, but had no discernible power source."

"Superior to any aircraft now in existence," Raeder agreed. "We're not traveling ten thousand miles for yak dung, my friends."

They laughed.

"Some of the philosophers behind National Socialism have interpreted these legends and reports," Raeder went on. "The American Madame Blavatsky, the Austrian Rudolf Steiner, the British medium Alice Bailey, Germany's Thule Society—all have contributed. If you've paid attention in SS seminars, you know their theories of Atlantis, Hyperborea, and Thule. Theosophy, Ariosophy, and other new scientific disciplines have established the history of race conflict and the origins of us Aryans. This is the new German science."

They nodded.

"Blavatsky herself posited three principles: that God's instrument is an electrospiritual force that embodies the laws of nature, that creation is a cycle of destruction and rebirth, and that all is unified—the soul and the material, the tiny and the great. Manipulating this unity, she preached, is the secret of supernatural power. Our *Führer* Adolf Hitler himself studied her philosophy and incorporated its teachings into National Socialism. We sail with a rich philosophic tradition."

"*Heil* Hitler," Eckells breathed quietly, like a prayer.

"Our ancestors from the north may have branched to Tibet. One of our tasks is to determine if this is true. Wilhelm here will search for racial evidence with his calipers."

"Just so he doesn't measure me," Muller growled. He thought the head measuring was anthropologic nonsense. Julius had little use for the social sciences.

"Yes, don't let him practice one of his plaster masks on you," said Diels, who'd tried it. "It's like being suffocated."

"Such a discovery in itself would be enough to garner us all global fame," Raeder went on. "It would reunify the Aryan and prove to skeptics that Germany's racial theories are true. Julius will add to our understanding of the physics of the earth, and Hans its human history. Franz will bring back movie footage of ceremonies never witnessed by Western man."

"If all goes well," Eckells amended.

"But there's more at stake here than that. We've all heard of the strange theories of Einstein, Heisenberg, and Bohr. A universe of the vast and the small, ruled by laws very different from what we perceive in everyday life. Some physicists think these ideas hint at strange and wicked new powers at the level of the atom."

"But that's Jewish science," Kranz objected.

"Even a Jew might stumble on a truth. And we must never let the Jew have a monopoly on a new kind of power. We true Germans are far ahead of them, I think. Haushofer founded the Vril Society two decades ago to search for the power source that stories attribute to Shambhala."

"What's Vril?" Muller asked. "I don't remember this from my physics texts."

"A convenient name, taken from an old novel, of what the *Reichsführer* thinks may be a very real power source. These ancients understood the natural world in ways we've forgotten, and found a way to tap fundamental energies far more powerful than gunpowder or gasoline. This power can be directed by the mind to build or destroy. It is power that may still exist in fabulous cities that, many writers and thinkers believe, lay hidden under the surface of the earth—cities that are the origin of the idea of hell, perhaps."

Diels took a swig of schnapps. "You're taking us to hell, Kurt?"

"Or heaven. Somewhere may be hidden the most fabulous city since the Aztec capital of Tenochtitlán. A new El Dorado! Not because of gold but because of power. The ignorant would call what travelers have sought 'magic,' but it's in fact simply a spiritually higher mastery of science and the cosmos. It restores man from a plaything of physics, a victim, to its central mover. We become not pawns but kings. Not mortals but gods. We become not the product of creation, but its manipulator. Has not our *Führer* demonstrated this kind of 'magic' already? Hitler is destined to be the true King of the World, and our mission is to help him. This is both a religious expedition, gentlemen, and a scientific one. We're being sent to find, essentially, supernatural powers—powers that our Aryan ancestors once possessed and ruled with, but which have been lost for millennia."

"But how were they lost?"

"We don't know. Perhaps they were deliberately hidden, to await reemergence of a fit people like us of the Third Reich." The first Reich was the heroic prehistoric world of Aryan god-men, the Germans knew. The second has been the chaos of history caused by the cursed philosophies of Jew and Christian. Now they were at the dawn of the third, the Reich of National Socialism. "We, gentlemen, are the apostles, the knights, the angels, who may bring the greatest secret in history back to the Fatherland. If we do, Germany conquers all, easily and completely. And then our species' evolutionary destiny can truly begin, unpolluted by human vermin."

"We're going to steal this Vril from the monks of Tibet?" Muller tried to clarify.

"Not steal. Re-find. Tibetans are sunk in ignorance and poverty. They've forgotten their own genius. We're going to plumb their legends to find if the legends of our ancestors are true, and learn where Vril is hidden. Tibet will be our new ally, on the flank of Russia, China, and British India alike." He took his own swig.

"Never has so small a group of men been given the possibility of achieving so much."

"But how will we find what no one else has?"

"Reichsführer Himmler has been researching these legends. He's found maps that date from the Middle Ages and the time of Frederick Barbarossa. We'll combine those clues with what the Tibetans know."

"Barbarossa!"

"There's evidence Barbarossa was interested in these mysteries himself. And belief that he may have left us a key."

"What key?"

"I'll reveal that to you when the time comes."

"And if we fail?" asked Diels. "What if there's no Shambhala and no Vril?"

Raeder looked at them seriously. "In that case, we might have to consider never returning to Germany. That is not a message the *Reichsführer* cares to hear."

78 • WILLIAM DIETRICH

9

The Skagit River Valley, United States
September 4, Present Day

North of Starbird Road, Interstate 5 dips toward the Skagit River Valley and paradise opens up. The peaks of islands in Washington's inland sea hump on the northwest horizon: Fidalgo, Lummi, Cypress, and Orcas as green and precipitous as a child's crayon drawings. To the northeast is the snowy volcanic cone of Mount Baker and the cutover foothills of the Cascade Range. Between is a plump platter of farmland, a onetime bay filled with sediment at the end of the last ice age. The result is some of the richest soil in the world. A hundred crops are grown there: tulips in spring, berries in early summer, and potatoes, corn, and grapes approaching harvest on this day.

The timelessness should have reassured Rominy: the gleam of glaciers, the meringue of clouds, and the orderly phalanx of ripened crops were reassuring. The overcast was breaking and the surface of the Skagit sparkled like sequins, while the valley's overall palette was toned sepia by September's golden glaze. She often came here on weekends, bicycling and kayaking to escape the tedium of her cubicle in Seattle. But now the beauty had a sense of menace. Was she really being pursued? Where was Jake Barrow taking her? The old pickup whined as the journalist kept it at seventy-five mph.

Rominy had managed to regain some composure after their escape. Her cheeks were rubbed dry, annoyingly red, her posture as prim as a princess. With time to think, she'd decided to wait and observe, since Jake didn't seem immediately threatening and she didn't want to be abandoned somewhere, waiting for skinheads to drive by. Since the insanity on the freeway he'd been quieter, watchful, brooding, checking his mirrors like a fugitive on the lam. Occasionally he'd glance her way and give a half smile, as if reassuring a child or a dog, but he radiated tension the way a stove does heat. The unease made him seem more human, believable, persuadable. Maybe she could talk her way out of this, whatever "this" really was. She thought he'd take side roads, but he seemed more interested in making distance. Half an hour had passed.

"Where are you taking me?" she finally tried. "Do you live up here?"

"You do."

"What? No!"

"I'm taking you to property you don't know you own."

She groaned. "It might relax me a little more if you began making sense."

He adjusted the rearview mirror for the thousandth time, the little bullet hole in back sighing like a leaking tire. "I'm about to, but I get rattled by car bombs and bullets. I just wanted to get some distance from the skinheads so I have time to explain. What I'm going to tell you is more than a little surprising." He tried the half smile again. "We *could* do this at a Starbucks."

The name conveyed a spark of reassurance. Steamed milk in public. She had a Starbucks card in her wallet.

"But I'm going to suggest something more refined."

"Don't go to any trouble." She didn't try to keep sarcasm from her voice.

"There're a couple of wineries up the valley. Your humble rescuer wants to share a bottle of pinot noir while we sort this out. Skagit's an excellent *terroir* for that varietal."

Jesus H. Insanity. Kidnapped by a wine snob. Well, serves you right, Rominy. Should have gone for a Republican in the canned foods aisle. "You know, if you'd come on to me in wine or spices, this might have gone better."

Now it was Jake's turn to be confused. "What?"

"Never mind." She winced. "My knees hurt."

"Oh, yeah, sorry. I should have said this before. There's a first aid kit in back of the seat with some antiseptic pads."

At least the moron looked chagrined.

The space behind the seats was piled with a mildewed tent, sleeping bags, pads, and other gear. "I like to camp," Jake said as she rummaged.

"You're not taking us into the woods, are you?"

"Not exactly. It's a red plastic box."

She found the first aid packet, bandaged her own knees, and sat annoyed at her disarray. Rominy was no supermodel, but men had been known to give her a second glance. She took pride in looking good, and she'd worn a skirt to the store. Now she was dirty, scraped, and tear-stained, and she didn't like Jake seeing her that way. Her eyes were an intriguing hazel, hair dark with an auburn tint, skin just slightly olive, which helped her avoid that Seattle winter-worm look, and she wasn't afraid to be seen in a swimsuit.

But now? She drew confidence from her appearance, and this weird flight from the Safeway parking lot had drained it.

Was that part of Barrow's plan?

"Here, I'll take that." He held his hand out for the antiseptic pad she'd cleaned herself with and glanced at the stain. "Blood."

"Heck, yes, it's blood." She could still feel the sting.

"I know you're mad, but it will be worth it. You'll see." He dropped the pad into a plastic bag he had hanging from the dash. The truck had old-fashioned knobs instead of buttons. If this was what Jake could afford on his investigative reporter's salary, how good could he be?

Judging, Rominy. Right now she was a step or two behind this guy. She had to get a step or two ahead.

They passed Mount Vernon and Burlington and took the Cook Road exit off the freeway, heading east up the valley. Barrow seemed to relax a little. The mountains began squeezing in toward the Skagit River like a funnel, piling up toward the rocky crests of North Cascades National Park. The foothills were snowless in late summer, the land somnolent and satisfied as the harvest came in before the autumn storms. Pasture hemmed by dark forest, the way she imagined a place like Germany might look. She'd never been to Europe. The Skagit River ran green to match the forest, thick and deep.

Elk were grazing in one meadow.

They passed through Sedro Woolley, Lyman, and Hamilton, each town smaller and each mile taking her deeper into the mountains and farther from the likelihood of any help. Her cell phone remained a useless paperweight, and he hadn't even asked if she needed to pee. At some point he'd have to stop for gas . . .

"Here we are."

They lurched off the highway onto a road called Challenger and coasted up past trim, modest frame homes set on a hillside above the river. Their lawns were brave bright badges against the darker forest. He braked at a small vineyard with a sign that said Challenger Ridge. Neat rows of grape vines led uphill to a wall of maple and fir. Old farm buildings, barn boards weathered and mossy, formed a cluster on either side of the road. Jake parked and got out, stretched, and walked around to jerk open Rominy's door.

It creaked, and Barrow took her hand to help her out. His own hand was large, hard, and callused for a newspaperman. He had an athlete's easy poise. "You can run if you want, but you'll get a glass of wine if you hear me out."

She stepped down stiffly. A sleepy collie came over to nose them. The tasting room was a cedar-roofed, single-gable house with wooden porch. It had twin American flags and flower planters made from wine barrels. Picnic tables tilted slightly on grass dotted with clover.

"Where's Norman Rockwell?"

"The house dates from 1904," Jake said. "Hobby farm turned medal-winning business. We did a story on them once in our weekend section, and I like their pinot. They do some nice blends with Yakima grapes as well."

Yep, she'd gotten her wine guy. "There's no one else here."

"Kind of the point. It's quiet on a Monday, and we need space to talk. It helps you had today off to go grocery shopping."

"That's me, lucky girl."

"I know this is hard, Rominy."

"Comp time. We were working up a presentation until eight P.M. Saturday so the boss could give a presentation in the Bay Area while we stayed home. Canceled a date that night to clear my calendar for . . . this." She shook her head. "I guess skinheads work Mondays." Her ability to joke surprised her.

"Was it a serious date?"

She glanced. He was genuinely curious. "Not yet." Her frown was wry. "Not after standing him up. Not now."

He swallowed. "Hope you like the wine." He gestured to the buildings with his hand. "Challenger is on the way we need to go."

Rominy felt like a rabbit uncertain when the trapdoor is raised. The air was clean, insects hummed, birds tweeted. The world remained surprisingly normal. "Where's the bathroom?"

"This way."

It was a Porta-Potty—not exactly Napa—but then they went into the tasting room with its overstuffed couches, gas fire, and dark paneling. Cozy as a sleep sack. The young woman who sold them a bottle introduced herself as Cora and Jake chatted her up, almost flirting, which unexpectedly annoyed Rominy. Then the woman pointed them up the hill. "Nice view. Do you need a corkscrew?"

"If you please." Barrow smiled as if this whole thing was a lark.

Cora gave them plastic drinking cups as well.

Rominy and Jake ascended to a wooden table resting beneath the canopy of a three-trunked cedar tree, the painted planking littered with needles. The view was soothing; purposely so, she assumed. Vines marched in soldierly columns down to the main highway, trees, and the green Skagit beyond. Across the river, rank upon rank of forested hills receded. Early autumn gave everything that honey glow.

Rominy was sore, tired, frustrated, and curious. She could run, she could scream, she could beg to use the winery phone . . . and she did none of these things. Watching Barrow work the corkscrew, the river and highway a distant murmur, the shade cool but not unpleasant, she felt oddly relaxed. Was this the Stockholm syndrome, where victims identify with their captor? Or had Barrow really saved her in order to tell her something important? Certainly nothing remotely this interesting occurred in her cubicle at work.

Rominy spent most days staring at either pixels on a glass screen or the gray fabric of her office enclosure, and more evenings than she cared to admit staring at another glass screen at home. Her abode was an apartment on Seattle's Queen Anne Hill she couldn't really afford; she kept the heat at 65 to justify premium cable. She went to a gym three mornings a week, belonged to a book club, purposely limited her gossip magazine time to the monthly stint at the hairdresser, club-hopped with girlfriends, and dated with more wariness than excitement. She shopped at IKEA but waited for the Nordstrom sale. On a package to Mexico she'd used her high school Spanish, wore a swimsuit it took two weeks to select, and applied sunblock with religious zeal. She wrote press releases for software engineers who alternately treated her with disdain or flirted from boredom. Her ambitions were to buy a bungalow, own a significant piece of art, or visit Africa, but her dreams were hazy after that. If anyone had asked—and they didn't—she would have said she was happy.

Yes, something had at last happened.

"A toast." He poured the wine and hoisted his. "To your illustrious ancestor!"

"My what?" She took a sip, eyeing Jake over the rim of her glass. Not bad, both him and the wine. Her moment of contentment confused her.

"To your great-grandfather, Rominy. To the famous and infamous adventurer, explorer, curator, and secret agent Benjamin Hood."

"Whatever."

"Apparently disgraced, however. Stripped of his prerogatives and effectively exiled to the murk of Skagit County at a time, World War Two, when his country might have needed him most. If you think this is rural now, it was the end of the earth then. A man lost to history, and even to his own family. Meaning you."

"I have a great-grandfather?"

"Everyone does, trust me." He smiled. "You were adopted, correct?"

"Yes. How do you know that?"

"I told you, I've been investigating. It's my job."

"My parents died in a car accident when I was a baby."

"And no other family that you knew about?"

"There wasn't any."

"But there had to be at one time, right? One's parents have parents. Didn't you ever wonder?"

"Mom and Dad—my adopted parents—said they didn't know. I haven't dwelled on it, really. They never made me feel adopted—I was an only child, *their* child. We didn't obsess on the accident. It's not what you want to talk about, you know?"

"Of course. Icy road. Mountain plunge. And you mysteriously found: abandoned, but bundled, in a cradle in a Forest Service campground . . ."

"Not abandoned." She flushed. All her old dread at the rumors, and her frustration at her adoptive parents' evasions, was coming back. "No. Not a suicide. Something terrible must have been going on, and they left me for a moment to go get help, and the ice . . ." She felt the threat of tears again and willed them back. It didn't make sense. It had never made sense. It annoyed her that he'd obviously looked at the old clippings. It seemed an invasion of her privacy, of a tragedy buried by time.

"It wasn't a suicide, Rominy, of course not." He took a quick swallow. "So you know your name isn't really Pickett?"

"It *is*. This is what this is about? You bring this up *now*? *Here*?"

"It's your adoptive parents' name."

"It's *my* name, the one I've had as long as I can remember. And my poor dead parents were not named Hood."

"But your mother's mother's father was. I'm going to show you the genealogy, and your descent from him is on the female side. But that's not my point. It wasn't a suicide, I agree. But it *was* murder."

"What?"

"By the same crazy fanatics who just tried to murder you."

She shook her head in bewilderment. "Skinheads killed my real parents?"

"Not skinheads, Rominy. Nazis. Neo-Nazis." He took out his own cell phone. "Which reminds me. I've got to make a call about your inheritance."

10

Kangra La, Sikkim
July 28, 1938

Kurt Raeder looked back from the Himalayas to a
flat world gauzed with haze, the steel of India's
great rivers faint threads of orientation. The Germans
had escaped the hot, damp hell of the British Raj and
were climbing toward their goal, the heaven promised
by old Tibetan texts that Himmler had sent along in
a steel box: Shambhala, the lost kingdom that would
violently redeem the world.

On Raeder's neck, kept warm by his own body,
was the vial that reputedly held the antique blood of
Frederick Barbarossa.

The explorer found himself lightening as they
climbed. For more than a month he and his four
companions had felt trapped in British India as news

from Europe grew more ominous. Traveling through Calcutta and the Himalayan province of Sikkim was the quickest way to Tibet, but it was getting harder for both sides to pretend England's relations with Germany weren't fraying. Meanwhile, the monsoon came in full force, rain pouring down. The humidity on the Bengal plain became suffocating. Snakes slithered from drowned burrows. Mosquitoes rose in clouds. His companions chafed and quarreled. The heat, the bugs, and the sheer bureaucratic sloth of a dying empire all weighed on them. England was in decline and Calcutta was crowded and chaotic. As Hitler tried to reunite a Germany brutally disenfranchised after the Great War, the old enemies grew jealous again, seeking to hem in the Teutons. So had the German Tibetan Expedition been corralled by the arrogant, frightened English! For that, Raeder held them in contempt.

Where, the officials in Calcutta had demanded of him, are your permits to travel to the Forbidden Kingdom of Tibet? Of course there could be no permits, since there was no permitted travel, and there could be no permission until the Germans met personally with the three-year-old god-king's regent in Lhasa. But they could not meet, because none but the British consul was permitted to travel there. The Germans stewed under the circular and self-serving reasoning of Whitehall and Calcutta.

What the British didn't take into account was German will, coupled with advice from the kind of Englishman who'd first built the empire.

Before sailing from Genoa in allied Italy, Raeder had received a peculiar letter from Sir Thomas Pickford, the octogenarian Himalaya explorer and hero of the siege of Gyantse, where thousands of Tibetans who believed themselves invulnerable to bullets had been slaughtered by British firepower. Pickford had served on Francis Younghusband's military expedition to Tibet in 1904 that forced it into reluctant relations with the British. Now, thirty-four years later, Pickford had corresponded with the young German he'd heard lecture in London. Rumor of Raeder's impending SS expedition had circulated in academic circles, and Pickford had advice.

A few Englishmen understood what the Reich was trying to do, he explained, the racial spirit Germany was trying to revive. A few sympathized with the power of Hitler's vision in this new, corrupt, decadent age called the twentieth century.

Don't wait out the bureaucratic intrigues, the crusty Englishman wrote. *My country is giving up its civilizing mission, but yours is seizing it. Germany is alone in displaying the character of our race. We are cousins, after all, and Tibet must not be allowed to exist in seclusion and hide its secrets. Take any opportunity and simply go, borders be damned.*

If a German had written this to an Englishman, the Gestapo would have called it high treason. But the English, like the Americans, felt free to say anything to anyone. Curious idea.

I have seen the sun set on the Potala Palace with a radiance that speaks of God, the old Englishman wrote. *I know there are things to seek in that land we can scarcely dream. If you want to see them, make your own way across the border as Younghusband did in 1904.*

Now Raeder had.

In Calcutta, the Germans had first falsely announced their intention, given the diplomatic delay, of returning home. Then, in the dead of night, monsoon thundering and streets awash, they'd loaded their theodolites, chronometers, earth inductors, shortwave radios, anthropological calipers, cameras, movie film, guns, cases of schnapps, and boxes of cigarettes into the specially designed, rubber-sealed cargo cases crafted in Hamburg. They'd hired trucks to taxi them to the station and bribed their way onto the express train north, arriving at its terminus a night and day ahead of any pursuit. Mountains rose as enticing as a mirage.

Paying in Reich gold, the Germans swiftly bought two freight cars on the next conveyance, a popularly dubbed "toy train" with tracks just two feet apart that puffed its way, at twelve miles per hour, to the British hill station of Darjeeling and its warehouses of tea. This would elevate them to 7,000 feet. The Nazis were moving on this second leg of their escape by the time bemused authorities in Calcutta realized they were gone at all.

"It's Jew gold we use," Raeder told his companions. "Confiscated from the rats fleeing Berlin. So does Providence assist our mission."

Up and up the locomotive crept, past banana plantations at first, and then through jungle so high that it arched over the tracks, the canopy shuddering in the downpours. The journey reeked of rotting orchids, foliage steaming.

Indian laborers rode an open freight car pushed by the bow of the train. When monsoon landslides blocked the track, they dutifully clambered out to clear them. Raeder, impatient and restless while the coolies dug, took his rifle into the jungle to look for tigers.

He saw not a living animal. The bamboo was still as death.

Tea plantations hove into view as they neared Darjeeling. There, between Nepal and Bhutan, they could see the beckoning crest of the Himalaya through breaks in the rushing clouds. The peaks were topped by snowy Mount Kanchenjunga, which at 28,000 feet was almost as lofty as Everest.

Diplomatic telegrams awaited Raeder, protesting their progress and demanding a return to Calcutta. But the German Foreign Office was putting pressure on the English to leave the Germans alone and it sent its own telegrams, seeking to bog the debate down in an exchange of diplomatic notes. While consuls argued, Raeder bluffed his way past the British constabulary, hired a train of oxen, and pushed on toward the Sikkim capital of Gangtok.

He knew how Asia worked. You butted your way, arrogant and impatient, or got nowhere. Now he marched up the hairpin turns of the riotously green Tista Valley with their animals, each ox plodding from four cases of equipment strapped to its back.

Still the monsoon sluiced down.

From every slope sprung a hundred white waterfalls, and in the gorges the rivers roared with chocolate fury. The Germans cut upward, first through birch and dark fir and then through whole forests of rhododendron, clouds of bright butterflies hovering over every puddle and wet leaf. The air was so thick with moisture that climbing was like rising from the bottom of a pool. They struggled through mud, crossed precarious log and vine-cable bridges, and drove their oxen along cliff ledges. The men were smeared with goo, lard of the earth. At the end of the day they'd stand under cataracts to sluice it off, roaring out beer hall anthems.

The rain cooled as they climbed, a promising sign of progress.

The British were fools to let them get this far, Raeder thought.

The oxen, powerful but ungainly, were exchanged at Gangtok for nimbler mules, better adapted to the narrower trail ahead. It took twice as many animals to carry the cases. Mounted with brilliantly colored saddles and blankets, and tethered by yak-hair ropes, the cantankerous animals brayed in chorus to the ominous throbbing of the drums and long *dungchen* trumpets of the Gangtok monastery. Hooves clacked on the muddy route's rocks. German boots splashed through brimming puddles. Higher and higher they climbed, whole hillsides seeming to peel away in the deluge. Sometimes they had to halt to build a new trail across a slide.

At Dikchu, the Devil's Water, the old rope bridge had fallen away. They winched a new one across its thundering chute, then hauled and whipped the balking animals across and up it toward the snowy crests above. The trail seemed evermore narrow, evermore wet, evermore slippery. When the rains paused it was foggy. At each stop they spent several minutes peeling leeches from each other, the odious creatures bloated with blood. Most clustered on calves and ankles, sucking greedily, but a few fell from overhanging limbs or ledges to feast on shoulder and neck.

Only rarely did the Germans meet the occasional pilgrim or merchant. These stood aside on the precarious downslope while the Europeans pushed brusquely past, hugging the cliff.

A wool caravan descending with wide, thick-haired yaks finally blocked their way. The horned animals filled the trail where it ran on the side of a precipitous gorge, leaving no room to pass. The wool drovers with their powerful beasts refused to yield to the Reich's train, and yet trying to back the recalcitrant mules down to a wide spot, even if possible, risked losing the animals and their cargo into the precipice.

Raeder pushed forward. He was wearing a pith helmet marked with the lightning runes of the SS and carried a birch switch in his left hand like a riding crop. As mule nosed with yak, the German confronted the Uygur leader. This man, a Turkic-speaking Muslim with a battered British Enfield—*likely stolen from a murder victim*, Raeder thought—bellowed in defiance and shook his weapon. He kept pointing down the mountain path, clearly insisting with his flinging arms that it was the Germans who must turn around. His men behind were squat, dark, and sullen.

Neither spoke the other's language.

Raeder considered a moment, reached in his field jacket, and pulled out a Luger. Before anyone could react, he pointed the muzzle at the forehead of the leading Uygur yak and fired.

The animal jerked, grunted, and then slowly leaned out from the edge of the cliff with a long sigh, its nostrils bubbling red. Its eyes rolled. Then it heavily and majestically toppled off. The yak fell free for a hundred feet and then bounced and skidded down a scree slope, skeins of wool exploding from its ruptured packs as rock flew like shrapnel. The beast churned up a tail of spray and mud.

The Uygur chieftain stared at Raeder, openmouthed, forgetting the rifle he held in his hand. Raeder smiled. He liked shooting things.

The German calmly stepped past the tribesman to the next animal and fired again and, even as that yak fell on its forelocks, pushed past its heaving flank to fire at a bellowing third. This time the shot went slightly wide, into the neck, but the shock was enough to send this animal into the gorge as well. As if following a lead, the second yak plunged the way of its fellows. The animals plummeted and slammed, cargo flying, as the Uygurs shouted and panicked. They'd encountered a madman!

The other Germans hurriedly broke out their guns, readying for what they expected would be battle on a precipitous ledge.

But the added firepower proved unnecessary. Raeder had a crazed glint to his eyes, his Luger smoking, and as he considered the next animal in line the chieftain ran past him and hastily ordered his own caravan to wheel and retreat.

"Now, after them!" the German snapped.

The mules were kicked and lashed forward, chasing the rumps of the lumbering yaks, until the latter came to a wider shelf and huddled next to a cliff. The Europeans pushed arrogantly past, jostling the Asians, the Uygurs looking at them with hatred. Their chieftain howled at Raeder's back as the Nazi ascended, gesturing with his rifle, but he didn't aim it. Raeder ignored him. And then the Nazis and their porters were around a bend and had the cliff to themselves, panting in the thin air.

"My God, Raeder, are you insane?" Muller asked. "All we had ready was your pistol. What if the Uygurs had fought?"

"Strike with surprise and you crush their will," Raeder said, reloading the Luger. "We're outnumbered a million to one, Julius, and have to act like we're the superior. That much I've learned from the British."

"Are we going to fight our way into Tibet?"

"We won't have to," the zoologist said, looking back. They could hear bells on the yaks as the surviving animals hurried down the trail. "Word of this will spread, and they'll give us the respect we deserve."

Hans Diels stepped forward and clapped the *Untersturmführer* on the shoulder. "Now I know why Himmler picked you to lead us," he said. "You understand how things are."

"And how they should be."

"Life is struggle," Kranz agreed. "We need ruthlessness."

"Then be prepared to follow, my friends."

They surmounted the canyon and came out into alpine meadows full of purple gentians, blue poppies, and wild strawberries. Raeder ordered a rest while the others changed their caps for the more imposing SS pith helmets. Then they lashed red pennants with the Nazi swastika to the pommel of each mule. The men were nearing Tibet, and he wanted the diplomatic nature of their mission made clear.

Ahead, clearing skies were dark as a lake. Peaks dazzled in the blinding clarity of pure air. Mountain snow was flawless. Buttresses of rock glittered in the sun. Behind them, the great Plain of Bengal was lost in cotton clouds.

Heat gave way to nighttime cold, and the progress slowed still more as Muller used his magnetometer to measure the magnetic field of the earth. Anomalies, he said, might show the caverns of underground cities.

Anomalies might reveal Shambhala.

Kranz made measurements of the Tibetans and Bhutanese they'd hired. He pinched their heads with calipers and cast plaster masks of their faces, tubes jutting from nostrils to prevent suffocation. "No Jews here!" he announced. Since eyes were closed for the casting, the result made their masks look like those of dead men. Word of this torture spread, too, and soon Tibetans kept warily away from the anthropologist.

"Are they Aryans?" Muller asked his colleague skeptically.

"Maybe."

Eckells did double duty by both documenting their progress on film and deploying the expedition's aneroids to record atmospheric pressure. Raeder insisted on the scientific measurements, saying it would legitimize the expedition by contributing to German science.

"We'll win fame from the government and respect from the academies."

It was July 25, 1938, when a British lieutenant named Lionel Sopwith-Hastings, riding a lathered mule, finally caught up with the SS expedition and presented orders from the consulate in Gangtok to return to India immediately. The Germans were not, the orders read, to risk a diplomatic uproar by violating the border of Tibet.

Sopwith-Hastings waited stiffly for response. He tried to muster the authority of a British imperial but at age twenty-two, with just a blond wisp on his upper lip and a frame so thin that he'd traded his military cap for that of a *khampa*, a fur herder, to stay warm, he was not a very intimidating presence. His pale blue eyes betrayed unhappiness at his mission, and he kept glancing at the Nazis, one by one, as if counting the odds over and over again. The Germans were brown, dirty, and bearded, with the lean athleticism that comes from years of exercise. They'd watched the Englishman approach from miles away, and arrayed on the rocks of their little encampment were three rifles, the submachine gun, boxes of cartridges, and Raeder's Luger pistol.

"But we do have permission," Raeder said mildly.

"Not according to the British consul," the lieutenant said. He licked his lips. "I'm to escort you to Gangtok and from there to Darjeeling and Calcutta to present your case to the authorities."

"Ah, to present our case. We'll get a fair hearing, then?"

He colored. "This *is* the British Empire."

"Well." The German stood. "You've displayed remarkable energy to catch up with us."

"You're fast. I had to leave my police attachment and push ahead." He gave a peek at the guns. "I can assure you they are still coming."

"Yes, but right now you are entirely alone."

"I met some Uygurs who were quite upset."

"They didn't understand the rules of the road."

Sopwith-Hastings stood as tall as he could. "Are you going to obey the directive?" His eyes strayed to the guns again.

"British pluck can only inspire Germany," Raeder said. "We've extra mules, now that we've gone through some food, and two are lame. It will be efficient if you take them down for us." He sat on a boulder and picked up the Luger, working the mechanism. There was a click as a bullet slid into the chamber. "Then it will be faster to follow."

Diels sat, too, picked up a Mauser, opened the bolt, and examined the weapon as if for dirt. "Perhaps you can also mark the way, where the trail is badly eroded,"

Hans said. "I've no doubt those Uygur yaks have worsened it."

Sopwith-Hastings stood at attention, looking from one to the other. Then he gave a short nod. "Very well. On your honor."

"We'll be on your heels unless the trail collapses," Raeder assured. "There's nothing up here, as you can see. It's pointless to go on." The little swastika pennants snapped in the wind.

"I will await you in Gangtok." The Brit saluted, wheeled, and went to fetch the lame mules.

As soon as the lieutenant disappeared from view, Raeder ordered camp broken and a quick last push to the pass at Kangra La. As the others started this final climb, the German retrieved five pounds of high explosive from one of the trunks.

"Come on, Muller. I'm tired of the English following us."

"Are you going to start a war?"

"I'm going to make it impossible to have one."

They went downslope to a precipitous pitch above the winding trail and climbed a hundred yards above, setting the charge on a hump of fractured rock.

"Kurt, I don't know if this is wise," Muller said. "This is a trade route, a lifeline. Do we have to destroy it? If word gets out, the natives could turn against us."

"I thought you liked to make things go boom, Julius."

"For science and research. Not vandalism."

"Reichsführer Himmler will be interested to hear you describe the necessary advancement of this expedition as vandalism."

"That British boy is no threat to us."

"That boy could bring men." He began walking back, unreeling the fuse cord. "When Cortés reached Mexico, he burned his ships."

"That's not reassuring."

"We can't go home this way anyway. It will be through Persia or China or Russia."

Muller resignedly helped splice the wires to the detonator.

"Now, twist the plunger," Raeder ordered.

"You do it."

"No. I want you to take a hand. I'm not the only National Socialist here."

Muller scowled but twisted. With a roar, a gout of rock flew outward and down, hammering the path and dislodging it. A rock avalanche thundered into the ravine. Stone and noise bounced in the fog.

"Whoo!" Raeder hollered. His shout echoed away down the canyon.

A hundred-yard section of the trail was gone. It would take weeks to carve a replacement.

"Alas," Raeder said. "It's become impossible to follow the lieutenant."

Muller looked down at their destruction. "I had no idea, Kurt, that university zoologists were so single-minded."

"I learned some things in '34 with Hood in Tibet," Raeder replied.

"Demolition?"

"No. Not to give your enemies any chance at all."

Let the British try to follow them now.

They traded the mules for yaks at a border village, reloaded their luggage on fewer animals, and trudged on. The trail's surroundings were treeless now, brown where barren rock prevailed and green in watered swales. The Kangra La itself was a barren saddle marked with a cairn of stone and fluttering prayer flags.

"Each flap of the flag sends a prayer to their gods," Raeder told his companions.

"What's our prayer, Kurt?" asked Eckells.

"Power."

They were at seventeen thousand feet. Around them, peaks shot ten thousand feet higher, draped with glaciers blue as fine diamonds. The sky was cobalt, the sun burned heatless. Wind whipped over the pass, snapping their clothes and pennants.

"Tibet," the German announced, pointing at a horizon of endless mountains. "This is what Cortés felt when he gazed on Tenochtitlán, or Moses at the Promised Land."

"Cortés had gold to entice him," Kranz said.

"Tibet has gold, too. Tons of it, in Buddhist temples. They are rich, and oddly weak."

"Ah, so that's your secret motive, Kurt? We plunder? I've been wondering as we've panted."

"Of course not. Mere treasure hunting is a relic of history. In modern times, the gold comes from the real prize, scientific discovery." He smiled. "But if we come away with gold as well, it will be just compensation, no?"

"Power in this oxygen-starved, arid, medieval backwater?" Muller said skeptically, gazing at the emptiness.

"The world's greatest secret." Raeder's eyes shone, as if he might pry a revelation from the slopes of the mountains ahead. "We are looking for the force, my SS brethren, that animates the world."

11

Hong Kong, China
September 28, 1938

B enjamin Grayson Hood traveled more miles in
nine days than Raeder's expedition had sailed and
marched in nine weeks. Hood's first three thousand
miles were by train from New York to San Francisco
by way of Chicago, aboard the gleaming *California
Zephyr.* Then by seaplane more than eight thousand
miles across the Pacific. The Martin 130 *China Clipper*
flown by Pan American averaged an astonishing 163
mph, hopping to Pearl Harbor, Midway, Wake Island,
Guam, Manila, and Hong Kong. Each was an oasis of
calm and safety, far removed from the aggression of the
Japanese Empire in China.

Hood's ticket for this race against the Germans had
cost a staggering $1,600, or as much as two new cars.

But then he'd had a private cabin with bunk, wash-stand, and the finest cuisine the airline could conjure. He relished the shrimp and steak while he could, and didn't turn down the company of one Edith Warnecke, either. She was a pretty and bored thirty-five-year-old double divorcée traveling to meet her newest husband in Singapore. Edith smelled Hood's money and pedigree; Hood, opportunity. She liked red wine, chocolate, and sex, and rode the American adventurer ragged three miles above the Pacific, moaning like another propeller.

He was willing to oblige since the days ahead would be privation enough. And yet the amusement was oddly unsatisfying. Edith was an unhappy woman, looking for distraction. Ben realized (somewhat to his own sur-prise) that he was increasingly dissatisfied with distrac-tion. Life should *mean* something, and not just society outings, specimen expeditions, and museum tolerance of his stooping to be a scientist. *Sex* should mean some-thing, someday. After the *Clipper* skidded down on its pontoons into Hong Kong harbor, he stepped out on the dock, annoyed with his own conduct. Since the Tibet scandal he'd been embroiled in four years before, he'd been marking time. Now, he thought, his time had come.

Mrs. Warnecke, sensing his mood, stalked off with-out a good-bye to drink by herself until the next flight to Singapore.

What am I doing here? Hood said to himself as he watched the minuet of the junks traversing the harbor. It certainly wasn't to fulfill some secret mission for Duncan Hale as errand boy for Uncle Sam. It was to complete what he'd long suspected was unfinished, his business with Kurt Raeder and Keyuri Lin.

Astonishing that Raeder had dared return.

Somewhere, in central Asia, was what he'd backed away from before: the test of being a man.

Hood had arrived at the edge of chaos. One couldn't tell that in Hong Kong itself, with its stately British warships, regal banks and ministries, and bustling streets where coolies pulled rickshaws at a steady trot and Chinese women of high fashion minced in narrow silk dresses slit just high enough, to the knee, to make maneuverability possible. Sampans choked the quay and liners gleamed like mammoth wedding cakes, their stacks pumping out energetic streams of smoke. All this played out against a beautiful backdrop of steep green hills as extravagant and improbable as an opera set.

Beyond, however, was the mainland. Shanghai and Nanking had fallen to the Japanese the year before. Nipponese warplanes had sunk the American gunboat *Panay* in the Yangtze River in December, creating a diplomatic uproar. While the beleaguered Chinese army had won an impressive victory at Shantung this spring, now the Imperial Army was counterattacking toward Hankow. Their warplanes, rising sun on the wing, ranged like raptors. Munitions destined for Chiang Kai-shek were safely stacked on Hong Kong wharves under British protection. But once they were on railroads to the mainland, they ran a gauntlet of air raids.

The British trader Sir Arthur Readings explained all this when Hood called on him in the imperial oasis of Hong Kong called Happy Valley, site of the colony's racetrack. Since British Intelligence had been alerted of Hood's mission and agreed to help, Hood had been instructed by Duncan Hale to go to Readings for advice. Sir Arthur knew finance, good liquor, and China.

"Ordinarily, old chap, you'd pull up here and call the journey done," Readings said when the two met for whiskey and dinner at his club. Apparently Sir Arthur did secret work for his empire beyond his shipping and sweatshops, and that work included liaison with mysterious agencies from the United States.

"It's not like '34 when you were here before," Sir Arthur went on. "I know China was a bit of a scrimmage then, but it's full-scale war now, millions killed, and the Japs are bombing the Kowloon-Canton Railway. I'm not sure whoever sent you entirely realizes what the situation is. Can't blame Washington, tucked as it is on the other side of the world."

I can, Hood thought to himself. "You said, 'Ordinarily'?"

"Quite. The truth is, we live in perilous times and I'm told your mission could have real importance. You're in for a bit of a romp. Accordingly, I have an idea. Just enough to get you killed, I suspect."

"I'm not sure that will rattle my employers. Though I am cheap labor; paid my own way, mostly. A patriotic cog to counter the deficits of the New Deal."

"By God, you won't see a British lord doing that. That's bloody marvelous, or bloody insane. So you're English in one way; a bit balmy, are you?"

"My country is counting on it. So I've got to get to Tibet, and crossing China is the quickest way."

"That's like saying crossing the battlefield of Waterloo is the quickest way to Brussels. It's sheer havoc out there, man. Chiang's generals are at each other's throats, the Nips have seized most of the coast and industry, and the Communists have created a bandit state of some sort up in the northwest. This Mao character won't stand and fight, but he yaps and snaps like a little terrier. The only way Chiang has slowed the Japanese is to break the dikes on the Yellow and Yangtze rivers, flooding a thousand towns. Might as well go to the moon."

"Arthur, if it was up to me I'd take your 'ordinarily' advice and board the *Clipper* back to Hawaii, finding another high-class tart to while away the monotony."

"Another? You had one on the way here?"

"More interesting than looking at the ocean."

The Englishman shook his head. "You Yanks always manage to make things a lark, don't you? But then I wish I still looked like you." Arthur was bald, sixty pounds overweight, and red as an apple. "And you've got a hankering to see the Roof of the World again?"

"Something like that. It appears the Nazis are trying to beat us to it."

"Nazis! Good lord, they seem to be everywhere, don't they? And which Nazis this time? The German military mission has abandoned the Chinese. Their new Japanese friends made them do it. Everyone's choosing up sides, trading this dance partner for that one."

"This Nazi is different. Old partner of mine named Raeder, an explorer and scientist on his way to Tibet. Capable, but perhaps too capable. I'm to catch up to him and find out what he's up to."

"Dominating the world, I imagine. That seems to be the German obsession these days." Sir Arthur sniffed, glancing at his own empire's clubs and racetrack. It was hard to imagine such established opulence ever being threatened. "Well, if you want to chase after Jerry, more power to you. Just take gold coin for bribes, ammunition to shoot your way through, and a good quart of scotch, because you're not going to find any in Tibet. Worst cuisine in the world, I hear."

"And some of the most glorious country. Their valleys are higher than the crest of our Rockies."

"All the more reason not to go there, if you ask me. Dreadful climb. But say, here's my idea. Have an eye for the ladies, do you?"

"Just the normal male appreciation."

"Have you heard of Beth Calloway?"

"A looker?"

"A flier, though I hear she doesn't look bad, either. A regular Amelia Earhart, this girl. A tomboy, what you Yanks might call an oddball. She showed up to shoot down Japanese, and while the Chinese won't let a woman do that, Madame Chiang put her to work doing other things for the Chinese air force."

"What things?"

"The male mercenaries monopolize the fighter and bomber planes, so they put Beth to work as an instructor. She also scouts airways and airfields to India and Burma, now that the Japanese are clamping off the Chinese coast. She's flown over more of Asia than any woman, and more than any man, probably."

"Really?" Hood sat straighter. "Tibet?"

"No idea, but you can spend three months walking there and being waylaid by bandits and warlords, or three days flying. I'm thinking you might be able to hire this girl away for a week or two, if Madame Chiang thought you were on the generalissimo's side. I could write a persuasive letter. Jolly romp to go with a comely aviatrix, no? You can drop in on these Nazis while they're still sweating uphill."

"You think she'll take me there?"

"The truth is, she's done some timely jobs for the Crown here and there and we've had some contact," Sir Arthur said. "She's earned a penny or two doing it. I've also had some correspondence from your Mr., er, Hale, and he, too, suggested her." The merchant sipped his drink. "Everybody wants to speed you on your way, it seems."

"Reassuring." Hood slugged his whiskey.

"Calloway has certain flair. If you can get to the new Chinese capital of Hankow alive, you can't miss her. As often as not, she's got cowboy boots and a Colt .45. Bowie knife, too, I imagine. Lovely girl." He smiled. "Resourceful."

"You make it so enticing."

"Better than the rogue Genghis Khans you'll otherwise meet, I assure you. Just keep your head low when the Nips strafe. And never trust the Jerries."

12

Summit Bank, Concrete, United States
September 4, Present Day

Your descent from Benjamin Hood is on your mother's side," Barrow said as they continued driving up
the Skagit Valley, Rominy purposefully numbed after
emptying more than half the wine bottle. She was an
occasion-only drinker, but had decided this qualified as
an occasion, even if she'd been slightly embarrassed at
having a third glass in front of Jake. "If the records
are correct, your grandmother, Hood's daughter, was
an only child. When she married she lost her maiden
name, and the chain of descent continues through your
mother, who also took her husband's name. It's no surprise, given the circumstances, that you haven't heard
of Benjamin Hood."

"So how have *you* heard of him?"

"It started as a historical feature story on a local figure everyone has forgotten. Tibet explorer moves to rural Washington and dies in unappreciated obscurity, that kind of thing. But then I began digging up these enigmatic documents suggesting that Ben Hood hadn't just gone to Tibet, he'd found or seen something there that other people wanted. Federal government people. But access to his old place is barred by some nutty Dotty Crockett type upriver, and the only person with right of entry is an heir. Which, I eventually figured out, is *you*."

"What did Hood find or see?"

"That's unclear, but the Nazis were after it, too. So I think, wow, this is the kind of yarn I could sell to *American Heritage* or *Smithsonian*, or maybe get a book contract, once it ran in the paper. Nice Depression-era mystery. But then there were odd clicks on my phone, and I found a bug on my desk."

"Bug?"

"Listening device." He waved his hand as if this was an everyday irritation. "I realized some other folks were looking into this story, too, but not just to make a free-lance fee out of it. Either they want what Hood found or they want to make sure no one else ever gets it. It turns out there were Nazis in Tibet, too, and suddenly I'm being shadowed by skinhead goons. I realized I'd better find you and figure out just what exactly is going on."

"I have no idea what's going on."

"But you have the genealogy to find out."

"I didn't ask to be dragged into this!"

"Of course not, but you're key. Which is why you're in danger. And it was dumb luck I learned enough to warn you. And there *is* an inheritance, apparently. You can thank me later."

"After my knees heal." She felt truculent about being caught up in something without being asked first. It wasn't fair.

"That wasn't planned. Before we could be properly introduced, 'boom'! And, well, here we are."

"Here we are *where*?"

"Concrete." Once more he turned the pickup off the main highway, driving them past some gigantic dull-gray concrete silos that, in faded red letters, indeed announced Concrete. "Guess what they made in this place? It built some big dams upriver."

"Benjamin Hood lived in Concrete?"

"Nah, he's up on the Cascade River, which is where we have to go. But he did his banking here, and that's where you come in."

Rominy looked out at a rain-stained, pocket-sized town punched into more of the valley's lush forest. She'd heard of it but never been here.

Barrow turned onto Main Street. "This burg is actually modestly famous, because De Niro and DiCaprio made *This Boy's Life* here. The Tobias Wolff memoir? Wolff lived up in the Seattle City Light company towns, Newhalem and Diablo, but he came down here for high school. Hollywood, baby."

They parked. Downtown was a block-long clump of architecturally uninspired buildings about as charming as a gas station and as typically American as baseball and Barbie. Tavern, hardware store, Laundromat, food bank—unsurprising, since there was no sign of money—and, more heartening, a surviving movie theater. Many of the time-warp buildings were built (as she should have guessed) of painted concrete. There were old lodge halls for the American Legion and Eagles and an eight-foot carved wooden bear, incongruously rearing under a gazebo built to keep the rain off. Summit Bank had a reader board displaying the temperature (67 degrees) and a sign, SINCE 1914. Inside was utilitarian as a post office. Paneling painted white, forest green carpet, and the kind of fluorescent lighting that gives off the warmth of Greenland's ice cap. The clerks, however, smiled. A vault door gave a peek toward safety deposit boxes.

"When Hood lived up here, this was the State Bank of Concrete," Barrow explained. "He left a will and a safety deposit box for his heirs, but guess what? No heirs. Until you. And a mystery seventy-plus years unsolved. Until now." He grinned and went up to a teller. "Mr. Dunnigan, please."

"I'll see if he's available."

"Tell him Mr. Barrow and Ms. Pickett-Hood are here to see him. He's *expecting* us." Jake stood tall like it was his birthday, glancing around impatiently. Rominy studied him again. Her companion, she admitted, was intriguing, smart, and a bit of a stud. He was built like a fitness freak, and his eyes seemed lit with blue fire. Certainly more interesting than another evening home with Netflix and Häagen-Dazs. Instead of savior or kidnapper, Jake was making himself, she realized, a partner.

Curiosity kept her with him. And it was reassuring he'd taken her somewhere dull, like a bank.

"I still don't get what I'm supposed to do here," she whispered.

"Inherit, remember?" he whispered back.

Mr. Dunnigan was a balding, portly bank vice president in a white no-iron synthetic shirt and JCPenney sport coat, who reigned behind a Formica desk of faux oak. He picked up a stack of manila folders and took them into an adjacent small conference room with wooden table and hard chairs, looking at Rominy as if she were a ghost. Which she supposed she was in a way, if what Barrow claimed was true. The missing heir of Benjamin Hood! Who?

"Congratulations, Mr. Barrow," the banker began, dropping the folders with a thump. "As you know, I was skeptical of your research."

"You sound like my editors."

"The DNA test, however, convinced me."

"DNA?" Rominy asked.

"Yes, Miss, it's been so long since Mr. Hood's death and his family history is so truncated—goodness, such tragedy—that a mere genealogical table wasn't going to convince me an heir still existed. That's when Mr. Barrow suggested the use of DNA evidence, which is surprisingly quick and affordable. We had a rather gruesome relic . . ." He paused, looking at Barrow.

"A finger." The reporter shrugged. "It must have meant something, because Hood kept it in his safety deposit box after he lost it from his hand."

"He was *attached* to it," Dunnigan said, smiling. Apparently, bankers in Concrete possessed quite the wit.

"Wait a minute," Rominy said. "You matched my DNA to his?"

"Yes, dear. An impossibility for earlier generations, but science marches on."

"But how did you get *my* DNA?"

Dunnigan looked surprised at the question and turned to Jake. He in turn looked uncomfortable.

"How did you get my DNA, Barrow?" Rominy asked again.

He cleared his throat. "Saliva."

"Saliva? *When?*"

"I got it off a Starbucks cup. I fished it out after you left a store."

"Are you joking? When was this?"

"A week ago."

"You've been following me to get my saliva?"

"To let you inherit, Rominy," he said patiently, as if she was a little dense.

"That's *illegal.* Isn't it?"

"My bank cannot condone anything improper," Dunnigan added.

"Of course it's legal," Barrow said blandly. He turned to the banker. "My newspaper's lawyers checked this out. As long as you're not taking samples from a person's body without permission—like clipping their hair—it passes the test. We've done this before. It's fine, so long as it's from discarded organic material."

Dunnigan frowned, then shrugged.

"Discarded like a Starbucks cup," Rominy said.

"Yes."

"That's sick."

"Do you think you would have let me run a swab inside your mouth?"

"Maybe, if you'd ever explained yourself in a normal way."

"I had to be sure or you would have run like a rabbit. 'Hi there, you might be due a missing inheritance so do you mind if a run a Q-tip?' It sounds like molestation. You would have dumped espresso down my pants and been furious if it wasn't a match. So I did something that didn't disturb you one iota, and we compared Hood's finger to the saliva you left on the cup."

"That's disgusting."

"Maybe so, but because of it you're sitting in a bank about to get a look into Benjamin Hood's safety deposit box. How many times do I have to tell you I'm trying to *help* you?"

"You're trying to help yourself." She closed her eyes, momentarily wishing she could will this day away. But when she opened them they were both still looking at her with troubled and not unkind expressions. There was sympathy there. And Jake did have that compelling little scar. She sighed. "The DNA shows this Hood character and I are related?"

"Yes," Dunnigan said, visibly relieved she wasn't going to throw a fit.

"What happened to all the other descendants? After three generations, there should be a zillion of them by now."

"Only children after mysterious accidents to their mothers," Jake said. "A drowning, a car crash. Nobody ever put it all together because of the changes of names and growing fear of even discussing the Hood relationship, I'm guessing. Nobody put it together until I did. And I realized there was one final survivor: a survivor because she was left in a campground, adopted by strangers, a girl who knew nothing of her own past."

Had her real parents been protecting her? Had they known they were about to die? Were they being chased? "And you think this was somehow the work of Nazi fanatics, leftovers from World War II, who didn't want whatever my great-grandpa found ever getting out?"

"Possibly." Jake glanced at the banker, and then shrugged. "Or the American government."

"The Americans? But Great-grandpa was American."

"He left a hero, a government agent, and came home a dropout. Why, we don't know. That's the mystery I'm trying to unravel. I thought we had more time until that bomb went off."

"What bomb?" Dunnigan looked alarmed.

"Watch the news tonight, Mr. Dunnigan. But don't worry, we're well past them. Don't call the press and they won't call you. But let's not linger, shall we? What if reporters find the same paper trail I did and trace Rominy up here? Or cops do? Or Nazis?"

"Exactly." Now the banker was brisk. "Let's get the pretty lady on her way." He took the folders and began spreading papers out on the table as if dealing cards, suddenly in a hurry to have them gone. "Here are the genealogical tables Mr. Barrow assembled, birth certificates, address reports, news clippings, and the DNA testing documentation. It's been quite an exercise in investigation, because Benjamin Hood was apparently quite the recluse. We never saw him; he was a complete hermit. He was represented by a woman; possibly your great-grandmother. But we have the will, the bank records, and information on the Cascade River property." He glanced at Rominy. "Are you a fan of compound interest, Ms. Hood?"

"Of what?"

"The way savings can accumulate over time. Mr. Hood left a relatively modest savings account here when he died in 1944 and it by rights now belongs to you. It was a little over $8,000. Which has become with compounding interest . . ."—he searched a table of figures—"a healthy $161,172, after deductions for the safety deposit box, taxes on the Cascade River property, and our administrative fees. Would you like a cashier's check? We'd like to clear out the account."

She was stunned. First her car gone, now this? Was she on drugs? She looked at Barrow.

"Now do you understand why this is important?" he asked. "And this is just the tip of the iceberg." He turned to Dunnigan. "We may need travel money. I suggest thirty thousand dollars in cash and a check for the rest."

"That's quite a lot of cash to carry around," the banker cautioned.

"Not for long. She'll be careful."

"I'm afraid the young lady is going to have to speak for herself."

Rominy was dazed. "Thirty thousand?" Her annual salary wasn't much more.

"Just for a day or two until we figure out if we need to go to Tibet," Jake said.

"Tibet!"

"Hang with me just a little longer, Rominy. It will make sense."

"Right." She threw up her hands. "In twenties, please." Wasn't that how they did it in the movies? It didn't seem like real money. "And you can transfer the balance to my account in Seattle." Her voice sounded small even to her. But she wasn't taking a check Barrow or neo-Nazis could run off with.

"I think we may have difficulty accumulating that many twenties in this branch. Now if you could give us a day or two . . ."

"Whatever bills you have, Mr. Dunnigan," Jake said. "As much as you can spare. We're a little pressed for time, remember?" He gestured toward the door. "Don't want anyone following us here."

"Yes, yes, of course. Sign these forms, and I'll start the arrangements."

Hand shaking at the thought of so much money, Rominy signed everything put before her. Then the bank vice president gave her a small brass key. "This is yours for the safety deposit box, should you decide to keep it. I trust you want to look inside?"

She still had a headache, but what answer could she give?

"Yes. Let's see what all this fuss is about."

13

The Lhasa Road, Tibet
September 2, 1938

The Tibetan Plateau averages three miles in height and sprawls across an area four times the size of France, but it is not the simple tableland the name implies. The German "descent" from Kangra La (*La* was the Tibetan name for "pass") was in fact a journey into an unending sea of treeless, arid, undulating mountains, swell after corrugated swell that ran on without obscuring haze until limited by the curve of the earth. It was magnificent desolation, only the highest peaks capped with snow at the end of summer. Tibet was grass-and-rock emptiness completely different from humid Sikkim, its brown folds meandering and stark. Rock cliffs broke through its grassy felt with vivid bands of ocher, yellow, and white. Rivers braided their way across gravel bottoms in deep valleys like the silver strands of a necklace. The sky was a deep, violet blue—Prussian blue, Raeder told the others, though his companions thought it purpler than that—and sunrise and sunset were yellow-green in the icy sky, dawn and dusk more electric and urgent than at home. Clouds and cliffs cast deep shadows that made a pinto contrast to the sunny ridges, and everything had a sharpness that confused any sense of distance. The Germans could pick out snowy peaks—Muller said one of them was Everest—that on the map were nearly a hundred miles away.

The air was thin but more precious because of it, and breathing reminded Raeder of drinking champagne. Lungs sucked greedily, throats raw and chilled from the draft, and there was a curious feeling of giddiness. The druglike euphoria countered the ache of muscles from the ceaseless climbs and descents.

At first, this side of Tibet—different from the Chinese border areas a thousand miles to the east that Raeder had explored with Hood four years before—seemed utterly empty. But then the explorers realized the dark humps they might mistake for distant boulders were in fact grazing yak, and that the black smudges were not patches of heather or thorn but nomadic felt tents. Southern Tibet was essentially steep pasture.

As the Germans marched, dirty, snot-nosed nomad children would sometimes run out to the dirt trail to fruitlessly beg. Or herdsmen would gallop on their ponies to pull up and stare at the German caravan as it passed, their faces dark and angular and their bodies wrapped in their *chuba*, a cloaklike fleece coat. The Germans kept their guns in view, Diels wearing the submachine gun and Raeder slinging his hunting rifle with scope across his back.

On three occasions the *dugchen* offered them tea, and Raeder and Eckells would then amuse the herdsmen by competing at shooting at rocks up to four hundred yards away. The men shouted approval at each puff of dust. But once, when Raeder aimed at a distant antelope, a chieftain gently shoved the muzzle aside. The Buddhists would not abide unnecessary killing.

When Raeder and Eckells were alone, however, they amused themselves by picking off animals that showed white against precipitous cliffs. They left the carcasses to the vultures.

The few Tibetan soldiers they encountered still practiced archery, since they had no spare bullets to expend on practice.

The Western show of arms was balanced by the little red swastika pennants that jutted up from the German pack animals like sturdy stalks, the wind snapping what Raeder hoped the natives would take as a familiar goodwill sign. Certainly they spotted similar swastikas inscribed or painted on doorways, monastery porticos, and farm carts. In some the swastika arms were extended into the intricate circular geometry Himmler had called a sun wheel. It was an encouraging suggestion that the Aryans were, indeed, finding ancient cousins.

The villages, made of mud brick with flat clay roofs, blended with the dun-colored hills and were hazed by yak-dung fires. With the only trees growing in remote river bottoms, the dung was a substitute for wood. It was slapped into bricks by young girls and stacked at each residence for winter fuel, proudly lining the top of every courtyard wall and reaching to the sill of every window.

The village roads were dirt, each plod of the yaks raising a plume of dung dust. Ill-fed dogs would bark and snarl as the Nazis passed, lunging against felt-rope tethers. The Germans shared the winding, lumpy lanes with scarlet-robed monks who hiked down from monasteries perched like forts on nearby hills. There were also barley farmers, herdsmen, shopkeepers, and migratory traders. The women were pretty, the Germans noticed: high-cheeked, dark-eyed, with hair like black silk. But they were modestly wrapped against the wind in colorful dress and striped apron called a *pangden* that discouraged much discernment of their form. The SS men were restless for women, but had no idea how to obtain any in this strange, contemplative culture.

Raeder wanted one to dominate, to hear her cries, but he dared not risk it. The mission required discipline. The craving made him moody, and when Diels tried to joke with him about the dung and the dust, he snapped in reply.

Submission was what he'd wanted from Lotte, until she hinted to her family about his tastes. The marriage became too complicated and had to end. And the accident was nearly that, an accident—he'd not planned it at all—but when the muzzle swung to follow a flight of rising ducks and traversed her body, his finger had acted on its own. He'd pretended *that* shotgun had been at the bottom of the boat, accidentally set off, and had just enough celebrity to discourage too many close questions. So Lotte died in surprise, sprawled in the bottom of the boat, the top of her head gone and the rest gushing blood, her mouth gaping with questions he himself couldn't answer.

She'd been beautiful, innocent, naive, and uncooperative. He needed to find something great here, something truly colossal, to cement his place in history so that he'd finally be able to sleep.

"What are you brooding about, Kurt?"

"Victory."

Raeder wondered if titans like Himmler had their own demons.

Religion was everywhere. Prayer flags were strung at every sacred hill. Prayer wheels spun on the walls at each holy site. Pointed white chortens, reliquaries for souls and saints, poked up at town entrances like upside-down turnips, or gigantic, golden-topped spark plugs. Every second male seemed to be a monk, and the monasteries seemed the only real industry. People shuffled while working *malas*, Buddhist rosaries of 108 beads.

But Raeder's quintet was drawn more to the old abandoned military forts, called *dzongs*. These medieval strongholds were empty and haunted, replaced by the monastic strongholds of an overpowering religion. The SS men felt more at home in these fortress ruins than in the dark, smoky monasteries with their ominous chants. Raeder's men scrambled through their labyrinth of rooms like boys at a German castle. Here, they speculated, their Aryan ancestors would have ruled.

"It was a more heroic, military age," said Kranz, their archaeologist. "Now all they do is pray."

The valleys were planted in mustard and barley because wheat would not grow at this altitude. *Chang,* the odd beer, was made from barley. Incised into cliffs above the farms were red-daubed Buddha statues, or painted black and white ladders symbolic of the long prayerful climb toward nirvana.

Tibetan technology was primitive—there were virtually no wheeled carts—but the Germans did occasionally encounter a waterwheel. One, near Gyantse, was used to mill barley. Another used the waterpower only to turn prayer wheels outside of a monastery, each revolution a radio beam aimed at God.

Lakes were turquoise or cobalt, vivid against the treeless hills, and birds hung over them like kites, rotating in the wind. The Germans' porter Akeh, one of several Tibetans they'd hired, pointed out sites for sky burials, where the dead were dismembered and left for vultures to hasten the cycle of returning to the earth. The carrion birds were holy.

"Poverty, superstition, ignorance, prayer, and barbarism," Raeder summed up one night as they camped by Lake Yamdok Tso, enjoying the luxury of a wood campfire fed by a nearby copse of stunted trees. "Reichsführer Himmler might begin to doubt that these Tibetans are or ever were Aryans, or that they could have left anything worth rediscovering."

"We certainly haven't found ruins of a nobler race," said Muller. "Just crude forts."

"Or any food beyond yak meat and barley cakes," moaned cameraman Eckells. The *tsampa* cakes were as tasteless as they were commonplace.

"And yet we're closer to heaven," said Raeder. "The stars tight as a ceiling, the air sharp as a shard of ice. I think I know why they're obsessed with religion. It's the only occupation that makes sense here, a way to make use of this weird clarity. In such a case, might a civilization not make discoveries obscured to empires in lower, murkier places? Could the legends of Vril be true?"

"I don't know, Kurt," said Muller. "My God, they labor like peasants."

"But they may have lost our secret wisdom," said Kranz. "We need the help of the Tibetans, and for that we have to convince them that Germany and National Socialism are their natural allies."

"With our runes and our swastikas," said Diels.

"Our machines and our modernism," said Eckells. "Our guns and our magnetometers."

"Yes, and with our mysticism and belief in the past," said Raeder. "Tibetans are a people lost in the past, and we seek it, too. They believe in lives beyond this one, and so does our *Reichsführer*. We're the new druids, my companions, the black knights who will lead the world to the purity of ice. Come, let's build up our fire and sing for our porters."

Their fire blazed higher, light reflected on the lake, and red sparks climbed to mingle with cold stars overhead. The Germans began singing a Reich military anthem, voices carrying across the water.

Flame upraise!
Rise in blazing light.
From the mountains along the Rhine.
Rise shining!

See, we are standing
Faithful in a blessed circle,
To see you, flame,
And so praise the Fatherland!

Holy Fire,
Call the Young together
So that next to your blazing flames,
Courage grows . . .

They seized burning brands and began marching, circling their camp as the mules shifted nervously. Then they paraded down to the dark lakeshore and, at Raeder's command, hurled the brands high over the water. The torches fell like meteors, hissing into the frigid water. Fire and ice, World Ice Theory.

Everything a struggle between light and dark, white and black, hot and cold, the immaculate and the corrupt.

Then they toasted one another with schnapps, howling at the moon like German werewolves.

The Tibetan porters watched silently from the shadows.

14

Hankow, China
September 29, 1938

The shadow of the Nakajima fighter flickered across the train just before the bullets did, the soldiers aboard as startled as squirrels beneath a hawk. Hood was riding atop a boxcar to escape the crowding and the heat, and watched the havoc stitch toward him as men yelled and instinctively ducked.

The carnage was transfixing. There was only time for a shout of warning at the rising snarl of the engine and then the fighter's machine guns chewed down the length of the lumbering cars, wood flying and the wounded yelping. Newly recruited Chinese infantrymen were blown from rooftop perches like chaff. The painted twin meatballs of the rising sun were clearly visible on the wings as the fighter banked overhead, and then it was coming for them again, hundreds of excited soldiers shooting a fusillade into the sky as the train engine's whistle screamed warning.

It felt like they were crawling.

Hood pulled out the .45 that Duncan Hale had issued him and balanced on his knees as the plane came toward them again. The gun was slick and heavy. He wanted to hide but inside was no better protection; each strafing bullet was the size of a forefinger and could punch all the way to the roadbed. Their tormentor seemed to swell in size until it filled the whole sky. Hood's pistol bucked as he fired, jarring his wrist and making it hard to aim. He vowed to take more practice. His rifle and shotgun were stored in his duffel below, and he suddenly incongruously worried that his belongings might take a bullet.

The tops of the freight cars ahead seemed to heave upward as the machine-gun fire struck, men jerking and tumbling, a catastrophic rupture that tore from car to car.

Hood braced himself for the explosion of his own flesh.

But then the machine guns stopped flashing, the Nakajima roared by, and the excited Chinese were left to fire their rifles at an empty sky. Hood actually felt the suck of the propeller. Then, as abruptly as it came, the plane was gone. Their train whistle kept shrilly blowing at nothing.

Maybe they wounded the pilot. Maybe the fighter ran out of bullets. Maybe it was low on fuel. But Hood knew that the only thing that saved his life during his harrowing journey to the chaotic new Chinese capital was that the plane aborted its second strafing run just moments before the stuttering spray reached him. Splinters rose in a fountain, a mesmerizing eruption, and then the fountain abruptly ceased one car ahead.

Born with a silver spoon in your mouth and dumb luck to cover your ass, Hood thought. *Must have done something right in a previous life. Or you're supposed to do something in this one to earn it.*

The attack left chaos in its wake. Cars were splashed with blood, men moaned from the impact of the slugs, and whole boards had been knocked askew. But the train, its engine unmarked, didn't slow. They chugged doggedly on, while the dead were rolled off to make more room for the shaken living.

Hood reloaded his .45 and tucked it back in its holster. The big pistol was less accurate than hurling rocks, but if it ever hit a target, it tended to stop it. This was his first combat, and he was relieved he'd had the presence of mind to shoot back.

They reached Hankow that night, the rail yard light a combination of kerosene lamps, paper lanterns, and bonfires steaming in light rain. Soldiers, coolies, nurses, nuns, and generals milled in the chaos of the depot. Blood was still dripping from the floorboards of Hood's troop train when he stepped down, the leakage diluted by the wet. Fog and smoke mixed with the hissing steam of locomotives. A distant rumble was not thunder, but Japanese and Chinese artillery. Their reflected flashes were like sheet lightning.

The remaining dead were stacked like cordwood. Soldiers kept beggar children away from looting the bodies, so they swarmed Hood instead until he swatted them off. Old women pressed close to sell tea and steamed buns.

He ate one to reassure himself he was still alive.

You always knew it wasn't over with Raeder, he thought.

A rickshaw took Hood toward Chiang's headquarters. Weaving through the crowded streets was like pushing through syrup. Everywhere were guns, munitions, heavily guarded pallets of rice, tins of fuel, and refugees. That's what the Japanese were attacking, Hood decided: syrup. China was an endless sea of viscous honey that would ultimately swallow any invader.

In the meantime, millions would die.

Sir Arthur Readings had given him a letter of introduction to Madame Chiang Kai-shek, the Shanghai-born, American-raised Wellesley College graduate who had become the fluent link between China and the United States. Because of her interest in aviation, she was also secretary-general of the Chinese Commission on Aeronautical Affairs. In other words, the generalissimo's wife ran the Chinese air force. Hood would need her permission to borrow Beth Calloway.

Madame Chiang was a petite Chinese woman with a large head who was not especially pretty anymore—power had hardened her—but who carried the commanding presence that comes from the blessing of a strong-boned face and incandescent eyes. She had a disconcerting southern accent from Georgia where she was raised, and a smile and animation that beamed with the energy of a lighthouse. China was fighting for survival, and this dynamo who bridged two worlds would do anything it took to save it.

"Tibet!" she exclaimed after examining the documents of introduction he'd been given by the Americans and British. "Even for us Chinese, that's the edge of the world, a place of mystery and misunderstanding. And you say Himmler is sending an expedition there?"

"So I've been told. The mission's leader, Kurt Raeder, is a man who accompanied one of my expeditions several years ago. Moody, but highly competent. And a Nazi. So I've been asked to learn what he's up to, but he has a long head start. Which is why I need to borrow an airplane. Sir Arthur suggested an aviatrix named Beth Calloway."

"Sir Arthur would. As would any man, I suppose." She looked at him slyly. "She's one of our best pilots, you know."

"That's what I need to fly to the highest country on earth."

"I'm actually interested that you prove the feasibility of such flights, Mr. Hood. Aviation is China's future. It's the one technology that can stitch a very big, very crowded, very complex nation together. My husband agrees. And because we have no aircraft industry of our own, we must cobble together Soviet, German, American, and British planes to fight the Japanese. In doing so, the invaders are learning we're not just a nation of ignorant coolies."

"The whole world admires your courage."

"The whole world knows we're in retreat. Which is why we can't risk leaving our backs unguarded. Were the Germans to somehow gain influence in Tibet and turn it against us for their new allies the Japanese, we'd have enemies on two sides. This can't be tolerated. So yes, I'm going to order Ms. Calloway to fly you to Lhasa. We need to know what Herr Raeder is up to, don't we? Have you flown in a biplane before?"

"I was hoping for something more modern."

"Anything more modern is fighting the Japanese. Have you met Beth Calloway?"

"No. Sir Arthur described her in flamboyant terms."

"Flamboyant is an interesting choice of word. You're in for an experience there, as well. I'll write an order giving you transport in one of our Corsairs. It can just barely clear the Tibetan passes, but it's durable, repairable, and old enough to be expendable."

"You're so reassuring."

"Miss Calloway has ingenuity, I assure you. She'll get you as close as she can as fast as she can. Dress warmly, and take a gun."

"I have several, and fired one at a Japanese fighter."

"Splendid. Did you hit him?"

"I don't know. At least he went away."

She smiled. "I wish I could say the same for the entire Japanese army."

"Thank you for your help and advice, Madame Air Secretary."

"Thank you for your service, Dr. Hood. I understand you're a wealthy man and a respected curator. I know you don't have to do this."

"Actually, I've thought about it and I do." He turned to go.

When he got to the door she called after him. "Oh, and, Dr. Hood?"

"Yes?"

"You might want to return through British India. We're doing our best, but Hankow may have fallen to the Japanese by the time you want to go home. *If* you've survived."

Beth Calloway didn't have a Bowie knife, but she did have cowboy boots, Western jeans, a denim work shirt dirty from engine grease, and a Brooklyn Dodgers baseball cap with its bill turned backward. A .38 was holstered on one undeniably fetching hip, and her blond hair was cut in a practical bob. She was twisting a wrench with masculine determination on the engine of a mustard-colored two-seater biplane scout. A thatched roof served as a hangar, flies buzzing on black pieces of machinery as if they were carrion. A Santa Claus calendar from 1937 advertised Coca-Cola.

The plane's patched wings, nicked propeller, and two bullet holes through its thin metal fuselage didn't inspire confidence. To Hood, the Corsair looked barely capable of clearing the runway, let alone the Tibetan plateau.

"So the Wright brothers had a garage sale."

She glanced up, squinting across a dust of freckles. Her eyes were sky blue. "Afraid of flying, Mr. . . . ?"

"Hood." He strummed a strut. "Afraid of falling. Dr. Hood, actually. Ph.D."

She straightened. "You must be the egghead the Chinese warned was coming."

"Museum curator."

"And expert on aviation." Calloway let her arm fall with the heavy wrench and Hood stood for inspection. He was taut and tanned in that country club way, with the confidence that comes of breeding, money, and schools with crests on their jackets. He carried a duffel bag on a sling that was nearly as long as he was, and had taken care to be washed, combed, and cocky.

Beth's knuckles were scraped, her nails short, and her lips bare and pursed with skepticism. Pretty enough in a wary way, but not as impressed with him as he was used to. In fact, she looked as if she were surprised he'd made it this far.

"I'm just cautious of machines with holes in them," he said.

"This Vought Corsair is only ten years old. Easy to fly and it can be fixed with chewing gum, if you have to. "

"Perhaps I should buy stock in Wrigley." He rapped on the plane and, when she didn't respond to his wit, decided to be less sarcastic. "Beats walking."

"So charmed to meet you." Her tone made it clear she wasn't.

"And you, Beth Calloway. So Madame Chiang did send orders to introduce us? You'll take me to Tibet?"

"Dear me. In this? With a woman? Are you sure you want to?"

"Unfortunately Madame Chiang says this crate, and you, are all that can be spared. *Expendable* is the word they all keep using." He looked in one of the cockpits. "Is it any bigger than it looks?"

"Much smaller, after the first ten hours. Don't like to fly, Dr. Hood?"

"Call me Ben. I flew to Hong Kong on the *Clipper*. We dined with silver cutlery and had a choice of wines."

"I dine with a tip cup and boil water before I drink it." She put down the wrench and ran a wrist on her forehead. Even a grease smudge looked good on her, he decided, but she didn't flirt. Maybe she didn't like boys.

"I guess this will have to do." He gave her his best smile.

"Christ. You look like you were sent by Pepsodent."

He reddened. "I do brush my teeth."

"Iron the ascot, wax the limousine, starch the collar. Yes, I'll take you to Tibet, Great White Hunter."

"You flatter me. I only collect scientific specimens."

"Madame Chiang is the one who flatters you, *Professor*." She finally held out a greasy hand, palm up. He wasn't sure if it was a greeting, demand for payment, or a gesture of warning. "She reports you're a fine shot of rare and defenseless animals, which you stuff and cart back to the States."

"And you have a reputation as the best American woman pilot in China. Also, the only American woman pilot in China." He took her hand and squeezed it. Their fingers slid, not unpleasantly, from the oil. He thought she hesitated just a moment before pulling away, but it was one of those signals best to receive two or three times to confirm. "A pleasure to meet you, Miss Calloway. It's not lucky for a passenger to disparage his aircraft, is it?"

"Not lucky to do *what*?"

"Dis . . . to criticize."

"My, my. They did send our best, didn't they? A real college boy."

"I'm a zoologist with the American Museum of Natural History in New York. And I've walked to Tibet before. I'm simply in more of a hurry this time."

"I wouldn't care, except that Madame Chiang does."

"I need to confer with authorities in Lhasa."

"No one gets to confer with the authorities in Lhasa. It's forbidden."

"I have to un-forbid it."

"For your museum?"

"My present employers require discretion."

"Your what requires what?"

"My new bosses told me to keep my mouth shut."

"Well." She regarded him a long minute, gazing up and down. "How much do you weigh, zoo-owl-o-gist?"

Without meaning to, he drew himself up. "About one eighty-five." Maybe one ninety, after those *Clipper* meals. "Why?"

"Big words, vague mission, fussy flier. I got a feeling that whatever extra fuel I can squeeze aboard is going to be a lot more useful than *you*."

This one was going to require some charm, he thought.

Or taming.

15

Cascade River Road, United States
September 4, Present Day

The mountains rose higher and drew tighter as Rominy and Jake drove up the Skagit, the twists in the highway giving an occasional glimpse of ramparts of snow. At Marblemount the valley broadened briefly into pasture, modest homes perched above the steep riverbank, the Skagit muscular as a snake. Then they turned to cross the river on a steel two-lane bridge and headed up the side valley of the Cascade River. This tributary poured from a forested canyon onto a pan of gravel bars. Ahead were hills steep as sugarloaves, rocky crags somewhere above. The new river was translucent as a jewel, the rocks of its bed bright coins.

Their banker had found an old Christmas cookie tin in the branch lunchroom, tapped out dry crumbs, and put Hood's safety deposit box curiosities in it for Rominy to take with her. There was an old Army Colt .45 that Barrow suggested she take for "home protection." The fact that the journalist was willing to arm her, even with a presumably unloaded pistol, reassured her. The weapon was as heavy as a brick, however, and she'd never fired a gun in her life. More intriguingly, there were three gold coins with some kind of curious Asian design embossed in the metal. A white silk scarf. A dented compass, black with a silver arrow. A brass key, apparently to a padlock left by authorities to secure Hood's cabin, Dunnigan had told her. And, dramatically, the mummified finger of her great-grandfather, shrunken and slightly bent. Was it a last defiant digit upraised against the unfairness of the world?

"We don't know if any of these has meaning," Dunnigan had said as Rominy laid the articles out on the counter in the safety deposit room, the bank of stainless steel drawers glowing green in the weird light. "Beyond meaning to your great-grandfather. The gold could fetch a couple of thousand dollars at today's prices, and the gun may have antique value, I don't know. The real money is the interest from the old savings account. Mr. Hood left a hefty deposit to rent the safety deposit box before he died."

The cash they'd requested was hypnotizing. Rominy settled for $28,500, since Dunnigan said the bank couldn't come up with more on such short notice. It was in twenties, fifties, and hundreds, the thousand-dollar packets wrapped with white paper bands. She'd never seen so much cash in her life. Jake fetched a day-pack from his pickup, stuffed the money inside, and handed it to her. "Yours."

"How did he die?" Rominy asked the banker of her great-grandfather. Given the suspicious demise of her other relatives, at least according to Jake Barrow, she half expected something truly exotic, like snakebite or Ninja throwing star.

"Natural causes, the papers said. A coroner's guess. Someone found the body up at his cabin in the spring, and he'd passed some months before. Wouldn't have liked to have walked in on *that*. There wasn't much left, I suppose. Anyway, most important was his will in the box here, leaving any possessions to unspecified heirs. Which apparently means you, since you're the last one."

"So I get this key to his cabin?"

"You get his cabin. Don't expect much. Taxes have been minimal due to the low assessment, and there's been little maintenance."

"I didn't expect anything at all a few hours ago."

"It's astonishing how fortune can turn, isn't it? And all thanks to Mr. Barrow." Dunnigan had beamed at him, and he'd done his best to look modest.

So now they were deeper in the woods than ever, the vine maple already turning scarlet and the fir that leaned over the road as high as a skyscraper. Creeks cut down from the mountain above, turning white when they flashed from the underbrush and tumbled over boulders into culverts.

Jake eventually turned left onto a dirt driveway, a tunnel in the brush. A piece of weathered-gray plywood with crudely painted house numbers was the only thing marking their exit. They traversed up the flank of a mountain above Cascade River Road, the pickup bouncing in the ruts.

"You can bet I had a hard time finding *this* one," Jake said, "and then Ma Barker greeted me with the muzzle of her shotgun. That's called an upriver hello."

"I'm a long way from the cops, aren't I?"

He glanced at her. "But not from friends."

They drove a hundred yards up the dirt lane, a strip of grass in the middle and salmonberry scratching the pickup's sides. Then they came to a clearing. There was a lichen-spotted singlewide mobile home, the color of its paint having turned indeterminate at least a decade before. The flat roof had a crew cut of moss. Smoke drifted from a pipe chimney elbowing out of the trailer, and all the curtains were drawn. Then there were the requisite junk cars being subsumed by blackberries, an old chicken coop, a weathered barn leaning like a drunk, and a scattering of rusted and plastic junk in unmown weeds. Two hounds came racing out from under a rotting deck, barking as if the place were Stalag 17. They put their muzzles up to the pickup door windows and bayed. Rominy instinctively shrank against Jake, who viewed the animals as calmly as if they'd stumbled on a petting zoo. After a minute or two, the hounds seemed to realize nothing was happening, or they ran out of breath. They quieted, pacing up and down the side of the pickup, snorting and slavering. Then an old woman appeared on the sagging porch and the dogs started up again.

"Thunder! Damnation! Shut up!" She waved a stick for emphasis. No, it wasn't a stick, it was a gun. Good lord.

Rominy turned to Jake. "Dogpatch is where my great-grandfather lived?"

"Up the road farther, but we have to tell Mrs. Crockett—er, Clarkson—what we're up to or she's likely to have half the neighborhood using us for target practice. Mostly Tar Heels up here, out from the Carolinas to log the woods."

Delphina Clarkson fit every stereotype. Wild gray hair, Carhartt overalls, rubber gardening boots, a double-barrel that dated to cowboy days, and a smile that hadn't seen a dental hygienist for just as long. The dogs raced around howling as she strode up, doing their best to earn their supper by being obnoxious.

"Down, you two! Thunder, quiet! Dammit, Damnation . . ." She rapped on Jake's window with the barrel of her gun and Barrow cranked it a hand's width down.

"Hello, Mrs. Clarkson. Remember me?"

"I told you to git!"

"And I told *you* I was trying to find the rightful owner of the old Hood place, to which this road is legal access. You know as well as I do that the deeds grant a right-of-way. The heiress is going up to view her property."

"Heiress?" She squinted at Rominy. "Her? That's a city girl."

"It surely is." He'd summoned a cornpone accent.

The dogs started barking again and Mrs. Clarkson started whacking them with the butt of her gun, swearing like a sailor. "Damnation, you stupid . . ."

"The name of your dog is Damnation?" Rominy asked, surprised she could find her voice.

"Hell, yes. Named for Damnation Crick, and for what I said when this pup ran loose up that rat hole of a waterway. I had to chase him through devil's club and deadfall. He's lived up to his name ever since." She seemed slightly less hostile talking about her dogs.

"Mrs. Clarkson, this is Rominy . . . Hood," Barlow said. "The great-granddaughter of Benjamin Hood. I tracked her down like I said I would and she is now your new neighbor. We've got a key to the cabin, and we'll be up there for tonight, at least."

"You two together?"

The idea startled Rominy. She realized it was almost evening but she hadn't thought ahead to where she might be sleeping. And it certainly wasn't going to be with Mr. Jake Barrow, no matter how cute he was. And yet here she was in a pickup cab she couldn't get out of without his help, her MINI Cooper reduced to shredded aluminum foil, her apartment two hundred miles away. Nor did she want to curl up with Calamity Jane here, along with Thunder and Damnation. And the river road was not the easiest place to hitch a ride. They hadn't passed another car in ten miles.

"We're business partners only," Barrow said briskly. "You can rest assured that Ms. Hood has displayed every capability of resisting my charm."

"Girl has some sense, then."

"But we'll both be in the cabin since we've nowhere else to go. I'd appreciate if you kept the hounds on your own property and don't call the sheriff when you see lights in the old cabin."

"Call the sheriff? I could raise eight children in the time it would take a deputy to get up *here*." She squinted at the journalist. "But you treat this young lady with respect or I *will* set the dogs on you, Mr. Business Partner. You hear?"

He smiled. "Yes, ma'am."

She looked at Rominy. "Watch yourself around men. That's my advice."

"Yes, ma'am."

She frowned, considering. "You comin' up here all the time now?"

"That's up to Rominy, but I don't think so," Barrow said. "We're just trying to learn about the past."

"Hmph. What's past is past, and that's the best place for it, is what I've learned." She looked at Rominy. "You want to sell the place, you let me know first."

"Yes, ma'am."

"You ain't gonna want to keep it." She stepped away, cradling her shotgun in one arm. "I already see lights up there, sometimes. This place of yours, young lady, is *haunted*."

16

Potala Palace, Lhasa, Tibet
September 20, 1938

The winter palace that would soon house Tibet's toddler god-king mimicked the majesty of the surrounding mountains. It stacked toward the clouds, tier upon tier of white and red, its walls sloping inward in the Tibetan fashion to give the edifice the firmness of natural cliffs. It was a royal crown the color of snow and dried blood, roofed with gold, and set high atop a hill above the capital of Lhasa. When dawn sun hit the Potala Palace and made it glow, the shrine seemed to be absorbing energy enough to lift free of its escarpment entirely and ascend into heaven like a stone balloon. Birds soared beneath the uppermost windows, and purple and yellow banners marked the royal apartments. Scarlet-robed monks kept watch from terraces, and a thousand windows looked out to green mountains and Kyi-Chu, the Lhasa River. To Raeder and his Germans the four-centuries-old palace was a fever dream, the fantasy of ten thousand long miles turned real, a storehouse of Asian mystery and (reports went) incalculable amounts of religious gold. Now the regent of the kingdom, who ruled until the recent reincarnation of the young Dalai Lama could come of age—a regent named Thupten Jampel Yishey Gyantsen, the Reting from the Rinpoche monastery—had agreed to see the Nazis.

He did so over heated British objections. The Reting wanted to hear what these foreigners might offer, or threaten.

Raeder had already wooed Thupten by sending presents. The Reting had torn wrappings off a telescope, radio set, and music box stamped with the Nazi swastika. Raeder also sent copies of several of Himmler's favorite books—in German—along with a letter translated into Tibetan by a hired monk. It proposed that the German and Tibetan races might share Aryan ancestry.

The gifts must have provoked curiosity, because now the quintet of SS men were ascending the steep switchbacking staircases that led to the palace's primary gate, wearing their hastily pressed black

Schutzstaffel uniforms trimmed with silver. Despite their conditioning from crossing the Himalayas, the Germans still panted. There were 2,564 steps in the palace, a physical reminder of man's difficult rise to nirvana. The edifice itself was a dizzying five hundred feet high, a stone skyscraper broad as a dam.

From the red-and-gold gate topped by the heads of seven white lions, Lhasa below looked like a scattering of brown cubes on a cultivated valley floor of yellow barley, an arena encircled by green, grassy mountains. The river curled like a *khata* scarf, silver where hit by the sun. Monasteries clung to the foothills, and the golden roof of the Jokhang temple in central Lhasa was an answering wink to the gleam of the Potala. The view was one of the most breathtaking Raeder had ever seen, earning his respect. Perhaps the people who had built this *did* have secrets that could help the Reich triumph.

If so, they must be learned. And stolen.

The Germans were greeted by the dinosaur bellow of the Tibetan long trumpets, the *dungchen*, a mournful, underworld serenade that echoed against the sloping walls. They passed through gate and passageway and a steward led them into a labyrinth of dark rooms, steep ladders, and dim passageways of the Red Palace, their porter Lokesh translating as they penetrated deeper into a shadowy maze. Gloomy chambers were built around gigantic images of Buddha, each serene and buttery smooth from a fabulous overlay of gold. Ventilation chimneys plunged down story after story like empty elevator shafts, butter lamp flames dancing in the resulting currents of air. There were metal mandalas the size of waterwheels, the sculptures representing exquisite miniature temples that symbolized the universe, each of them gilded with gold and studded with jewels. Adjacent to this artisan glory, the painted wood of the hand-trimmed posts and beams gave a curious mountain lodge feel to the place. The floors were beaten earth and pebbles, tamped into a dry concrete on ancient joists.

"There's wealth enough here to buy a dozen panzer divisions," Raeder murmured, "guarded by medieval sentries who could be overcome by a platoon of storm troopers armed with machine pistols. We are conquistadors, comrades, able to view treasures equivalent to the Inca Atahualpa, and yet now we must bow and scrape in order to achieve a greater goal. If Himmler is right, this treasure is mere dross."

"Dross! Compared to what?" Muller whispered. Slit-eyed Buddhas, golden lamas, and gilded saints looked sternly ahead. The palace was a museum of frozen gold, hundreds of statues, thousands, in a bewildering pantheon.

"Shambhala," Raeder replied. "The real Shangri-la."

"That might be Himmler's fantasy. *This* is real."

"For us, what's real is what the *Reichsführer* says is real."

Sufficiently awed and subdued by the splendor, the Germans were taken across the eastern courtyard to the White Palace, its icy color a symbol of peace. More than a hundred people waited in the plaza: guards, monks, emissaries, and petitioners. It was hot in the sun, cold in the shade. After a wait of forty-two minutes— Raeder timed it on his Junghans military watch—the Europeans were led up a short pyramid of stone steps to wooden ones so steep they were almost ladders. Banners with a purple symbol of infinity flanked the door. Inside was dimness that kept only tentative rein on a riot of color, a kaleidoscope of painted reds, golds, blues, greens, and purples on every pillar and beam. The designs could take a year to fully examine and decipher. It was the very opposite of the cold, intimidating austerity of the Third Reich. White, obelisk-shaped posts rose to a mustard-yellow ceiling in the throne room. Cushions were Vatican red, while bowls of ceremonial water were Viking silver. The inside was as baroque as the mountains were bare.

Various functionaries, monks, and hangers-on sat on padded benches in the smoky shadows, murmuring and humming prayers. Light was cast by wicks flaming in tubs of yellow yak butter, the air pungent with incense. The place smelled like every one of its four hundred years.

"Never use a thousand colors when a million will do," murmured Kranz. "It's like the explosion of a child's paint-box set."

"Look," whispered Hans Diels, "swastikas!" The symbol was sewn onto tapestries.

"As foreign as this seems, we have, I suspect, in some sense come home," Reader told his men.

Tibet's regent sat cross-legged on a padded throne, draped in robes and crowned with a peaked saffron-colored hat that descended over his ears and back of the neck like bird wings. The Reting was a serious-looking, smooth-cheeked, large-eared young man who didn't look entirely happy about his weight of responsibility. He ruled while the new Dalai Lama, whom he'd helped discover the year before, was coming of age in Kumbum monastery. The majesty of the transition was unsettling. Reting had had a dream of where the reincarnation of the deceased Thirteenth Dalai Lama might be found, and a retinue of holy men had made a pilgrimage to a remote rural home. Eerily, the peasant toddler had picked out the belongings of the dead holy man, shouting, "Mine, mine!"

while ignoring other choices. Even to a believer, actually finding a reincarnated presence had been shaking. Soon His Holiness would be brought to Lhasa, but for now Reting was the monarch of the Potala and responsible, with his council, of deciding what to do with these Germans.

The Europeans were stocky, sunburned, hard-looking men, who seemed to want to suck experience in with their mouths instead of feeling it with their souls. The Tibetan thought their eyes darted like those of rodents, their limbs trembled with restlessness, and their black uniforms were forbidding. They wore death's heads at their collar. Pale, anxious, unhappy men.

The world was squeezing Tibet, the regent knew. There was war to the east between China and Japan. The British had bludgeoned their way into Lhasa more than thirty years before. The Soviet Union was a secretive dark dictatorship hulking beyond the Kunlun Mountains. Airplanes and radio waves were violating the sanctity of distance that had always protected the sacred kingdom. Reting himself had been alerted of Raeder's approach by British radio. And now these Germans had come claiming some kind of ancestral kinship! Everyone was suddenly Tibet's friend, because everyone wanted to turn it against their enemies. Which nation should be trusted and which kept out?

How could these giants, with their steel machines that groaned and spat fire, be played off against each other?

And then the German spokesman, a man named Raeder, gave a solution.

The handsome visitor began by presenting an album of pictures of Nazi Germany and its leaders, pointing to the National Socialist symbols that seemed inspired by ancient Tibetan iconography. The *Führer*, like Reting and the future Dalai Lama, was not just the political leader of Germany, Raeder explained. He was the spiritual leader as well, a new kind of god, for a new kind of man.

Some of the pictures depicted huge rallies for him, all the people standing curiously in line, as rigid as posts. They wore helmets and looked like lines of beetles. Reting wanted to laugh at their rigid stiffness but knew that was impolite. He passed the album back.

This *Führer*'s lieutenant, Himmler, was intensely interested in the origins of mankind and the history of the Aryan race, Raeder explained. Tibetan nobility had the fine bone structure of the Aryan, and it was in this beautiful country that ancestral proof of their relationship might be hidden. The Germans had come to Tibet to learn if their peoples were related.

"There are even Western theories of ancient powers that might have been found and lost in Tibet," Raeder said. "My friend Kranz here has been casting masks of facial characteristics and finding remarkable correlations between your citizens and ours. My friend Muller has been making scientific measurements of magnetism and gravity to hunt for hiding places where such powers might reside. My friend Diels wants to study your history, and my friend Eckells to record your ceremonies. Reichsführer SS Heinrich Himmler has sent us here to offer our help."

"We hide nothing," Reting said. "In another chamber I can show you a Buddha made of a thousand pounds of gold. No crypt is needed to secrete it. Our faith is our life. And this life is but a step toward the next one."

"There is much we can learn from such wisdom," Raeder replied, even though he believed no such thing. "And much we could share. Some Germans, like Reichsführer SS Himmler, believe in reincarnation, too."

"Then why did you hunt, when you came before with the Americans?" Clearly, Reting knew more about Raeder than was expected. "Why have you shot animals this time, when you thought we weren't watching? You killed what may have been your leaders' ancestors, reincarnated in animal form."

Raeder shifted uncomfortably. "That was for science."

"You left them to rot. You must not kill while you are in our kingdom."

The German gave a curt nod. "We apologize for our custom. We accede to your wisdom."

"The sanctity of life is a path toward nirvana."

"We Germans appreciate your beliefs."

Reting shook his head. "I've seen your books and movies. We believe in an escape from passions, and you believe in heightening them. We believe in losing our desires, and you believe in feeding them. We believe ambition leads to dissatisfaction, and you believe ambition is life's purpose. We believe in exploring what is within, and you believe in exploring what is without."

The Germans looked at each other, murmuring. Then Raeder tried again.

"It's true there are differences, but there are similarities as well. You believe in perfecting your soul through many incarnations, and we believe in perfecting all mankind through natural selection and the discipline of National Socialism. We both believe in past ages better than the present, and a future of promise. We are both, your monks and we Nazis, idealists in our own way." He took a breath. "But we also believe in the importance of *this* life, and use science and engineering to improve it. The world is shrinking, regent, and you'll want powerful friends if your giant neighbors press too close."

"Friendship is why we didn't arrest you as you approached Lhasa."

"And friendship is why more Germans should come here to protect you. We can teach your soldiers."

"More Germans? With your American friends?"

"The Americans are not our friends. I was here on an academic partnership on that earlier expedition, but their leader, a man named Benjamin Hood, was jealous of my achievements and tried to thwart them. You must never allow Americans here. They are a greedy, shallow people. They care only for money."

"And you do not?"

"We Germans are scholars and idealists. We could help search for lost secrets that could help us both."

"Ah, secrets. What everyone seeks."

"There are reports of a lost kingdom of Shambhala, are there not?"

"There's a mural of it here in the Potala," Reting said. "It is our Olympus, our Atlantis, our utopia. It is a kingdom ringed by impenetrable mountains, accessible only to the most holy. There, poverty, hunger, sickness, and crime are unknown. People live for a hundred years. At the center is a glittering palace where the sacred Kalachakra teachings are kept. And someday, when wickedness is rampant and the world is engulfed in catastrophic warfare, the mists that hide Shambhala will lift and its king will ride forth with his host to destroy the forces of evil and establish a new Golden Age that will last a thousand years."

"Not entirely different from the prophecies of the Christian Bible."

"Which were inspired, perhaps, by Shambhala, if your theories of ancient connections are correct."

"Or Shambhala by the West. Who knows?"

"Once, in the distant past, all was one. Just as in the universe."

"Yes. The northern legends of the Germanic people have similar echoes. So perhaps we were indeed, our people and yours, once one. And now we share symbolism." Raeder pointed to a swastika.

"But not necessarily alliance. Tibet doesn't want the world's quarrels."

"And yet the world is quarreling."

"And what do you want for your friendship?"

"What if Shambhala is true in some way and could be found and learned from? That is what the *Reichsführer* believes. Its secrets could ensure the security of your country and mine for a long time."

"If any Tibetan has found Shambhala, he has not returned."

"But my men are willing to look *for* you, with your guidance. We believe it exists. But we need your help to find it."

"Shambhala exists as much as anything exists in the dream we call life," the regent said. "But I believe the journey to it is within one's heart as much as upon one's legs, and to understand one's heart is perilous indeed."

Raeder smiled. This was the kind of Eastern nonsense that would keep these societies in the Middle Ages while the master race took control. "Then let us Germans take the risk for you."

"You have the right consciousness?"

"We have the right will. We condition our hearts to probe the wilderness. I respect your inner journey, but Shambhala is a physical place as well. Do you know where the kingdom is supposed to lie?"

"The traditional belief is a lost valley deep in the Kunlun Mountains at the head of a disappearing river, far from every trade route and habitation. There, the voices of the dead inhabit the wind. Difficult to find and, by reputation, dangerous to penetrate. There are impossible gorges and impossible mountains."

"Impossible until it is done."

The young regent considered his visitors. He'd heard a hundred stories. Tibet's past was a fog of history and myth, a fog one could get lost in—but a fog rising from a lake of truth. These Europeans had no idea of the hazards ahead, or the terrible things they might discover. "You think you can do this when we have not?"

"Only with your help and permission. As you said, we explore the world when perhaps we should be exploring our souls. But we are very good at exploring the world."

"And if you found what you are looking for?"

"We would share what we found." The Germans nodded.

Reting looked into the shadows of the room. There, on shelves, were stacked thousands of holy books, *peche*, unbound leaves wrapped in cloth and tied with wooden end pieces, dating back centuries beyond counting. The books were enigmatic, but had many clues. One remarkable young nun had been compiling those clues. She'd met Westerners before, and had prophesized this moment. She'd warned that modern Tibet must rediscover Shambhala before foreigners did, or ensure that it could never be found.

Her perspective had been poisoned, Reting knew. There were rumors upon rumors about Keyuri Lin.

Still, he and she had made their plans.

The Reting's visitors were tough, restless men, obsessed with the longings the Buddha taught should be escaped. But here they were in the Potala, which they'd been forbidden to approach. Where else might they reach? What if they *could* give Tibet real power in a dangerous world?

"Perhaps we can make a partnership," he said, watching the Germans.

The Westerners' eyes lit with ambition and greed. "The world's crisis is growing darker," Raeder said. "Time is of the essence. Do you have any trucks or cars that would speed part of the journey to the Kunlun?"

The regent smiled. "The British do. Ask them." Let the Europeans quarrel among themselves. He wasn't going to risk his own motorcar, shipped in pieces on animal backs and reassembled in Lhasa so he could drive on the palace parade ground. So he'd heed Keyuri and work with these interlopers to either retrieve rumored secrets or get rid of the Germans entirely. The woman had counseled that perhaps they could do both—this odd woman who studied things that were rightly the province of men.

The Germans shifted. "The English will not help us," Raeder said. "We fought a war with them a generation ago."

Reting shrugged. "We have a scholar, a most unusual nun of most unusual curiosity, who has studied the Shambhala legend more than any monk. Does your culture allow you to work with a woman as a guide?"

"Of course," Raeder said, not admitting that he agreed with the Nazis that a woman's best duty was raising children. "European nations have been ruled by queens as well as kings." The Germans glanced at each other. This seeming cooperation was more than they'd hoped, and they were both elated and wary.

Reting clapped his hands, once, and monks bowed and disappeared in the shadows. A short time later, they led a young woman into the reception area. Her head was cropped as short as a boot camp recruit in the fashion of both monks and nuns, but she was quite pretty, her features fine, her lashes long. She advanced with eyes low, a sheaf of papers and maps in her hand.

"Keyuri Lin will give you what guidance we can," the Reting said.

Raeder started. His companions looked at him curiously, but he had eyes only for this female scholar, his face suddenly pale. She lifted her head.

It was the woman Benjamin Hood had taken from him.

Each waited for the other to shout warning, but neither did.

17

The air over western China
September 9, 1938

The Corsair biplane had two cockpits. Hood would sit in front of Beth Calloway as she piloted, in a basket about as comfortable as a barrel: a metal seat, hard ribs, and welded flange to hang on to behind a snarling engine. It was 1,400 miles to Lhasa, and each one was going to be bumpy, cold, and noisy.

"We'll fly close to the ground at first and put down if we spot any Japanese," she said. "Then we'll follow the Yangtze to Chongqing and break due west for Chengdu. After that, it's mountains, mountains, mountains."

"How high can this crate fly?" Its mustard yellow was spattered with mud from rough landings.

"More than eighteen thousand feet if we stay light. That's high enough to clear any passes. Beyond that, you have to hike."

"Just get me to Lhasa at twelve thousand. If I can reach the authorities fast enough, I can do what I'm supposed to do, I hope."

She looked him over: jaunty Filson bush hat that would blow off if he didn't put it away, oil cloth packer coat, a .45 automatic that would identify him as an American, a bandolier of rifle and shotgun shells like some Mexican bandit, and high-lace mountaineering boots shiny with waterproof wax. All he lacked was a merit badge. In the humid heat, he was sweating. She pointed skeptically. "What's that?"

He was shouldering his sling canvas duffel, fat as a sailor's and long enough to stuff a body. He swung it off for presentation. "My gear. Where does it go?"

"It doesn't. Not with us."

"I'm going to need this in Tibet."

Calloway swung open the door of a compartment behind her own seat. "You're not getting to Tibet unless we carry these." Three petrol canisters took up most of the space. "The Corsair's maximum range is less than seven hundred miles. We've got two refueling spots, but we'll have to put down and top off with these on the leg to Lhasa."

"Then we need a bigger plane."

"We don't have a bigger plane, unless you packed one in that duffel."

He frowned. "I miss the *Clipper.*"

"I miss flying by myself. What's in there, anyway?"

Reluctantly, he handed her the bag, which bent her over with its weight. "You're kidding, right?" She dropped it on the hangar dirt and began pulling the contents out. "No, no, no." Shirts, underwear, trousers, and jackets were tossed to one side. So were extra boots, binoculars, compass, canteen, and sleeping bag.

"What are you doing?"

"Curbing weight and space. Here." She picked out a sweater and threw it to him. "It will get cold past Chengdu. The rest is too bulky. What's this?" She held up a bottle of single-malt scotch, Glenfiddich, which Sir Arthur had recommended.

"Replenishment."

"Weight." She tossed and it shattered.

"That's twenty-year-old scotch!" She was a madwoman.

"The monks don't need it and neither do we. And what's this?" She pulled out two guns by the stock, a .12-gauge shotgun and a Winchester Model 70 hunting rifle with scope. "Jesus Lord. Going hunting again?"

"In a manner of speaking. Those we *do* bring."

"No room, college boy."

"I've already been strafed on this trip."

"No room."

"*You* carry a pistol."

"And so do you. We've no room for long guns."

"They go in the cockpit with me. We'll leave *you* behind if we have to."

She put her hands on her hips. "You're going to fly this plane by yourself?"

He looked her up and down. "How hard can it be?"

The insult won a smirk, her first concession of respect. She nodded reluctantly. "You bring a Zero down with one of these and I'll be impressed. So let's do a trade for these guns. Something else has to go." She stepped up on the wing, reached into his cockpit, and hauled out a pack and harness. "This will give you more room, and incentive to aim true."

"What's that?"

"Your parachute. We'll leave it here."

"Great. What are *you* bringing?"

"The clothes I'm wearing, a box of tools, and chewing gum. And *my* parachute, since *I* travel light. You got money?"

"Chinese gold."

"Don't show it. Use a money belt. But you can buy robes and boots in Tibet for pennies on the dollar. Guns, too, I imagine."

"I like my own."

She gave him a leather flying hood, goggles, and white silk scarf. "Bugs and grit can hit like bullets when you fly. The scarf is to prevent chafing when you crane your neck. I want you looking for Japs the first hundred miles. When you get to the Potala Palace you can give it to the regent. Trading scarves is custom in Tibet; they call the scarf a *khata*. Now, be useful. You can turn the prop."

"We are in the Dark Ages."

"Don't do it until you get my signal. And step *backward* once it spins. I don't want hamburger all over my plane."

The engine roared to life, spitting a plume of black smoke. The propeller turned into a blur. He walked around the biplane wings to look at what the aviatrix was doing. Inside her cockpit was a stick, a pair of foot pedals, and a throttle. He *would* fly, if he had to.

"Here, use this!" she shouted over the roar of the engine. It was a jar of Vaseline she was smearing on her checks. "Fights windburn. Tibetan herders use red cream made from whey, but it stinks like hell and makes them look like demons."

He smeared his face, climbed up on the lower wing, and swung himself into his cockpit. Even with the parachute gone, it was a tight fit with his firearms. Their barrels pointed up, rattling with the vibration.

Beth pushed the silver throttle and the biplane shuddered and began to move. Then she used the rudder pedals to turn and soon they were bouncing down the dirt runway. The engine roared, climbing toward a whine, and they raced, skipping now. Then a pull of the joystick and they lumbered into the air, a posse of Chinese children running after them and waving.

Could have carried another fifty pounds, Hood thought sourly, but his spirits lifted with the plane. Maybe he could still catch Raeder. Houses turned to toys below. People became insects. He settled back for the ride. It was too noisy to talk.

The view was panoramic, the wind bracing, and the experience entirely different from the *Clipper*. He felt as farsighted as a bird. China became a green quilt buttoned with tile and thatch roofs. They skimmed just a few hundred feet above, peasants pausing to peer up at them. Behind, on the horizon, plumes of smoke rose from the Sino-Japanese front.

Hood did spot the wink of sun on a plane back toward the war, so as precaution he took up his rifle, opened the bolt, and slid in a shell. He turned half around, resting the barrel on the rim of the cockpit.

Calloway pushed it aside. "Idiot!" she shouted. "You'll take my head off before you hit something going three hundred miles an hour! I was joking about downing a Zero. Put it away!"

He saluted but rested the butt of his Winchester on the floor of his cockpit again, safety set, one hand on its stock. If a fighter came near him again, he was going down shooting.

The Yangtze was a broad silt road, third-longest river in the world. As they flew east the land grew hillier, China a hazed, rolling ocean. Everything from steamships to sampans crawled below, peasants stooping and oxen plodding in a tableau that hadn't changed in a thousand years. Then the land rose still more and they began flying through a succession of magnificent ravines, green mountains rising higher than their wings.

"The Wu Gorge!" Calloway shouted. Forested mountainsides reared like the skyscraper canyons of New York. The sediment-laden river twisted like an orange intestine. Villages clung to narrow shelves still in shadow.

Somewhere ahead was Raeder.

They spent their first night in Chongqing, Hood dazed and stiff from the long hours of engine noise, fumes, wind, and cramping. He paid the pittance it cost to buy them two rooms at a makeshift inn near the grass runway. It was dim inside—electricity hadn't reached this far—and smoky from the charcoal brazier. Calloway looked weary from the day's flight, and was about as flirtatious as Eleanor Roosevelt. She bolted her rice and vegetables like a dog. Hood tried to make conversation.

"You're a smart-mouth like my sister. I enjoy that."

She snorted. "Your sister."

"How'd you learn to fly?"

She looked at him tiredly. "Watched some barn-stormers and saved up for flying lessons." Her reddened eyes wandered around the room, as if sociability was almost too much to endure.

That just made it interesting. "Shows initiative."

"It's called gumption in Nebraska."

"And you're a girl."

"Quite the observation, deadeye."

"It's unusual, that's all."

"We're half the population. And unusual isn't impossible. I wanted to do more than peel spuds and have babies."

He waited for her to ask more about him, but she didn't, so he plunged on. "It's a long way from Nebraska to the Chinese air force."

Beth looked at him directly this time, over the rim of her teacup. "You *are* educated. So, okay. I'm a tomboy, a runaway, and a mercenary. And the weather's better."

"Everywhere's better than Nebraska."

"And the money's good."

"Yes, your wealth is apparent."

She chewed. "You haven't seen my closet full of shoes."

He smiled at the joke. Progress.

"I also get to work for a woman."

"Madame Chiang?"

"Remarkable, isn't she?"

"Forceful. And so are you, Miss Calloway. You've flown me five hundred miles and haven't strayed off course once."

"How would you know? Besides, I was following the Yangtze."

"That shows wisdom right there."

"You don't need to flatter me, Mr. Hood. I'm not impressed by your museum, your money, your conversation, or your skill at killing helpless animals. I'm far too tired to want to sleep with you, and too well read to expect anything you say to be particularly enlightening. You're an assignment."

"You flatter *me*. I thought I was a mere chore." Yes, progress. She'd volunteered more than one sentence in a row.

"The leg to Chengdu is two hundred miles shorter, but you'll excuse me for going to bed. I'm guessing you'd rather have me alert tomorrow. And I'm sure you can fascinate yourself." She stood.

Hood remained seated. "Do *something* by myself, anyway." He threw her a few gold coins. "For the first leg of the trip."

She didn't pick them up. "We leave at dawn."

They went on at six A.M., the plane bouncing as they slowly climbed west. It was another long, cramped day, and after landing at Chengdu and refueling, Hood wearily sat with his back against the tail of the plane, watching the sun go down in a haze of fire behind the mountains to the west. He'd stuffed cotton in his ears beneath his helmet for the flight, but they still rang from the long hours in the air.

Calloway had been her usual laconic self upon landing, wordlessly directing coolies to gas up the plane and checking an engine that ticked as it cooled. Most people got to Hood's family and money sooner rather than later, but she'd shown no interest in either. She was professional, guarded, and working hard to be unimpressed. Hood considered that a sign of character, but still.

Beth finally wiped her hands with a rag and stood in front of him. "Are you just going to lean on my plane, or find us a place to sleep?"

"I'm postponing the inevitable. There are more fleas inside than out."

"I think you're sulking because I broke your scotch."

He looked up at her, squinting against the late glare of the sun. "And I think you were showing off by breaking it."

She bit her lip. "So were you, by bringing it. I knew what it cost."

He looked back down across the airfield. Pretty women had the luxury of being annoying, and she was managing to annoy him. Pepsodent my ass. "Sorry to have offended you."

Beth suddenly looked hesitant and abruptly walked around the plane again, thrumming the wire wing supports for tension. Then she plopped next to him on the grass. "Look, it was stupid."

He studied her, the girl too tough to ever risk being hurt. "You don't allow yourself to enjoy much, do you?"

"I don't allow myself to be disappointed. It's a fault." She shook out her curls to loosen them from the packing of the helmet. Of course she didn't go so far as to actually look at him or offer a pleasantry. That would be too polite.

But she didn't move away, either. They both had goggle rings around their eyes, like raccoons.

She stared at the sky, too.

"I never knew riding could be so tiring," Hood finally tried again.

Silence.

"I'm still vibrating from the engine. It doesn't go away."

More quiet. Then, "Ready to walk, college boy?"

"Why do you call me that? I'm a specimen collector, not an intellectual. You already claimed you're a reader as well, though damned if I've noticed any evidence of it."

"I was reciting Thucydides all day. You just couldn't hear over the engine."

"Baloney. I'll bet the only thing you've ever read is *Ladies' Home Journal* and engine manuals."

"*Ladies' Home Journal!*" She barked a laugh. Then she finally looked at him to recite, proud as a school-girl. "*The secret of happiness is freedom. The secret of freedom is courage.* Thucydides said that."

"*E Pluribus Unum.* A nickel says that. See? We're both eggheads."

She finally laughed. "Out of many, one."

"But you're the lonely aviatrix."

"I just rely on myself."

"And you're free."

"To a point."

"And courageous."

"To a point."

"And contemptuous of any man who isn't you."

She seemed warily interested in his assessment. "Women, too."

"I've never sat home counting stock coupons, which I could afford to do." He knew he sounded defensive. "I'm paying my own way on a mission for my government. I'm in the middle of nowhere, going to find a man I'd just as soon forget. It takes courage to fly in a plane like yours, with a pilot like you, in a place like this, but I don't feel free at all."

"Or happy?"

"The best I've managed is to be amused."

"So what the devil are you doing here, Dr. Hood?" She was cross-legged and leaned forward a little, curious now.

"It's secret, of course." He could think of no better way to irritate her.

"To save the world," she guessed. "It's got to be *something* important to fly to the end of the earth."

"Why do you care?"

"You've taken me with you. It only seems I'm taking you."

He plucked at the grass, recognizing the truth of that. He considered how to answer her. "All anyone ever manages is to save themselves—I know that. But give me credit for doing what I can. The fact is, the luck of my birth embarrasses me. I envy ordinary people."

"Then you're a fool."

"People are happier being ordinary."

"Nonsense. You're the kind of man who does everything he can to keep from being ordinary. I've seen your type in China a hundred times. Terrified of being bored. Deliberately eccentric to fit the adventure stereotype. Achievement as penance."

"Penance for what?"

"You tell me."

"For being envied by people like you." He looked square at her as he said it.

That stopped her for a moment. Then she nodded. "So tell me, Dr. Benjamin Grayson Hood. What are you *really* doing here? Why go to Lhasa now? Nobody goes to Lhasa."

"The Nazis have sent an expedition to Tibet."

"Nazis!"

"SS officers. I'm to find out what they're up to."

She looked more puzzled than ever. "Why you?"

"I've been to the edge of Tibet twice before, on museum expeditions."

"So the American, British, and Chinese governments send a curator?" It clearly made no sense to her.

"When we came before, we had an international group. One of the scientists was a German named Kurt Raeder. An able mountain climber, crack shot, and trained zoologist like me. It was a natural partnership."

"You mean you know German?"

"Yes, but I mean I know Raeder. He's the leader of this new Nazi group, coming back to a nation we visited before."

"Ah. So you can approach him, as a friend, to learn what he's up to."

Hood gave a humorless smile. "Actually, he's an enemy."

This intrigued her. "Really? You had a falling-out? Tug-of-war over a carcass? Argument over the right scientific Latin name?"

She was teasing, but he decided to be honest. The truth was, she *was* risking her life just taking him there. And she was obviously intelligent. "Argument over a woman."

"Ah."

"Her name was Keyuri Lin. Her husband hired on as a porter and guide and she came with him to cook and clean. Raeder had his eye on her from the beginning; she's very pretty. He and the husband were out one day and Mondro fell off a cliff. Or so Raeder said."

"What do you mean?"

"Perhaps he was pushed. It was the first thing I thought, anyway."

"That's quite the accusation."

"Maybe, but I didn't like the guy. Too . . . driven."

"Look who's talking."

"Raeder turned his consolation of Keyuri into something else pretty quick. He's as striking as she is, and perhaps she'd encouraged him, either knowingly or unwittingly. You know how people are."

"Lusty. Clumsy. Stupid." Now she stretched out her legs. She had a fine set of them, and knew it.

"They no doubt hoped they could be discreet about the whole thing, but nothing is secret in an expedition camp. There was no evidence of murder, and ordinarily none of it would be my business. But then she began to look frightened."

"Of what?"

"Raeder. I think there's some Germanic dark spot on the man's soul. He didn't just want to possess her, he wanted to consume her, or hurt her, to make her a kind of slave. I warned him to be careful and he exploded at me, warning me off."

"Is that so surprising?"

"No . . . but the change in his personality, the switch from dignity to rage, was so complete that I began carrying a loaded pistol even in camp. There's something dark in him beyond the usual Nazi bravado. I was afraid he'd try something violent. Finally Keyuri crept to me at night and pleaded for rescue. She . . . showed me her body. There were cuts and burns and she feared for her life."

Calloway gave him a sideways glance.

"I decided to fire him. But he was stirring the others against me, complaining I was trying to steal his woman, this fragile widow, and people began choosing sides. I feared it would rip the camp apart, and possibly result in violence. I . . . was wary of Raeder."

"Chicken, you mean. And it's been eating you ever since."

Hood frowned at the assessment but didn't dispute it. "So one night I simply took her and fled with some of the animals, leaving a note that my financial support of the expedition was over. Some blamed me for their failure to complete their scientific objectives. Raeder felt humiliated. And it was worse than that."

Beth was enjoying the tale now, absorbed without pretending sympathy. Two men, one woman? Old story. "Worse how?"

"I fell in love with Keyuri myself. And eventually we *made* love, but we were all mixed up. The expedition had been derailed. She felt guilty about whether she might have played a role in the death of her husband. She was angry at Raeder, but embarrassed at having embarrassed him as well. The victim began to feel like the culprit. So one night she left *me*, too. It took quite a while to get over it."

"And you *are* over it? This has nothing to do with why we're flying to Tibet?"

"The last I heard, she'd entered a Buddhist nunnery."

"So you're going back to salt the wound." It was a judgment. "Good move, college boy."

"I'd just like to set things right."

"You can't set things right. That's the whole point of history."

"Well, this history is what you're flying to, which is what you wanted to know. And maybe I can write the future."

"What does *that* mean?"

"Keyuri is still there, as far as I know. I'm going back so Kurt Raeder doesn't hurt anyone else, ever again."

18

Hood's Cabin, Cascade Mountains, United States
September 4, Present Day

The last home of Benjamin Hood was a swaybacked cabin of weathered gray logs, its chinking as gapped as the teeth of a punch-drunk prizefighter and its mossy roof shaggy as a bear. The place listed like the *Titanic*, and Rominy thought its intention was to sink back into the earth. Her new property was not shelter, it was a trauma victim in need of emergency infusions from Home Depot.

Jake once more opened the pickup door from the outside—the need to do so made it seem like they were on some kind of ludicrous date—and then dug a lantern out of the toolbox in the bed of the pickup. While he did that, Rominy burrowed behind the seats to get the first aid kit again to re-dress her knees. A wink of brass caught her eye. It was almost entirely hidden under his camping gear, tucked at the edge of a floor mat. She instinctively reached. It was a small shell casing for a bullet, she saw, empty of powder.

Jake said he didn't have a gun. A leftover from an earlier owner or outing? She considered asking but he was preoccupied in the toolbox. The casing tickled her memory, but she wasn't sure why. She pocketed it for later.

"Come on, heiress!" He swung the lantern to help beat a path through high weeds and blackberries to the cabin's sagging porch. When Rominy stepped up, a piece of deck broke through. Something furtive skittered away. Great.

"Another piece of my fabulous inheritance?" she said, pulling her heeled shoe free of the rot. "I should have worn waders."

"Another piece of the puzzle, I hope. And I've got some spare boots in the truck I can loan you."

"You have my size?"

"Maybe. Old girlfriend left 'em when she dumped me."

"Now why would a woman do that?"

"That's what I asked." He stepped over some animal droppings and went to the plank door. "You never get an answer."

"But now you're Prince Charming and I get a hand-me-down glass slipper?"

"I'm on the trail of a story and you might need to walk in the woods."

"Gosh, she was wrong. You *are* romantic."

She'd joke with him now.

The key from the safety deposit box was to a padlock on a rusty hasp, and Jake had to twist and jerk to force it open. The door swung with the proverbial creak, or more precisely a squall of protest, and let out an exhalation of must. The cabin was dim inside, lit by greasy multipane windows that hadn't seen a wash in decades. The thought that Hood had decomposed here, until his discovery months later, gave her the creeps.

The place was also a time capsule. There was a Depression-era iron bed frame but no mattress, an old drop-leaf table with three painted wooden chairs, a counter with porcelain basin and hand pump, and a river-rock stone fireplace. The fur rug was so decayed as to make the species unidentifiable. The joists and rafters were bare, the underside of the shingles stained where rain had leaked through. There was even a bookshelf, and Rominy inspected the volumes. Faded tomes on Tibet, Buddhism, zoology, and flying, time having glued their pages to a pulpy mass that mice had chewed. Droppings dotted shelves and floor. Hanging on a peg on the wall was a calendar with a faded scenic of Mount Baker, turned to September 1945. It was as faint as a ghost negative.

"Is that when he died?"

Jake nodded. "Apparently. Remember, he wasn't found right away. That calendar page is right after the end of World War II, and they found him the next spring."

"He sat out the war up here."

"Yep. And this is the edge of the edge. To the east of us is a hundred miles of mountain wilderness."

She turned, reluctant to touch anything. "All right, Woodward and Bernstein, what are we supposed to find?"

"The story, Lois Lane. What happened to Great-grandpa? He goes to Tibet on the eve of the war, comes back to play the hermit here, and dies forgotten. Except his descendants meet untimely deaths, and a great-granddaughter who doesn't even know he exists is almost blown up in her MINI Cooper. So finally we have access to his cabin, and to his safety deposit box, and suddenly you've got enough moola to buy several new cars, thanks to me. All you have to do is give me the scoop of the century and I'll be on my way."

"Slam, bam, thank you, ma'am."

"I wouldn't put it so crudely. We're partners now, Rominy. If I'm Woodward, then you're Bernstein."

"I want to be Woodward. *You* be Bernstein."

He smiled. "You're on."

She glanced around. "The place is a sty."

"Let's call it a dusty attic of nostalgia." He glanced up. There were cobwebs enough to festoon a crypt. Mice and spiders and flies, oh my.

"But someone's been here." Rominy was looking at scuff marks in the dust on the floor. "If this place is haunted, the ghosts leave tracks."

Barrow frowned. "Kids, maybe. Through a window? Or drifters looking for food."

"Or your skinheads. Shining lights around and acting spooky."

"I don't think they'd know enough to look way up here."

Rominy dragged her finger in some dust. "Yeah, for their sake. I think my neighbor would answer the Hitler salute with buckshot, and they'd probably contract a disease in this dustbin. No self-respecting ghost would take up residence."

Jake smiled. "We're safe, then." He sat on the old bed frame, springs groaning. "Welcome home."

"I hope you don't think that's seductive." Rominy walked to the kitchen window, looking over the enameled sink basin. Outside there were claustropho-bic walls of fir in every direction. It was like being at the bottom of a green well. "It *is* odd that he came here and died here. But just because I'm his descendant doesn't mean I have any clues."

"You now have the contents of the safety deposit box."

"Geez, a fossilized finger? Thank you, Grandpa. Was it the middle one?"

"In that case I think he would have left the entire hand."

She sighed. "Okay, let's think about it." She sat at the painted table, using her forearm to shove off some dust, and emptied the cookie tin of what they'd found at the bank. "A scarf. It's a memento, I'd guess." She held it up to the light. "Part of it ripped away, and dirty from someone's neck. Nice. What else? The Chinese gold pieces are cool. And this is quite a heavy pistol." She lifted the .45 so it fell back with a thud. "You could use it to drive nails."

"Army issue from back then."

"A compass to find our way, if we had a direction to follow. If it's not just memorabilia, that suggests a des-tination and even a map, don't you think? But no map."

"Maybe the finger means pointing, like Sacajawea with Lewis and Clark," Barrow hazarded.

"But no Sacajawea to go with it. And this cabin? He dies at the end of the war. Why? He leaves . . . what?"

She glanced around. "No pictures, no maps." Shelves and cupboards held rusty cans and utensils. The books were ruined. "Hidden passageway? Secret compartment?" She fingered the rock on the fireplace and then had to dust off her hands. She paced around the tiny cabin, Barrow watching her think. Or maybe just watching her. Guys did that, she knew. Just not quite the right guy, yet.

So who *was* Jake Barrow? Savior, abductor, stalker, or partner? "So what else do you report on, when you're not rescuing damsels?" she suddenly asked.

He shrugged. "All kinds of stuff. Reporters are generalists. I like science, actually. Talk about spooky."

"What do you mean?"

"Just that the world is a lot weirder than it looks to us, when we peer up at galaxies or down to subatomic particles." He slapped the bed frame. "Do you know this is all an illusion?"

"I wish it were, but okay, I'll bite. An illusion how?"

"That things aren't solid in the way that we think. Atoms are mostly empty space. You make a nucleus the size of a tennis ball, and its electrons are like BBs buzzing around a mile or two away. What keeps us from falling through the floor isn't matter, exactly, but physical forces that keep atoms together and then repel other atoms. Our eyes give us this illusion of solids, but if we could really see at that level, we'd see this oscillating fuzz of force fields, all the little bits jumping like pop-corn in a popper. A lot of it is chance, particles bounc-ing like dice, but it adds up to normalcy. It's very, very strange down there at the smallest level."

"Except you still can't walk through a door."

"But what if you could? I mean, if we *really* under-stood how matter and energy works? You know, the Bible says, 'Let there be light,' and the universe really started as light. Some energy later became matter, and yet this frozen energy can unthaw again in an atomic bomb—all interchangeable. Physicists talk about extra dimensions, multiple universes, and all kinds of bizarro ideas. But it's no stranger than electricity would have seemed to Galileo."

"This is what you think about?"

He laid back, the old web of iron squeaking. "When I'm not thinking about other guy stuff. Beer, breasts, and baseball. Men are pathetic, but occasionally we lift our minds above the ooze, you know."

"*Very* occasionally, from my experience."

"What do women think about?"

"Nuclear fusion." It surprised her that she was com-fortable teasing him. But a lot had happened in a very short time.

"See? Partners. I like mysteries and your great-grandfather is a crackerjack conundrum. What the heck happened? Isn't it fun to try to figure it out?"

It *was* fun, but exhausting and frightening, too. She'd been grabbed by the most intriguing guy she'd ever met. *Concentrate, Rominy. You're here to solve a puzzle, not moon over the mysterious Jake Barrow.*

She went to the calendar, studying it. It was hung on a narrow wood peg, maybe whittled by a lonely hearts Benjamin Hood out here in exile. Except Dunnigan said there was a woman who represented Hood at the old bank, and was that Great-grandma?

The odd thing was that the view of the mountain looked like it was taken from across Baker Lake, which gave her a chill. That's where her parents—her adoptive parents—told her she'd been found, in a Forest Service campground. Had her biologic parents taken her to that spot deliberately?

She lifted the calendar clear and turned a leaf over, so she was looking at August. "There are two dates, circled," she said. "His birthday?"

Jake came to look. "August was the end of the war. Ah, interesting. August sixth and ninth. Kind of chilling, really."

"Why?"

"Those are the dates Hiroshima and Nagasaki were bombed."

"Ick. Hood didn't have anything to do with *that*, did he?"

"I don't think so. Maybe it wrapped things up for him, you know? The Japanese surrender."

She flipped the pages. They held other faded scenics: hardly a clue to world war mysteries or even her great-grandpa's personality. Not even a Vargas girl pinup. You're not going to get your scoop, Mr. Reporter, because there's no scoop to be had. Maybe Benjamin Hood was just a cranky old hermit who simply hadn't accomplished whatever he was supposed to accomplish in Tibet. Try, fall short, retire, die. That about summed it up for most people.

And then she noticed the stamp.

It was blue with what looked to be some kind of animal in the center, a cat or deer. The creature was surrounded by graceful writing like a cross between Arabic and Chinese, or the Elvish of Middle Earth. At the bottom, in English lettering, it read, TIBET.

Her heart began hammering. The stamp was folded over the edge of an old calendar page, except it was *two* pages, she now realized. They were stuck together. If she hadn't thumbed the calendar she wouldn't have noticed it. She used a fingernail to slit the stamp and then gently pry the aged paper apart. What had been stuck together were two blank back pages of the calendar. Except they weren't blank.

They opened to reveal a curious design. Carefully inked lines ran sinuously like elongated ripples in a pond, filling the pages with an abstract pattern. It looked familiar, but how?

Barrow had come up behind her. Now he grasped her upper arms and leaned over her shoulder, his breath hot by her cheek. "You found something."

"Doodles." She wasn't sure whether she had or not. She was very conscious of his holding her, and not sure what she thought about it.

"No, it's too convenient to be in the only calendar, the only hanging, in the place, but hidden. It's a map, I think."

"If so, it's a map of a maze." She turned to release her shoulders from his grasp but when she did so she was between the wall and Jake, looking up at his annoyingly handsome face, her hands trembling slightly. Yes, she'd found *something*. And he was standing very close.

He hesitated, considering for a moment. "I think it's a contour map," he finally said. He stepped back.

She exhaled. "What's that?"

He took her elbow. He did seem to like to touch her. "Come to the table and I'll show you."

They spread the old calendar out. "A contour map uses lines to show elevations. These swirls here actually mark ridges and mountains, I think. See, here's a mark for what might be the cabin, a square. This is a map of the surrounding hills, I'm guessing."

"But why?"

"To direct Hood, or us, to someplace near. Don't you think? Wait. I've got a Geological Survey map in my truck."

Jake's map was green and much more finely drawn. "Here, I've marked where we are, so we just need to orient Hood's map to our own."

They studied the two.

"They're nothing alike," Rominy finally said. "Yours shows the river, but Hood's is just lines."

Barrow frowned. "You're right. I don't get it."

"Maybe his map is of Tibet."

"But where in Tibet? Damn!" There was ferocity in his frustration. He wanted this story very badly. Maybe his career depended on it.

"Or maybe it's some other clue entirely."

He glanced at her. "What?"

"I don't know, Jake. I'm so tired." She slumped into a kitchen chair. "I'm hungry and I've had a headache all day. All I've had is wine."

He glanced from the map to her, fingers drumming, clearly impatient. But then he nodded sharply. "Yes. Yes! I'm an idiot. Look, I've got food in my toolbox, too. Stove, sleeping bags in the cab, the whole nine yards."

"What are you, a Boy Scout?"

"Eagle. Be prepared. I'm going to cook up something on my camp stove and we'll think about it. Sleep on it, even. We're close, Rominy. Closer than I've ever been. But we need to eat and think. I'm missing something."

So they did eat. The can of spaghetti, with carrot sticks as salad and M&M's for dessert, apparently stretched Jake Barrow's cooking skills to the limit. No wonder he'd been in frozen foods. While he heated she changed into some old-boy jeans he loaned her, cinching them in with a belt. Her heeled shoes were set aside for the boots, which *did* fit. She wondered about the girl who'd worn them but didn't ask. Then she swept the place out with a fir bough, throwing away the ratty fur rug.

It got cold as the sky darkened. Jake had gathered some wood and now he lit a fire in the old fireplace, the flames pushing aside the musty feel. The crackle and scent of smoke was reassuring. Rominy was more comfortable in the new clothes and warming cabin, but it also felt like she was losing her identity. She'd fallen down a rabbit hole.

Jake heated water on the camp stove and used powder packets to make hot apple cider. The warmth relaxed her. Rominy still felt trapped at having to sleep here, but it was too late, and she was too tired, to think of any alternative. She unzipped one of the sleeping bags and draped it on herself like a quilt as she sat in the chair, considering it a shield against the chill of dusk and anything Barrow might try. Not that he tried anything. And not that she wouldn't have been curious if he *had* tried something. He seemed to be leaving any move to her, which was good, except for the ways in which it wasn't.

She realized she'd phoned no one, since she had no phone. The radio had never been switched on. Had the MINI Cooper been identified with her? Was somebody searching? Her adoptive parents were gone and there was no real boyfriend at hand, but what were her friends thinking?

She would miss work tomorrow. It seemed on another planet.

"There's obviously no mattress but I brought pads," he said. "We'll sleep on the floor and figure out what to do in the morning."

"We?"

"You can sack out as near or far as you want. No drama."

She wished there was drama, just a little, so she could have the satisfaction of telling him to stick to his own side of the cabin, but he seemed as weary as she. So they bedded down on either side of the fireplace, a Puritan six feet between them.

Rominy begged for sleep to come but her mind kept nagging at where she'd seen Hood's pattern before. Some art museum, maybe, or a child's book of mazes. Why couldn't she think of it? She needed sleep! She sneezed from all the dust.

And then it came to her with a bang like the explosion of her beloved car. She sat abruptly upright in her bag. It was utterly dark in the cabin, inky and spooky.

"Jake, I've got it!" she hissed.

No reaction.

So she crawled out, still in jeans and her morning's knit top—she wasn't about to give him a peek at her panties, although she *had* considered it—and shook him. "Jake!"

"What?" He'd already fallen asleep. Men!

"I think I've got it! Hood's map—it's not contours, it's a fingerprint."

"Huh?"

"Light the lantern."

When he did so, both of them shivering in the cold of the cabin now that the fire was only dull coals, she reached inside the cookie tin from the bank and took out Hood's mummified finger. Carefully she rolled it in the dust of a kitchen shelf and lifted the hissing camp lantern to study the dust. It had left the faint impression of a fingerprint. Then she looked at the inked calendar page. "This one." Jake bent close. "See? This ridge has the same pattern as his finger."

He sucked in his breath. "What does *that* mean?"

"I've no idea. It's midnight in the middle of nowhere."

He grinned, looking up at her. "I rescued a genius," he whispered in triumph. And then, before she had a chance to think about it, he kissed her.

19

Lhasa, Tibet
September 21, 1938

The close cropping of her hair had the effect of emphasizing the beauty of Keyuri Lin's face: the dark eyes, the fine ears, the sculpture of cheek and chin and brow as she and Raeder stood in the glow of butter lamps off the main audience hall, the serene gaze of a gigantic Buddha filling the chamber like a cloud. She had the regal bone structure of a Nefertiti. There was also a calmness that Raeder didn't remember from before. That crazed religion, he guessed.

Serenity made him uneasy.

Her presence in the Potala Palace was the worst luck, and yet he still felt the old desire. She was exquisite! Once more he ached to possess her, especially since as a nun she was more unobtainable than ever. Yes, the

Germans were tormented by longing, as Reting had said, but wasn't that what made them succeed?

At the same time, his weakness irritated him. A fabled power at stake, and he wasted feeling for this woman? Any woman? Discipline!

She studied him with an objectivity that surprised him; why wasn't she more afraid? Maybe she thought she was untouchable because of the protection of the Reting and the nunnery. That was nonsense. Everyone was vulnerable. In the end, you had to rely on yourself.

"You've come a long way from washing camp dishes," Raeder began.

"And you from hunting specimens for a museum, Herr Raeder. Now you're a diplomat for Himmler and Hitler?"

"I represent my country. It's humbling."

"I very much doubt that."

Again, that disquieting self-confidence. "Does your regent know about our past together?"

"He knows I'm a scholar of Shambhala. Its purity intrigues me."

If she was trying to insult him by referring to his impure tastes, he wouldn't acknowledge it. "Why do you think Reting is willing to help us?"

She thought. "The Reting is curious if you could actually find Shambhala, but isn't unhappy at the thought of your failure, either. If you search for what you seek, there's a good chance you'll never return, and the problem you represent is solved. If you do return, he'll take the secret from you. I suspect he finds humor in putting us together, a woman and the uniformed Nazis. And my research has alarmed him."

"Alarmed?"

"What if myth is true? Dangerous opportunities. Delicious dilemmas."

Which was why he was here. "Why did you become a nun?"

"You know that better than anyone." Now she betrayed some coolness, a flash of bitterness, that actually reassured him. As long as he understood her, he could control her. He was already sifting possibilities.

"Why do you study?"

"You Europeans talked of these tales during Hood's expedition, and after experiencing what I did, it was time to retreat and think. As the Buddha pondered, why is there suffering?" She held his eyes with her own, her hands splayed at her sides. "So tell me, Kurt Raeder, what I still wonder in the dark of every night: Did I cause my husband's death by being friends with you?"

"Of course not," he lied. "His fall was an accident; I told you that."

"I wish I could believe you."

"You should believe your friends. I wanted to be a friend, Keyuri."

That lie hung like incense smoke above the lamps. Raeder had told it deliberately to provoke her. To maneuver her to doing what he hoped.

She tried to mask her own calculations. "As to the legends, I wanted to learn the truth myself, before anyone else did. What if Shambhala *does* exist? Your Western curiosity incited my own. What is Tibet's responsibility, then?"

"Your regent says *your* responsibility is to work with us Germans. To help *us*. What are you going to do?"

"I'm hearing you out."

"Do you think it's in the Kunlun Mountains?"

"That's the most likely place."

"Is it possible to get there?"

"It would take months. Winter is coming on."

He nodded. "The British held us too long in India. What if we had trucks or motor cars?"

"You've seen Lhasa. There are none, except the Reting's ceremonial car and those of the British. A wheeled vehicle could go only partway anyway."

"But cut months to days, no?"

She glanced at the Buddha, massive, serene, a golden genie. "Yes."

He took a breath. If she really knew something useful, he had to try. "I loved you, Keyuri. In my own way. I've . . . reformed. Help me hire the British cars. You'll be our guide, a nun above reproach. In return, we'll share what we find with your kingdom. Germany is on the rise. It will be a partnership to save you from everyone—the British, the Chinese, the Russians. National Socialism will protect you."

"Maybe Tibet can save itself."

"Has it so far? Have Tibetans found and harnessed Shambhala?"

She was silent.

"Can the Tibetan army fight a modern invasion?"

She looked up at the Buddha. Its stare was to infinity.

"Time is short," he pressed. "The world is about to go to war. How will your country survive it?"

She shook her head. "The British won't rent to you."

"Then you must get the cars for us. The Reting must. Buy the trucks. Steal them."

She looked at him with her great, dark eyes, or rather looked above him, as if studying some aura above his head. "Let me make inquiries."

She was going to do it. She was going to betray him as he hoped! Keyuri thought she was misleading him, but he could read the calculation in her eyes as easily as the text of a newspaper. Her hatred would prove to be the swiftest way. He bowed. "Even if we can't be friends, we can be partners." He smiled, the effort feeling like a crack in stretched parchment, his mind aghast at the irony, the karma, of having to deal again with this woman at all. But the Germans couldn't afford to sit in frustration in Lhasa as they had sat in Calcutta. By next spring there might be world war.

He would not play the Tibetan and British game.

He would not let anyone else have Shambhala.

"We're facing treachery, my friends," Raeder told his SS companions when they reassembled in their hostel in the city below the palace. Outside, donkeys and yaks jostled, vendors cried, monks chanted. A medieval backwater.

"Treachery?" replied Kranz with surprise. "I thought we just won Tibetan help in finding what we seek. My God, did you see the gold in that edifice? I do feel like Pizarro! What else might be awaiting us in these mountains?"

"That young woman is beautiful, too," said Diels. "What I wouldn't give for a taste of that. I wonder if she has sisters?"

"I recognize that nun from my previous travels," Raeder said. "We can't trust her. We can't rely on her to guide us until we ensure we're in control."

"A nun?" asked Muller. "I'd think she'd be the one person we *could* trust. A nun or a monk. What's wrong with that?"

"She wasn't a nun when I knew her," Raeder said.

"What was she, then?"

"A widow. She worked on the Benjamin Hood expedition, her husband died, and I consoled her. Eventually we had a falling-out."

"What the hell does that mean? What's going on here, Kurt?"

Raeder hesitated. "I'm afraid she fell in love with me. Of course I had to leave her behind. The gap between our cultures was too great."

"My God. And this is who Reting chooses to guide us? Does the regent know?"

"I'm not sure what that Oriental bastard knows or doesn't know, or exactly what kind of help or interference he's offering. You can't tell what Asians are thinking."

"But why this woman?"

"She became a student of the same mysteries I was curious about. I suppose I inspired her. Perhaps becoming a nun gave her access to secret records. Who knows? Reting Rinpoche is probably a simple man and simply thinks her knowledgeable—and expendable—if things go wrong." He had to be careful his companions didn't learn the full truth.

"Did she recognize you?"

"Of course. You saw us talk."

"Do you think she's still in love with you?"

"I've no idea. Well, yes. Probably. She may be hurt, or jealous, which is why we must tread carefully here." The question of love was irrelevant, he believed. Raeder had bound her to have fun, out of earshot of the other scientists. She'd protested, which he ignored, and then begged, which he'd enjoyed. Then she'd surprised him by daring to crawl to Hood to complain, and the American had interfered. The expedition had broken up, Raeder hastily claiming he was the loser in a love triangle. Hood had agreed not to tell the truth, barely, in return for the German letting her go without a violent showdown that would have destroyed their reputations.

I should have killed them all.

But no, everyone's scientific status was salvaged. And now, was there to be surprising reward from his mercy? Would Keyuri Lin be useful after all?

Raeder still remembered how ripe she'd looked. Women could pretend they didn't enjoy his appetites, but he knew better. That hatred when she suspected he'd killed her husband was also a form of respect, he believed, obeisance to the victor. It was foolish to feel shame for being human. Why did he have to be embarrassed by what was natural? Himmler was right. Religious commandments were a plot to emasculate the strong. He'd assumed the bitch Keyuri would disappear into some Tibetan marriage, and yet here she was in Potala Palace. A nun? A scholar of Shambhala? Was God laughing?

No. This was luck that could be turned to his advantage.

"I've paid one of our guides to follow where she goes," he said. "She'll try to betray me like Judas betrayed Jesus, so we have to move first."

What if he could not just use her but have her back?

What if he could gain not just Shambhala but her submission?

He was flushed, feverish, at the possibilities. Muller looked at him warily, and Raeder decided he didn't like the geophysicist anymore. Julius was too judgmental. He wasn't loyal. He wasn't *trustworthy*.

Their Tibetan guide Lokesh *was* loyal. At dusk he brought back word that Keyuri Lin had visited the British legation. Reader had expected that. Now they must get a move ahead of their opponents.

"Lokesh, how would you like my black SS uniform?"

The man's eyes brightened. The costume was very stirring.

That night a column of Tibetan soldiers silently surrounded the hostel of the German visitors. After listening to Keyuri Lin, the British consul had warned the Reting Rinpoche that the Nazis represented not aid but subversion. He'd obtained from the Potala a writ for the Germans' arrest and interrogation, in joint action with Tibetan police. Ever since getting wireless warnings from Calcutta, British authorities had wondered what Raeder's approaching party was up to. Now Lin had told them. A search for ancient powers? When the Nazis had no business being in southern Asia at all? Absurd. The sheer cheek of Himmler and his fellow bandits was breathtaking. It was time to teach the Hun a lesson.

A full company of one hundred and fifty Tibetan soldiers, under the advisement of Captain Derrick Hoyle, readied to charge. An old artillery piece from Younghusband's 1904 expedition was positioned opposite the hostel's front door. One of the army's two heavy machine guns was set up at the rear.

The Germans could be seen moving through the small, dim windows.

Finally a shrill whistle was blown and the British led the charge. Doors were smashed, entry forced. Hoyle shouted in German that Raeder was under arrest!

No shots had to be fired. Their quarry meekly raised their hands.

The soldiers took into custody five Tibetan porters attired in the full-dress uniform of Himmler's SS.

Raeder's own men, equipment, and weapons were gone.

Captain Hoyle snapped his swagger stick in frustration.

Several miles away, a British motorcar and heavy truck with a squad of English soldiers were racing north from Lhasa, winding up a dirt road to a pass that led to the broader plateau. Far to the north, the remote and mysterious Kunlun Mountains waited.

A young Tibetan woman was guiding from the front seat of the lead car, having assured the English that they represented a more logical alliance in the hunt for ancient secrets than the restless Germans. The British legation thought this choice made perfect sense. If war was coming, the British Empire and nearby India would surely prevail. England was Tibet's natural ally. The British truck towed a trailer loaded with extra fuel, food, explosives, and climbing gear. The vehicles wouldn't get over the final worst terrain, but caravan trails would get the hastily organized expedition close enough to make a forced march feasible before winter descended.

With luck, the Nazis who'd escaped India were already interned in Lhasa.

And in return for Keyuri's help, the English had sworn to turn over whatever they found to the Potala. Reting had nodded gravely at their offer, not believing it for a moment.

The moon was up, the mountains silver, and the plume of dust from the hurrying vehicles was pewter in the gloom.

Then a dark blockage loomed. The British driver of the lead car slammed on the brakes.

A shaggy yak stood tethered in the roadway. Boulders prevented the vehicles from going around either side.

"What the devil?" said Major Howard Southampton. He bounded out to investigate.

Four men dressed in the yak-hair robes of Tibetan herdsmen materialized from the gloom. Bandits! Before the English could reach for their own weapons, the muzzles of German weapons were pressed to their ears.

"Careful," said Eckells in English. "I'm an Olympic shot."

"Hello, Keyuri," the lead herdsman greeted, holding a Luger. "So convenient that you've gotten us an early start to Shambhala."

It was Kurt Raeder, his yak-wool cloak giving him the look of a shaggy bear.

"It's them!" she cried. "It's him!"

But the British were already disarmed.

"Thanks for delivery of the motorcars," Raeder said. "Fortunately for you, it's a downhill walk back to Lhasa."

"This is not just theft," Southampton sputtered. "It's an act of war!"

"It's an act of expediency forced by your own malfeasance in trying to interfere with Reich research and to benefit from Reich discoveries. It's your attempt to arrest *us* that is an act of war." Jabber, jabber, the currency of diplomacy. Hitler was right. Guns made the point more strongly.

The Germans began loading their own expedition's equipment into the car, truck, and trailer.

"You'll have to come back this way," the major warned. "The whole Tibetan army will be waiting for you."

"And us, them, with whatever we find. Your shoes, quickly!"

"Shoes? That is beyond bounds, sir!"

"Be happy I'm only slowing you, not shooting you."

Then, the vehicles commandeered, the Germans sped on toward the mysterious mountains of the north.

Eight British soldiers and their three accompanying porters were left standing, barefoot and disarmed, a humiliating hike from Lhasa. Except for the Reting's limousine, there were no other cars in all of Tibet.

In the backseat of the lead motorcar, Raeder regarded his new captive. She'd betrayed him exactly as he'd expected, and led the British away from the protection of the Tibetans. Fortune was smiling on the Ahnenerbe.

"How sweet to complete our reunion," he told her.

She turned away. "Beware what you desire."

He laughed. Buddhist rubbish. Then he pounded Diels on the shoulder. "Drive faster!"

20

Flying to Lhasa, Tibet
September 10, 1938

O n the third day of Hood's flight from Hankow, China began to rise like a lumpy loaf of bread. Hills became a universe of forested mountains, cut by deep, shadowy valleys that were seamed by rivers. He and Calloway crossed the upper reaches of the Yangtze and the Mekong. The little biplane jounced as it cleared each ridge crest, land falling dizzyingly away and carrying Hood's stomach with it.

If Ben couldn't catch Raeder in Lhasa, it was going to be hard to track him in the vastness that was Asia.

The trees thinned and then largely disappeared. Clouds scattered, and the sky became a vast bowl of blue. Snowy ranges occupied the horizon in all directions, like distant whitecaps. Their plane was an insect buzzing across eternity.

Ben was jostled from a doze when Beth pounded him on the shoulder. "Check the gas!"

The fuel tank was in the upper wing and fed the engine by a tube strapped to a strut. Next to it was a glass gauge that gave a simple eyesight reading of how much gasoline was left.

"We're almost empty!"

"See why we needed those cans?" She glanced around. "There's pasture in that valley. Maybe flat enough to land." The biplane began to descend.

It was like entering a room, the mountains rising around them as they sank, narrowing the sky. Hood could see a few tents at the upper end of the valley and was uneasy about landing where there were people. Farther on, animals grazed. Calloway swept down over the herdsmen and sped down the length of the valley, dropping until the plane was skimming only twenty feet off the ground. She leaned out, studying. Rocks and bushes flashed by. To Hood, it looked like the kind of place where once you landed, you didn't leave.

"Looks risky!" he shouted.

She pulled on the stick, climbed, and banked. Empty mountainside flashed by the wingtips. They'd stirred the herdsmen's camp and people were running, pointing, and fetching horses. A final tight turn at the valley's head and Beth was aimed down the valley again, her touchdown picked.

"I saw a red flag back there!" she warned.

"So?"

"Those aren't just herdsmen. They're Communist mercenaries!"

"So?"

"Drafted bandits. Hang on!"

They drifted down the last few feet as the plane felt for safe purchase. Hood could hear grass whickering at the spinning wheels. They touched, bounced, touched, and bounced again, and then they were roughly down. A boulder loomed ahead but the plane slewed to miss it, coming around to point back toward the tents at the head of the valley. The engine coughed and stopped, the propeller jerking to a halt.

"We'll take off into the wind," she said. The breeze blew exhaust smoke back into their faces. "Get out and pass up those petrol canisters."

"Yes, ma'am."

Ben opened the compartment behind the pilot and boosted the five-gallon cans up to where Calloway balanced by the upper wing. She used a funnel to pour the precious fuel, its color a whiskey peat. Periodically she glanced up-valley like a wary bird.

"Company," she finally said, pointing.

A party of men on tough little ponies was galloping toward them.

"What do you think they want?" Hood asked.

"Whatever they can take, I imagine. Or to arrest us and steal the plane, if a commissar is looking over their shoulder."

"Then let's get the hell out."

"Not until we're refueled." She sounded grim. "You'd better figure out a way to slow them down."

Hood took his rifle out of the cockpit. He'd shot at animals a thousand times, but China was his first war. His gun had a German Zeiss scope. He rested it on the fuselage and sighted. The horsemen were carrying their own rifles.

"Should I try scaring them?"

"If you just want to make them angry."

"Maybe we can negotiate."

"With what? Me?" They were bandits impressed as guerrilla soldiers, she explained, and their idea of mission and discipline devolved from the Mongol hordes.

"Big target to start," he muttered. Hood aimed at the breast of the lead horse, held his breath, and squeezed. The rifle bucked. The horse jerked out of his scope's view and he looked up. The animal had fallen, its rider tumbling. The others reined up in momentary confusion. Dust swirled. He could hear surprised, angry shouts.

"Are you done?" he called impatiently.

"Still pouring. We don't want to have to do this again."

"Christ." Now there was the sizzle of bullets whipping by, the bandit rifles thankfully inaccurate at five hundred yards. Then pops as the sound of the shots reached them. Puffs of smoke hazed their attackers. The Communist cavalry was fanning out into a semicircle.

"I told you you'd just make them mad. They'll rape me and bugger you before they kill us. The killing part will take a day or more."

"Great airport you picked." He aimed again. They were riding hard now, an arc converging on their plane.

"I was told you were a great shot." Her voice was cool, but there was just a tremble.

He fired, worked the bolt to feed another cartridge, swung his muzzle, and fired again. And again. And again. One, two went flying from their mounts. Just three hundred yards now. He could hear the whap of bandit bullets hitting their airplane and he unconsciously tensed, waiting for one to strike his own flesh.

Beth pulled a pistol and rattled off several shots from her wing perch while a funnel finished draining, not really trying to hit anything. Then she leaped down, ramming the empty cans back into the fuselage. She vaulted into the cockpit and set the ignition. "Now, now! Crank the prop!"

Hood shot and a pony went tumbling. He threw the Winchester into his own cockpit and ran to the propeller, giving it a heave. The engine roared. The plane was already moving when he sprang onto a lower wing and hauled himself aboard. They bounced over the lumpy field, aiming at their assailants. Yips heightened. Still at least a dozen of them.

He climbed into his own seat. "I can't aim with all this bouncing."

"Neither can they, I hope." But then a bullet shattered part of the windshield above her instruments, fragments bright as they flew. "Dammit, that stung! Throw off their aim, Ben!"

Hood scooped up his shotgun, an over-and-under with two barrels. The plane was slowly gaining speed as it skipped across the ground, but each second brought them closer to their wildly firing assailants.

One horseman set his course directly for their propeller, as if determined to drive his horse directly into it. Maybe he would, leaping off his steed at the last minute.

Hood stood, hauled himself onto the top biplane wing where Calloway had been, and aimed the shotgun above the arc of the spinning propeller. He dare not fire through it, lest he chew off their propulsion.

The gunman spotted him and aimed his rifle. They were just yards apart. The rifle fired and the shotgun bucked and the pony tumbled, the rider's rifle flying. Lead sizzled past the curator's head. The aircraft vaulted, the undercarriage bouncing as they clawed over the careening horse, wheels given a quick spin. They were past, bounced, and jumped up in the air again, engine howling. Another horseman came galloping alongside, taking aim at Beth. Hood pivoted, fired, and the bandit threw up his hands and pitched backward.

"Yee-hah!" Calloway shouted. Her cheek was bleeding.

Hood allowed the wind to push him down into his cockpit again. The horseman had tumbled into the dust, to his immense satisfaction.

This was more exciting than museum meetings in New York!

The others hadn't given up. They were riding hard behind, bullets peppering the wings. Hood stood, bracing with his knees, and broke the shotgun open to reload. When it snapped shut he aimed backward over Calloway's head and fired. Bam, bam! Buckshot sprayed. Three more swerved, leaning like drunken men, and then the ground was falling away as the Curtis strained, reaching for the sky. They swept over the tents, men still shooting, red flag snapping in the wind.

A cliff loomed.

"Bank!"

They cleared it by inches.

Finally they had enough altitude to pivot back toward the west. Far below, horsemen milled in frustration. Hood could see the specks of bodies he'd dropped.

He didn't feel guilt; he felt relief.

"Nice shooting!" She pounded him on the back. He turned. She was grinning beneath her goggles.

"Couldn't you have picked a quieter place to land?"

"I'm not that lucky. But you are, maybe."

"Are you hit?"

"Scratched, but they didn't get our gas, or our engine, either. We're going to make it to Lhasa, Ben."

He put a finger to her cheek, wiping blood away. The wound had coagulated. "I wish we had that bottle of scotch."

She laughed. "Me, too! It could stretch our fuel!"

That dusk they came down on little more than fumes into the valley of the Kyi-Chu. The sun had sunk behind the encircling mountains, the golden glow of the roofs of the Potala winking out. A few lamps burned but Lhasa was still unelectrified, dark and remote. There *was* an airstrip, however, and the Curtis touched and taxied to rest next to two other derelict biplanes, a British aluminum transport with no wings or engines, and a stone corral of yaks.

Was Raeder still here? And what would Hood do if he was?

How many men had he killed today?

Hood and Beth dropped to the ground, shaken, exultant, exhausted. There were bullet holes all over Calloway's biplane, and shell casings littered his cockpit floor. Thwarting death makes you feel alive. Besting men makes you feel strong. And her wire-and-chewing-gum crate was a tough little bastard after all.

He smiled. It was primitive. Elemental.

Beth watched him as he walked around the airplane. Her hair was a ragged mess after being crushed by the flying helmet, her face smudged with soot and blood, and her fingers still smelled of fuel. But her eyes were very, very bright.

He came to stand close. The barrels of his guns still jutted from the cockpit. No one had come out to the grass strip to greet them. They could hear the river running in the distance.

"Now you'll see this Tibetan woman you left?" she asked.

"Maybe. I'm dreading it, actually. What am I going to say? I think I'll ask the British what they know and decide how to approach Raeder." He stared toward the river. "Now that I'm here, I'm not exactly certain *what* I'm supposed to do."

"Save the world, right?"

"Yes. Or didn't we agree you can only save yourself?" He put his finger in one of the bullet holes. It was a miracle they hadn't been disabled. "And you, Miss Calloway, have gotten me this far. You're a good pilot."

"You're a good shot."

And then, because she'd finally tired of waiting for him to initiate things, she kissed him.

It took him by surprise, but then women were sometimes inexplicable. So he kissed back, enjoying the taste of her, and suddenly restless for release after the trauma of the last few days. She broke with a little gasp, her eyes wide as if surprised by herself, and he leaned in to kiss her neck.

"You smell like gasoline," he whispered.

"You smell like gunpowder."

He laughed, kissing her ear, her nape, the hollow under her neck in front. He opened a button on her shirt and nuzzled part of her shoulder. Her hands were pulling on him and he let his own roam over her rough clothes. She was the opposite of the society princesses and glamour models he grazed through, and a hundred times more desirable because of it. She was *real*. He lifted his face and she kissed him fiercely, cupping his head with her hands, eyes moist and urgent.

Then the two of them were down on the grass as the moon rose over the mountains, fighting out of their clothes. He tarried while peeling hers off, enjoying how she allowed his hands and mouth to explore. She made little sounds, not the tough aviatrix but only a woman hungry for connection. And then they fused.

This one meant something.

They kissed more tenderly, still locked together. In fact, he was so busy kissing that he didn't notice the dozen Tibetan soldiers who materialized out of the dusk and surrounded them and their plane, peering down at their pale bodies in the moonlight.

"Benjamin Hood?" one finally interrupted in British-accented English.

Ben started and jerked around. Beth shouted and snatched at clothes to cover herself.

"What the hell?"

"Apologies, Doctor. But you are under palace arrest."

21

Hood's Cabin, Cascade Mountains, United States
September 5, Present Day

A kiss is just a kiss, the old song went, and Rominy had been perfectly prepared to tell Mr. Jake Barrow not to take any liberties, thank you very much. But he kissed her at midnight at the end of the most traumatic day of her life, after explosion, chase, wine, inheritance, and Nancy Drew mystery madness at the hour she felt most vulnerable and puzzled. He smelled smoky, with a masculine scratchiness on his firm jaw. She kissed back—where was her discipline?— and somehow it advanced to the inevitably awkward comedy of unzipping the sleeping bags and dragging the pads and struggling out of clothes.

So they did it, poor Benjamin Hood's creepy disconnected finger left forgotten and alone on the shelf above. Too weary to make it explosive, too tentative and clumsy to make it sublime, but a release nonetheless. It left her warm, and worried that she'd made a mistake. *Stay away from men, that's my advice.* So why did it feel so right? They fell asleep, his arm across her until he rolled over, and she didn't wake again until the approaching dawn had turned the windows milk-gray.

She blinked sleepily, looking at unfamiliar shadows, stretching stiffly on the sleeping pad. Jake's breathing was heavy but so far he didn't snore. Point for Barrow. There were also the sounds of field mice or worse skittering around. Yet the cabin was also small and snug and cozy, and birds were starting up in the trees outside as the light strengthened, and. . .

Someone was at the window.

Her eyes opened wide and her head jerked up. A face seemed to float in the glass like a pale moon, young, cruel, with thick, snarly lips and a Mohawk stripe on an otherwise shaved head. A silver ornament dangled from one ear.

The face stared back, with deep dark eyes as soulless and unblinking as a shark's. Then it disappeared.

Rominy sat up, heart hammering. Had she really seen it? "Jake!" she hissed.

He grunted and moved closer.

"Jake, wake up! I saw someone!"

"Who?" he mumbled.

"Some bald guy, like a skinhead! He was at the window but then he wasn't." She was whispering without knowing why.

Barrow opened his eyes and looked over her shoulder. "Where?"

"There, above the sink."

"Are you sure?" He stood, naked, and went to the window. "Up here in the sticks?" He looked out other windows, then cautiously opened the door. He glanced around and shut it. "There's no car. You were dreaming."

"I don't think so." She was trembling. "What if they've come?"

"It took me forever to track this place down. I don't think those guys have done it, or they'd have been waiting for us."

"That's not reassuring."

"He just looks and leaves? And Delphina's dogs don't go crazy? No, I think you had the edge of a nightmare." He came back to the sleeping pads, sat, and pulled her down. "Or maybe you saw a raccoon."

"Jake, we don't even have a gun and we're in the middle of nowhere."

"We have Great-granddad's gun, which looks menacing enough. And we're in the middle of nowhere so we don't need a gun. This is the safest place to be right now, trust me. And I have a hunch we're going to find what we're looking for today." They were spooned together, his arm across her shoulder and against her breasts, with all the rest of him against her back and butt and legs in a quite delicious way. She could feel *that* part coming to life again.

"But what if somebody's out there?"

"Nobody's out there, I looked. Anyone coming up that road we'd hear from a mile away. Maybe you saw old lady Clarkson's ghosts."

"It was so *real*."

"It was a dream. Settle down. It's too early to get up."

She wiggled against him, glad of his warmth and nearness. "*You're* up."

"I'm just glad to see you, as Mae West said."

"You know, I didn't mean for us do that last night," she whispered.

"*I* did. I like you."

"And I still don't know anything about you, Jake, not really."

"You will. This is a good start."

"I'm usually more reserved."

"I don't doubt it. Unusual circumstances."

"*Extraordinary* circumstances."

"Spec-*tac*-ular circumstances," and he began to laugh, so she had to turn to kiss him to get him to stop and, well, another half hour went by.

Finally he told her to rest in the warmth of the bed while he got up to build a fire and put water on the camp stove. She watched him as he pulled on his jeans. Yep, he was as fit as she'd surmised in the Safeway store, eye candy in Dogpatch. He seemed in awfully taut shape for a keyboard jockey, so he must really be trying to get his money's worth from a health club membership. Was he too vain?

Stop being so judgmental! One minute Rominy is buying Lean Cuisine, and the next she's in a wilderness cabin with stud muffin reporter. Was *any* of this real? She lazily viewed him as he pulled on his shirt.

"You've got a tattoo." It was on his right shoulder.

"Yeah. Almost a cliché these days."

"What's it of? A circle something?"

"A sun wheel. Old traditional art. Tibetan, among others. I liked the design."

"Chosen after three beers too many?"

"Oh no, I thought about it quite carefully."

"I like it," she decided.

"It's supposed to be good luck."

She had a vague memory of having seen something similar somewhere before, but couldn't remember where.

"We've still got a mystery to solve, you know," she said.

"We're not supposed to indulge our appetites until we do," he agreed.

"But now I'm hungry."

"So we'll eat and then we'll figure this out." The camp stove kettle whistled and he poured hot water into a mug with instant coffee. "I've got a Kellogg Variety Pack."

"You do know how to impress a girl. Will you turn your back while I dress?"

He sipped, looking at her. "No. I don't think so."

Which was not entirely bad, since he did seem appreciative.

The sun eventually came up, lighting the trees and cabin, and they turned again to Hood's odd map with its fingerprint contour lines. It still looked more like a Rorschach blot than a treasure map, but there had to be some meaning to Hood's weirdness. Had he cut off his finger just for this, like van Gogh sawing off his ear?

There was a directional arrow on the map, with an N presumably marking north. Jake oriented it with his survey map, but there was no obvious correlation between the two.

"It's like half a clue," said Rominy.

"I hope he was sane when he did this."

She went back to the cookie tin with its contents. "He left us a compass, too."

"To use that, you have to know which way you're trying to go."

"It's amazing it still works." She turned, to watch the needle spin. Nothing happened. "Except it doesn't." She turned again. "It's broken. Frozen."

"What do you mean?"

"The needle always points the same way on the dial. Sort of northeast."

Jake took it from her and tapped the instrument. The needle didn't budge. "You're right."

"What if *that's* a clue?"

"Why would a broken compass be a clue?"

"What if he fixed the compass so it wouldn't turn and then put it in the safety deposit box with his finger?"

"You mean it's a bearing, a heading?"

"Yes."

"But from where?"

"I think we have to assume this cabin. Find where we are on your survey map, use the compass bearing, and draw a line."

Jake did so. The line crossed several mountains, but it still wasn't clear which, if any, was supposed to match Hood's fingerprint. "We're still missing something. What next, Woodward?"

She pondered. "Elementary, my dear Bernstein. The other stuff in the tin has to mean something, too. The only question is, what?"

He shook his head. "Oh boy, this is not like jotting notes at a press conference. My brain does not work like this. A pistol and a scarf? It makes no sense, this calendar has no guidepost, no . . . wait a minute. Is that gun loaded?"

"God, I hope not. I waved it around in the bank. With seventy-year-old ammunition?"

He picked it up, aimed it away, and worked the mechanism with an efficiency that surprised her. Did Jake know about guns, too? A shell, green with age, was ejected. It fell on the floor.

"Oh my, what if it had gone off?"

"Well, it didn't." He picked the round up, studying it curiously. "Look." He moved the bullet to the calendar. Its diameter matched the hole that had been made through the pages to hold the calendar up. "The hole is ragged. I think Ben Hood shot through this baby before he drew his map, or finger, or whatever the heck he was doing."

"Why?"

He pointed at the open pages. "To give a reference point. Either where we're going or where we are."

"Yes!" She liked this collaboration. "Where we are, I'm guessing. Our starting point. So your compass bearing can be drawn from the bullet hole."

Using the *N* to orient the broken compass, Jake drew a line from the hole the .45 bullet had made across the calendar map to the northeast. It crossed Hood's fingerprint. "Which means?" he asked.

"I don't know. The scarf. What's that for?"

"Your great-grandfather was a lunatic, wasn't he? Or completely paranoid, locking everything away until a relative comes along to claim it—someone who likely wouldn't be with the government, or Tibet, or the Nazis. And here you are, junior detective." His tone was admiring, which she liked. Rein it in, Rominy.

She picked up the scarf and examined it. The silk was dirty, frayed white, and unremarkable in every way. Had it been given to him by some potentate in Tibet? Or was there something hidden in its meaning? What would a junior detective do? Or a man at the end of his life at the end of a terrible war? She held it up to light from a window. Parts seemed cleaner than others. Which meant . . . what?

"Jake, light your lantern."

"Sun's up, Rominy."

"Light it anyway. I need some heat but I don't want to hold this by the fire and risk setting it ablaze."

The lantern was the old gas type, and its mantles flared to life with a familiar hiss. In short order the glass cylinder enclosing the mantles was too hot to touch, and Rominy held the scarf near the light. "This is something we used to do as kids."

"Hold scarves to lanterns?"

"Invisible ink. You can use juices, honey, diluted wine, urine, you name it. Coke, even. You mix with water, write, and let it dry. You can't see it."

"Until you heat it?"

"Yes. Voilà!" Brown characters had appeared on the scarf. Rominy pulled it away and they read.

360/60/60=1"

"That's perfectly clear," Jake joked.

"No, it obviously means something. Is it a date? A year has 365 days, not 360."

"The ancient Babylonians and Egyptians started with that as the length of the year, before astronomy was refined. And that's why we use it for bearings today. I think three hundred sixty means degrees, like compass degrees. This is another bearing, perhaps. Sixty . . . plus sixty. That's one hundred twenty, about opposite where the needle is fixed. And one is . . . I don't know."

"Why have another bearing?"

"To cross the first?"

"But it wouldn't cross. It just leads in the opposite direction. That doesn't help."

"Let me think." He pursed his lips, studying the relics, in a way she thought was irresistibly cute. Yes, she'd fallen. "Have you ever used a nautical chart?"

"No," she said, silently condemning her own lack of caution in affairs of the heart, but then sometimes magic just happened, didn't it? And . . .

"The nautical mile is based on the length of one-sixtieth of a degree, or one minute of one degree of latitude on the earth's surface. That's a distance just a little longer than our land mile."

"But his invisible writing has two sixties."

"Which would suggest a nautical *second*, which my boating days taught me is about a hundred feet. A hundred and one, I think."

"So one inch on his map equals a hundred feet."

"Is that all? That means to his fingerprint from the bullet hole is only a few hundred yards."

She looked at the cloth again. "Wait. Is this another number?"

They peered. Less distinct than the first were more numerals: 72.1.

"Look at your contour map again."

"So?"

"What if it's seventy-two point one times a hundred and one feet? Where does that put us?"

He multiplied it out. "That's seven thousand two hundred eighty-two feet. That could be"—he looked from modern map to Hood's fingerprint and back again—"the far side of this peak here, Lookout Mountain and Teebone Ridge, toward Eldorado."

"Plot it on your USGS map."

"Here, about. Below Little Devil Peak, above Marble Creek Canyon."

"And what are the coordinates?"

He read them off.

"I think that's where we need to go," she said. "A little tricky to find in the woods, I'm guessing."

"Not necessarily," he said. "I have GPS. We can use it to walk exactly to this spot."

"Cool! Then what happens?"

"I don't know. He seemed to go to a lot of trouble to plot this, but then make it obscure. If you didn't have the contents of his safety deposit box, nothing would make sense. Maybe our interpretation is still off. But I think you're on to something, Rominy. We follow this frozen bearing the required distance and find . . . treasure. Maybe." His tone was cautious. He was trying to control his hope. "What are the coins for, then?"

Rominy thought a moment and then beamed, triumphant. "That's easy. You said yourself these mountains are riddled with old mines. We're going to find a gold mine!"

"I like your optimism."

"Maybe he found something in Tibet to help him mine."

"I'll get the daypacks," Jake said.

"I'll clean up the breakfast. When you go out, could you check for ghosts and skinheads?"

"And raccoons."

Jake had started a garbage sack the night before. He was out by his old truck, dragging stuff from his big toolbox and poking around in the cab, when Rominy stooped to scrape leftovers into the bag. She saw he'd lumped in some perfectly good recyclables: the spaghetti can and two plastic water bottles. Odd for a Seattle boy; he was no tree hugger. She decided to fish them out for proper disposal. When she did so, something small, round, and shiny dropped from some crumpled paper towels where it had been caught. Had Barrow lost a coin?

Diving past strands of spaghetti, she picked it up. Not a coin but some kind of small battery. Odd that he'd think to toss one here.

Then a thought occurred. She glanced out the window; he was still busy. So she opened her purse, took out her cell phone, and opened its back.

Its battery was missing.

She put the discarded one in. The phone still didn't power on.

22

Toward the Kunlun Mountains, Tibet
September 30, 1938

The Germans drove seven hundred miles north and west of Lhasa, first on a winding caravan track through a maze of mountains, and then on the trunk road that led across Asia toward Kashmir and the Karakoram. A hundred miles before Karakoram Pass, they turned north again into wilderness, so high and unpopulated that they no longer encountered any nomads. Animals watched them curiously and without fear, not understanding what the two-legs were. Raeder itched to kill some—they wandered near enough to try the submachine gun—but hunting would only slow them down. The distant peaks were getting whiter as autumn began, the snow line lower each morning.

The Kunlun Mountains, a two-thousand-mile-long range that parallels the Himalayas, forms the northern border of Tibet. It lay along the horizon like a white wall, remote as the moon. Keyuri Lin had combined her fragmentary clues from the old *peches*, or books, with ancient legends to turn Tibetan mystery into a tangible goal, a gamble like Columbus's sailing west to go east. Now the roof of the world swallowed them as they drove into a geographic vacuum. Maps were blank here.

When the British motorcar broke down after thirty straight hours of dirt roads and steppe trails, its tires blown, Kurt Raeder's party siphoned its gas tank and unceremoniously rolled it off a hillside. They whooped as it bounced and spun, pieces flying off like bright marbles.

The truck and trailer made it for three more days, some of the Germans riding like coolies on the towed cart.

Then they came to an impassable gorge.

It was as if God had taken the earth into two mighty hands and cracked it across its crust. This was not a canyon, it was a rock crevasse, a split in the plateau that extended as far as the eye could see in either direction. Water glinted at its depths, a thousand feet down. The lip of the other side was a tantalizing fifty yards away. The rift was effective as a moat.

"Now what?" asked Muller.

"We cross it," said Raeder.

"Impossible," said Diels. "We need a balloon."

"Nothing is impossible for National Socialists. And your idea of a balloon is not a bad one, if we had means to make one." Raeder inventoried the truck and trailer. "Unfortunately I don't see how."

"Maybe we can drive around it?"

"Through those boulder fields? How far, and what if the Tibetans are pursuing? Detour and delay could ruin everything."

"We could throw a light line to someone on the other side," Eckells said.

"Do you see anyone, Franz?" Muller asked. He sat on a rock.

"One of us climbs down and up the other cliff." Eckells peered over the edge. "But we don't have rope enough for the entire route. A single slip . . ." Their cameraman/political officer was the most eager of the group, and the most stupid.

Raeder paced the edge like an impatient animal. "Let me think."

"Perhaps this is why no one has ever found Shambhala," said Muller.

Raeder ignored him, scratching a design on the dirt with the toe of his boot. "What if we could shoot a line across? Eh, comrades? A rope to shimmy across?"

"Shoot with what?"

"Our truck. Look. I have an idea."

The truck's exhaust pipe became their cannon muzzle. The vertical stakes of the front grill were dismantled, crossed, and bent to make a grappling hook. The lightest line they dared trust a man's weight to was tied to the hook's cross and carefully coiled next to their makeshift launcher. Gunpowder became the charge, and a revolver was dismantled to provide a trigger and firing pin.

"We're going to blow our eyes out," Kranz said nervously.

Raeder grunted. "You sound like my mother."

"I'm going to film it on camera," promised Eckells. He backed away. He was not as stupid as the others thought.

A sloped trench had been dug and the butt of their launcher braced against the dirt. The muzzle of the exhaust pipe pointed across the canyon, the pole of the grappling hook inserted like a ramrod. Someone had to get down in the trench to pull the trigger.

"I'll do it," Diels finally said, "if someone else is first across."

"That will be me," Raeder said.

Diels closed his eyes and squeezed. There was a boom, the tube jerked, and the archaeologist yelled as hot metal lacerated his arm. The butt of the makeshift cannon had burst. But their hook was arcing like a rocket, line unreeling like a writhing snake. The grapnel struck ten yards beyond the far side and Raeder pulled until it caught on a boulder.

He swiftly tied their end to the truck. "Back enough to give it tension!"

Then he slung a heavier rope coil on his shoulder, grasped the line, wrapped his legs, and pulled himself out into thin air. It was like watching a spider bob in the wind, a thousand feet above a maw of rocks.

Foot by foot, he pulled himself across, the line sagging but not breaking.

"*Heil* Hitler!" he called from the far side.

In astonished acknowledgment, they raised their arms.

The heavier line was pulled back across the chasm. Flywheels from the truck were unbolted to make a crude pulley system for a rope cradle. By the end of the day even Keyuri had been conveyed across, along with all the food, water, and ammunition they could carry. The truck was left, bottomed on rubble and leaking oil. The remaining canisters of gasoline were left in the trailer.

Raeder turned to Keyuri. "Are we close enough to trek from here?"

"Somewhere on the far side of that." She pointed to a horizon of snow-dusted hills ahead.

He nodded. "I know you *could* lead us into oblivion."

"My people want Shambhala's secret, too." She shouldered a pack.

"Yes. And if you mislead us, you'll never see Lhasa again."

"If we find it, I may not see Lhasa, either. No one has ever returned, Kurt."

Raeder didn't tell Keyuri the Germans wouldn't return to Lhasa either. Maybe they'd sneak through China to the Japanese. Or go north to the trans-Siberian railroad and take ship at Vladivostok on the Pacific to avoid Communist scrutiny in Moscow. But the safest route might actually be west, through the wilds of Afghanistan to Persia. A direction in which no power, including Tibet, was likely to stop them. A route that brought them and the secret of Shambhala safely home to Germany.

He'd no intention of sharing anything with the holy men of the Potala Palace, despite what he'd promised. The prize was to help conquer the world.

Nor would those holy men even hear what the Germans had found, until it was too late. Raeder had no intention of leaving Keyuri Lin alive.

The Nazi leader had reestablished his domination of her the first night, muttering to the other Germans not to come near. He'd pitched a British tent out of earshot of the others, ordered Keyuri inside, and pointed his Luger. "Take off your robes." He was master, she was slave, a game that delighted him.

Shaven or not, she was ripe as a young peach under her religious cloaking. But Keyuri was annoyingly indifferent to his attentions. She didn't respond to his caresses, didn't protest, and didn't fight. Her mind fled.

Raeder had been angry at her surrender and took her quickly, his rutting savage. All he felt afterward was disgust. She did curl and weep, but that only added to his dissatisfaction. Where was the fire they'd felt in Hood's camp? Where was her fear? Where, even, was her hatred? She was nothing like his fantasies.

He hadn't touched her since.

Worse, the other men had grumbled. Muller was disapproving. "What did you do to her, Kurt? Look at her, she's a whipped dog."

"She's pretending."

"Why do you get a woman and we don't?" complained Eckells.

"Take her yourself for all I care." But he would kill Franz if he did, and somehow the man knew it.

"I'm not taking anyone. I just say there should be women for all of us, or no women at all."

"Yes, we need a guide, not a concubine," grumbled Muller.

"And I need a geophysicist, not a nanny." He scowled at them. "All right, she asked me for it but from now on she sleeps alone. She's only here because she has maps and clues. We brought her for National Socialism, comrades. She stays until we find Shambhala."

Keyuri hiked in the center of their file. She'd acquiesced to her new destiny with the curious fatalism of the Asiatic. She didn't seem terribly surprised that Raeder had successfully ambushed the British, nor that he would drive their vehicles to ruin without hesitation, nor that he'd bridged a chasm no normal person could cross. That was who Kurt Raeder was. Had she actually been *waiting* for him to return, a secret she withheld not only from her nunnery and Reting but from herself? Did a flicker of attraction still exist? Kurt still thought it possible, but she hid all signs of it. Was indifference her way of punishing him for what happened before? Had her study of the old books infected her with the same lust the Nazis had: to find Shambhala and harness its powers? Was she, the Buddhist nun, as greedy as any of them?

Yes, that was it. Raeder didn't believe anyone could shed longing, no matter what religion they claimed. Longing was what humans *were*, one convoluted mass of longings. People were defined by desire. Keyuri could pretend to spiritual superiority until the sun went cold, but her soul was still his. He'd caught her eyeing the death's-head insignia, the blue gleam of weapon barrels, the hard forearms of his company of SS knights. She was secretly fascinated, he was sure of it. Serenity was a facade.

He was determined to see some kind of final lust in her eyes, a desire for *something*, before he had her murdered.

So they marched. The utter emptiness of the land had begun to strike the Germans as eerie. There was desolate beauty, of course. Much of their route led by lakes three miles high, backed by snowcapped peaks one to two miles higher. The water ranged from indigo to the iridescent green of a hummingbird's neck, as if the plateau were a succession of watercolor cups. The sky remained deep and clear, as roofless as outer space. Everything was immense, shrinking their party to insignificance. The other Germans whispered. Did the Tibetan woman hope to lose them in this wilderness? Would it swallow the Reich's finest as the Reting had warned it had swallowed all who sought Shambhala before them? Were they being led astray?

No, Raeder assured. The Tibetans were as curious about the legends as the Germans were. They'd work together until the inevitable betrayals at the end.

There were no trees at this altitude, and the grass, brown and desiccated at the end of the season, was sparse on the stony ground. As they marched, the blue and brown snouts of bulldozing glaciers came more sharply into focus, descending from the sea of peaks ahead. Clouds clung to the summits, casting gray shadow. The explorers drank from pothole lakes that had a fringe of ice on the shore, and woke in pup tents that each morning had a coating of frost. There was no wood or dung for fires. Their fuel for cooking was dangerously low.

Then the ground heaved up into the hills Keyuri had pointed to and they climbed upward, the air thinner, the wind more shrill. Early snow puffed. The men wrapped scarves over their beards, their eyes pinched into narrow slits. Keyuri coughed but never complained.

"Is this the Kunlun?" Muller asked Keyuri.

"This is only its porch."

They trudged up on old snow patches until there was no more up and they were on a summit of shrieking wind and stinging flakes.

"Kurt, where's Shambhala?" Kranz gasped.

"There."

The setting sun broke through to their left. They could see ahead for a hundred miles. Another vast, frigid basin, a desert dotted with frozen lakes, stretched before them. Beyond were higher mountains yet, icy, mist-shrouded, implacable.

Raeder pointed. "The Kunlun?"

Keyuri nodded.

"Come. Let's get down into the basin as far as we can before nightfall."

They made eight more miles and camped.

When he roused them at dawn their clothes were stiff. Their only liquid water was what they'd kept in canteens close to their chests. They shuddered as they ate cold food, ice mountains behind them, ice mountains ahead.

And marched on.

Then they came to the disappearing river.

A milky glacial stream ran from the mountains, seeming to emerge from nothing—a wall of cliffs far ahead—and sink into nothing. It fanned out onto the stony plain in a braid of channels, getting smaller instead of bigger as it poured from its source. It was obviously seeping into the ground. Its last tendrils disappeared in a bed of rocks. As they hiked upriver along its bank toward the Kunlun range, the flow paradoxically grew stronger.

"It's very peculiar," said Muller. "Following this feels like walking backward in time. Who ever heard of a river bigger at its source than downstream?"

"There're no tributaries to feed," said Keyuri. "The plateau drinks it. I'm guessing that in winter, when the source glaciers stop melting, it disappears entirely. But this is what the legends talk of, a river without end. I thought they meant endless, perhaps circular, but instead they meant it never reaches the sea."

The running water cheered the Germans up. Before, the immensity seemed too quiet, except for the ceaseless sigh of the wind. Now they walked beside the chuckling sound of a glacial stream, familiar from their treks in the Alps and Himalayas.

The longer they followed the river toward these highest mountains, however, the more forbidding their goal became. The Kunlun loomed white, storm-whipped, forbidding. There was no valley or pass promising entry. Glaciers ended like gray palisades, their leaning snouts cracked and leaning. Huge moraines of gravel ran out on the plateau like tongues. Plants were shriveled and stunted. It was the Ice Age. The stream itself sprung improbably from a wall of black cliffs, which made no sense at all.

Then they topped a small hillock next to the now-roaring river, foaming tan with glacial slurry, and saw where the water was coming from.

There was a vertical cleft in a cliff that Muller estimated at two thousand feet high, as if some giant had split the wall with an ax. This canyon was no wider than a room, its walls sheer as a castle's, and it was from this narrow gate that the stream erupted, shooting into the air like a fire hose before falling a hundred feet to the plain they stood on. There was no obvious way up this waterfall to the canyon, and certainly no way through the canyon to whatever the source was. The roaring river filled the cleft from wall to wall, its mist coating the slit with a rime of ice.

They stood, dismayed.

"This can't be right," Raeder told Keyuri.

She looked baffled as well. "But everything else is as the stories describe. A river that becomes a gate. Beyond it, the legends say, is a valley nestled from all storms. And from there, an entrance to Shambhala."

"It's a trap," Muller muttered.

"A trap is something you can get into," Diels disagreed. "This we can't even enter."

"But what a sight, eh?" said Kranz. "Have you ever seen a canyon so narrow? This is more sheer than that gorge! Made from an earthquake, perhaps? Or a lightning bolt. Franz, you must get some pictures."

Their cameraman was already setting up his equipment. "Look, you can see a glimpse of white beyond it," he said. "There's a glacier in there I think, giving birth to this river. This will excite the geographic societies."

Raeder was studying the wall with his binoculars. The cliffs soared up to precipitous slopes of snow that went into the clouds, the white mantle scarred by avalanche tracks. At the crests, wind blew the snow into sharp cornices, their edges swirling away like smoke. "We've no ability to get over the mountains," he said. "If there's a valley in there, it's guarded like a fortress by this canyon gate."

"And if we can't get in, no one else can either," said Muller. "We're chasing a myth about an inaccessible place, I think. That's why Tibetans could invent stories about it. A valley with no entry? Why not pretend a secret kingdom lies within? Who will contradict you?"

"Wait," said Raeder. His binoculars aimed at the canyon. "There's a path, maybe, or at least a ledge. Here, take a look." He handed the binoculars to their geophysicist.

"You can't be serious," said Muller, focusing. "What path?"

"There's a ledge in that canyon twenty feet above that rushing stream. Too narrow for most animals, I'm guessing, and maybe too narrow for us. If we fall into the water and don't drown, we go straight over the falls. It looks ludicrous, and yet it doesn't appear to end. The ledge goes on into the shadows, as if it were hewn."

"You want us to follow *that*?" Kranz said, taking his turn through the binoculars. "It's suicide, I think. That *is* a trap."

"Or a test," said Raeder. "If Shambhala was easy, it would have been found long ago, no? We need to at least get up there and see if it's really a trail, and what might lie on the other side."

"And then what?"

"We leave our extra equipment and sidle our way in there. If we fall, we die. But if we turn back now—if we return to the *Reichsführer* and say yes, we saw something promising, something that fit the legends, but prudently turned back—then I think we die anyway."

Eckells nodded. "The Fatherland does not permit failure."

23

Summer Palace, Lhasa, Tibet
October 2, 1938

So much for Agent Hale's diplomatic letters of introduction. Since his arrival in Lhasa, Benjamin Hood had been kept prisoner in a gilded cage, a meditation pavilion with a pagoda roof. His jail was a serene retreat built on a stone island in a rectangular pond on the summer palace grounds of the Dalai Lama. No one could approach his flowery Eden without permission, nor could he could leave it. Soldiers guarded the bridge. It was a claustrophobic paradise, the terrace girded with a carved stone railing. Ducks and swans floated in the green pool, and trees turning golden with the fading year showered the water with leaves the color of bright coins.

Hood had demanded an audience with the Reting Rinpoche and been denied. He'd demanded release and been ignored. He'd demanded an explanation and been met with the Buddhist chant: *Om mani padme hum*. It was a mantra open to endless interpretation, but in general called its practitioner to the correct path. Which path was that?

From one corner of his little island he could see past the trees to the winter palace called the Potala on its spectacular hill, its golden roofs as remote as heaven. Was Kurt Raeder up there, laughing at him? What had happened to Beth Calloway? Flown the coop, he assumed. Did his museum or government even care where he was? The lack of all communication was maddening.

So it was with cautious relief that he heard the thump of drums and the guttural moan of the *dugchen*, the Tibetan long trumpets, so huge that they had to be rested on the ground. It was like a growl from the bowels of the earth. Some kind of monkish procession was coming toward him, a ribbon of scarlet and purple.

From another direction a file of Tibetan soldiers trotted up, rifles ready, and took up position around the perimeter of the lagoon where Hood was kept. They wore pith helmets and British field uniforms with puttees. Another file of ceremonial archers in long robes drew up on either side of the gravel path that led to the stone bridge, as handsome and taut as their bows.

Between their ranks came the aristocracy of Lhasa, stately as a wedding procession.

A single robed figure with high peaked cap detached himself from the column and walked forward, the soldiers snapping to attention. He brought no escort, carried no weapon, and seemed to have no fear of the American. So why was Hood being held?

The man approached slowly, as if not to spook a wary animal. In his hands was a white silk scarf, a *khata*, of greeting.

"I am the Reting Rinpoche, the regent of Tibet, who rules in the name of the Dalai Lama before His Holiness comes of age," the man said. He bowed, and held forth the scarf. "I welcome you to our kingdom."

Alerted to this custom by Beth, Hood dipped his head to take the cloth. He offered his own flying scarf to the regent. It was smudged, but Reting took no notice.

"It's a pleasure to at last make your acquaintance," Hood said carefully.

"I apologize for your incarceration, but I'm afraid it's necessary. Events needed time to occur before we could have this meeting. We've made you as comfortable as possible."

"Comfortable but anxious. I'm Benjamin Hood of the American Museum of Natural History, and I've come here to warn you."

"Yes, we've been expecting you."

"Expecting me?"

"The scarves signify peace." Reting gestured toward the pavilion. "Should we sit and enjoy it?"

Clearly, Tibetans preferred to take their time. The two men retreated to rest in the shade. The small, brilliantly colored army on the other side of the pond waited stiffly.

"You've come very far," the Reting began.

"I've been sent by my government on a diplomatic mission . . ."

"I know all about your mission, Dr. Hood."

"But how? I haven't been able to speak to anyone."

"Word of your approach came to the British legation from their counterparts in Hong Kong two days before you arrived. I myself spoke to the English authorities on a wireless set that a German delegation thoughtfully gave me as a present. As you might imagine, what the British had to say about you, and the Germans, differed a great deal from what Herr Kurt Raeder, *Untersturmführer* of the SS, told me."

Hood was taken aback. The Tibet he'd seen in his previous travels had been technologically backward and preoccupied with religion. He'd expected complacency and lassitude in the Potala, not a wireless. Yet the young regent seemed calm and knowledgeable, not a naive potentate easily manipulated by the West.

"You know about Kurt Raeder?"

"I've conferred with him."

"Where is he?"

"Searching, I presume, for the ancient powers of Shambhala in the Kunlun Mountains, far to the north and west. He's promised to share anything he finds with my government." The Reting smiled, as if he'd made a joke.

"Do you know what kind of a man Raeder is?"

"More than you think. I've had the remarkable counsel of a young nun who knows about Shambhala, Raeder, and you."

"Me?"

"Her name is Keyuri Lin." He waited for the American's reaction.

My God, what's going on here? Hood made no attempt to mask his confusion. "She's alive?"

"Very much so."

"She serves you?"

"She serves her religion. But, yes, she's a patriot of Tibet."

"Is she why I'm being held captive?"

"Oh no. She's why you're going to be let go."

"I can see her?"

"Not unless you can find Kurt Raeder."

"What do you mean?"

"Keyuri is with him."

Hood's face fell. "Not again."

"By her choice, not just his. But not for the reason you think."

"I'm confused. I came to warn you about Raeder . . ."

"It's not warning we need." He looked about. "It's a crisp morning, breathing of winter, but the air is pleasantly clean, is it not? This is the best time in Lhasa, when the trees turn yellow and the first storms sprinkle the distant mountains with snow."

Hood shifted, impatient. "Your soldiers took me and my companion, Beth Calloway, by surprise. It was embarrassing."

Reting looked serene. "It was natural. Things happen as they're meant to."

What did *that* mean? "Perhaps then you can tell me what's going on."

The Reting arranged himself, his robes fanning like a dress, thinking about what to say. His air of gentle patience seemed alien after New York. In a world sliding toward war, he was eerily calm.

"Approximately one month ago, the British consul called on me in the Potala to report that a German delegation of SS men had left Calcutta without permission.

Lhasa was their announced destination. Messages to that effect had arrived to the British legation via wireless from India. The consul suggested that I mobilize troops to stop the interlopers and turn them back toward the British Raj. He warned me they meant no good for Tibet."

"So Raeder eluded you?"

"Oh no. We knew where he was at every moment and could have stopped him at any time. But a Tibetan Buddhist owes the weary traveler hospitality, and in any case I was curious who would be so bold as to approach our kingdom uninvited. So the English gave me the names of the Germans who'd been in Calcutta, and one of my scholars exclaimed at mention of one."

"It was Keyuri who exclaimed about Kurt Raeder, wasn't it?"

"Yes."

"She's a scholar? A woman, in Tibet?"

"Miss Lin is an unusual young woman. Four years ago she elected to enter a Buddhist nunnery after serving on a Western research expedition."

"The expedition was mine."

"And both you and Kurt Raeder had been involved with her shortly after she had been widowed, she confided."

Hood bowed his head. "Yes."

"Her experience with Westerners had greatly troubled her. Part was their worldly ambition. Part was their ability to thrive and travel in a land so far from their own. Part was the strength of their desire: their madness, if you will. You are formidable. And restless."

"We're scholars too. But Raeder . . ."

Reting held up his hand. "It was Raeder who gave Keyuri the impetus to study legends of ancient Tibetan powers. She fears the West and wants my people to be ready to cope with it. So I spoke with her for many hours in private, getting her story and pondering what to do. The easiest thing would have been to turn the Germans back. But was it the wisest thing?"

"They're Nazis, and Hitler preaches world domination."

"Yes, but they're skilled and unafraid of the legends that inhibit us. They've instruments to probe the earth that we don't have. They are scholars of the Tibetan past and have the ability to understand technology that might elude us. So Keyuri suggested a solution. She proposed that we cooperate with these SS men."

"But Raeder abused her!"

"Shambhala has long been rumored, but never seriously sought. We Tibetans know the difference between legend and history. Yet what if part of the legend is true? Could these ambitious Germans find it? And understand its secrets?"

"Understand only for Germany, I warn you."

"Of course." Reting looked mildly away, studying the paddling ducks. "Keyuri's plan was to go with Raeder and see what he could find, learn what he could learn. She knows he's still obsessed with her, because in the end he couldn't have her heart. Our nun went to help the Germans and yet spy on them. To share in discovery, but bring it back to the Potala."

"More intrigue than the Buddha taught." Hood was wary of this game.

"These are perilous times. Will the coming storm reach my people? And if so, how will we shelter from it?"

"Maybe China can protect you."

"China is our greatest fear of all."

"Keyuri offered to Raeder to go along?"

"Of course not. He'd never expect her to after his treatment of her."

Hood looked surprised.

"Yes, she showed me some of the scars," Reting said. "We had to be cleverer than that. Instead, she betrayed the secret of his mission to the British, who immediately set out to find Shambhala for themselves, as we knew they would. Raeder also knew they would, and he arranged to ambush them north of Lhasa."

"My God. You planned all this?"

"The British were unharmed, but their vehicles—the only ones in Lhasa capable of such a journey—were stolen. So was Keyuri, as the Tibetan with the most knowledge of what the Germans seek. So now they hunt the legend together."

"You're crazy! Raeder will eat her alive! You'll never learn a thing about Shambhala the Germans don't want you to know!"

"My nun is quite aware of this, but fortunately she has a solution."

"Which is?"

"You." He gave a slight smile.

"I don't understand."

"You've been confined here while we give the Germans time to find what they're looking for. With the motorcars, they quickly outran any feasible pursuit. But we'd heard you planned to fly here, and that gave us our solution. We want you to pursue Raeder by airplane, learn what he learns, deal with the Germans in whatever way you see fit, and bring Shambhala's secrets, and Keyuri, back to the Potala. Beth Calloway has been promised sufficient fuel to return to China in return for helping us with this task. She's been employed patching your flying machine."

"Me, instead of the British or your own officers? I'm not a soldier."

"No, but you have one attribute that recommends you to the Tibetan government and persuades us that you will do the right thing, which is to return to Lhasa with what you learn."

"What's that?"

"That you're still in love with Keyuri Lin."

"She told you that?"

"*You* told me that, by coming this far at all."

Hood flushed. He realized that what the Reting said was true, and that the Reting had known this truth before he had.

Now he wanted one woman he was falling in love with to take him to another.

"There's only room for two in Beth's plane."

"I hope that many survive," the Reting said calmly. "Ah." He stood, listening. "That's Miss Calloway's plane now. She'll land just outside the palace grounds, and you'll be on your way."

24

Eldorado Peak, Cascade Mountains
September 6, Present Day

Rominy and Jake started on a trail to Monogram Lake, took a fork toward Lookout Mountain, and climbed to the spot where it made sense to cut through the forest. This was not the most direct way— they could have plowed straight uphill from Hood's cabin—but even the switchback misery of the Forest Service trail was better than scrambling across logs and breaking through the salal and sword fern of thick Cascade forest. Rominy wore the women's boots Jake had provided—half a size too big, she estimated—and had cut off the oversized jeans at mid-thigh. It was nice Barrow had the gear, but after the revelation about the saliva and the Starbucks cup, Rominy was suspicious of his story. Had Jake learned her shoe size, too? Was he an investigative reporter or a stalker?

Had he deliberately disabled her cell phone?

If so, had he simply been buying enough time to sell her on this wild story? She also remembered his caresses and couldn't believe her instincts were *that* wrong. Christ, he could kiss. He'd found her inheritance, too.

But the cash had been put in his heavier backpack, not hers.

Rominy had thought of trying to sneak the old .45 into her own pack for protection, but it was as inconspicuous as an anvil and she was doubtful it would even fire. Her Safeway skirt was packed away, her purse was in the truck, her identity stripped. Jake said he was taking the money for safekeeping. "Better than risk it lying around the cabin, just in case you *did* see someone," which was not exactly reassuring. "Don't worry, I'm trustworthy as a bank."

"Like *that's* reassuring, after the Wall Street meltdown."

He laughed.

The money was in a zipper pocket of his backpack, about as fat as the other one that carried energy bars. Rominy thought about demanding to carry the cash, but he'd found the inheritance and she didn't want an argument to break the mood of partnership. Instead she quietly did take one secret scrap along for herself, just so she did something Jake didn't know about. She tucked the old Tibetan scarf with its invisible writing in her bra between her breasts. It wasn't much, but it was something *she* did, not Mr. Reporter. She needed to regain a measure of control.

But she also wanted to get to the bottom of this crazy mystery, and so far they'd made a great team. So she'd play along, learn about her ancestor, and then if necessary run screaming for the cops.

Well, it was a plan.

Barrow was certainly fit. Not unusual in this part of the nation, but he soon had her panting as he chugged up the trail with the determination of the Little Engine That Could. Rominy had done her share of hiking— guys saw it as a cheap date—but her idea of alpine adventure was driving to the parking lot at Paradise on Mount Rainier and meandering with the mob through the wildflower meadows until pavement ended. If God had wanted people to walk on dirt trails, why had he provided asphalt? This path seemed to be made of equal parts mud, rock, roots, and brush, and was empty for good reason. There was no view, just monotonously steep forest rising above the Cascade River Valley. It was shadowy and still. Few birds lived in these deep woods.

"Did you bring a flashlight?" she finally remembered to ask.

"I've got two, plus GPS, working compass, climbing rope, Swiss army knife, and food for two days. We could invade Afghanistan."

"You seem awfully prepared."

"I was an Eagle Scout, remember."

"Why aren't I surprised?"

"Ski Patrol, lifeguard training, CPR, and ballroom dancing."

She didn't know if he was kidding. "Ballroom dancing, really?"

"I took some lessons."

Intriguing. "I thought newspaper reporters hung around bars and stayed up late and ate bad food."

"I *do* eat bad food. Haven't you noticed?"

"But you know about wine and you have all this outdoor gear."

"I'm a backpacker and camper, and I knew about Hood's cabin. I just couldn't get to it without your help. I've been preparing this for a long time, Rominy. I didn't expect the car bomb. Or how clever you'd be."

"I don't feel clever. I feel bewildered."

"Or how pretty."

Male bullshit, but she liked it. Even now, huffing and sweaty, she felt a kind of satisfied tingle from their lovemaking. Why wasn't anything ever simple? "What do you think we'll really find? Did Hood come back from Tibet with some kind of treasure? Is that why he hid out here?"

"I hope so. Not for the money but for the story. I've already got a good story, of course: you, the bomb, the ancestor, and the safety deposit box. But I've got a hunch I still don't have the *whole* story. And why are those skinhead goons after you? What happened to your relatives? Why did Ben Hood make this a game of Clue? I hope we're hiking up to all the answers."

"Each answer just seems like it poses new questions."

"Kind of like life, isn't it? Too many questions, and then you die."

After two hours of steady climbing, Jake took a reading from his GPS, consulted his contour map, and announced it was time to leave the trail and strike due east—still up—on their own.

"Just make sure we can find our way back."

"I've got a satellite to guide me. But if worse comes to worst, just head downhill. Eventually you should hit the Cascade River Road, if you don't starve or get eaten by a cougar or a bear."

"Thanks for that, Jake."

Fortunately, the trees had already shrunk in size at a mile in altitude, so the downed logs were more hurdles than walls. It was slow going through huckleberry and silver fir, Jake shouting once in a while to warn any bears away from their plowing. Slowly they broke out into heather meadows with a view to higher peaks. Rominy caught her breath. A great rampart of rock and snow, glaciers hanging, loomed above a densely forested valley. Alpine meadows were a bright Irish green between the dark trees and the snow.

Jake looked from his Survey map to the horizon. "Dorado Needle, Triad, Mount Torment, Forbidden Peak."

"Cheery."

"And that one is Eldorado. Appropriate when looking for a gold mine, no?"

"Except El Dorado didn't exist."

"Or Oz, Shangri-la, or Camelot. Or did they?" He smiled, fetchingly.

"Lead on, Dorothy."

Jake would stop periodically to take readings from his GPS and then plot their position on their two maps, his USGS green contour one and Hood's fingerprint chart. They steadily closed in on their target. The entire idea of using satellites in outer space to plot their position in the Cascade Mountains struck Rominy as little less than magic, and using clues from a petrified finger as little more than weird. The entire day was fantastical, the air crisp, the sun bright, the distant glaciers gleaming, and this new man beside her who'd come out of nowhere and seemed able to do anything and everything. Her heart beat faster just watching him move. His mystery made him frightening and fascinating.

What wasn't magical is how the coordinates forced them to work in and out of ravines, scramble across downed timber, and get clawed at by underbrush. The morning dragged into hard work, only the excitement of a treasure hunt preventing the bushwhacking from getting dispiriting.

And then they were *there*, supposedly.

It was a steep mountainside in a stand of alpine firs twenty to thirty feet high, dropping off below to a cliff that fell down to the forested gulf between them and Eldorado. There was no striking outcrop, no "X marks the spot," no gleam of gold or skull. The spot seemed utterly unremarkable.

"I don't get it," Rominy said.

Jake squatted, studying his GPS and his maps. "If we guessed right in the cabin, we should be here." He peered up at the sky as if the satellites might give him a different answer. "Maybe we figured the clues wrong."

"Great." She looked around with her hands on her hips. "All that sweat for nothing." She felt dirty and uneasy.

"Maybe your great-grandfather miscalculated a little. He didn't have our instruments, after all."

"Maybe my great-grandfather was crazy as a loon. Well, let's check around. Could be we're just off by a hundred yards, though it looks to me it's more likely a hundred miles. You go back up, I'll go down."

"Just don't step off that cliff."

They began scouting in opposite directions. It was just more trees and brush. Rominy grazed on huckleberries as she moved cautiously down the slope. She and Jake would shout, "Hey, bear!" once in a while to keep each other in earshot.

Suddenly she slipped on something slick, soil or wood, and fell on her butt, sliding down. She panicked a moment because it was in the direction of the lip of the cliff, but heather and huckleberries quickly braked her. Now all she could see was leaves. She stood up to look back toward Jake but he was hidden. She was in some kind of hollow. More important, she wasn't near him, and *he* had the maps, GPS, and compass. Not to mention her money. "Jake?"

No answer.

"Jake!"

"What?" He sounded too far away, and she wanted him closer.

"I think I found something!"

After a while she could hear him thrashing toward her. Meanwhile she inspected her position, since she'd have to justify calling him over. It *was* a depression, like an old crater, about a dozen feet wide and three feet deep.

"What is it?" Jake looked down at her from the lip of the hollow, poking up out of the huckleberries like a bear himself. He was sweaty.

"It's a kind of pit, like where people dug."

He looked skeptical but clambered down to join her. "Maybe just a hole where a tree went over, its root ball pulling out of the ground."

"Trees don't grow that big up here, and where's the log?"

"True." He looked around, considering.

And then, with an ominous crack, the ground around them split and the hollow caved in.

They spilled down into darkness.

25

Shambhala Canyon, Tibet
October 3, 1938

I f Shambhala Canyon was a gate to paradise, it was
designed to discourage all but the boldest. No sun
penetrated the rift from which the disappearing river
exploded. The canyon walls were coated with great
tapestries of icicles as dramatic as the limestone drap-
ery of a cave. Its end was hidden.

Raeder's party had to climb the waterfall cliff first.
This precipice actually leaned out, the curtain of water
allowing an icy backstage behind, and the climb was
impossible for all but the most experienced mountaineers. The Germans were alpinists, however, survivors
of the Eiger. They had to leave their scientific instruments behind—too bad, because Muller couldn't measure for underground cavities—but among the goods

they'd carted since abandoning the truck were pitons and rope. They also shouldered their rifles and the submachine gun and crammed their pockets with bullets.

"If you have to choose between food and ammunition, take ammunition," Raeder instructed. "Food we can seize from the Shambhalans on the other side."

They strung a route next to the roaring cataract, the climbing line taut enough so that even Keyuri could haul herself up the cliff. Her small booted feet scrabbled for purchase on the slippery face.

Raeder, Muller, and Diels went first and pulled themselves up to a ledge above the brow of the falls, their perch not much bigger than Himmler's old desk in Berlin. The shelf was slick with frost and tilted outward, as precarious as greased glass, but it connected with the trail Raeder had spied with his binoculars. This path was hewn into the western cliff in a seven-foot-high groove that led into the darkness of the canyon. The roof of the groove leaned out over the trail, its eave draped with ice. The overhang had the advantage of keeping the worst moisture off the path. The cliff trail itself was just two feet wide. Below was the river, white and roaring, a mad slurry of racing foam. If they fell in they'd be hurled into space by the force of the waterfall, and then drop a hundred feet to their deaths.

The canyon bent slightly so they still had no idea what lay on its far side. Raeder, however, was exultant. He put his hand to his chest, where a vial of blood from the legendary Frederick Barbarossa stayed warm near his beating heart.

"Someone built this!" he shouted above the roar of the river to Muller.

"Madmen," the geophysicist muttered. "We can't get through that, Kurt. We can't haul our supplies. We'll slip into the river."

"We can carry what we need. Get Keyuri up here."

The woman was dragged up, her hair streaming, a coat of frost on her clothes.

"This canyon," Raeder demanded. "What's on the other side?"

"Supposedly, Shambhala," she said. "Open to the chosen."

He frowned. *Chosen* reminded him of the tribal Jews, but also the SS, the master race. "Like men who brave this trail?"

"It's all legend, metaphor, and symbol. I can't promise there's anything on the other side." She looked at the forbidding trail. "Maybe this is a natural fault. Maybe this used to be a road thirteen feet wide and the rest of it has caved into the river and it's now impassable. Maybe the tale-tellers all stopped here without going on and invented everything we think we know."

"And maybe no one has dared this since ancient times." His eye gleamed. "You wouldn't be here, Keyuri, if you didn't believe that yourself. You wouldn't have tried to betray me to the British if you didn't think there was something to find."

She blinked, looking into the canyon. "Do you believe in destiny, Kurt?"

"You mean fate?"

"Fate that you met me."

"Yes. Things happen for a reason. Opportunity comes for a reason."

Her eyes were solemn. "Pain happens for a reason?"

He nodded. "Yes. Yes!"

"I'm going into Shambhala with you. But never think I'm truly *with* you. This is for my country, not yours."

"Of course. Each of us has our loyalties. But destiny has brought us this far together." He held her shoulders. "Let's see where else she takes us." *Until I don't need you anymore*, he thought.

The climbing rope was reeled in and a fresh piton driven above the ledge where they crowded. Kranz looked excited, Muller doubtful, Diels like a fatalistic infantryman resigned to making a charge. Eckells, who'd come up last because he'd insisted on bringing his cameras, was muttering *Heil Hitler* to summon Nazi courage. They squeezed like a single organism.

Then Raeder went first, his face to the cliff, sidling sideways, his Mauser hunting rifle slung across his back. The cataract roared and sucked at the cliff face twenty feet below his boots. It was like mincing on a frozen pond. Rope spooled out behind him. At a hundred feet he drove in a second piton. When the rope was secured, the second German sidled forward. Each member of the party followed in turn, until they were strung like beads on a string.

"Now, stay still and hold on while I advance," he ordered them. Again he extended like a spider, fastening a line the others could follow. When the last German advanced, a slipknot let the first line come loose so it could be reeled in and used again. It was like the creep of a caterpillar.

Raeder always went first, with nothing to hold on to. *The leader takes the most risk.*

The canyon grew darker and colder as they penetrated.

What if they ran out of pitons?

Keyuri was shivering, but said nothing. She was sandwiched between Muller and Eckells and shuffled forward with them as her turn came.

Hour followed hour. They'd no idea what the sun was doing; it was eternal shadow in this crack in the mountains. They crept a hundred feet at a time, Raeder refusing the offers of the others to pioneer the route.

"I led us here, and I will lead us out," he said. "The Fatherland calls us to courage, my friends."

Muller rolled his eyes. Diels shared a sly smile.

After an eternity, the canyon seemed to be lightening. Raeder had Diels grip his pack while he leaned out over the rushing river to peer ahead. Then he gestured and was pulled back.

"I see the canyon ending," he said. "There's a wider valley beyond, and distant snow. I think we're coming to Shambhala, comrades."

"What does it look like, Kurt?"

He winked. "Paradise."

All he had glimpsed was the white of ice. But his men began shuffling faster.

They could see where the trail broadened at the end of the canyon, two hundred yards ahead, when the pitons at last ran out.

"What if we need them for this Shambhala?" Muller asked moodily.

"I'll send you crawling back to get them," Raeder snapped. Then, even though he couldn't possibly know, "Don't worry, we're past the worst." He addressed the others. "We're almost there. From here we balance. You've seen me do it. We're almost off this hellish path."

They'd made another thirty yards, legs trembling from the strain of mincing along the icy ledge, when there was the flicker of a shadow above. The others might have missed it, but Raeder's senses were honed by the concentration required when hunting. His head jerked upward. A vulture?

No, a plane! It flashed a moment in the narrow ribbon of sky above the canyon and then disappeared behind the other rim. An airplane here? The Tibetans had none. Was this some British trick?

He could hear the craft circling. "God in heaven," he muttered.

"Not God, Kurt," Keyuri said. "Benjamin Hood."

"What?" For just a second his practiced composure was gone. He looked back to where she clung on the canyon wall.

"He's pursuing you," she said. "You've led him to what he's looking for."

"You're lying."

She looked at him evenly, and he knew she wasn't.

"How do you know this?"

"I planned it. As did the Reting."

"Damn you!"

She allowed herself a smile.

The other Germans looked bewildered.

"The American?" asked Diels. "In Tibet?"

Raeder thought. "He can't land ahead in the valley of Shambhala, or he'd be doing so already. We'd hear the drone of his motor. He'll have to come in the same way we did. But we're first, and ready for him."

"You're going to shoot him?"

"Stop him."

"But if he brings the British or Tibetan army . . ."

"No one is bringing an army." He glanced around the precipitous canyon. "You others, go around me. I'll be last."

"Go around you?" protested Kranz. "We'll fall off!" The river thundered below, steaming as if boiling.

"I'll jam my mitten into the crack here to brace myself. I'll be like a root in this cliff. Hold on to my pack and squeeze by." There was another flicker and a faint sound of engine noise. The biplane again. "Hurry!"

One by one they crept around him, clutching his pack, trembling at the strain, and then continued sidling on the narrow trail, creeping toward where it widened to a shelf in what must be a valley. Muller, Kranz, Diels, Keyuri . . .

Eckells was last.

The Nazi cameraman was exhausted. The movie camera and tripod were awkward and unbalancing. He grabbed Raeder's pack, began moving around, and hesitated, his limbs shaking from exhaustion. His gear was hauling him backward. A foot slipped, and he leaned out over the river.

"Franz, don't stop! Move, move!"

Eckells began to flail.

"Franz, you're pulling me loose! We'll go into the river!"

The cameraman's eyes widened as he panicked. He tried to make a sound, but nothing came out. All he could sense was the water below.

"Franz, you're peeling me off the cliff! Let go!"

Eckells clung tighter. Raeder began to lose his own grip.

So the *Untersturmführer* stomped on the cameraman's instep, the pain causing Eckells to release his grip in surprise. His mouth formed an *O* of pain and shock.

Then he was falling.

There was a splash and Eckells was gone in an instant, a dark form flashing down the racing sluice of a river, sinking from the weight of his own pack. In less time than it took to drown he would reach the falls.

And then it was as if their companion had never existed at all.

Raeder slammed himself back into the protection of the cliff.

The others froze, horror-struck. All were in front of their leader now, staring back.

Raeder took a breath, cursing, and then ignored them. He slung off his pack, put it on the slippery ledge, and hauled out some explosive.

"Kurt!" Muller yelled in alarm. "What are you doing?"

The zoologist jammed dynamite into the crevice he'd just clung to. There was no way to wire a detonator. He fumbled for a lighter and lit a fuse. "Sending the American a message!" he called. "No army can follow!"

"Kurt, no!"

"Silence!" He began following the others, facing forward on the trail to make better speed, ignoring the torrent below as he tottered. The fuse was burning. "Go, go, if you don't want us all to be blown off the cliff!"

"But how are we going to get back?" Diels shouted.

"By finding Shambhala and a new kind of power!" the German roared.

"You're a madman!" Muller cried.

"And you're dead if you don't move!"

Keyuri put her hand on Muller's arm. "It's all right," she whispered.

Muller stared at her. What did she mean?

"Soon it will all be over."

She's a witch, the geophysicist thought. *We're doomed.*

They crept on as fast as they dared, trying to put distance between them and the explosive.

It went off like a clap of thunder, the shock wave nearly shaking them off. Rock blew out from their side of the canyon to crash against the other wall before falling into the river. Where the precipitous trail had been, where Eckells had fallen, there was now only a bite out of the rock.

They had no more pitons, no means of ascending glaciers, no route home.

The biplane passed by one more time, a flicker as it flew from rim to rim.

Raeder laughed, lifting his arm in Nazi salute to the sky. "Try to follow me now, Hood!"

His companions huddled. They had become Shambhalans.

26

Shambhala Valley, Tibet
October 3, 1938

If Kurt Raeder hadn't set off his explosion, Benjamin Hood might never have confirmed the Nazis were there. Beth Calloway had shouted that their fuel was getting low, that they must turn back if they were ever to return to Lhasa. She wasn't about to abandon her precious Corsair by having it run out of gas in this desolation. But then there was a flash and smoke from what almost seemed inside the earth, and the Americans realized they'd guessed right. The Germans must be inside a narrow canyon, trying to reach the valley beyond. And the Nazis had seen them and were destroying something in reaction, Hood bet. The race was to its final sprint.

It was the end of a long, wearying day of flying from Lhasa.

When he'd met Calloway and her plane outside the summer palace grounds in the Tibetan capital, Hood was honest. This was a woman he'd last seen when they were making love, and now she'd been asked to fly him off the edge of the map.

"Do you know who we're going after?" he asked. Not what, but who.

"Your old lover and your old enemy." She said it matter-of-factly. The Tibetans had been candid.

"And this is okay with you?"

"Shut up and crank the propeller."

"It's dangerous."

"So I double my fee. To buy more shoes."

"Beth, I didn't expect to go after Keyuri again."

"But you hoped you would."

"She's not what this is about."

"Yes she is."

"When we get back, we'll sort all this out."

"*If* you get back. I'm flying this crate, and I'll be judging which of the pair of you is lighter." She smirked, menacingly.

He hunted for the right words. "Your plane is the only chance to catch the Nazis."

"The only chance after giving them time to find what the Tibetans want them to find. Right? The Germans are playing the Tibetans, and the Tibetans are playing us, and you're playing me. Everyone's got a bet in this fiasco, Ben, so don't worry about stamping out medals. Let's just do what we have to."

"What's *your* bet?"

She shrugged. "That your nun is unlikely to be alive by the time we get to her. Or as sweet as you remember. Or available."

"But if she is?"

"I'll save as many of our hides as I can. It's what I do."

They took off, the altitude forcing them to snake through passes instead of hopping over mountains to fly direct. The biplane followed the trace of dirt roads below, Hood watching for the Germans but finding only what he expected, herds of goats and caravans of yaks and oxen. The trade traffic thinned as they flew north and west of the city, and then nearly ended altogether. They followed the main trunk road that led west, a thread of connection in a vast plateau wilderness, the wind so biting that Hood almost wrapped his head like a mummy with the silk scarf Reting had provided in trade. Calloway had a *khata* of her own. The fabric hid her expression. Behind her flying goggles, he couldn't see her eyes.

"At some point they'll have to turn for the Kunlun!" he shouted.

"Watch for sign."

An hour later, he saw it. A lighter scrawl of dust on a tributary track suggested a place where dirt had been kicked up by more than animal hooves. He pointed and she banked, nodding at the line of tire tracks. They turned north. The biplane bucked in the cold air.

A hundred miles on, a glint of metal confirmed they were on the Germans' trail. It was the British motorcar, overturned, wheels up, slid down a hill. An accident? They circled twice, looking for bodies or survivors, but saw none.

"I think it broke down!" Hood said over the roar of the engine.

Beth nodded.

They flew on.

Three hours more and they came to an enormous crack in the crust of the earth. A huge canyon sat athwart the path, and the truck and trailer were beside it. A rope stretched across the chasm. Again, no sign of life.

"Pray they left the gas," Beth said.

This landing spot was even rougher than the one with the shoot-out, but there were no bandits this time. No Germans, either. Nobody at all, just the sighing wind of an emptiness even the Tibetans didn't want. Beth topped off her tank with the

German spare fuel while Hood got more by siphoning the German truck dry. She put three canisters in the biplane's storage compartment while he hid the rest behind a rock. If they survived, this was the only way they'd get back.

Then they took off again, the engine throaty as they clawed over the precipitous canyon. It was getting late.

There was a range of snowy hills they barely skimmed over, boot tracks in the snow, and then a barren basin. The Kunluns beyond were a frozen rampart that stretched as far as the eye could see. When they saw the river, Hood pointed and Beth nodded, following it. The waterfall was a white beacon miles away, and when they flew near, it seemed to be spurting from the cliff face. The canyon was a cleft too narrow to see into. Odd.

They circled. Down at the base of the waterfall, Hood spotted abandoned bundles of equipment.

"Go as high as you can! See if we can fly above the source of the river and get into the mountains!"

They pivoted upward like a climbing bird. There was a snowy saddle at the top of the cliffs that led toward white haze. A jagged black line represented the rift in the rock below. As they passed over it, he got brief glimpses of racing gray water.

Were the Germans somewhere in that chasm?

Beth rapped him on the shoulder and pointed. Several miles east, at the outer base of the Kulun range, there was a wisp of smoke. They saw a tracery of wall there.

Did someone live near the gate of Shambhala?

Then they saw the flash of the explosion, deep in the crack of the river.

"They're here!" he shouted.

"Where?" She peered over the side. The crevice was narrower in places than her wings.

"They must be pushing through. See if we can fly over the saddle. It must be where they're going."

"We're already at our limit."

"Climb anyway."

Shaking her head, she aimed where he pointed. "Pray."

Mountain piled upon mountain. They skimmed the snow. The engine was laboring in the thin air, wheels dipping toward a crash . . . and then the ground plunged abruptly away, sheer cliffs again, and they popped out over a hidden valley.

Shambhala was like a well. The vale was shadowy, ringed by towering peaks with glaciers that fed the river. Yet at the bottom it also had an improbable wash of green, totally unexpected in October. Somehow the basin below must be warmer than the bitter norm.

Beth dipped and circled, rotating around the curve of the mountain bowl. There was a party of people down there, hurrying through a jumble of old ruins.

"Can you land?"

"Where? Look at that mess."

"But the Germans must have blown the only way in."

"One of the ways, unless your Germans and your old girlfriend don't plan on ever coming back." She glanced around. Everywhere, mountains higher than their maximum altitude, her biplane a fly in a cup. Pass a few miles in either direction and you'd never suspect this secret hole was here.

"Christ," Hood cursed. "We can't climb over those cliffs, either."

"There *is* another way, college boy, but you ain't gonna like it." She kept them rotating. The party below had disappeared.

"What?"

"Jump."

"I wish." He looked down. If only he could step onto those snowy slopes, maybe he could pick his way down . . .

"Wish granted." She unbuckled straps, put the plane straight and level for a moment, half stood, and wiggled out of her parachute. "Tie the straps as tight as you can. When you fall, yank that cord there. You don't have much room, and need time for the canopy to deploy. You'll still land hard."

"I've never used a parachute!"

"Neither have I."

Hood groaned. "There's no alternative?"

"This is what you get for chasing your Tibetan sweetheart. I'll try landing back on the plain we crossed and check out that smoke. No house has only one door."

He closed his eyes. "Igloos do."

"So you'd better hope the Shambhalans weren't Eskimo. Hurry up, we're wasting gas! Pretty soon it might occur to Raeder to start shooting at you."

Hood lengthened the straps for his frame and awkwardly put the parachute on. It felt bulky and flimsy at the same time. "To think I was bored."

"What are *you* complaining about? Now *I* don't have a parachute at all. Go, go, it's getting dark!"

He glanced around. A cirque of mountains, frigid air, strange greenness below, enemies who'd vanished. The sun had long since set behind the mountains, and all was pale gray. Too awkward to jump with his rifle. He checked his Duncan Hale–issued government .45. Taking a breath and trying to think of as little as possible, he grasped the rim of the cockpit and boosted himself out, tensing as the wind hit him full force. He clawed for a strut, trying to get in position to jump. Every instinct screamed not to let go.

But then Beth abruptly tilted the biplane and the cold air plucked him off.

Hood fell toward Shambhala.

27

Eldorado Mine, Cascade Mountains
September 6, Present Day

R ominy plummeted, slid, and dropped again. It
happened so suddenly, in such disorienting darkness, that it was over before she could scream. She and
Jake tumbled into a tangle at the base of some mine
shaft, the rotting wood of an old lid piled around them.
As her wits returned from the blast of adrenaline, the
real fear began. What if they couldn't get out?

"Rominy! Are you okay?"

"I can move." She groaned, but when she tested her
limbs they all seemed to work, thank God. "Barely."
She coughed. "I'm covered with dirt, my body aches,
and I can barely see. I think my knees are getting
scraped down to the bone."

"I've got more bandages."

Dim light filtered down from where the cave-in had occurred above. It was like looking at the top of a well.

"You know, you're the worst date I've ever had."

Jake coughed, too. "Ditto."

She looked around. They'd tumbled at least forty feet and were in a wider cavity about ten feet high, which meant it was impossible to jump up to the narrow tunnel they'd fallen down. The walls and ceiling were rock, the floor dirt and rubble, and the darkness in every direction but up was profound. "This is very bad, Jake." She tried to keep any tremor from her voice. "What now?"

He stood up, weaving a moment from dizziness before straightening and brushing himself off. "I'm guessing you found where X marks the spot. Maybe Great-grandpa came back to be some kind of hermit miner."

"Great." She wobbled to a stand, too. Yep, nothing broken. Not that it mattered if they couldn't get back out. "It didn't occur to him to dig sideways?"

"I don't know. Maybe this is an old pioneer mine he found."

"So why is it on his fingerprint map?"

"You're asking all the right questions. Fortunately for us, I'm a Boy Scout, remember?" They'd fallen with their packs and he rooted inside for a moment before digging out a flashlight. "I'll keep the other in reserve. Let's see where this thrill ride goes." The beam was as welcome as coffeehouse neon on a cold Seattle night. Gloom shrank back to reveal a horizontal shaft that must run toward the cliff face they'd spied from above; the old horizontal shaft would have opened to a view of Eldorado.

Mine timbers at the ceiling sagged from age. In a hundred feet, the tunnel ended disappointingly in a wall of rubble and snapped bracing.

"Cave-in," Rominy said. "This place feels very unsafe."

"You've got all the instincts of an investigative reporter." He played his light on the blockage and then on the ceiling. Back and forth he shone the beam, like a paint roller. "Look at those streaks. Soot radiating from an explosion."

"Which means?"

"That maybe this mine didn't cave in, but was sealed. Dynamite, and boom. That closes the front door. We fell through the back."

"So no way out."

"Maybe there was a rope or ladder at one time. Would have rotted since the end of the war, of course." He kept staring at the ceiling. "Looks pretty firm to me, but I'm not a mining engineer. Probably best to go back to where we fell in while we figure out what to do. But, you know, I don't get it." He sounded more puzzled than worried. "What did Hood expect us to find here?"

"My guess is an old gold claim," Rominy said. "Maybe he thought his heirs could make something of this, but no way today. Too many environmental restrictions. I think we're on federal land in the exact middle of nowhere."

"Which means he definitely thought he *had* children, or a child. That's interesting, isn't it, because there's nothing in the records about one living up here. So where was Great-grandma? Mystery upon mystery."

"Jake, the mystery is how we're going to get out of here."

"Maybe I can lift you up until you can get a grip in that shaft."

"I'm not much of a climber."

"Consider the alternative."

And then Rominy stumbled on something that gave way with an audible crack, an object softer than rubble on the floor. "Oh, Geez! What's that? There's something creepy, Jake."

He shone the light. "Yuck. A shoe."

A man's dress shoe had been kicked out from the rubble by her stumble. There was a gleam inside. Barrow bent to peer.

"With a foot attached. You broke the bone."

"Oh, my God. I'm going to be throw up."

"It's just a corpse, Rominy. Dust to dust."

"Jake, let's go. I'll climb, I promise."

"No, this is important. Great-grandpa led us to a body. The ankle bone is attached to the shin bone . . ." He sing-songed, playing the light. "There." A bone projected from the loose rock, and near it was another shoe. "Hello. Looks like we really found someone."

"This is so sick!"

"What if this is your illustrious ancestor?"

"Dunnigan said they found him in the cabin."

"That's right. So, in that case, who's *this*?"

"I don't think I want to know. I can't take looking at bones, not when we're trapped like this."

"We can't just walk away, girl." He squatted and calmly began throwing aside rock. "Yep, there's a whole dude in here." What was *wrong* with him that he could just dig up the dead like that?

"Isn't this desecration?"

"My guess is he's been here since 1945 and either the explosion or subsequent rockfall covered him up. The poor guy has never had a decent burial. Maybe we can arrange one."

"But what's he *doing* here?"

"That's the million-dollar question, isn't it? Here, shine the light, can you?"

The flesh had long since rotted away, thank goodness, but the skeleton was still enclosed in shreds of decayed clothing. There was no obvious injury to the skull, and no indication of how the man had died. It was a man, because the other shoe was male as well. The clothing looked like . . . the ruin of a business suit. Out here?

"Not really outfitted for mining, was he?" Jake asked.

"What was he doing in the woods dressed like that?"

"We need identification." The flashlight danced. "Eureka!" He crouched again and threw aside more rocks to uncover a pack. "Look. Old oilskins to keep out the weather." He pulled it out, ignoring the mold and grime. Bones fell aside, fabric deflated. "And inside . . . Ah. A leather satchel. Maybe *this* is what your calendar map was directing us to, Rominy."

Despite herself, she was getting excited again. She played the light over what Jake held. "What's inside?"

He opened the satchel carefully. There were papers, documents with script in a foreign alphabet, curious diagrams, and maps. He carefully unfolded one. Central Asia. They could still read it clearly in the flashlight beam: *Tibet.* "Hallelujah," said Jake.

"So it *is* my great-grandfather?"

"In a business suit. A burial suit." He rocked back on his heels. "Was he a suicide? He makes obscure clues, hikes in his funeral best to an old mine, and uses dynamite to seal himself in? Man, that's grim. I don't get it."

"But they said they found him in the spring of '46. Dead of natural causes."

"Yeah. And this happy camper . . . has all ten fingers. Look."

"So it's not Benjamin Hood."

"Or that's not Grandpa's finger."

She shook her head. "I'm more confused than ever."

"Me, too. But I think this is some other guy, who maybe Grandpa sealed in. So who is it?" He began digging through the leather satchel, looking for a clue.

Rominy had spied something else, caught among the tendrils of decayed fabric and old ribs. It was a much smaller bundle. She didn't want to touch, but curiosity animated her arm. Besides, once they identified the body maybe they could concentrate on escape. Squeamishly she reached in, snagged the packet from the bones, and pulled it out.

Jake looked up from his papers. "What you got?"

"His wallet or something."

"Open it up."

It was a leather folder of the kind that carried official identification, stuck shut with moisture, grime, and time. Gingerly, the old leather cracking, she spread it apart. "It's some kind of government credentials," she read slowly in the beam of the flashlight. "A badge. Office of Strategic Services."

"OSS? That's the war's predecessor to the CIA." He frowned. "What was an overseas operative doing here?"

"There's a name, too, I've never heard of. Have you?" She held it out.

He looked, his head next to hers.

Special Agent Duncan Hale.

28

Shambhala, Tibet
October 3, 1938

Kurt Raeder's mother had taught him that life is a series of disappointments, where reality falls short of hope. She'd been widowed by the Great War and impoverished by that widowhood. She'd almost starved in the chaos of the Weimar Republic that followed Germany's defeat and become bitter because of it, a shrew for whom even the good was never good enough. She'd spent Kurt's youth recoiling from any suitors and railing against fate. In reaction, Raeder had retreated into adventure stories. His childhood strategy was to believe that if he just hiked hard enough, or climbed high enough, or won prizes enough, he could reach the end of the rainbow and flee his family gloom. His thick-necked, mustached father, who disappeared at Verdun, had glared balefully at him from a photograph fading in a tarnished frame; he'd sought to please the brutal ghost who had beaten him in his earliest years by fighting bullies, until he became one himself. Always, though, Kurt felt destined for something nobler than his mother's religion of pessimism and his father's eternal dissatisfaction. He would scale Valhalla.

Well, he had hiked and climbed now. He'd come to the very end of the earth, a place of thin cold air and epic vastness, a Hyperborea of ice and rock, seeking the victory of the hero stories he'd escaped in as a child. And here, finally, *was* the rainbow's end, the El Dorado he'd dreamed of all his life.

He'd found Shambhala. He was sure of it.

The survivors of their party had fallen silent when they emerged from the gorge into the valley. Even Keyuri, who had somehow betrayed him to Hood, had gone quiet in awe and trepidation. The valley into which they'd emerged was surrounded by cliffs so precipitous that it was craterlike, glaciers hanging above like half-descended curtains. A dozen waterfalls that cascaded down from those ice fields were drawn like wavering lines of chalk, feeding the river they'd just inched along. The river, gray and cold, bisected the valley. There was no pass at the upper end, just towering mountains. The effect was claustrophobic but sheltering.

The valley floor was a wonder. It was green in this otherwise brown Tibetan autumn, not lush by any means, but full of grass and heather.

"The mountains must catch the clouds and wring out more rain," Muller speculated, as much to himself as to the others. "The cliffs trap warmth."

This pasture was broken by old ruins, a crumbled maze of roofless walls and pillars. Their style was vaguely Tibetan, the walls sloping slightly inward to mimic mountain slopes and brace against earthquakes. Yet in detail, the stonework was different from anything Raeder's party had seen. There was a hint of Egypt, Rome, and China, and yet the architecture was none of these and impossible to date. Abstract patterns created a frieze on some of the broken walls. Pediments, buttresses, and porches had carvings of animals both recognizable and fantastic, from lions and camels to winged serpents, shaggy yetis, and crocodiles the length of a Mediterranean galley. Here the remnants echoed Babylonia; there the geometry of the Yucatán. Erosion had taken its toll, but there were still bits of bright paint on the stonework.

"This place might once have been as brilliantly colored as the Potala in Lhasa," said Diels, the archaeologist. "The Egyptian and Greek temples were like that, too, before the paint wore away."

"We've found our lost city," Raeder announced, unnecessarily. He'd expected the others to cry out in wonder at this moment, or slap him on the back, but instead everyone seemed subdued and wary. There was something haunted about this place.

"Feel the air," said Diels. "It's warmer, is it not? Not warm, but warmer than outside. Isn't that strange?"

"There's an odd tingling, too," said Kranz. "Do you feel that? A silent buzzing, like electricity. The feeling you get in a generating plant. Could this be some trick of electromagnetism, Julius, like an energy field?"

"If we'd brought my instruments, I could tell you." Muller was grumpy.

"And if I had my cache of schnapps, we could drink a toast," quipped Diels.

"Are you mad?" snapped Muller. "Franz Eckells is dead! I can't get my instruments because our leader has destroyed our only escape. And you want to celebrate? Or comment on the temperature?"

"A scientific phenomenon." Diels sounded hurt. "We can't bring Franz back, and he was too much the Nazi brownnose anyway. Come, Julius, we're making one of the greatest discoveries in the history of the world! Don't you feel anything?"

"I feel trapped. Look at what you're seeing. The city's dead. There's no way out. We're led by a fanatic."

"And I feel on the brink of achievement," Raeder retorted. "Germany sent us here out of conviction that there were valuable secrets to be learned. This is what Heinrich Himmler dreamed of. Sulk if you want by the river, here, Muller, but the rest of us are going to explore Shambhala."

"Even her, this Delilah who somehow helped the American find us?" Muller pointed to Keyuri.

"Especially her, to interpret what we find. She can scheme all she wants, but the American can't follow us. And look at her eyes. She wants to explore this, too. You didn't really believe it, did you, Keyuri? You thought we were chasing a myth. But German will prevailed. National Socialism prevailed."

"Destiny prevailed," she said. "Remember, none have ever returned."

"I'll return. With Vril." He addressed the others. "Unsling your weapons. We don't know who might be hiding here."

"Ghosts," Muller said.

They advanced into the bowl, the geophysicist reluctantly bringing up the rear. The valley's sides had been terraced, Raeder realized, with the glacial streams feeding pools that at one time were part of a complex irrigation system. At some point in the past this had been an intensively farmed oasis. Why had this civilization tucked itself away like this? Who'd come to build it?

They found themselves walking on what must have been the principle avenue, many of the paving blocks heaved or broken. Their gun muzzles swept the road. The lost city's layout and order became plainer, but so did the fact that it had almost certainly been abandoned, contrary to myths of long life and perfect harmony. Had it fallen prey to catastrophe, or to the simple old age that doomed all civilizations? This find was the fantasy of any archaeologist—Diels was walking goggle-eyed—but Raeder's goal was a practical one, to find a new kind of power.

They passed two enormous statues of warriors or kings, each at least sixty feet high. The men, one on either side of the avenue, were holding staffs thrust forward in their fists. Their bodies were encased in a kind of chain mail. This was overlain by rigid armor across the chest and groin. Curiously, however, their helmeted heads were turned backward, as if looking for followers through the narrow slit of their visors. Their faces couldn't be seen.

"They don't know whether they're coming or going," joked Kranz. "Not the most heroic of poses."

"They're looking for something behind them, I think," said Diels.

"Or they're turning away," said Muller.

"Turning from the face of God," Keyuri said quietly.

"God?"

"Or his manifestation. The power of the universe. It's blinding, like the sun."

"Hmph," said Muller. "What do you think, Kurt?"

"I think all humans have historically worshipped the sun because it's the obvious source of life on our planet. We're dust and water animated by energy. Some theosophists believe there's a black sun at the center of our planet with similar power. Perhaps the Shambhalans tapped that, or brought their own energy with them. Look at those friezes. They could be ships, but we're thousands of miles from the ocean. They could also be flying machines, or rocket ships like the American Buck Rogers. Their suits could be spacesuits. Or they could be gods, with winged chariots."

"But why Tibet, in this valley?" said Kranz.

"If you wanted an outpost or base hidden from hostile natives," Diels speculated, "this is the very best place. It's too high for conventional civilization, and far away from roads and cities. It's on the highest plateau of our planet. The valley is hidden, but easily defended. Maybe they just stopped here to build something or repair something."

"*Who* stopped here?"

"The helmet men," Raeder said. "Gods, or visitors from outer space. The ancestors of us Aryans. They cast the seeds of civilization, completed what they wished, and moved on. Possibly leaving descendants, Germans, to rule the earth."

"Or they didn't leave but just died," Keyuri said quietly.

"Like any number of European explorers," Muller said. "Disease, starvation, despair. Maybe what they were seeking didn't work."

"Or they couldn't control it," she said.

"*I* will, if it's here," Raeder said. He looked at his companions. "Are we women, worried about the worst like Keyuri? Or are we going to get what we came for?" He pointed. "I think the helmet men are looking back at that tunnel entrance. See that glow? That's the real entrance to Shambhala. They aren't guardians. They're guides."

Just then they heard the whine of the airplane again. The sky was already twilight blue, everything in shadow. The biplane caught a last ray of the sun at its height and shone for a moment like a star.

"It's Hood," Raeder growled. "Looking for us. He could strafe us, even! Run to that cave before he spots us. He'll soon run out of fuel and turn back. If he ever finds his way in here, it will be too late. We'll have Vril and be ready for him." He jerked Keyuri's arm and began hurrying her. The other Germans broke into a trot as well. Ahead was an arched entry into a hill, the stone portal carved into a scrolling tapestry of what looked like mathematical and geometric symbols. From within came a faint green glow.

The opening was as big as a train tunnel. The causeway they were on peaked at the entrance and then sloped down into the earth. While the others ran under its roof a few yards, Raeder paused to look up at the sky. The biplane was circling aimlessly. There was no place to land. Hood had come all this way for nothing.

Satisfied, the German stepped inside. "Somewhere below is our El Dorado."

29

Shambhala, Tibet
October 3, 1938

The vault of the Shambhala tunnel was as riotously decorated as the painted pillars of the Potala Palace, but the intricacy was carved with stone instead of drawn by paint. A universe of images enclosed them as they descended on a gently sloping ramp: thick jungles with slant-eyed beasts peering through prehistoric fronds, high mountains with plunging waterfalls, vast temples, marching armies, strange ships that seemed to float on air instead of water, voluptuous dancers, stampeding chariot teams, grinning monkeys. The figures wound around each other in spirals and loops, a giraffe nibbling at a maiden's hair, a salmon leaping through a ring of fire, a soldier thrusting a spear at what looked like a dirigible. Here a prisoner had his heart torn out;

there figures erotically entwined. The artwork was in panels, as if telling a story like the stained-glass windows of a church. The panels were separated by geometric bands.

"Exquisite and barbaric at the same time," Kranz said. "It looks almost Mayan or Mexican. But also Indian, Cambodian, Minoan. Could the connections between ancient cultures be deeper and more profound than even the Ahnenerbe has dreamed?"

"Either these people copied from everyone," Diels said, "or the world copied from them." He was transfixed and wanted to stop and study, but Raeder dragged him on. Time for art history later. What intrigued and worried him was the mysterious force that infused the stone with a green, electric glow, as if the rock itself was somehow alive and illuminated from within. What caused that?

"It's the dream of madmen," Muller whispered, looking about in the ghostly glow. "Every surface is covered. And what is this light? Curie's radiation?"

In a hundred yards their progress ended at a massive gate, made of an unknown substance dull as pencil lead. It sealed the tunnel. The gate, divided into petals like the shutter of a camera, was a disk a dozen feet across. It bore a carved Tibetan mandala like they'd seen in the Potala Palace, a symbolic portrait of the universe. It was a map of a fantasy temple or palace as viewed from a bird or flying machine, a succession of canals dividing the utopia of palaces and gardens into circular bands. Each section was grander as the eye was drawn to the center: the Atlantis of legend was like that, according to Plato. The heart of the design was not a throne or king, however, but a literal heart—a carving of the human organ where the petals joined. At the center of *this* universe was the universal human pump of blood. A carved artery sprouted from it like the tube of a flower.

"That looks Aztec, too," said Muller. "Remember how the ancient Mexicans plucked out hearts? Is that a symbol of blood sacrifice and worship?"

"It's a way in," Raeder said.

"Why did they delve underground at all?" asked Muller.

"Because invention is not the same as wisdom," said Keyuri. "What these people were doing was dangerous. They hid it down here. They were seeking to protect themselves, or others."

"*Was* dangerous, in ancient times," said Raeder. "Dangerous before the rise of science. Dangerous before the rise of National Socialism. Dangerous before the research of the Ahnenerbe." He addressed them as a group. "We have a chance, comrades, to change world history. All it takes is courage."

"Providence rewards the bold," Kranz seconded.

"Not," said Muller with more practicality, "unless we have a key to this gate."

The barrier weighed many tons but had no handle or keyhole. The joint where the sections met was at the heart, but the means of opening was unclear. Diels pushed on the gate. It was as firm as a mountain.

"It's a blood lock," said Raeder.

"What does that mean?"

"Tell them, Keyuri."

She looked at Raeder with unease, surprised that he had guessed this. "The Shambhala legends say the ancients had keys that only one person on earth could open, the person with the correct blood. The mechanism could detect the worthy from the unworthy."

"That's nonsense," said Diels.

"On the contrary, isn't that what National Socialism teaches?" said Kranz. "Race is real. Blood is real. Heredity is real. Perhaps there's some code in blood that tells one man from another."

"Which we don't have," said Muller.

"Which is why I in fact may have the necessary key," said Raeder. He withdrew from his shift the silver vial, slightly bigger than a rifle shell. A small chain was attached to a metal cap. "I've been carrying this for ten thousand miles."

"What is it?" Diels asked.

"Before we left Germany, Reichsführer SS Himmler entrusted me with a relic that has been brought to the Nazi Party by German scholars of the medieval period. For eight hundred years it has been guarded, passed from custodian to custodian, as 'The Shambhala Key.' No one understood what that meant, until the research of the Ahnenerbe. It's Aryan blood from the mists of history, brought from here to Europe after being taken from the veins of our great German ancestor Frederick Barbarossa."

"Barbarossa?" said Muller. "Are you mad?"

"If I am, then so is Heinrich Himmler. Barbarossa didn't die in the Third Crusade, comrades. He secretly came here."

"Came for what?"

"To learn. And perhaps to lock this door until the time was right, until National Socialism had been created by Adolf Hitler and our people were ready to receive Shambhala's secrets."

"Wait," said Diels. "Barbarossa went to *Tibet* and back?"

"Maybe not back. But his blood did. And locked the door until his rightful descendants returned to make sense of what he'd found. See the hole in the heart, that artery?" He uncapped the vial and stepped forward.

The stone artery gaped like a little mouth, leading into the stone heart. "This is where I pour, don't I, Keyuri?"

She said nothing.

Raeder shrugged, carefully tipped the vial, and emptied the bright red contents into the gate. "As Wilhelm said, scholars of our Ancestral Heritage Research and Teaching Society contend that Shambhala's doors read something individual in blood, some code that we do not yet understand but which differentiates each of us from the other. This code is too tiny for even microscopes to see. Keyuri is right; only chosen individuals, somehow programmed by nature like the numbers of a combination lock, can gain access. And in reading, the door responds."

Indeed, there was a sudden whir and growl like the sound of a machine. Gears and levers clunked at the sides of the tunnel. Then the great stone gates groaned and an aperture began to slowly open. Dust puffed out to settle around them. The air that blew out was musty.

"This is crazy," Muller said. "Barbarossa was an old man by the time of the Crusade. How could he have come here?"

"A better question is why. What did he know or seek? I suspect he heard tales of this place in the Holy Land. Who knows who else visited here. Abraham? Jesus? Mohammed? A key to its entrance was our king's last gift to Germany. Perhaps this door was locked when he left. Or perhaps his bones are here and not in the Holy Land."

"You believe that?"

Raeder pointed. "The doors believe it." The massive petals had mostly receded into the tunnel walls, just a small portion of each still jutting out like the curved teeth of a shark. A circular entry led to more tunnel. The way was clear.

Raeder cautiously stepped through. Nothing happened.

The broad avenue sloped down as before, but this time the way ahead was dark; there was no green glow. The Germans hesitated.

"What does legend say is down there?" Raeder asked Keyuri.

"Revelation. And the danger that comes with it, like the apple in your Bible. Everything you believe is counter to my own religion, Kurt. Everything you strive for, my religion teaches is illusory. Go down that road, and you'll only bring misery to yourselves and the world."

"And I say everything that is wrong with *your* religion can be seen in the medieval barbarity of your country, Keyuri. You teach acquiescence and despair. We teach hope and triumph." He turned to the others. "This door has been waiting for the right men to open it: the triumphant heirs of Frederick Barbarossa. And it opened! *That's* the lesson here."

"Kurt, we can't go down there without lights," warned Kranz.

"Maybe we can make torches," said Diels. "Look, there's a rack of staffs to the side here. They must be antique weapons or tools. We tie on some brush, light a match, and proceed. If we carry several we can light the next with the last one and have some time to look about."

"Good idea," said Kranz. He strode and seized one, and . . .

It lit.

The upper third of the staff glowed. The German almost dropped the staff in surprise and then raised it higher, in wonder. When he lifted his arm, the tip shone brighter. In bright daylight the output would seem modest, but in the gloom just beyond the massive gate, it sent shadows fleeing. "What magic is this?" Kranz gasped.

"Shambhala," Keyuri said.

"See?" said Raeder. "It's a sign from God—our God—that we're on the right path. A sign that our nun's fears are groundless."

The others picked up staffs as well. With the touch of a human hand, each glowed. The light staffs tingled

the palm as they illuminated, and there was an odd
energy to the air, a feel like an approaching thunder-
storm.

"I hope it's not *black* magic," said Muller.

"No more magical than a battery torch would be to
a medieval knight," Raeder said. "We're encounter-
ing what we came for, a technology more sophisticated
than our own. Our theosophist philosophers dubbed it
Vril, but under any name it's the power that girds the
universe. We can't detect it, but these staffs absorb it
from the air or the cave walls. We're going to find it,
comrades. We're going to control it. And when we control it, we control the world."

"Then where is everybody?" Muller asked. "Why
were the doors sealed, opened only by special blood? I
sense a wickedness about this place."

"You've turned into an old woman, Julius. We've
got two nuns, not one!"

The other Nazis laughed.

"This from a man who's marooned us all? Who let
poor Franz fall into that river?"

"Who just led you to the most exciting find in all
history, if you have the sense to seize it. My God, here's
your magnetic anomaly, your underground cavity, your
source for a hundred scientific papers and everlasting
fame! And you don't want to walk down this ramp?

Fine! Then sit outside with the machine gun and keep watch for more interlopers like Benjamin Hood."

"You're not rid of me so easily. I want to keep an eye on you. I'm the only one here who retains common sense."

"Then stop undermining morale and help lead the way. Live up to the ideals of the SS, Julius. The fact that no one remains is a *blessing*. We can explore the city in peace." Raeder's eyes burned.

They descended, Muller in reluctant lead. The main avenue remained the size of a train tunnel, and from it opened doors on both sides, dark rooms beyond. They peered into a couple but they were empty, with stairs leading both up and down into darkness. "It's a vast hive, I'm guessing," Raeder said. "See the size of the steps? These were people, just like us."

They didn't pause to explore any other rooms. Instead they kept to the main path, noticing more decay and detritus as they did so. There was broken pottery and scraps of odd material, flexible like cloth but stiffer and harder—canvas, or oilskin, but from a substance they'd never felt before. The deeper they went, the more cracks appeared in the tunnel's walls and ceiling. From them water dripped, the leach-ate forming small stalactites. Some of the bas-relief carvings—presumably of kings and queens, courtesans and captains, royal pets and a zoo's bestiary—seemed deliberately defaced. If Shambhala had been sealed, it had not been when it was in pristine condition.

"They were fleeing, I think, and dropped things behind," said Keyuri.

"Or they were an army issuing forth," said Raeder.

"Or they were fighting each other," said Muller. "Rioting."

At last the ramp leveled and they came into an enormous cavern the size of a train station, the ceiling so high that it was lost in darkness overhead. Raeder guessed the stone hall was a lobby or assembly area for this underground maze. Arched doorways directly ahead led to what had evidently been a huge dining room, with stone tables and benches, some of them shattered. Beyond was a stone counter and ovens. On the walls were faded murals of fantastically opulent gardens and pavilions, with brilliantly colored birds, huge butterflies, and grinning apes. Eden in a cave.

"I suspect they worked down here but didn't live down here," Diels said. "There's too much love of nature. That's what the valley was for."

"Or they missed the nature they'd abandoned," Keyuri said.

"But why dig underground at all?" Kranz was baffled but fascinated by his own bafflement. Here was a lifetime of research and prestige! "What was down here?"

"Come, before these glow staffs decide to dim," Muller said.

"I don't think they'll ever dim," Diels said. "I think that's the tingling, that they replenish. Can you imagine a lightbulb that powers itself forever? That alone would make us rich, Kurt."

"I just hope you're right," said Muller. "It's a long climb back in the dark."

They went back to the cavernous lobby. There were more small doors to the left side, leading to dark, tight chambers. To the right, however, was a large, garage-like opening. When they explored this, they realized there was a hangar door half-attached. It had been knocked askew into this new room but still hung by one hinge. This gigantic door was metal, and a solid red from rust. Flakes littered the floor like cinnamon.

Beyond was a vastness into which their light would not initially reach. There was a sensation of cold, empty space, and their footsteps on the stone floor echoed.

"Lift the staffs as high as you can," Raeder ordered.

When the glow strengthened, its light was reflected ahead by vast, hulking machinery that filled the wall opposite the door. It reminded them of a factory or power plant, its engines extending into a cave hewn from rock. As they approached this apparatus, their light brightened even more and the staffs vibrated more. There was a faint insect hum.

"This is no ancient civilization," Diels murmured. "This is some incomprehensible future."

Some great beast of a machine, the size of a hundred locomotives, loomed above them, a great matrix of pipes, wheels, gears, drums, pistons, and levers receding into gloom. Cables looped like vines. Catwalks allowed access to higher levels. At the top, pipes branched out from the machine like the limbs of a tree to run and entwine along the ceiling. At the machine's center, these pipes gathered into a trunk that dived into a faintly glowing pit in the earth, as if this apparatus had organically grown out of some kind of hell.

Some parts were metal, but other parts, including the piping, were of dull-colored material the Germans couldn't guess at. There were no obvious wheels or buttons for control, and no obvious purpose to the contraption. It did have a focus, however. In the center of the machine, at floor level, horizontal tubes from left and right ended in a gap. In this gap was a stone cradle. And lying on this cradle was another staff, this one looking as if it were made of crystal. Its ends were aligned with the hollow pipes that ran in two directions from the machine.

These pipes disappeared into horizontal tunnels about ten feet in diameter at either end of the huge room. The tunnels themselves extended into darkness.

There were squat boxes at the base with blank screens. Diels passed his staff near one. It hummed, and then made a residual crackle when the staff lifted away. "Perhaps these boxes showed some kind of picture or signal," the scientist hazarded. "They could be the controls."

"But what does the machine do?" asked Kranz.

"I have no idea."

"There are tunnels at either end of this big room," Raeder said. "Let's check them."

These were more peculiar still. The hollow pipes near the crystal shaft became encased in larger pipes that ran through the tunnels, extending as far as their light would cast.

"Is it a pipeline?" asked Diels. "Is it to send some kind of oil or chemical from that machine, a refinery, to someplace else?"

"Or perhaps this is the refinery, and these tunnels conduct crude oil," Kranz guessed.

"It must go to other parts of the city." Raeder turned to Keyuri. "What do you know?"

"That to truly understand, we need wisdom."

Nunnish nonsense, and he was tiring of it.

"Should we follow it?" Kranz asked.

"I think we need to figure out this big machine first," said Diels.

"Look, more staffs," said Muller. There was a rack of them near the squat boxes at the base of the machine, like a rack of arms. Some were dull and black, like carbon. Some were crystalline. Some were metal. When Muller took one, it flared brighter and whiter than the ones from above. They blinked in its illumination. "I can feel it vibrating," the geophysicist said. "It's like it's a radio receiver for energy."

"Are they more powerful light sticks?"

"I think they're here to be charged in the machine's cradle," Raeder said. "I think they're instruments of Vril. Weapons. Wands."

The improved visibility from the new staff only deepened the mystery. Now they saw that some of the pipes at the ceiling had been torn and knocked askew. These walls, rough-hewn and undecorated, had black rays on them like blast marks from explosions. There had been some kind of accident.

And in the center of the machine, where pipes ran down into a circular well, was a high metal mesh to guard its perimeter.

Raeder took Muller's staff and walked over to this, looking through the grill to peer down the shaft. Far,

far below—impossible to say how far, but tremendously deep—was an eerie red glow. Heat wafted up. Stairways, pipes, and cables descended into the pit. On the sides of the shaft, gates led to new stone stairs that seemed to delve ever deeper.

"Perhaps I *have* led you to hell," Raeder told the others. "Or a chute to the center of the earth."

"What do you think the pit is for?" asked Kranz, looking down warily. It was dizzying how deep it delved.

"They're getting energy from the earth," Muller hazarded. "Heat energy, and perhaps electromagnetic energy as well. Or some new form of energy we can't guess at. Perhaps they mined into this valley for this very connection, or went underground because their experiments would only work in places deep and dark. Maybe it was so dangerous that they had to pick the most remote spot on earth. In any event, every machine needs fuel, and this one uses the planet's core, I'm guessing. The black sun, perhaps."

"But a machine for what?"

"For Vril." Raeder took the brighter staff and passed it near one of the squat boxes. The black rectangle on its top began to glow. There was a clunk, a groan, and a hum as the huge machine began to start.

Nothing moved, but some of its components gave that same ghostly green glow they'd seen at the top of the tunnel, and now the room was fully lit for the first time.

"It's coming to life," muttered Kranz.

They stepped back, unsure what the mechanism might do. It began to make a whirring sound. In the stone cradle before them, the crystalline staff began to glow.

"It's a generator," Raeder decided. "It's transferring energy from the center of the earth, or energy we can't detect, to these instruments or weapons. Look. Those pipes from the deep bring energy. The motors and gears transfer it to the horizontal pipes that extend into the tunnels. And they in turn feed power to that staff, charging it like a battery. But how could an ancient civilization master such a thing?"

"All their knowledge was lost," Diels hazarded. "Or they left here for another world."

"Left where? To prehistoric Germany, to our age of heroes? Did they give rise to the legends of the gods?"

Muller was looking about, peering into shadows. "Or they didn't leave at all," he said. "Look." He pointed.

Kranz followed his finger. "Oh my God!"

The hangar door, they'd seen, had been almost knocked from its hinges. But what they hadn't seen was that some blast or force from the machine had swept across the room and hurled everything against the far wall, in the shadow behind that door.

In that newly illuminated gloom there was a white shoal of bone, a bleached reef, including hundreds of blank-eyed human skulls. It was a ridge of bony remains.

It was a hurled heap of long-dead people.

30

The Lost Valley, Tibet
October 3, 1938

For one terrifying moment, after Ben Hood pulled his ripcord during his fall toward Shambhala, nothing seemed to happen. Then the parachute opened with a bang and he snapped hard against its straps, gasping. He looked up. The silk had blossomed into a reassuring canopy. Beth's biplane was a black dot against the dying light and then was gone, past the mountains.

Alone.

He looked down. The ground was coming fast.

He tensed for the shock until remembering to relax. The ground was dark and jumbled, ruined walls running in every direction and small canals descending from the mountains. Pools from ancient reservoirs were rectangles of gray. Nor did he have any idea how to control his direction. Obstacles rushed up, he lifted his knees reflexively, and then with a thud he was down, rolling, his chute snagging on some old parapet.

For a moment he lay still, stunned. Then he sat up to confirm nothing was broken.

There was no sign of Raeder or anyone else.

Hood unbuckled his parachute and let it sag over the wall, the strings trailing like long white worms in the gloom. Now what?

He had no food, no water, and no weaponry except the .45 on his hip. But Raeder must be here, and with him Keyuri, unless the bastard had already tortured and killed her. There'd be other Germans, too.

His one advantage, he hoped, was surprise. Judging from the explosion, the Nazis expected they'd blocked his pursuit by dynamiting the canyon.

Hood began navigating over old rubble, the dusk continuing to deepen. Then he came upon a clearer path, an old road with ruptured paving. He stopped.

There was a low hum. Was the ground vibrating?

The sound seemed to come from where the road led. There was the faintest green glow in that direction. Keeping to the deepest shadows and wary of ambush, Ben hurried as fast as he dared. Walls, turrets, and huge statues rose all around. The statues were looking backward, in the direction he was going.

Shambhala looked very strange.

If only Roy Chapman Andrews and Agent Duncan Hale could see *this*.

The road led to a tunnel sloping down into the earth. It was from there that the humming emanated. There was a faint, sickly luminescence that seemed to emerge from the walls of the tunnel itself, as if the rock were alive with energy. How this could be, Hood had no idea. Then, a hundred yards in, a circular entrance with a narrow pocket to either side into which some kind of aperture door had slid. Beyond was darkness. Except not complete darkness, because far, far below a yellow light glimmered, like a candle at the end of the tunnel. In that direction, too, was the source of the noise, a whir like a turbine.

The ruin looked centuries or millennia old yet trembled like a powerhouse.

Hood took out his pistol, wary.

Then there was a new rumble. The tips of the door's black petals began closing like an insect maw.

For just a moment he considered bolting. But then whatever he'd come for would be forever beyond his grasp, wouldn't it? He'd be haunted by incompletion, like last time. He stepped through and watched, die cast, as the door slammed shut.

He was in Shambhala.

It was dark, except for that distant light.

He carefully began to walk downhill.

As Hood descended he occasionally felt currents of air from what he assumed were openings on both sides of the central tunnel, and felt like he was being watched by the spirits of what had once been here. No one challenged him, however. There was only the murmur of spoken German ahead.

The humming grew louder and he saw light slanting out from a hangar-sized opening. It spilled into a cavernous lobby, a great stone atrium with carved pillars branching across a rock ceiling. Various doors opened to all sides. Now he heard excited voices to the right. He trotted lightly to where a massive iron or steel door had been wrenched askew. Shielding his own body from view, he peered inside the next room.

And there was Raeder and his party! It was startling to see his quarry after four years, standing in a ballroom-sized stone chamber barren of all furniture or decoration. He was as Hood remembered him, tall, handsome, and carrying himself with that peculiar Teutonic poise. Raeder and three other men he assumed to be Nazis were dressed in mountain boots and heavy jackets, their packs on the floor. A smaller, slighter figure was Keyuri; when she moved his recognition was instant. Her slim grace was like a fingerprint. Each of the five people held a long staff, he saw. From the tips a light shone, like a gas wick. And beyond was some kind of vast machine, high as a cliff, glittery from metal and somber with black pipes and boilers. This contraption glowed and emitted a low whine. Pipes from the machine led into low tunnels at each end of the room. At the center of this behemoth was a cavity. In this cavity was a rack, and on that rack rested another staff, but this one translucent, like a piece of agate. It was not shining like a lantern but instead pulsed with a golden glow, like a beating heart. Beyond was a pit that appeared to descend into the earth, its mouth reflecting red.

What ancient civilization had built this thing?

"I think the machine is energizing the staff with a power we've no knowledge of, the power of Vril," Raeder was saying to the others. "Something comes through those pipes in the long tunnel."

"What's the staff for?" one of the Germans asked.

"Think of legends and fairy stories. Remember the magic wand or wizard's staff? What if they were true? I think our forebears wielded these rods of power."

"It's dangerous," Keyuri warned.

"And hard to control," said a German who seemed unhappier than the others. "Why are all those bones there, Kurt? Where are all the inhabitants?"

"We've discovered exactly what the *Reichsführer* sent us here for," Raeder said, ignoring his question. "What matters is Germany."

Hood looked to the shadows beyond the twisted door. There was a great, ghastly pile of human bones, the dead of this civilization in a macabre tableau. What the devil had gone on here? Why was this place so secret, so remote, so buried?

"Touching the staff may be like touching a hot wire," another of the Germans cautioned.

"Or like holding the butt of a gun," said Raeder. "Most savages would be afraid to pick up a firearm. But not all." He hesitated just a moment, looking at the others. Then he strode decisively under the brow of the machine, stooped, and reached for the cradled staff.

"Kurt, no!"

"Stop sounding like an old woman, Julius."

Yet as he reached, the humming died with a sigh, and all the lights from the staffs they held dimmed. He paused.

"Somehow you've turned it off," one of the Germans called. "Like blowing a fuse."

"Or cooling a candle so you can touch it. This wand wants to be held." So Raeder hesitated just a moment more and then seized the staff and lifted it clear. It shone like amber, a beautiful six-foot-long staff of honeyed crystal, pulsing like life itself.

Unlike the other staffs, this new one didn't cast light but instead purred with it, honey and amber flowing up and down its length. "I can feel its energy," Raeder reported. "From my hands to my toes."

"Energy for what?" one of the Germans asked.

"It's an elixir." Tentatively, Raeder moved the staff through the air. It gave a hum. When he swept it in an arc it hummed louder, an odd chord that echoed in the vast room. "It makes music!" He laughed.

"Unearthly music," one said.

"The music of the spheres, perhaps," Raeder told them. "The music of the cosmos. It isn't wicked. It's beautiful!"

"We've come ten thousand miles to a hole in hell for a toy?" the grumpiest German said. "This is what Franz died for, Kurt? This is what you blew up our only route of retreat for? A music stick? We're going to starve in this cellar while you wave your baton around?"

Raeder looked annoyed. "We make a greater discovery than King Tut and you call it a toy. A machine bigger than a battleship and you think we've come for nothing. You're a coward, Julius."

The German flushed. "But what does it *do*, Kurt?" The man named Julius pointed toward the bones and

Hood shrank into the shadows. "Why is Shambhala a catacomb?"

"Every city has bones. Look at Rome."

"Why is no one left to attend the machine?"

"We're attending it. Maybe the builders got what they wanted—Vril—and left, locking it for the return of the descendants of Barbarossa. Preserving it for *us*."

"You're risking our lives without careful consideration. Let's be cautious here. Experiment. Test. Use the scientific method."

"I'm seizing what I need because the Buddhist bitch here fetched her American boyfriend. This is not an archaeological dig, it's a treasure hunt, and we may be in a race with the Americans. And I'm tired of your criticism, Muller." He pointed the staff at his companion.

"I'm tired of your reckless leadership."

And then there was a flash, bright as lightning, a terrifying crack, and with a cry the complaining German went flying across the machine room and crashed into the far wall, sliding down.

He was grotesquely burnt, clothes smoking.

Everyone froze in shock. The man named Julius had been killed. His flesh had blackened and peeled. The corpse sat on the floor, mouth frozen in a gasp of pain, and then huge parts of him sloughed off bone. He'd not just been blasted, he'd half disintegrated.

"Great God!" one of the other Germans cried. "You murdered Muller!"

Raeder was white with shock. "I did nothing . . ." His protest hung in the air.

Keyuri stepped back from him.

" . . . except think it," he finished in wonder. He stared at the staff in his hand. "But I didn't mean for it to happen. It reached out for him at its own accord."

"Like your wife, eh, Kurt?" one of the other Germans said shakily.

Raeder rounded on him. "Don't you dare mention Lotte."

The man swung a submachine gun around. "You're going to fry me, too?"

"No. No! Dammit, I don't know what happened!"

"It's wicked, I told you," said Keyuri. "A sword or gun from ancient Shambhala. Its power comes from the deepest pits of the earth, the core of the universe, and you've no idea how to control it."

Raeder let the staff fall to the floor where it clattered. "It fired on its own." He stepped away. "I never meant to harm Muller. I needed him, dammit. It's his fault, his criticism, his whining . . ." He glared at the others. "None of you can tell Himmler. I won't have my career ruined."

"It won't be if it's really a weapon, Kurt," one of the other Germans said. "You're still a hero, if this is what Himmler wanted us to find." He looked at the disintegrating corpse. "It's too bad about Muller, but I'm sorrier about Franz. If only we had his camera to document this! My God, a handheld lightning bolt? A ray gun? Imagine an army of these! No nation could stand before us."

Hood had been calculating the odds. One German had let his submachine gun drop, dangling from his shoulder, and another had rested a hunting rifle on the floor. Raeder had shed his own rifle. All had pistols on their hips. But would he ever have a better chance than this, when the Nazis were in turmoil over their own fiasco?

He stepped out from the shelter of the wrecked door, pistol leveled, and closed the distance as quickly and quietly as he could.

Then Raeder fastened on Keyuri. "This is *your* fault. You knew this was going to happen." He was tired of moralizers. Everyone was always questioning, whereas his need was to *act.*

"I did not point the staff."

He pulled his pistol. "You should have been a better lover."

"Because I don't enjoy your assaults? You're going to murder me, too?"

He blinked. "I don't need you anymore."

Hood was within twenty feet. "Freeze!" He aimed at Raeder. The Germans whirled.

The muzzle of Hood's .45 was pointed at his enemy's head.

Raeder looked at him in bewilderment. "But I blew up the path."

"I dropped in anyway. Keyuri, take the staff!"

She hesitated.

"Hurry, pick it up! And if they go for their guns, use that witchcraft on them!"

"I don't know how."

"Neither did Kurt, but a man that dared talk back to him is dead. How did it feel, Kurt, to have the finger of God?"

"He's alone," the German said to his companions. "He can't escape us. We outnumber him. When I give the word, use your weapons."

"Keyuri, now!"

"Hans!" Raeder shouted. The archaeologist jumped and Hood instinctively swung his gun toward him. And as Keyuri bent for the amber staff, Raeder grabbed for her and it.

Shots blazed.

All their light abruptly vanished.

31

Eldorado Mine, Cascade Mountains
September 6, Present Day

I t just gets weirder than weird," Jake said, studying the sad heap of bones. "What in the devil was Special Agent Duncan Hale doing in an old gold mine in the Cascade Mountains, with city shoes and a business suit? It had to have something to do with Benjamin Hood."

"My great-grandfather took him here," Rominy guessed.

"Or forced him here."

"If he worked for the government, he should have been on Grandpa's side, shouldn't he?"

"Let's review what we know." Jake was squatting, thumbing through the papers in the satchel, now the businesslike investigative reporter. "Grandpa is recruited to go to Tibet. He comes back, but instead of returning to New York he becomes a hermit up here. Somewhere there's a child, who will turn out to be your grandmother. And Hale comes calling. To lure him out of retirement? To find out what he knows? What if Hale was stealing this satchel?"

"What if Great-Grandpa Ben lured him here? Or was hiding here, or the satchel was here, so Agent Hale comes up the mountain . . ."

"Or was killed at the cabin and brought up here. Carried like a sack of potatoes."

"I don't think my ancestor would do that. Can you imagine carrying a corpse up that mountain? And wouldn't the OSS have come looking for him?"

"And found Benjamin Hood. And . . . killed him." Jake stood up.

"That's pretty melodramatic."

"Well, all we know is that everybody died. Except your grandmother. Except maybe she was murdered, too, eventually."

Rominy shivered. "So who was her mother? Who did Hood marry?"

"You don't have to be married to have a child, Rominy." He stopped shuffling the papers and pulled out a photograph. It was a faded shot of a woman standing next to an old biplane, in flying helmet and pants. "Take her, for example."

Rominy craned to look. "She's pretty. You think she's my great-grandmother?"

"It's possible."

"Who is she?"

He turned it over. "It says, *Beth Calloway, 1938.* Maybe there's more in here about her."

"This is so strange, finding people who've been dead so long and having some obscure connection to them."

"Not obscure. A blood connection. Blood is thicker than water. Descent is important. Ancestry is important."

"Don't talk about blood down here. It's creepy."

"Historically, it used to mean everything. You were who your parents were. Children inherited the sins of their fathers. Now genealogy is just a hobby, nations are mongrelized, race is politically incorrect. But blood is who we really are."

"No. Too confining."

"I'm talking about family, Rominy. DNA. Self-identity. Belonging. As an orphan, you should understand that better than anyone."

"Belonging? To a race? Yes, Jake, politically incorrect."

"You want to know how to become a messiah? Tell your followers they're chosen. Jews, born-again Christians, Muslim fundamentalists, it doesn't matter. Tell them they're *chosen* and they'll follow you anywhere. You think Hitler didn't understand that? People long to be told they're special. Blood, my dear, makes the world go round." He turned the flashlight so it lit his face from below, drawing deep shadows like a Halloween mask. "The trick," he said in a deep voice, "is deciding who's *really* chosen."

She looked at him in confusion. Now he was frightening her. "Who *are* you, Jake?"

He turned the light away, becoming a silhouette in the dark. "I'm a reporter, remember? I just try to see the world clearly, without all the self-censorship crap that goes on these days. We don't burn witches, we fire the blunt from media jobs. Well, I speak to truth. Isn't that what journalism is all about?"

"Why did you take the battery out of my cell phone?"

"What?" He cocked his head.

"I found it in the trash this morning. That's why my cell wouldn't work, wasn't it? You'd taken the battery out."

"I took the battery out *because* it wouldn't work. I was trying to fix it. When it was obvious it was really dead, I tossed it. What, you think I sabotaged your phone?"

"Yes! Somehow. Way back at Safeway. I wanted to call and I couldn't."

"Because your battery was already dead! How could I get your battery out? Do I look like Houdini? Come on, don't be paranoid. We're trying to help each other here. Figure this out together."

She sighed. He was right, the battery *was* dead. "I'm so confused."

"Jesus, I'm not. Did last night mean nothing?"

"Jake . . ." she groaned.

"I'm falling for you, Rominy. You've got to trust me on this. We're onto something big, really big. It's going to make all the difference. Come on, let's walk back to the shaft we fell down where it's light, and look at what's in the satchel."

She was consumed with doubt. She was falling for *him*, too, at the same time every instinct told her this was way too sketchy. Hadn't she been wary the first time she spied him? But now he looked a little wounded, boyish, and she still buzzed inside from the night and the morning. Which instinct was true?

"How did you get that scar?"

"What scar?"

"On your chin. Like you've been in a fight."

He looked at her as if she were a lunatic. "I flipped my bike when I was ten."

Now she felt foolish. She flushed. If he was some kind of rogue, why was he trapped down here with her?

Deep breaths. One step at a time. Get out of here, and *then* think. Everything was happening too fast. She needed a day—heck, a *month*—to decompress. To figure out if anything with this guy was real. She was falling in love with a man she didn't entirely trust, which wasn't smart, cubicle girl. Get gone, get focused, get clear.

Meanwhile, the satchel was a treasure trove. Maps, diagrams, diaries, photos—the raw remains of a strange, truncated life. There was a crude drawing of mountains with a bowl-like valley, with coordinates. A diagram drawn in a circle, with arrows and boxes. And a journal with the title page reading, *For the heir, only.* Jake solemnly handed it to her. "I think he means you."

She thumbed through it, unable to resist excitement. *This* was real. The handwriting was surprisingly neat, almost feminine. Well, they did teach penmanship in those days. The diary appeared to be about some kind of journey, fleeing from some terrible thing. But also notes to return there, *When the time is right.* And underneath it, *Wisdom before invention.*

Maybe this would explain the whole story.

Her old life seemed so trivial.

Jake was peering at the map. "My God, I think he's telling exactly where we need to go."

"Go? I thought we were already here, in a hole in the ground."

"No, in Tibet, to find what he found."

"Tibet! That's the other side of the world."

"Don't you see? His death, your relatives' deaths, the skinheads—it all must come back to this. There's something wonderful there, something *huge*, and it's been waiting for *you*—the heir to get into this safety deposit box, the heir to find this mine—to go find it again. We're supposed to go to Tibet and retrace his journey." His eyes were alight. He'd found his treasure map.

"Jake, we can't even get out of this mine. We're going to crumble into bones like poor old Duncan Hale, and some other descendant is going to find this satchel and our stash from Summit Bank."

He laughed. "We haven't had time to make a descendant yet."

"Actually, we have, except I'm on the pill."

"There you go. But look, if we're going to Tibet we'd better focus on getting out." He stood, peering up at the shaft. She didn't understand his confidence. He didn't seem like a newspaper nerd, he seemed like a commando.

"I'm not going to Tibet, Jake. I'm going to where there's a shower."

"They have showers in Tibet. Listen. I'm going to boost you up and you're going to grab that ledge and that root. If you can pull yourself up into the chimney you can wedge, back against one side and feet on the other, and inchworm your way up."

"*Then* what?"

"Go get help. There's rope in my truck. You'll be back for me by tomorrow morning. Unless you were *really* dissatisfied with my performance."

"I don't want to go down the mountain alone!"

"Well, maybe you can throw down a log I can climb out on. First step is to get you up there."

She sighed. What choice did they have?

He was strong, surprisingly so, and he hoisted her up on his shoulders. "Can you reach?"

"Just barely . . ."

"Try to pull yourself up. I'll push your feet."

It was like her worst memory of gym class. "Jake, I don't have any upper-body strength . . ."

"Try, Rominy. We've got to get out of here."

She reached, straining, and he took the soles of her shoes in his hands so she wobbled as she tried to pull herself up into the shaft. It felt like a cheerleader stunt. She got so her waist was even with the bottom of the hole, grabbed a root, and pulled. Her legs thrashed now that she was above his reach, arms shaking. She was hanging helplessly, looking for something higher to grab. Nothing! Then it was as if a pin burst her effort. All strength left her and she fell back into his arms. He sat down hard, with a woof.

"I can't. Jake, I'm sorry, but I just can't lift myself." Her voice shook.

"We've got to try."

"I *did* try."

"Can you lift me?"

But that was even more useless. She tried to boost him but he was nearly two hundred pounds of hard muscle, and it was like trying to hoist a piano. They collapsed together, Rominy crying.

They were going to die in this hole.

They lay awhile, panting.

And then there was the baying of some hounds. He sat up. "Listen!"

The baying came closer. There was the sound of thrashing brush, and then frantic barking. There were dogs at the lip of the shaft.

Rominy sat up, too, drying her cheeks as hope filled her. Rescue?

"Thunder! Damnation! What the hell did you find?" It was Delphina Clarkson, her new neighbor!

"Mrs. Clarkson, we're down here!" Jake called.

"That you? What'd you do with that girl?"

"She's down here, too. Can you call Search and Rescue?"

"I don't need no Search and Rescue. Hell, I'd be raccoon meat if I waited for the likes of them. I know this hill like my own La-Z-Boy." She peered over the lip. "Missy! He treating you right?"

"Yes, Mrs. Clarkson, we fell in accidentally. We need help getting out!"

"Yeah, let me tie a rope to this tree. City folk!"

A line slithered down. Jake boosted her once again and this time, with something firmer to hold on to and the promise of salvation above, she managed to climb. Once she got her feet and legs working in the shaft, it was much easier. Jake was right behind her, hauling himself and boosting her when she needed it, while also carrying both their packs and the satchel.

They crawled out of the hole, dogs sniffing and yipping, and collapsed, the sky a miracle.

"What the devil is down there?" Mrs. Clarkson asked.

"Old gold mine, I think," Jake said. "We found this depression and wondered what it was and then boom, cave-in. We're really lucky you came along."

"I'll say. What are you doing over here? You're way off the trail. You know there's a cliff right there?" She looked at them suspiciously.

"Yes, ma'am."

The dogs tried to lick Rominy, and she pushed them away.

"I tracked you with my hounds," Delphina said. "Started with your truck at the trailhead and followed you on up."

"Thank goodness, but why did you do that?" Rominy asked.

"Because you're all over the news, Missy. There was a bomb down in Seattle, and nobody knows where the heck you went or who you're with, be it city slicker here or the Taliban. You got half the cops in the state looking for you. You know that?"

"I had no idea. Everything has been happening so fast . . ." She realized Jake had never played the truck radio. She couldn't even remember if it had one.

"Yep, you're lucky I had the sense to hunt you. Me'n my dogs, here."

"We'll pay you for your trouble," Jake assured.

"Oh, no need for *that*." She picked up her shotgun and swung it on them. "There's a fifty-thousand-dollar reward out for the two of *you*." She nodded. "They think you might be terrorists, or worse. Neighbors, you are under *arrest*."

32

Shambhala, Tibet
October 3, 1938

ood dared not fire, lest he hit the woman. The
Germans were under no such compunction, and
muzzle flashes blazed in the blackness. Luckily the
American had thrown himself flat, and bullets ricocheted with an awful whine while Raeder shouted at
them to stop.

"Listen! Listen for his footsteps!"

Sound echoed away. Hood inched across the floor.

"I think we hit him, Kurt."

"You almost hit me, you idiot."

"Do you have the girl?"

"No, she bit me!"

"*Scheisse!*"

"Where's the staff?"

"I don't know."

"I can't see a thing. I didn't know it could be so dark."

"We're dead men. Muller was right."

"Shut up, shut up! Listen!"

Something rolled across the floor. Hood snaked on his belly toward it and reached. The staff. As his hand closed upon the smooth crystal, it was as if his finger was inserted in a light socket. A jolt shuddered through his arm and he winced.

The staff glowed, illuminating their tableau.

Keyuri was on her belly, a dozen feet away.

The Germans turned.

Raeder, his rifle on the floor, sprang with a knife, his boot coming down on Hood's wrist that held the .45. The SS dagger swept down, to pinion his other hand, which held his staff.

Hood twisted as the knife struck, feeling a sharp pain in his ring finger and meanwhile losing hold of his gun. Then Raeder's boot slipped off his wrist and stamped on the staff.

There was a bang, like a short circuit. Some mysterious but stupendous energy kicked the German backward and he fell and skidded, with a grunt.

The American picked up the strange weapon in a bloody grip, wincing, and swept it toward the Nazis, not knowing what to expect.

Something bright, hot, and terrifying stabbed out. It also stabbed in, to Hood's injured hand, and he shouted.

There was a boom like thunder and lightning that was blinding. The Germans shrieked, hands to their eyes and ears, frozen in the flash. It was like looking into the sun. Then there was a crack on the ceiling and stone rained down, slamming against the floor and bouncing. The staff and Hood went skidding away across the floor, shot like a puck, his teeth clenched in agony. Finally it was dark again, except his eyes were filled with sparks from the dazzle. He could dimly hear the Germans shouting, and he wondered if any had been hit by the debris. What had happened? It was as if the staff had a life of its own, or as if his thoughts had merged with its properties to eject some kind of thunderbolt. If this is what Shambhala held, he wanted no part of it.

Yet he didn't let go. As his night vision returned, he realized the thunder stick still glowed dimly.

Light footsteps, and someone seized his arm. "Hurry!" It was a hiss. Keyuri. "I have your pistol."

"Then shoot them."

"I tried. It's jammed."

Hood staggered up. The third finger on his left hand was hanging by a tendon, blood gushing. The hand, seemingly electrocuted as well as sliced, felt on fire.

Meanwhile his gun hand had been stomped on. The room echoed with German curses. Keyuri clutched his arm and forced the tip of the staff to the ground to mute its illumination, like an aisle light in a dim theater. Numbly, he followed her pull. He thought at first that she'd lead him past the bones and onto the main causeway they'd descended. But the Germans were between them and the door. Instead she was pulling him toward one of the tunnels that led away from the side of the machine.

There was the crack of a revolver and a bullet whined off machinery. They ducked around a massive metal arm, making themselves invisible, just as the submachine gun went off with a stutter. More bullets pinged and buzzed.

"Stop! They're ricocheting toward us!"

"But they're getting away!" The Germans began arguing some more.

"Where are we going?" Hood whispered to Keyuri.

"Where we close one door and open another, if you can use that magic staff again." They entered the tunnel, a stumbling trot taking them along horizontal pipes. He looked back. There was a faint whitish glow; the German light sticks must have reignited. Hood's body ached, and he mentally cursed Raeder. That madman made a mess of everything.

"They've gone the wrong way!" he heard the German cry. "We've got them trapped."

"Leave them," another said. "Muller was right. This place is evil."

"No, I want her and I want the staff. She knows more than she's telling!"

Keyuri caught Hood's arm and they stopped a moment, looking back. "Seal us in."

He looked at her questioningly.

"There's supposed to be a second door, a back door, somewhere deep inside this underground city. Use the staff, seal us in, and we'll look for it."

"This is legend?"

"This is our only chance."

He lifted the staff again, feeling energy surge through it and him, his arm shaking. It glowed bright, and he heard the Germans shout and begin to run toward them. Blood dripped from his grip to the floor. Gritting his teeth, he aimed toward the ceiling of the tunnel entrance. Another crack and boom, the recoil excruciating, but then with a rumble a section of rock roof gave way and crashed onto the pipes at the tunnel mouth, a cave-in that blocked that entrance. Dust blew back at them, grit swirling.

Hood's head ached and his ears rang. They were in a tunnel about ten feet high that stretched as far as he could see, large pipes running through it at breast height.

"Bravo," he said. "Sealed us in. Trapped like moths in a jar."

"And them out, for a while."

The staff's illumination was dimmer than before. Was it weakened like a battery? Keyuri pulled at him again and they went on, deeper into Shambhala.

"Where's this second door?" he asked.

"I don't know."

"I think this fire stick is losing its power. Will its light go out?"

"I don't know."

"Should we run?"

Now she pulled to stop him. "No." She wiped her mouth free of a smear of blood. "He hit me," she said when his look was questioning. "What happened to your hand?"

He clenched his half-severed finger. "Raeder cut me. And the recoil from this devil weapon didn't help, either. Hurts like hell." He felt dizzy from the craziness of the last hour. "How did the Shambhalans use these things?"

"Open your hand."

Wincing, he did so. She placed it on one of the huge pipes so the damage to his digit was more apparent. It was throbbing and covered with blood.

"Now, kiss me."

"What?" She was looking at him with her great dark eyes, her features fine as polished porphyry, her lips insistent, her hair still short but growing out since leaving Lhasa. She seized his head with one hand, bent him to her, and kissed him fiercely, not like a nun but a lover.

Then the pain from his hand seemed to explode, and he roared. She'd chopped with another knife and completely severed his finger!

"God Almighty! What did you do, Keyuri?"

"I'm sorry, but we've got to bind it. Give me your scarf."

She took the white silk Reting had given him in Lhasa and ripped off a portion, using it to wrap and gap where his finger had been and cinching down on the dressing.

"Couldn't you warn me?" His eyes were watering, it hurt so bad.

"That would have made it worse." She inspected her dressing. "We've got to get the bleeding to stop or you might faint."

He sat down hard against the pipes. "That might happen anyway. I've had quite a day." He couldn't quite believe where he was. Probably the greatest discovery in his museum's history, and he'd just deliberately caused a cave-in. Roy Chapman Andrews would have shot his way out by now.

She knelt beside him. "Me, too." She picked up the severed finger. "I may use this for a blood lock."

"A what?"

"The locks of this place, like to the door of that main tunnel, can be opened only by the right person's blood. Raeder said he had the necessary blood from a long-dead German hero."

"That makes no sense."

"He thinks the Germans and Shambhalans are cousins. Aryans."

Hood laid his head back. "And to think he and I were partners, once. Scientific colleagues. I sure know how to pick 'em."

"He's still embarrassed you fired him. Ashamed of what he is, but unable to change." Keyuri looked at him, her own cheeks wet now with tears. "I'm sorry I had to do that to your hand. I'm sorry destiny made you come back here." She leaned and kissed him again. "I'm sorry you picked me, not just Kurt. But we were meant to be together again, Benjamin."

Despite the pain he kissed back, the communion an instinctual antidote to everything that was going on. Her lips were full, ripe, soft, everything that was opposite the machine nightmare that was Shambhala. Pressing against her seemed to lessen the pain, and then she was pressing against *him*, and he groaned with sudden lust and longing.

He broke from their kiss, panting. "Keyuri, I'm sorry, I can't help myself, I know you've taken vows . . ."

"You must have me now." Her voice was commanding, insistent. "I think we may die in here, and I want you to make love first."

"For God's sake, we're in a cave running from a lunatic."

"The tunnel is sealed. Now, Ben, it's important! I want to erase the memory of Raeder. Now, now, please!" She was crying. "Please, to undo what he did to me."

She was clawing at his clothes, unbuttoning his pants, and to his own surprise he was responding. What was wrong with him? She was a Buddhist nun! This was as crazy as the Nazis, but of course he didn't care. She pulled him down on top of her, her robes pulled up, knees high, hips lifted, and in seconds they'd fused. She clung and rocked urgently. "Please, we may never have time again."

She was impatient. A few thrusts, she bucked, he finished.

"I'm sorry, you took me by surprise . . ."

She put her finger to his lips. Rather than be displeased with his speed she seemed fiercely satisfied, pulling him as deep as she could, hips quivering as she gently rocked. "It's good."

At least he'd forgotten about his hand.

Keyuri let out a loud, shuddering breath, squeezing her eyes shut. Then she reached up to pull him close again and kissed, fiercely, and then just as abruptly pushed him off her. "We must go, but this was my only chance for salvation."

"That's some salvation." He looked at her in wonder. "What about your vows?"

"He already raped me again."

"Raeder? Did the other krauts know?"

"Yes and no. I don't know. What does it matter?" There was sorrow there, a profound sense of loss and doom. "I just didn't want him to be my last. Now, tend to your clothes. We have to hurry to find the second door."

"I thought you said you sealed the Germans off? Seems to me we have eternity." He looked down the tunnel into the dark.

"To Westerners, everything is a line. To us, all is circular. Look down the tunnel. How far can you see?"

"It's dim . . ."

"The pipe doesn't extend forever, it disappears, like a ship going over the horizon. This tunnel gently curves."

"What does that mean?"

"The tunnel is a circle. If you walk far enough from this end of the machine you will come to the other, like walking around the world. The beginning is the end, and the end the beginning. These pipes stretch to infinity, they never end. And yet they go nowhere at all."

"Is that some kind of Tibetan riddle?"

"Whatever is in these pipes, it's meant to come back to where it started," she said. "That's not a riddle, it's a mandala, a map of the universe."

He stood. "But if this tunnel leads back to the machine . . ."

"Yes. They can come at us from the other end. We have to hope it will take them a while to figure that out."

"Maybe they've given up. And we've got this crazy staff."

"Raeder would give you up. Even give *me* up. But not the staff."

Hood took a breath, furious at Raeder for Keyuri all over again, but also oddly renewed. She hadn't depleted him, she'd tapped new strength. She'd recharged him, like the machine apparently had done to the magic wand here. By blazes, was she in love with him still? Was he in love with *her*, as Reting and Beth believed? What happened to the three of them if they got out of this nightmare?

But Keyuri, he sensed, didn't expect to.

"Okay," he said. "Listen for Nazis coming the other way. The light from this staff keeps getting weaker, and I've got a feeling there's not much pop left. I think it's low on ammo. Give me back my pistol."

"You can't carry it in your injured hand and I told you, it doesn't work."

He grimaced. "We need to find that second door. Then we can destroy the tunnel in the other direction and escape."

The rock tunnel they were fleeing down had no decoration on its sides, and no doors. It just ran on and on, mile after mile, a tube in solid rock. The pipes were mute beside it. They ran, then jogged, then trotted, wheezing from exertion. Mile followed mile. Hood left bright drops of blood on the floor like a spoor trail.

"How long is this tunnel?"

"Not long enough," said Keyuri.

And then there was a burst of machine-gun fire.

Bullets whined and pinged as they bounced down the curving tunnel. It was a German coming from the other side. They were trapped.

Hood clenched the staff. "Better to go down fighting," he said. "I can try to blast with this, or maybe hide in the dark behind the big pipe and clobber them. You've got your knife . . . Keyuri?"

He turned. She'd fallen down.

"Keyuri!"

Blood was pooling out beneath her onto the smooth rock floor.

One of the Germans, not Raeder, shouted. "Give it up, Hood! I have a machine gun! Surrender the staff and I let you live!"

The Nazi wasn't coming close, however. He'd seen the explosion at the other end of the tunnel and was keeping a wary distance.

Hood knelt near the nun and gently turned her over. The front of her coat was sticky with blood and she was wheezing. It looked like she'd been hit in the lower lung. Not instantly fatal, but not good.

"Keyuri, I'm going to drag you between the pipes and the far wall. At least it will protect you from a stray bullet."

She moaned. "Maybe he'll go past us," she whispered.

"No, he'll see the light of the staff. How do we turn it off?"

"I don't know."

The beam of a flashlight stabbed toward them. The German kept a cautious fifty yards away, too far for accurate submachine-gun fire but also far enough to be out of easy range of their thunder stick.

"Hood, I know you're there! Come out with your hands up if you want to live!" he called in English. "Come out, and we spare the nun!"

He and Keyuri stayed silent, hiding behind a pipe.

"You can't escape, you blocked your own retreat. Come out, American, and we negotiate, eh? Do you want the girl hurt?"

Hood squeezed the shaft with his left hand, feeling the familiar jolt of power. His only hope was that he got a shot at the German before the German saw him.

Then the Nazi flashlight went out.

The staff glowed brighter. Amber illumination peeked from under the piping.

"Ah, there you are. You ran with the wrong man, Keyuri. He led you into a trap."

Why not at least save her? She wasn't dead yet. "I'm going to surrender in return for your life," he whispered. "Raeder still wants you in his own twisted way. He may still spare you."

She shook her head. "If he does, it will be to destroy me slowly. He needs to destroy people, Ben. You know that."

They heard footsteps, a heavy tread, coming toward them. Slowly, cautiously, inexorably. "Don't make me kill you!" the German called.

"Let him come closer," she whispered. "Then erase him."

Feisty for a Buddhist nun. Hood rose and braced, dreading to have to fire the painful thunder stick again. Would it bring everything down on top of them? Then the flashlight came on, blinding. Its cone of illumination fell directly on him, and then played over the pool of Keyuri's blood.

"I see you! Stand, stand!" The stubby snout of the machine gun gleamed, dark and oily in the gloom. The German was nervous but excited. "Come out, come out, it's your only chance! Come out or I machine-gun the girl!"

Slowly Hood put down the staff.

"No!" Keyuri groaned.

He didn't care. The German was too far away. A thunderbolt could bring the whole tunnel down on them. He had to save her.

"Raise your hands! Climb over the pipes!"

He began to do so.

The German raised the submachine gun. "Now. We finish this and get out of here." He nodded and aimed.

And then there was the crack of a pistol. Several shots rang out and the German jerked, a hole appearing in the middle of his forehead, and he slowly toppled backward. A tendril of blood ran down his face. His torso was punctured, too. His submachine gun fell with a clatter. He sat down with a woof, looking at where a new light blazed from the ceiling. His mouth opened, as if seeing an apparition.

And now a new voice came down, as if from heaven. "This way, college boy. And bring baldy there with you."

33

Eldorado Peak, Cascade Mountains
September 6, Present Day

Y ou can't arrest us, Mrs. Clarkson," Jake said patiently, eyeing the muzzles of Delphina's double-barreled shotgun. "You're not a police officer. And we're not terrorists."

"Which is just what Osama bin-Lunatic would say, I figure. This is a *citizen's* arrest of two highly suspicious young people who seem to be mixed up with bombs and banks and who knows what all, and by the Grace of the Lord, my dogs could smell the evil on you when you came up that driveway! Now march, before my finger gets tired and sits down on this trigger."

"But they bombed *me*," Rominy exclaimed. "We're the *victims*. We're escaping from the terrorists, if that's what they are. You have to help us, Mrs. Clarkson."

"I'm helping you into a holding cell where you can sing your story to great big guys with buzz cuts and badges. Move, woman!"

Rominy was in shock. First the cave-in, and now this? She'd never touched a gun except for her great-grandfather's old pistol, and now one was being pointed at her. The twin muzzles looked as big as manholes. Jake handed back her pack but kept the satchel and the backpack with the money on his own shoulders. Then he winked, as if this were all part of some game, part of his mysterious, irritating, admirable, enviable self-confidence. Was that supposed to reassure her? He could dig through bones and wink at a loaded gun? Who *was* this guy? Rominy led the way, the dogs flanking her, with Jake behind and Delphina Clarkson's shotgun behind him.

"I'll bet you Seattle people figured I wouldn't have TV way up here on the Cascade River, didn't ya?" their captor said as they retraced their route to the trail. "You think I never go into Marblemount for a buffalo burger and a beer? Oh yes, the Safeway bombing is *all* over the news, and Miss Rominy Pickett's picture is getting more airtime than a politician with his pants down."

"So I'm missing, right? *That's* what the reward is for."

"And you know what? Not one newscaster has said anything about some heir of Benjamin Hood. Not one newscaster talked about pretty-boy newspaper reporters, or musty old mysteries. You know what? I don't think that's your cabin at *all*."

"So at least I won't be scooped," Jake murmured.

"What's that?"

"I said I'm glad you're a vigorous news consumer, Mrs. Clarkson."

"Shut up with your fancy talk."

They hit the trail again and started down it. No amount of reasoning seemed capable of getting the crazy old woman to lower her gun. The only good news was that she seemed to have no curiosity about what they'd found down in the mine or what might be in the decaying old satchel. She couldn't think past the possibility of a payday. Rominy tried to calm down. Once they were in the hands of the police, they'd be safe, wouldn't they?

Just get dotty Delphina to swing the muzzle away or take her finger off the trigger. How could she connect with her?

"Mrs. Clarkson, I'm impressed your dogs could track us."

"My dogs could sniff out a Brussels sprout in a meat-packing plant."

And then there was a hiss of something slicing through the air, a lethal whisper, and a soft thud as it hit. Damnation, one of Clarkson's dogs, gave a sudden jerk, squealed, and flipped over. The shaft of an arrow jutted from his flank. Where it met flesh, the dog's chest rose and fell, pumping blood.

Rominy whirled. There was a man in the forest who was dressed in camouflage and drawing back a bow. His head was shaved with a strip on top, like a Mohawk Indian.

It was the same guy she'd thought she'd seen in the cabin window. Another arrow loosed, and then both shotgun barrels went off with a roar next to her ear.

"Run!" Jake raced past and jerked Rominy like a rag doll, leaping off the switchbacking trail and straight down the forested mountainside, crashing into brush. With his hand on her arm they half ran, half plunged down the precipitous slope. There was a frantic yelping and cries of outrage behind. Rominy tensed for the sting of another shotgun blast but none came. The gun had swung at the skinhead, and then they were far enough downhill that the woods gave them screening.

"That crazy bitch is too old to follow us this way! Run, run, run!"

She leaped like a gazelle, heedless of obstacles, bounding over logs she'd hardly dare crawl over in normal times. A single misstep and she'd break a leg and yet their flight seemed charmed, magical, even exhilarating as they fell through the forest. They came to the trail again, which zigzagged the other way, but simply leaped it and continued straight downhill in a barely controlled plunge.

There was another gun blast, but far up the mountain. Faint shouts, too.

Step, leap, step, leap, as trees flashed past. She was not so much out of breath as breathless, stunned, afraid, excited.

They hit the switchbacking trail again and Jake pulled up, gasping. He was grinning, too, the bastard. "Geez, Rominy, what was *that*?"

"It was that man."

"What man?"

"The man I saw in the window."

That sobered him. "It's them. Skinheads. Come on."

"I thought you said he was a raccoon."

"I thought wrong."

They ran again, but down the trail now, Jake sometimes drawing ahead but then slowing so she could catch up. Her legs were jelly, her feet ached, but she dared not rest. What if shotgun lady was chasing them? What if Mohawk man was doing the same? For the thousandth time, *what* was going on?

"Jake, why do skinheads care about my great-grandfather?"

"Nazis. They were in a race with Hood for something important, and these neo-Nazis know more than I thought. They tracked us here, which means they know about the cabin."

Her eyes darted as they ran. Every tree seemed to hide an archer or street tough with a swastika tattoo. The towering fir and hemlock blocked out the sun, casting their escape in shadow. The world had become nothing but menace.

"Let's cut through here," he said. "I don't want to run into a bad guy waiting at the trailhead." They left the path again, skidding down through sword fern and salal toward a growing light: the road. There was a final embankment she almost pitched over but instead slid on her butt, hitting the road shoulder in a shower of dirt and gravel. Her bare legs were a mottle of scratches and dirt. Jake was already crouched, peering up and down the lane.

"There." He pointed.

It was a dusty black SUV, windows tinted, pulled off on the shoulder. Jake's truck was out of sight, in the small trailhead parking lot.

"You think that's their car?"

"I saw it before at Safeway." He started toward the Explorer.

"What if somebody's in it?"

"If they were, they'd already be out the door and in our face by now."

He trotted up, chest heaving, and peered through the windows. Then he jiggled the handle. "Locked."

"What are you *doing*? Let's get out of here!"

"That *is* what I'm doing." He began feeling the driver's-side wheel well, and beneath the door. "Bingo." He pulled out a magnetic case. "Hikers don't like carrying keys."

"You're going to steal the Nazi's *car*?"

"*We're* going to steal it, because I've got the key for my own truck and I don't want Mr. Bow Hunter following us any longer. This ends, now. He can walk out to Marblemount. If Delphina Clarkson hasn't finished him."

"We go to the police?"

He unlocked the doors, jerked open the door, and climbed in, waiting for her to join him on the passenger seat. The rig still smelled new and had every bell-and-whistle accessory that Detroit could invent. Apparently, skinhead Nazis had money. Or they'd stolen the car themselves. The engine started with a roar.

"No way." He shook his head. "We go to Tibet."

BLOOD OF THE REICH

34

Shambhala, Tibet
October 3, 1938

Beth Calloway had shot the German while hanging upside down from an airshaft that rose from
the ceiling of the tunnel. A stone door had slid aside to
reveal the chimney. Now she turned, tucked her smoking pistol into her belt, and dropped lightly down onto
the big pipe running to infinity. She glanced in both
directions.

"Any more of them?"

"Not yet," Hood said.

"What's down here, anyway?"

"Deviltry." He held up the amber staff with his
mutilated hand. Blood dripped from the bandage.

"No good on your lonesome, are you? What
happened?"

"We were fighting over some kind of goddamn magic wand. SS cutlery is pretty sharp. Actually, Keyuri here finished the amputation."

"She chopped off your finger?"

"With a kiss." He grimaced.

"No wonder you're smitten. She's not dead, is she?"

"Not yet. Wounded, though."

"You're going to have to boost her up. There're more nuns above."

"Nuns?"

"There's a nunnery outside the valley with tunnels into this anthill. The abbess gave me blood to unlock the booby hatch I just dropped from. She said they use blood like a key. Can you believe that?"

"Unfortunately, yes. My surgeon has already saved my finger for that quaint custom." He bent under the pipe. "Keyuri, help has come. We're going to patch you up, all right?"

The young woman groaned.

Beth stooped to examine her. "Wow, that's bad. Okay, I'm going to use my flying scarf to bandage her up. Then we're going to boost her on top of the pipe, I'll get in the shaft that goes upstairs, and you lift her to me."

"You're saving her life, Beth. You probably saved mine."

"Damn right, Professor. So let's move, or do you want to spoil my track record?"

He looked up the hole she'd dropped from. There were torches flickering far above, and a halo of shaven figures peering down a well at him, clad in scarlet. The women's eyes were wide and fearful.

As gently as they could, they lifted Keyuri atop the pipe and climbed up themselves. Then Beth leaped for a handhold in the shaft, hauled herself up, swung her head and arms upside down again, and braced to lift the nun. Hood felt awkward having the two women together. He'd made love to both of them. Keyuri, however, was going into shock, and Beth seemed intent simply on escaping.

Then the earth quivered slightly.

There was a clunk, a whine, and a pale illumination came on in the tunnel below. It came from everywhere and nowhere, from the rocks and the air and the motes of dust, spangling the corridor.

Raeder was starting the machine again.

Hood called up to Calloway. "How did you find us?"

"After I put the biplane down I hiked up to that smoke we saw. Turned out to be this crazy nunnery. These nuns stand watch until the time is right, the abbess said. They were buzzing like a disturbed hive because no one had approached for centuries, and then those Nazis climbed in like human flies. When I told them you'd *parachuted* in, it was like announcing Herbert Hoover had snuck back into the White House. They went nuts. Then we heard this gawd-awful noise. What the hell do these Germans have? A Big Bertha cannon?"

"It's a stick that shoots fire."

"A fire stick? We're Indians now?"

"In our technological understanding. There's stuff down here that looks like it's out of Buck Rogers, Beth. Heaps of bones, too. Something went terribly wrong."

"I'll say. Is your pal Raeder still down there?"

"Yes, I think he just started the big machine again. I think it reloads a fire stick. A magic staff like this one." He held it up. "I don't think we should let a man like Kurt Raeder have it."

"I'll say. Well, let's start with Keyuri. I'll drag her up to the nuns."

Hood lifted the groaning, half-conscious Tibetan, watching her small, dangling feet disappear up the chimney. In the dimness, it was as if she were floating skyward. Then Beth dropped back down to the hole in the roof of Hood's tunnel, holding out an arm. "You next."

He shook his head.

"Thanks for coming back for me, but I was sent here to put a stop to this. I think Raeder's going to try to take another one of those thunderbolt staffs back to Adolf Hitler. I don't think I can let him do that."

"How you going to stop him?"

"Just two krauts left, I think."

"Then I'm coming with you, Ben. Even odds."

"No. This isn't your fight."

"The hell it isn't! That bastard dragged my biplane to the middle of nowhere." She looked at him expectantly. Keyuri was shot, Hood desperate. This was a way to cement their partnership.

"No." He shook his head decisively. "I might not make it. I want you to take this staff of mine to the surface. It's too low on juice to fight with, but I think we need to show it to the American government. War's coming."

"We can leave it with the nuns for a minute. We get Raeder, and *then* we worry about the shaft."

"No, Beth. I want you to fly it, and Keyuri, back to Lhasa."

"I'm flying *you* to Lhasa!"

"Listen. There's only room in the biplane for two. If I don't survive, none of this matters if we can't report what happened. Somebody has to get out alive. Somebody has to warn the Tibetans, so they can arrest Raeder if he tries to escape overland. There's something strange about how this place feels, like it does something corrupting. So stay clear. If I stop him, I'll come back here. If not, Keyuri and you have to tell what happened. And Keyuri is shot. You have to make her well."

"I'm no doctor! *You* make her well. Maybe we can just seal Raeder in."

"And maybe he'll blow his way out, if we let him play with this infernal machine long enough. Please go up and wait."

"This is nuts." It was the end, Beth could feel it, and it tore her in two. She liked this guy. He was an egghead, all right, but an egghead with gumption, dammit. "Leave the fanatics down here to play with their machine, Ben. If he's got another magic wand, what chance do you have if you give this one up? Where's your pistol?"

"It jammed, and Keyuri's carrying it. But I'll take the submachine gun of the German you just shot. I'll get the drop on them."

"Ben . . ." She was pleading.

He wearily held up his bloody hand. "I've been lucky my whole life. Rich my whole life. Catered to my whole life. And rarely had much I cared *about*, except shooting blue sheep and falling for both of you. Now I've fallen into something important, against a man I know better than anyone. Kurt Raeder and I have been destined to come back together ever since the death of Keyuri's husband."

Beth's faced twisted. "I don't want to lose you."

"And I need to straighten things out. It starts with Shambhala."

"This isn't Shambhala," Beth said. "Not this evil power. This isn't what the legends promise."

"Well, whatever it is, we need to button it up before all hell breaks loose in the world. I was told it wouldn't be difficult for me to kill Kurt Raeder, and I realize Duncan Hale was right. Go, seal the door until it's over. Save Keyuri."

The aviatrix shut her eyes. "Try not to lose any more fingers."

"I wish we'd kept that scotch."

"I could use a swig myself."

The nuns called down "Hurry!" in English.

"At least I've got a flashlight for you in case the lights go out." Beth handed him one and glanced at his holster. "And take my pistol."

"No, I'll have the machine gun. I can't leave you unarmed."

"You're the one going to a gunfight, and you'd better have a backup. Take it, dammit, so I can go heal your girlfriend. Meanwhile I'll fix your forty-five."

"She's not . . ." He stopped, frustrated. "Thanks." He took the revolver, a cowboy six-shooter, and jammed it in his holster.

"Don't get too grateful. There's just one bullet left. It's for you, if you get trapped in the cave."

"Oh."

"I think ahead."

He smiled, tiredly. Then he went to the body of the dead German lying in a flower of blood. Calloway was quite the crack shot with a pistol; there were three holes in the bastard. He picked up the machine gun, lighter and more practical than anything Americans had.

"Good-bye, Beth."

"We'll be waiting." She said it without conviction.

He watched as she climbed up out of sight. A stone door slid shut, fitting so tight he could barely see the joint. How many access points were there?

Then he stepped off down the tunnel to hunt Kurt Raeder.

35

A Boeing 747, over the Pacific
September 7, Present Day

Rominy had never flown business class before, but Jake persuaded her that they needed the indulgence to rest before the tiring journey ahead. "And we need room to inspect Benjamin Hood's lost satchel with some measure of privacy. You want to do a treasure map in the middle seat, coach?"

Since the money she'd just inherited didn't seem real, she'd acquiesced to the surreal $5,000 one-way cost for the two of them. She was betting on Jake Barrow, despite her doubts: in for a penny, in for a pound. His sense of purpose, confidence, and journalistic mission had cast a spell. They'd raced from the Cascade River road in a stolen SUV, taken back roads to Darrington and Granite Falls, and driven to Seattle's airport without stopping. She'd asked to get fresh clothes at her apartment and he'd refused.

"Too risky. The skinheads might be watching. We'll buy a few things at the airport."

"Jake, the police are looking for me. I can't just disappear."

"You have to, for a while."

"*How?*"

He thought. "Your adoptive parents are retired, right?"

"In Mexico. They don't keep track of me."

"Close relatives?"

"No."

"We just need a few weeks. We're going to stop at the Business Center at the airport and set up a new e-mail account. Write your boss that you're alive. Mention something only you and he would know you're working on, so he knows it's you. Then say you quit."

"What!"

He glanced at her, gaze opaque behind sunglasses he'd found in the glove department. "You've got more than a hundred thousand dollars in the bank, a dead-end job, and the adventure of a lifetime, as they say on TV. Do you want to go back to your cubicle? An e-mail will save police the trouble of looking for you. The money gives you a year or two to look for a job. To travel, first, if you want. To see what happens between us. And if you decide to bail on me . . . they'll probably hire you back."

Probably not, but yes, a door had cracked open to freedom. It was as terrifying as it was exhilarating. She bit her lip. "All right." She considered. "That doesn't explain the MINI Cooper."

"E-mail a friend that you've met a guy who's changed your life and you're on a journey of self-discovery. That's true, isn't it? I torched your car for the insurance to get some cash to travel with. You never thought it would be on the news, but don't worry, you're safe and happy."

She blinked at the audacity. "You're quite the liar, Jake Barrow."

"Some is true. I'm expedient."

"You think the cops will buy it?"

"No, but they get reports about a hundred runaways and messed-up chicks a day. It reduces the crime to insurance fraud, a low priority. And even if my truck was spotted at Safeway and they find it abandoned up by Eldorado, we'll be in Asia. We go cold case. Then we come back with the story, all will be explained, and it's book-and-movie-deal time."

"*Movie* deal?"

"Think who you want to play you. This is big."

It was crazy. Thrilling. Absurd. Hypnotic. "*If* you get the story."

"If *we* get the story."

To cut all ties and vault halfway around the world? Liberating. Irresponsible. Irresistible. "I feel like Bonnie and Clyde, not Woodward and Bernstein."

"I'm hoping it's more like Pierre and Marie Curie, discoverers of radium. There's a couple of things I have to tell you on the plane."

"I'm losing my old life, Jake."

"And gaining a new one."

He'd parked the stolen car in the half-empty lot of a discount store—"Leaving it here may confuse the police more than the airport garage, until we're out of the country"—and called a cab to take them to the terminal. To her objections that she had no passport, he produced two proclaiming them Mr. and Mrs. Robert Anderson (her first name listed as Lilith, of all things) along with the requisite permits to fly to China, of which Tibet was now a part. "I was hoping the story would take us this far," he said, "so I got these from a forger I met on the crime beat."

"A *forger*? Jake, we're going to go to prison."

"Not if you hang cool." He also had two simple gold wedding bands. "I got *them* from a pawn shop and carry them in my car. Every once in a while it helps to look married when I'm on assignment."

"What kind of assignment?"

"When I'm focusing and don't want to flirt. It's just less distraction."

That seemed unlikely. "You need two?"

"They came as a pair—probably an estate sale—and I put one on a photographer once when we were nosing around in a conservative hamlet in the Idaho panhandle, getting background on a religious sect. It relaxed a few sources still living in the nineteenth century."

"So long as your photographer was a woman."

He laughed. "Right! And Caroline made me swear not to tell the newsroom. So keep a lid on. I still kid her about it, though."

The marriage charade struck Rominy as almost sacrilegious, but they couldn't afford questions at the airport. It was weird having him hand her the ring, fraudulent and yet touching.

"Just for practice," Jake said. He actually blushed, which she liked.

Her heart hammered a little as she slipped the ring on.

At the ticket counter he paid in cash, which cost them an extra five minutes while the agent double-checked the no-fly list. And, yes, they only had carry-ons. "I won't pay those new baggage fees," Jake told the agent. "You guys are air pirates."

"Business class doesn't charge for luggage, sir."

"It's the principle."

Rominy expected her to trip an alarm for an air marshal, but the agent only gave a sweet smile. "Have a pleasant flight, sir."

In fact, Rominy expected arrest at any moment for arson, kidnapping, auto theft, or identity fraud, but none materialized. Instead, as she was trying to buy some emergency underwear in the Seattle concourse, Jake nudged her and pointed to four shaven-headed young men at a pub table, disturbingly attired in bomber jackets, combat boots, and tattoos. One of them kept glancing her way. Were they watching? So they hastily moved on, and she'd postponed her shopping until the two-hour layover in Los Angeles, buying jeans, sweater, and parka. From there they'd caught the trans-Pacific flight to Shanghai and then Chengdu, China, from which they'd fly to Lhasa.

"What is it with skinheads, anyway?" she asked as they waited to board. "Why do they want to intimidate people?"

"They just want to belong. That's the basis of all gangs, armies, and nations. The Nazi stuff is rebellious enough to get a rise out of people, which is an improvement if you've been poor and ignored your whole life. And there's a philosophy behind it, an idealism."

"Being a Nazi?"

"Look, the Nazis lost and didn't get to write history. Hitler told his followers to stick up for their own. That's what skinheads believe, too. So do Jews, blacks, women. Everyone's got a tribe, except white guys."

"Jake, they didn't stick up for their own. They tried to conquer the world."

"It spiraled out of control. But in the beginning the key Nazi philosophers were reformers who believed in self-improvement, discipline, classic art, and bringing back some of the old beliefs in nature and environment. People voted for them! Did you know the SS had a research division? That's why the Nazis were sent to Tibet. Heinrich Himmler wanted to build a kind of Vatican for the SS, a Camelot or a Valhalla, at an old castle called Wewelsburg. Just like Hitler wanted to make his hometown of Linz the art center of the world. I'm not saying they were right, but it didn't start with panzer divisions and death camps."

"I think it *did* start with that. I think it was embedded in what they stood for from the very beginning."

"And I think it got twisted, which is more believable than a nation deciding to get evil for a dozen years and then get good again."

She shook her head. This was like going on a blind date and learning your liberal agnosticism had been paired with a supply-side creationist. Just what *were* his beliefs? "I've heard of being open-minded, but this is ridiculous. And white guys are *the* tribe."

"It's not ridiculous. I'm a reporter, and I'm trained to look at both sides. Hey, I'm the one who saved you from the skinheads. I'm on *your* side. But I try to understand the other side, so I can write about them."

"What I understand is that they blew up my car."

"Which is why we're moving on."

It *did* feel reassuring to get away from Seattle, where all this madness had started. So did a Bloody Mary on the first flight, two martinis at LAX, and the welcoming champagne in business class. She'd fallen asleep soon after they flew over open water, and woke up somewhere mid-Pacific. It was dark, she was hungry, and Jake had saved her a bag of peanuts.

"Don't worry, there's another meal in an hour or two."

She felt groggy and uncertain. The intimacy she'd shared with Jake in the mountain cabin had been overwhelmed by the roller-coaster terror of falling into the mine and then careening downhill from madwoman Delphina Clarkson and the Mohawk bow hunter. Then sending the cryptic e-mails from the airport, the new clothes paid for from the stash of cash, and flinging herself into the void. Had the destruction of her MINI Cooper really been less than two days ago? Instead of her old life they had two backpacks, more than $21,000 in cash, a swollen bank account, a bag of peanuts, and moldy seventy-year-old documents taken from a skeleton.

"Good sleep?" Jake asked, brisk as a butler. He'd bought some toiletries and looked washed, combed, and competent, though he'd left the two-day stubble for that fashionable bad-boy look that, dammit, did look good on his strong jaw. Well, she was alive, richer, and an aisle curtain snobbishly separated her from the coach-class proletariat she'd long been accustomed to. One day at a time, Rominy. Maybe Jake was the answer she'd been waiting for. At least there were no skinheads in business class.

"I need some aspirin, actually."

"Got 'em. Picked up a vial at the airport newsstand."

He'd given her sunglasses and a sun hat to wear at SeaTac, where she was already old news in the twenty-four-hour cycle but where her picture popped up once on airport TVs. She'd kept her head buried in *People* magazine, reading about celebrity calamities that seemed ridiculously trivial compared to her own. No one had looked at her with even a flicker of recognition.

Now she was stateless, groundless, history-less, suspended in midair. "Water," she ordered from a flight attendant. "And a gin and tonic." Maybe adventure would make her an alcoholic.

"I waited until you woke up to dig out the documents," Barrow said. "They're really more yours than mine, though I think they're going to show us where to go in Tibet. I think we're thousands of miles ahead of any pursuit now, Rominy."

"If we get through Chinese customs."

"You're a missing person, not a fugitive. You won't show up on Chinese computers."

"What about you, Jake? What have you told your editors?"

"That I'm on the biggest story of my life and I'll be out of touch. They cut me slack because I'm good. It's only been a couple of days. By the time they start wondering about my clock hours, I'll have the biggest scoop of the year and they'll be drooling Pulitzer."

"I'm the biggest scoop of the year?"

"No, Shambhala is."

"Sham . . . what?"

"Actually, I did peek a little. That's what Great-grandpa was after, Rominy—Shambhala. A mythical kingdom in Tibet, a real-life predecessor to Shangri-la."

"How many Bloody Marys have *you* had?"

"The Nazis were after it, too, led by a man named Kurt Raeder. Ben Hood was in some kind of race for new powers, like the atom bomb. Captain America against Hitler. And I think they found it, or found *something*, according to this stuff. Maybe that's what agent Duncan Hale was after, too. Think about it: end of the war. Atomic bombings. Soviets in Berlin. The smart ones see a new arms race. And so Mr. Hale gets wind that the reclusive Mr. Hood just might have found something that could tip the balance of power. He comes out to Washington State, tracks Great-grandpa down, snatches the secret papers, but then dies in that mine. Maybe Hood trapped him with a cave-in."

"But why wouldn't Great-grandpa share it? It's his country, after all."

"I don't know. Why didn't he go back to New York? Why didn't he claim his family fortune? Why didn't anybody know he was dead for months? We're a team. We're going to learn the answers."

She sighed. "All right. We'd better start reading."

The papers were not in order. There was a journal of fragmentary entries, and a collection of sketches, maps, random notes, and coordinates. There was a crude map of a valley in a bowl of mountains and a drawing of a waterfall. There were clippings and torn textbook pages on amps, volts, and equations she couldn't make sense of, with graphs and charts. Hood had a fine, feathery hand, but she didn't see how Duncan Hale or anyone else could make sense of this without her great-grandfather's verbal explanation. There were sketches of some kind of machine, with things that looked like pipes, boilers, and stacks, but no indication of what it was for or how it worked. It was so incoherent that the notion he'd become eccentric at best, crazy at worst, seemed reasonable. She'd bought $5,000 in airline tickets based on *this*?

"I don't know, Jake. This seems pretty vague."

"It gives us a place to go to. No one's had these coordinates, Rominy."

"Coordinates to *what*? A mythical utopia? A waterfall?"

"To this, actually." He pulled out one of the diagrams. She'd glanced at it before, but it had meant nothing to her—just a narrow ring, a thin doughnut. It could be a circular plaza, the orbit of some planet, or someone's design for a wedding band.

"Which is?"

"It looks like an ancient design for a cyclotron."

"What in the world is a cyclotron?"

"An atom smasher." He smiled, as if his Super Bowl bet had just paid off.

"Okay, I give up. Why are we flying ten thousand miles for an atom smasher?"

"You know what they are, right?"

"They smash atoms." She wasn't about to admit she didn't care, until now.

"They break them apart so we can see what's inside."

"Scientists already have atom smashers."

"*Now,* yes—but this one looks to be hundreds or even thousands of years old. The principle behind them is very modern, very sophisticated: to accelerate atomic particles fast enough to smash them, you push them along with magnets, but it takes a long track to get up to speed, like a long ski jump. In 1929, Berkeley physicist Ernst Lawrence realized that if you could bend the beam, accelerating them in a circle, your track was essentially infinite. They just go around and around, faster and faster. With enough size and power, you could get things up to almost the speed of light."

"So Shambhala figured this out, hundreds or thousands of years ago."

"At a time when no one else knew atoms even existed. Imagine that, Rominy: an ancient civilization as sophisticated, or more sophisticated, than our own. There were some primitive attempts at cyclotrons in the 1930s, but we didn't really get going on them until the

1950s. Yet the Shambhalans, if these diagrams are real, had them when we were in togas or suits of armor."

She looked back at the diagram. "I'm sure this would thrill Indiana Jones. Why do Nazi skinheads care?"

"Ah. When you take little things apart you understand how they work, and when you understand how they work you can begin to manipulate them. Nuclear weapons are the most obvious example. Once physicists realized that atoms could be split, and that energy is released when that happens, it was a relatively short step to a bomb, even though the details were expensive and complicated."

"Neo-Nazis want this to make a bomb?" What was she mixed up in?

"Well, the original Nazis, the 1930s Nazis, wanted it to make something more controllable than that. Atom bombs are kind of indiscriminate. It would be nice to have such firepower that could be aimed."

"If you're a mad scientist."

"If you're trying to defend your country. When I started reading about your great-grandfather I stumbled onto all kinds of theories and legends about Tibet, Heinrich Himmler, and secret expeditions. Yet all of it was just that, stories, until I found you. Then we discovered, together, this satchel of documents. Hood was the guy who was the key, but he died and left clues only for his heirs, who have had a disturbing habit of dying off. Until you."

Only because he'd saved her life in that Safeway parking lot. "The Nazis killed my grandma and birth mother."

"Maybe. Maybe buddies of Agent Hale killed them, because the U.S. government wanted this secret covered up. They didn't know what Hood had hid, so they just discouraged any attempts to find out. Heck, it took me a long time to track you down. That's why it was so awkward in the grocery store. I didn't know how to start this conversation. 'Hi, baby, can I talk to you about Nazis?' "

"But if we've got cyclotrons there's no need for an old one, right?"

"Tibetan holy men have always been reputed to have magical or supernatural powers. What if those rumors have some basis in science? Our atom smashers are designed to break things apart. But this one, according to Nazi legend, was designed to put things together, to reassemble energy in a new way."

"How do you know all this?"

"I'm a science nerd, like I said." He took her hands in his. "Rominy, have you ever heard of a secret power source called Vril?"

36

Shambhala, Tibet
October 4, 1938

The noise of the great machine was growing louder, a rising whine more powerful than any sound Hood had heard before. He advanced down the tunnel cautiously, grateful it was lit but also feeling exposed. At any moment he expected another German to appear at the tunnel horizon from the other end, maybe with a bizarre staff that would fry him like the electric chair. But nobody appeared.

They were waiting in ambush for him.

No, they were preoccupied.

The circle of pipes was several miles in extent, and it took him an hour of cautious walking to get from Shambhala's "back door" to the machine room where he'd first caught up to Raeder. At the end of the pipeline tunnel he crouched and crept, the MP-38 ready, until he had most of the big cavern in view.

At the far end was a heap of rubble where the other entrance of the circular tunnel had been caved in by Hood's thunder stick. The main hall was still littered with rock from the blasted ceiling. Bones were tossed about like confetti. And the horribly mutilated German who'd triggered Raeder's wrath—or at least the wrath of the weirdly diabolical staff—still sat, half-disintegrated, against one wall. Raeder and the other surviving German were at the machine, a staff reinserted in its cradle. The weapon was pulsing amber, and presumably was being charged.

The two were arguing. Shambhala did not seem to induce harmony.

Hood stepped out, submachine gun in hand, and walked toward them. Raeder had another staff in his hand, the American saw. It, too, glowed.

"Let's try this again," Hood said. "Drop your weapons."

The Germans turned, momentarily disconcerted but then regaining their poise. "Ah, you found that the tunnel doesn't go anywhere," Raeder replied. "Yes, now we're back as we were. Except what did you do with Keyuri?"

"Your henchman shot her."

"Ah, too bad. And you shot him?"

"Something like that."

"It's gotten a little crazy, has it not, Benjamin Hood? We have here, I suspect, something more valuable than the gold of El Dorado." He shook his staff. "And instead of rejoicing we're fighting. Why is that?"

"Because you want to give it to a bunch of book-burning Nazi lunatics." Hood gestured with the muzzle of the machine gun. "You're finished, Kurt."

"Am I? Under whose authority?"

"The Tibetan government sent me here."

"To get this power for themselves."

"It's their country, isn't it? So I repeat: Hands *up!*"

"And what *proof* do you have that you work for anyone but yourself, Hood?"

"I have the machine gun."

"What happened to the staff you already stole?"

"It went cold."

"Keyuri is spiriting it away, that's what I think. We still have a destiny, she and I. And I have something entirely different from your primitive gun. Reichsführer SS Himmler called it Vril, and it makes that toy in your hand as obsolete as a stone club. I have a weapon as quick as thought itself, and just as mobile. I think, therefore I destroy." He lifted the staff slightly. "Imagine a tool that doesn't hammer on reality but rearranges it.

That's what I feel when I hold it, Benjamin. I've gotten hold of the fabric of the universe itself."

"Don't make me pull the trigger."

"Will you really shoot me down like one of your museum specimens?"

"Just like you fried your own man there, hurled against the wall."

The other German looked at Raeder nervously.

Raeder ignored him. "Who really sent you? The Chinese? The Americans? What faith they have, dispatching you all by yourself!"

"We're both scientists, Kurt. They sent me as a fellow scientist."

"To steal discovery. Alas, I got here first." And he raised the staff to point it.

So Hood fired.

The M-38 spat, the barrel climbing slightly as he fought to control the unfamiliar weapon. It stuttered like the guns in the gangster movies, shells flying like flung coins. Raeder should have been cut down.

Instead there was a blinding flash, a boom as loud as bells in the belfry of a cathedral, and the whine of angry hornets.

Hood's bullets flew all around the room, anywhere but at Raeder, having been deflected by the force in his crystal staff. The American, meanwhile, was cuffed backward by power like hurricane wind, flying off his feet and skidding on his back against the pipes.

The sound of Raeder's shot gonged off the walls before rolling away into a throaty rumble. The air crackled as if there'd been a bolt of lightning. It tasted like ozone. More rock rained down from the ceiling and bounced off the floor, the other German wincing.

"I've no idea how it works," Raeder called, "or what it can really do. If it hadn't had to deflect the energy of your bullets, I'd guess you'd be dead by now. So let's just finish what I started and bring the curtain down."

Hood scrambled for cover in the tunnel. Raeder aimed the weapon at the tunnel mouth. A thunderbolt flashed again and the cave quaked, the tunnel ceiling shattering and rock dropping down as Hood rolled under the pipes. It smashed onto the second entrance of the tunnel, burying it. Stray fragments bounced out across the floor of the main chamber and a cloud of dust shot out. The great machine itself seemed to shift gears and whine higher.

"Oh, I do enjoy that energy, even if it hurts. Hood? Have I killed you?"

"For God's sake, Kurt, let's *go*," the other German urged.

"Silence, Hans. Do you realize that at this moment I'm the most powerful man in the world?"

Diels lifted his own staff. "No, you're not. This one is charged, too. We both have Vril."

"Then go make sure he's finished. None of this slaughter would have happened without the interference of that damnable hack scientist and his nun. Keyuri Lin has my comrades' blood on her hands."

The German archaeologist walked warily into the cloud of dust. The Vril staff throbbed in his hand, casting light, but everything was obscured by the fog of the explosions. "I don't see him," Diels called.

"Escaped?"

"Buried, or trapped in the tunnel."

"Then help me puzzle out this machine. It's running higher and higher, and I'm worried it will race and break. With the tunnels sealed, we can work in peace."

Diels turned. "We've buried the piping at both ends. Maybe it's running too hot."

"Then let's try inserting another staff to absorb its power."

"We don't know what we're doing, Kurt. We should walk away."

"From godlike power?"

Then there was the bark of a heavy pistol and Diels's forearm shattered. He screamed, clutched it, and dropped his staff.

A figure rose out of dust and rubble, emerging from a pocket under the pipes. Hood was gray with cave dust, rock scratches bleeding, the submachine gun ruined beneath the rocks. He hurled Beth Calloway's now-empty revolver over Diels's head at Raeder, who instinctively ducked instead of lifting his Vril staff.

Hood charged and dove for the other one. Diels grasped, too, screaming as the American rolled onto his injured arm.

Raeder couldn't use his staff without incinerating them both.

Then the other German was knocked away, Hood rising to his knees, his captured staff swinging around.

Twin thunderbolts met.

The world went white. It was like a twin star exploding, two radiating coronas of energy. There was a shriek from Diels as its fury caught and dissolved the SS man, shredding him and throwing the spray of his body against the walls. What Hood and Raeder felt, encased in the energy of their own staffs, was far different. A pulse of dark energy punched through their bodies but lit them with a glow that was a transfiguration that infected every cell and corpuscle. Their air was sucked out, then punched back in. They were blind from the flash, and yet could feel the granular texture of time and space itself.

They saw a shimmer of force fields and fogs of particles, a part of the universe beyond normal human perception.

The machine was rising to a scream as it accelerated. In the cluster of pipes that led to the red glow below, something broke and steam shot upward in a geyser.

At last, Raeder ran. In fear.

Something was being unleashed he didn't comprehend. He retreated up the ramp that led out of this underground city.

Hood wearily pursued, half staggering, since every nerve seemed on fire. The irradiation of staff energy was painful, exhilarating, numbing. His senses had been heightened, yet ached.

At the entry of the machine room where the great door had been knocked askew and the bones piled, he turned back and aimed his weapon at the machine. A jolt shot out and there was a bang, more pipes punched and broken, wire unspooling. The machine whined higher.

He didn't want Nazis toying with this monstrosity again.

Then the American was running up the central ramp, following Raeder. There was an explosion ahead, and a rush of cool air.

When Hood got to the circular mandala door, he saw it had been blown to pieces. Raeder was somewhere beyond, on the surface of Shambhala.

Hood trotted out, his body not just tingling but almost sizzling, a boil of electrons alive with a strange new music. Was this what death felt like? Was he dead? But no, he could see his own flesh, but it had a weird, radioactive glow. He was translucent as amber.

Where was the mad *Untersturmführer*? It was night, the roof of the valley ablaze with stars, the snow glowing silver, the waterfalls iridescent lines of pearl. The entire valley was quivering from the tremors they'd unleashed. He could hear the rising shriek of the machine, far, far below.

How to stop this madness before it escaped into the world?

How to ambush Kurt Raeder before Raeder ambushed him?

And then he had an idea.

He ran down Shambhala's main surface avenue, broken ruins rising to his left and right, the walls snaggletoothed and sad-looking. Had its inhabitants buried what was too terrible to have in the open? Had they fled when the energies they unleashed proved uncontrollable? Or had they made something they needed and simply returned to the stars?

Then there was a crack, like a thousand whips being swung at once, and light seared by him and boomed off a valley wall. The whole cauldron shook. Snow and ice broke off the surrounding glaciers and avalanched down, bringing rock with it.

Raeder had taken a shot at him.

Hood turned and swept his own staff back at the ruins, letting loose a rippling sheet of fire that played over the devastation and turned the uppermost ramparts into shrapnel. Thunder rolled and reverberated. It was a battle of demons. Then he turned and ran again, down the river that ran through Shambhala.

He was making for the narrow slit of a canyon where Raeder had dynamited the only path.

Sheer blocking cliffs rose in front of him a thousand feet high. In the night it looked as if the river disappeared into a cave, so dark was the canyon, but he knew the cleft was like a sword stroke in the edge of a shield. He waited as the noise of their Vril shots grumbled away, trying to hear Raeder over the rush of the river. Where was the German hiding? Then he turned toward the gorge and lifted his staff, summoning every ounce of his will into bringing down those canyon escarpments. He pointed and thought.

The universe seemed to flash into rebirth, light blazing. His arm snapped, broken, and the staff flew wide, sailing into darkness. He roared with pain. The rock walls that gripped the river fractured and leaned precipitously, but didn't fall.

One more, but he didn't have it. His staff had broken on the boulders by the river. All the light had gone out of the amber crystal. His arm was shattered, his hand once more gushing blood. Hood turned to face the valley. The ground was shuddering from earthquakes below, and there was grinding as the machine in the deeps kept accelerating into overdrive.

"I still have the machine gun, Kurt!" he yelled to give away his position by the damaged cliffs. It was his bravest lie. "I can still shoot you!"

And then the biggest corona of all pulsed out toward him, the earth shook like a shocked muscle, and the mountain shattered.

37

A Boeing 747, over the Pacific
September 7, Present Day

No, Jake, I have not heard of Vril. Unless that's the new cleanser that cleans the bathroom so you don't have to." Rominy was smart, but she didn't spend her pretty little brain cells worrying about Nazi power sources. At least, not until now.

"It's a fictional name, a kind of code for what German theosophists hoped might be out there somewhere."

"German *what?*"

"Just guys who provided some of the intellectual underpinnings of National Socialism, the creed of Hitler's party. It did have a philosophy, you know."

"You bet. Blow up the world."

"In the 1930s many highly educated people took race and evolutionary theories quite seriously. After

Darwin, it seemed self-evident that if you wanted to improve the human species—if you wanted it to evolve—
then you bred the best with the best. People do exactly
that every day. They want to mate with the prettiest or
the smartest or the strongest or the richest. The Nazis
simply thought you could apply that common sense to
the group."

"Master race? Aryan supermen? Sore point for
Jews?"

"And Vril."

"Did I miss that *Oprah* episode?" She glanced out
the window. The view over the Pacific looked exactly
as it had hours ago. God, it was a long way to China.

"It sounds goofy, like looking for a way to turn
lead into gold, or the legend of King Arthur's sword,
Excalibur. Yet for thousands of years humans believed in a much more spiritual world than we do, in
which gods or ghosts manifested themselves. Then
along came science, everything opposed to science was
labeled superstitious heresy, and ideas of exotic power
sources like Vril were dismissed. Until modern physics
came along."

"Cyclorama."

"Cyclotron. But it's not just particle accelerators
or atom smashers. It's our whole concept of the universe. Now some people think the Nazis were on to

something. Maybe Himmler's Lewis and Clark expedition to Tibet wasn't so wacky after all. Maybe Vril, or whatever you care to name it, really exists."

"And you think Benjamin Hood discovered this?"

"Maybe. You know what an atom is, Rominy?"

"Jake, I *am* literate."

"Bear with me. It was the Greeks who came up with the term. They looked at the world and saw that big things could be made of smaller things. Buildings out of bricks. Beaches out of grains of sand. And even sand could be ground down into dust or flour. Tiny and tinier. But was there a point at which things couldn't get any smaller? Such a fundamental particle, they proposed, could be called an atom."

This was a moment in which women learned to humor men. You nodded as they held forth, and if you were really interested in the guy, you could smile in amazement or widen your eyes. If guys were smart, they learned that the inverse of this seduction was to pretend to listen sympathetically while the girlfriend kvetched about her day, and then rub her feet.

Barrow plunged on. "It turns out the Greeks were right. There are fundamental particles called atoms. They come in nature in about ninety-two sizes, or weights, and out of them you can build anything we see in the universe. It's like how you can make any English-language book from just twenty-six letters, or any song from just eight notes. You take the atoms of the periodic table and you can make *anything*. But here's the problem. By the beginning of the twentieth century, scientists knew atoms weren't the smallest thing after all. Do you know what they believed was smallest?"

"The unholy heart of Ronnie Hoskins, my two-timing high school boyfriend?"

He laughed. "Hey, I'm being serious, here."

"I'll say."

"Electrons, protons, and neutrons. Their number in an atom controls the type of atom it is. Now we're down to everything being made from just *three* things."

"Amazing." She widened her eyes.

"But then they wondered what would happen if they smashed those particles together."

"Boys do that with trains."

"It turns out there's smaller stuff still. Quarks, and there are at least six varieties of those. Neutrinos, muons, leptons, a whole bunch of stuff physicists call a particle zoo. There are separate families of particles, called tribes. It's bizarre, and confusing. A quark is a thousand times smaller than the nucleus of an atom, and remember I said that's just a pinprick of the fuzz we call atoms. More than 99.99 percent of an atom is empty space."

"Jake, this is sweet, but why are you telling me all this?"

"Because it drives physicists crazy. They're romantics. They believe the universe is not only simple at the tiniest level, but that it *needs* to be simple to be aesthetic and neat and religious and *right*. They want to explain the whole shebang with a single equation so short you could fit it on a T-shirt."

"Like $E=mc2$."

"Exactly! That explains the relationship of energy to matter, that they're two sides of the same coin. But then scientists have found four basic kinds of energy, too, the weak, the strong, electromagnetic, and gravity. It drives them crazy."

"I certainly hope so."

"At these smallest levels, everything goes woo-woo. A particle can be in two places at the same time. It can move from one spot to another instantly, without traveling through the intervening space."

"Oh, come on."

"Even worse is that all of the universe we can see, all that beautiful stuff that shows up in the Hubble telescope photos, isn't everything. In fact it isn't most things. Scientists think more than 96 percent of the stuff that makes up the universe is matter and energy we can't see, or even detect. It's called dark matter and dark energy."

"Earth to Jake. What does this have to do with Nazis?"

"So. Some of the Nazis believed in an energy source called the Black Sun, buried at the center of the earth. Woo-woo, right? Except not entirely different from our ideas of dark energy, an energy so mysterious we can't even detect it."

"How do we know it's there?"

"Something's driving the universe apart faster than it should. That 'thing' has been labeled dark energy."

"And you take these physicists seriously?"

"This is real! Okay, so now there's this idea that there's a smaller particle still, something a trillion times smaller than an atom, called a string. It's a one-dimensional line, meaning it's so small, this string has length, but no width."

She groaned. "Where's my gin and tonic?"

"And then when this string vibrates, it creates everything—*everything*—the way a vibrating violin string creates music."

"Music isn't *stuff*."

"This music is. It's all the stuff, all the energy."

"Why can't I hear it?"

"It's not *real* music, Rominy. We're talking metaphor. But you *can* hear it, too, since if these vibrations make everything—if they're really the fundamental building blocks of atoms—then they made this jet and your ears and the air the engine noise travels through. It's like the music of the spheres. The music of the cosmos."

She shifted in her seat, feeling something hard in her pocket poke her in the thigh. "And Nazis wanted the music."

"In essence, yes. What if you had a violin bow that could play these tiny, tiny strings and in so doing manipulate reality in ways we could barely imagine? I'm not talking just lead into gold. I'm talking matter into energy, and consciousness into action, and space into time and time into space. I'm talking extra dimensions, because string theorists think there may be a dozen or so we're not even aware of, besides the usual four. I'm talking about walking through walls and teleportation and, well, magic. The Tibetans believe in *tulpa*s, or beings created by conscious thought: that we can *think* things into existence if we understand how the universe really works. I'm talking about extraordinary abilities that the smartest people in the world searched for over many centuries. Wizards, alchemists, priests, and kings. It would be like the bow of God." He looked at her expectantly.

"Adolf Hitler wanted to play these strings?"

"No, Hitler and the Nazis had no idea they existed. There were these legends of Vril, but no one in Germany had an idea what it really was or how it might be controlled. But since then we've had all these amazing discoveries in physics and suddenly this crazy 1930s idea sounds more plausible. What if an ancient civilization somehow figured this out centuries ago? Or some alien civilization came down to earth? What if Shambhala was a research center? Think about it—Tibet is the highest plateau on earth, the closest to angels and aliens, a natural landing point for a visiting civilization. What if someone, at some time, figured out how to play the music of the cosmos, to draw a bow across the fundamental strings?"

"You think this is what my ancestor and the Nazis were after?"

"Yes."

She thought. "These strings are really small, right? I mean, we're talking about tiny violins."

"Teeny-tiny."

"So this is a tiny bow? Like, I'm not going to pick it up with my fingers?"

"I don't know. My suspicion is that they forged a great big bow that could play very little strings. You know, what's come down to us in legends and stories is the idea of a stick—a magic wand, or a wizard's staff— with magical powers."

"Like Gandalf."

"Exactly. And not just fictional wizards. Cardinal Richelieu carried a wand of gold and ivory his enemies thought had special powers. Newton was entranced not just by science but by alchemy and magic, and hunted for ways to transcend normal material boundaries. Nikola Tesla thought there was a connection between the mental and physical planes—mind over matter, if you will. What *I* think is that these legends have some basis in reality, that Shambhala devised very big tools—compared to subatomic particles—that could play this subatomic music and control the natural world with what we would call magic. What if they really existed? What if they *still* exist—in a hidden city that your great-grandfather found?"

"Jake, this is starting to sound a little bigger than a newspaper scoop. A little scarier, too. And a whole lot crazier."

"Conceded. But maybe my weirdness makes a little more sense to you now. I seemed crazy because the story seemed crazy, until your car blew up. That's when I knew this was real, and you had to be protected."

"I can protect myself," she said automatically, even though the idea of a protector was not entirely unappealing.

"Sorry. I mean you needed a partner. A friend."

She glanced down at the sheaf of diagrams. "You think the *skinheads* are after these staffs of Shambhala?"

"Yes. Or at least after the idea that there's *something* to the Shambhala legend."

Rominy sat back, thinking. She didn't know if she was sitting next to a lunatic or Einstein. But then a thought occurred. She knew what had poked her thigh—the empty bullet cartridge she'd found on the floor of Jake's pickup, behind the seats. Its meaning hadn't been clear, but all this talk of big things and microscopic things had jarred her memory. She let her fingers touch it, next to her leg, but decided against pulling it out. Instead, she remembered its size. It was small, smaller than she imagined most bullet shells to be.

In fact, the shell was the right size to hold a bullet that would make a small hole just like the one in Barrow's rear window when they were being chased on the freeway.

What was the shell from such a bullet doing *inside* Jake's cab?

Had that gunshot come from assailants she never saw as she was mashed down on the seat? Or from Jake Barrow himself?

Should she challenge him on it?

"Okay, but I still don't get it, Jake. You got me to go along, get the safety deposit box, find the mine, and retrieve the satchel. That's my part as the heir, right? Why do you need me now?"

He smiled, putting his hand on hers, covering where that gold ring burned on her finger. "Can't you tell? I've fallen in love with you."

38

Lhasa, Tibet
September 10, Present Day

L hasa gave Rominy a headache, but then it gave almost all first-time visitors a headache. At nearly twelve thousand feet, it was one of the highest cities in the world. Yet its dizzyingly perched airport was still tucked in the valley of the infant Brahmaputra River, the runway surmounted by taller mountains that glowed like green felt. The sky was a deep blue and clouds drifted overhead like galleons. The topography was so steep that she and Jake had to take a tunnel to get to Lhasa's neighboring valley. Golden willows and cottonwoods bordered gravelly rivers. Lines with flapping prayer flags were stitched from tree to tree like cloth graffiti, telegraphing prayers to the eternal. Buddhas peered down from niches in cliffs. Painted ladders symbolized ascension through reincarnation toward the final grace of nirvana.

Tibet was a jumble of time. There were more oxen than tractors in the barley fields. The stone houses with small openings looked like fortresses compared to the glass expansiveness of American homes, and they were enclosed by adobe walls instead of white picket fences. Yet their geometry was more proportional and pleasing than a McMansion, with trapezoidal windows, walls alternately whitewashed or the color of the earth, and prayer flags fluttering from the four corners. There were bands of black and ocher at the eaves of the roofs, the tops flat because it so rarely rained.

The sun burned with an intensity never felt in sea-level Seattle. Everything was crisp, the clarity defeating attempts at perspective because there wasn't enough haze to judge distance. Shadows were intensely black; rock glittered. Even the facial bones of the Tibetans seemed sharp like their mountains, their skin the color of the earth. If you wanted to contemplate the workings of the universe, this was the place.

Rominy had expected Lhasa to be backwardly quaint, but the city was a burgeoning, car-crowded metropolis of more than 400,000 people in which native Tibetans were a minority. Han Chinese had flooded in to dominate Tibet's capital. The Potala Palace was as awesome as Jake had promised, an otherworldly edifice of more than 900 rooms, but opposite were the huge concrete parade grounds beloved of totalitarian states, complete with a musical electronic billboard. Pedicabs jockeyed with honking taxis. There were billboards for Budweiser beer, shops for Italian clothing, and stores full of glistening motorcycles and Mercedes.

"The Chinese Communists invaded Tibet in 1950," Jake recounted, "and by 1959 the Dalai Lama—the one who was just a child when Benjamin Hood was here—had to flee into exile. The same guy has since become a global celebrity, but we can get into the Potala as tourists while he can't as regent. The wars and upheaval are said to have killed more than a million Tibetans. Meanwhile Chinese have moved in, so you have this country that's half traditional and half modern, everything put on overdrive by go-go capitalism ruled by Communist dictatorship. Even now, if border guards find a book with mention of the Dalai Lama, they confiscate it."

"You seem quite the expert."

"Ever since I got on the Ben Hood story, I've been reading about Tibet."

Some of old Lhasa remained. East of the Potala, around the golden-roofed Jokhang temple, the Barkhor neighborhood of historic buildings and markets sustained sights and sounds Kurt Raeder might have encountered in 1938. Here the streets were narrow and winding, jammed with booths with cheap clothing and globalized souvenirs. The smell was charcoal braziers and cypress incense. A single stall of scarves—a brilliant bank of pinks, reds, purples, and yellows—was a detonating rainbow.

"They like color, don't they?" said Rominy.

"Wait until you see their temples."

In the rectangular plaza in front of the Jokhang, men and boys flew kites that looped and dueled in the blue breeze, trying to slice each other's lines. On the foothills to the north, the Sera, Nechung, and Drepung monasteries clung to the hillsides like old-man eyebrows, limpets of medieval glory overlooking the modernist bustle below. And around the mount of the Potala, a constant circuit of pilgrims shuffled in a clockwise direction called a kora, turning prayer drums and working their rosary malas.

Jake and Rominy checked into the Shangri-la Hotel.

"If we're traveling incognito, isn't the name of this place a little obvious?" she whispered.

"Nobody knows we're here," said Jake. "Besides, we won't stay long. But you can't just run around China willy-nilly, you need a guide with permits. I e-mailed ahead to a booking service and they found one last-minute, which probably means no one else wanted him."

"Great."

"It won't matter. We just need his paperwork." He turned back to the desk clerk. "A room in the back, please. And yes, double, not twin."

Rominy didn't contradict him.

In their room, Jake hugged her. "Take some aspirin and a nap to help acclimate to the altitude. I'm going to pick up a few things in the market and will see you for dinner."

Their guide was an American expat in khaki cargo pants, REI hiking boots, and a torn Led Zeppelin sweatshirt, a genial-looking nobody of the kind Rominy had spent half her life meeting at Seattle coffeehouses and passing over as amiably directionless. They all seemed to have the goals of a fourteen-year-old: play hard. This one had made a living of it, guiding in Tibet, but if what Jake said was true, they'd drawn the bottom of the barrel. He was traveler-shaggy, with a mop of dark hair that hadn't seen a shower for days, a weedy beard, and just the beginning of beer pudge. He wore peace beads at neck and wrist and had a sweat-stained camouflage Booney hat from L.L.Bean. He wandered into the restaurant tapping an iPhone, absentmindedly bumping the Tibetan waitress.

"Sam Mackenzie," he said, sliding into a chair at their table and offering a large, horny hand. "Hear you're looking for an expert."

Jake gave Rominy a sideways glance. "Bob and Lilith Anderson," he replied. "We need someone to get us to the Kunlun Mountains. None of the Tibetan guides seem anxious to go there, so the travel agency suggested you."

"The Kunlun? Heck, you want to see mountains, I can show you several from the sidewalk. What do you want to go to the Kunlun for? They're kinda off the beaten path, my friends."

"And I could show you two entire mountain ranges from Seattle, Mr. Mackenzie, but we flew halfway around the world anyway," Rominy said. "We want to see mountains not everybody's seen before."

Mackenzie considered her. Cute. "Fair enough. Better than 'Because it's there.' Yeah, I might get you to the Kunlun. I got the permits to go through the Chinese checkpoints. I got the Toyota Land Cruiser. I got the maps. It's a trek, however. Late in the year. Your butt will have calluses from the washboard road and you'll eat so much Top Ramen you'll think you're made of monosodium glutamate. It's actually kind of a long, monotonous, rugged, wheezy, kidney-killing trip. A mountain's a mountain but, hey, you're right, the Kunluns are special. High, higher, and highest." He smiled encouragement.

"You've been there?" Jake asked.

"Close enough." He waved his hand. "I can get us wherever we need to go."

"Can we fly?"

Sam laughed. "If you want to play tag with the Chinese air force. This is Tibet, not Topeka, Mr. Anderson. Nobody flies who doesn't have the permission of the Communist government. No private planes. So you get off the main highway and the roads are tracks, and you get off the tracks and the roads are trails. AAA is one hell of a long ways away. There are no doctors, no search and rescue, no gas stations, and no bushes to pee behind. If you pardon my French, Mrs. Anderson."

"I get the picture."

"Yeah, the Tibetans who guide, they're not anxious to go to the Kunlun. Takes a long time. There's nothing there except old legends and enough ice to restock Canada. They tell ghost stories about the place. The Kunlun Mountains are two thousand miles long. Do you care which Kunluns you see?"

"Yes, we have coordinates to a specific place," Jake said. "The western half of the range, approaching the Hindu Kush. I'm a writer, and we're following a historical mystery."

The guide squinted from under his hat. "I love a mystery. What is it?"

"We'd rather not say."

"So what exactly are we looking for?"

"I'd rather not say."

"I see." Mackenzie considered them and then scratched his chin. "Yep, the Kunlun are a sight to behold. If you want mountains, they're an outstanding example. But a trip like this is kinda pricey. I'm thinking a couple thousand yuan a day, or three hundred bucks." He waited for protest and, getting none, plunged on. "And, gosh, we could easily eat up three weeks getting there and coming back, so that's what, six thousand . . ."

"I'll give you ten thousand dollars," Jake said. "Cash."

Sam blinked. "Really?"

"Plus money for supplies. If you can do it in less time you keep all the money. If you know a shortcut, by all means take it. If you want to pack something besides Top Ramen, I'll give you another thousand dollars to do so." Rominy was alarmed at how Jake was burning through her money, even if it was necessary to hire such people and get the rugged trip over with. But then the cash didn't seem real anyway. It felt more like they'd robbed Summit Bank than withdrawn money from it.

But she made a sudden decision. That night, when he was asleep, she was going to peel off $5,000 of their bankroll for emergencies and keep it in her own pack.

And not tell him.

Shouldn't she trust a man she was sleeping with?

She did, mostly. But she wanted some things for herself, like the *khata* scarf from the cabin, tucked near her heart like a good luck charm.

"You must really want to see those mountains," Mackenzie said.

"We're tourists in a hurry, Sam."

"Gotcha." He looked from one to the other. "You're not really Mr. and Mrs. Anderson, are you?"

"We're whoever we tell you we are."

"Listen, I don't care, but I don't want to squirrel my deal with the government. I mean the guiding is supposed to go to Tibetans, but I kind of grandfathered in and get the Yank jobs no one else wants. You're not spooks, are you? And no guns, right? I don't want to see the inside of a Chinese prison."

"Tourists, Sam. Just like our visas say."

"Awesome. Well." He looked at them uncertainly, then shrugged and stood. "A thousand bucks for supplies? You like beer? I could bring some beer along."

"Bring whatever it takes. But we need two axes, two shovels, a pry bar, and two thousand feet of climbing line. If you can just rent some of it, great."

"Rent for how long?"

"Three weeks, I thought you said."

"There's something at these coordinates, right?"

"We hope. By the way, does your iPhone work here?"

"I don't hold it to keep my ear warm. The Chinese have much better reception than the States. They're leaving us in the dust, man. We bicker, they build. This country is so smart, it's scary."

"India, too."

"Everyone has their turn in the sun."

"Can we leave first thing tomorrow?"

Sam squinted again. "When's first thing?"

"Eight."

He frowned. "Sounds good. But maybe nine would work better. Ten if I have trouble rounding up supplies. I'll meet you in the courtyard. And the money . . ."

Barrow counted six thousand in American hundreds into Sam's hand, the guide's eyes going wide. He stuffed the wad in his pants, glancing around the restaurant to see if anyone else was watching.

"The other five when you get us there and back," Jake said. "And a bonus if we find what we're looking for. A report to the Chinese police if you screw us."

Sam saluted. "You got it, bwana."

39

Lhasa, Tibet
September 11, Present Day

Mackenzie didn't show until eleven, a delay that left Jake fuming. Their guide explained he'd been assembling supplies enough for Armageddon, "or at least for the absence of convenience stores in northern Tibet."

The odometer on the faded white Land Cruiser indicated 83,418 hard-won miles, but Sam assured them the rig was indestructible. "Taliban seal of approval, man." Its storage area had been expanded by putting down half the backseat, and it was crammed with jerry cans of gasoline, camping equipment, food, water, beer, a spotting scope, a camera, two board games, a Frisbee, and coils of brightly colored climbing rope. Inserted into the pile were the digging and prying tools Jake had asked for.

"As we drink down the beer, we'll buy more jerry cans with gasoline. There's a station about four hundred miles from here, and then we'll turn off into the backcountry. I tried Google-earthing where you want to go, but that part of the world is pretty fuzzy. As near as I could tell, there's nothing there."

"That's exactly what we're hoping you'd see," Jake said. "It will explain why we're the first to see it."

Sam cocked his head. "I like your logic, man."

They inched through stop-and-go traffic to get out of Lhasa and then broke out onto the main highway, Mackenzie demonstrating an apparent belief in the assurance of reincarnation by recklessly passing crawling trucks on narrow, twisting roads. He did seem to handle the four-wheel-drive vehicle well, and popped in a CD of bemusing Buddhist folk pop. He enjoyed telling them more about Tibet.

"What you got is the most religious country on earth ruled by the least religious country. The spiritual versus the material. The next life versus this one. So there's tension, man, and more machine guns than *Scarface* whenever Chinese pooh-bahs fly in for a visit. It's too bad, you know? What's cool about Tibet is that they're *not* like everybody else, that they had this theocracy and their own laid-back spiritual thing. And now comes China, which is desperate to keep its billion-zillion contented by giving them the Western good life. You want the story of the twenty-first century? We're driving through it."

"Can't they coexist somehow?" Rominy asked.

"That's what the Chinese say. And they do, to a degree. The Commies have allowed the monasteries to reopen after decades of suppression because Tibet is a great tourist draw, not just for Westerners but for the rising Chinese middle class. But is South Dakota run under the precepts of the Sioux nation? The dominant culture dominates. So I don't see an end to the tension anytime soon. The Chinese are just waiting for the Dalai Lama to die, and with him the last hopes of Tibetan independence."

"But hasn't some of the change been good for Tibet?" asked Jake. "Roads, power, water, manufacturing?"

"I suppose. I don't know if it's made anyone any happier."

Jake looked out the window. "You can't stop progress."

"You can bitch about it, though."

Sam Mackenzie thought his clients were more than a little eccentric. What was the pretend marriage gig in this day and age? But he was accustomed to getting the oddball Americans the Tibetan guides didn't want and heading off to oddball places the Tibetans didn't want to go. The Tibetans had families to come home to, and Sam just had himself. Weirdness was his business.

What he didn't like was complicated baloney. "Now that we're out of town and set to camp together for three weeks, who are you really, Mr. Anderson? Shouldn't we level with each other?"

Jake considered. "I guess it wouldn't hurt. I'm Jake Barrow, a newspaper reporter from Seattle. And that's Rominy . . . Pickett, who's been helping solve an old mystery concerning her family. It's a genealogical quest. Where we're going has meaning to her."

Sam looked in the rearview mirror. "You have family that came to Tibet, Lilith? I mean, Rominy?"

She glanced up from some old papers she was studying. "I guess so. I'm sort of here for my roots."

Interesting. Most of Sam's clients came to check off another global experience on their bucket list, bagging enough Buddhas to fuel entertaining dinner party conversation back home. Digital SLR with full-motion capability, sunglasses propped on hair, SPF 50 sunscreen, sacred strings tied around wrist, a tantric tattoo or two, altimeter, iPod, Kindle, pedometer, compass watch good to one hundred meters underwater, boots with more pieces to their assembly than the space shuttle, down, fleece, Gore-Tex, and a determination to rough it, once they got over their disbelief there wasn't a power outlet and a Porta-Potty round every bend. Those tourists were okay. They came, they looked, they paid.

More problematic were the seekers of enlightenment, the Buddhist devotees and questing Christians who desired desperately to break free from desire, and preferably do so sooner than their friends or neighbors so they could brag about it. The worst of them were spiritual snobs, contemptuous of anyone who didn't share their particular muddle of mysticism, guessing ahead as to which Buddha statue was which like a bright child eagerly lifting its hand in class. Sam had quested, too, but then seen it through the eyes of too many fellow American pilgrims, and now he didn't think you had to fly to enlightenment, or that high elevation produced anything but light-headedness. But if you played along, complimenting the women without flirting and hanging with the men without pretending to be their equal, the seekers might leave a good tip. For a week you became their confidant and then never saw them again, to the relief of both parties.

This pair was different. Barrow seemed about as religious as a hedge fund trader shorting the investment trash he'd sold his clients. Something about the newspaper tag didn't sit right. Mackenzie had gotten drunk with journalists and this one was too . . . what? Smooth. And free spending. He had a wad like a Mafia don. The girl was oddly tolerant of Jake's bullshit, having perhaps been well and truly fucked one too many times. She was bright but in love—a disastrous combination—and was probably convinced her dude was deeper than any dude could ever be. In Sam's considered opinion, any attractive woman who preferred her own feckless companion to Mackenzie charm had, by definition, terrible taste in men. Rominy was pretty, and if Anderson-Barrow wasn't around, Sam might have a go at her.

But there was more to their oddness. Barrow spent money with the ease of a man who hadn't really earned it, and both of them seemed after more than family memories. They were going for Their Precious, Sam guessed, and the guide worried what their reaction would be when they inevitably didn't find it. There was *nothing* in the Kunlun, which is why Lhasa's Tibetans didn't want to go there. Travel often disappointed, and when it did, some people took it out on their guide.

Meanwhile, Barrow passed the time with dorm room philosophy.

"What makes us happier is the real question, isn't it?" Jake said after staring out the window for a while. "Money? Flush toilets? Enlightenment? What did you come for, Sam?"

"God. Didn't find him, but I stayed for the people. The Third World is homey."

"You know, the Germans came here in the 1930s."

"Did they now?" He hated it when clients tried to lecture *him*.

"The Nazis, and I guess they tried to sell the Tibetans on some kind of alliance. But the gap was pretty wide. And then came the war."

Mackenzie decided to humor Jake's Trivial Pursuit. "The krauts came to Tibet? I'll bet that went over big. Let's be friends with crazy Adolf!"

Jake laughed. "The weird thing is, Hitler did some good things in Germany they could have used here. The autobahn, employment, the Volkswagen."

"I don't think Tibet needed an autobahn in the '30s, since they had no cars. And I don't recall Hitler doing much good, Mr. Anderson. I mean Barrow."

"Jake. That's because it's the victors who write history."

Holy-moley, Sam thought. Was this guy a Holocaust denier? Wouldn't that be fun to prattle on about for the next three weeks? "So why didn't Hitler stop with the Volkswagen?" Sam asked in his most carefully calibrated neutral guide voice. "What was his thing with the Jews?"

"Psychologists have had a field day," Jake said matter-of-factly. "Hitler the prude: a grandfather who had some illicit affair with a Jew. Hitler the mama's boy: the doctor who cared for his mother when she died of cancer was Jewish. There are rumors young Adolf contracted syphilis from a Jewish prostitute. That he was insulted by a relative of the Jewish writer Kafka when he was down and out in Vienna. That he was in love with his niece and got twisted over her suicide or murder. That he only had one testicle, and some Freudian thing was going on."

"I go with the niece theory. Nazis just weren't good with girls, were they?"

"Actually, most were happily married. If anything, they were socially conservative, family-values types. Hitler didn't marry because he thought bachelorhood made him more politically appealing."

"The messiah."

"There were more than a few Germans who thought that. Not that they'd admit it afterward."

"You, too?"

"Of course not. I just study the period. Rominy puts up with it."

"Jake calls it open-minded," she said from the back.

"And what do you call it?" Sam asked.

"Nutty." She flipped a page, and Jake laughed. "You'll be sorry you got him started, Sam."

"I admit it," Barrow said. "I like to argue."

Sam didn't like Jake's casual confidence because he was jealous of it. The other thing about the tourists he guided was that they were usually paired, like Jake or Rominy, or bonded in some mountaineering fellowship. They always belonged—either to each other, like the Three Musketeers, or to some place Back There, where they'd come from and where they'd return to. They were *anchored*. They had careers, money or the expectation of it, maybe family, at least friends, Facebook . . . *something*. And Sam, the drifter, the broken home kid, the college dropout, stung from one too many dumpings by indifferent ratty-haired girlfriends, and one too many lazy betrayals by self-centered traveling mates, and with one too many fuckups from one too many drinks or joints or dumb-ass decisions . . . had only secretly sensitive Sam for company. His very own self, indivisible, with liberty and restlessness for all. Reduced to accompanying people he didn't know and sometimes didn't like, for a fee, like a Craigslist whore. What the hell was he doing with his life, driving to Outer Bumfuck and trying to make conversation about Nazis? Driving *belongers* around. Barrow, he thought, gave all the signs of being in some kind of tight fraternity. A let-me-challenge-political-correctness nerd who Sam decided was annoying as hell.

Rominy, he liked.

"But Adolf can't get over his own private frustration?" Sam challenged. "So he kills six million Jews, and six million more besides? Poles, Russians, gypsies, retarded people, homosexuals, Freemasons . . . I mean, come on."

"Let's assume he did," Barrow said mildly. "Some people think he was possessed by the devil. Hitler's own explanation is simpler. He was gassed during World War I and said he had a vision while in the hospital of saving Germany. He thought Jewish financiers and leaders had cost Germany the war."

"You defend this guy?"

"I try to explain him. Unlike most people, I've actually studied him. If we could understand *Hitler*, maybe we could understand anyone. Even ourselves."

"Good luck with that." Yep, Barrow was a smug little prick. Or maybe Jake was just fascinated with the Third Reich, like any number of people who pause to look at accidents, tour torture museums, and walk the gravel of old concentration camps.

"You know what's funny?" Sam asked. "He goes after the Jews and gets Israel. Be careful what you wish for. That's why I'm laid back, man. Why the Tibetans are laid back. Mind your own business and look after your own soul—if everyone did that, the world would be happier, right? That's what Jesus said. That's what John Lennon said."

"One crucified, the other shot."

"That doesn't make them wrong."

"No, but their world would be medieval."

"John Lennon's world would be medieval?"

"Their laid-back world, I suspect, would have no Land Cruisers," Barrow trumped.

"We wouldn't miss Land Cruisers if we didn't have them," Sam said doggedly.

"It's a long walk to the Kunlun Mountains."

"We wouldn't miss the Kunlun Mountains."

"Look," said Jake, "I've studied Hitler because where we're going is where the Germans went in 1938. I'm curious what they found. Curious what they were looking for. Rominy here is an heir to someone who got wrapped up in it all, an American explorer. So the more I understand about the Nazis, the more idea I have of where they might have gone."

"The Kunlun? They went to Nowhere Central, man. They went to where there's no there there." He glanced at Barrow. "You really got the hots for Hitler, don't you?"

"I just think he was complicated, like everyone, and interesting, like everyone."

"Complicated? That's an *interesting* way to put it."

"What if he was an idealist in his own way, driven into wars he didn't want?"

"That's not how I heard it went down, bro."

"Yes, get real, Jake," Rominy chimed in. "Don't be provocative just to be provocative."

"A lot of people followed him for *some* reason." Barrow sounded defensive. "I'm just saying, if you want to make sense of history, let's understand what it was, not parrot cowboy-and-Indian dogma about who was right and who was wrong."

"Sorry, amigo, I saw the movie. The Nazis were wrong."

"That's my point. All you've seen is the movie."

Holy-moley. "Hey, you want a picture of some yaks?" Sam pointed. Time to change the subject before he got too steamed.

Rominy was in the backseat, trying to ignore the debate of the men while sifting through the satchel documents again. The more she read them, the more she came to believe that Benjamin Hood hadn't written them. The script was in a feminine hand, and the maps and diagrams had a vagueness that might come from someone getting the information second-hand, from memory. There were no measurements or dimensions, no logical depiction of a machine with interlocking parts. The entire packet was impressionistic.

Could that mean it was myth, that they were chasing a fairy tale?

Or did it mean that someone like the woman pilot in the picture had befriended Ben and taken his dictation or descriptions? *Beth Calloway, 1938.* A good deal of the journal seemed incoherent, more a collection of notes than a narrative or diary. There were names: Kurt, Keyuri, Beth, Ben. Was her great-grandmother's name Beth? Rominy considered. Maybe Calloway and Hood pursued the Nazis together, Beth flying a plane. So they get back to the Cascade Mountains, and Beth tries to make sense of it all. Maybe Hood was disabled. But the journal was riddled with question marks, arrows, and blanks, as if it were a jigsaw puzzle only half put together.

Maybe Rominy could put it together here in Tibet.

Maybe she was supposed to finish what her great-grandmother started.

Maybe the journal would make sense in Shambhala.

40

Concrete, United States
September 7, 1945

S o this is where the elusive *Benjamin Hood has gone
to ground*, thought Duncan Hale, special agent of
the Office of Strategic Services. His agency had been
created in the cauldron of the recently concluded World
War II and had absorbed his old Army Corps of Intelligence Police.

I've arrived, Hale thought. *Backwater, USA.*

It wasn't until the end of the war that Hale had realized the necessity to start tracking the man he'd sent
to Tibet eight years before. Rumors of Hood's discoveries had been fantastical, and his disappearance per-
plexing. The millionaire had gone mad, most thought,
and withdrawn like a hermit crab somewhere into the
American wilderness.

Then, with the wartime explosion of science, the fantastic had become commonplace. The German V2s. Jet fighters. The atomic bomb. And suddenly an anonymous letter had arrived that made the strange rumors more compelling. Just what *had* Benjamin Hood discovered in the nether reaches of Tibet? And would any of it be of use in this new, uneasy embrace with the bearlike Soviet Union?

With the help of the FBI, banking records had led Hale to this tiny burg at the edge of the known universe, the aptly named Concrete, Washington. Now, as he stood on the train station platform near the junction of the Skagit and Baker rivers, Hale could look uphill to a one-block downtown that slumbered under a haze of morning mist and coal smoke. With gas rationing still in effect, not much moved on the roads. The war had ended only three weeks before. But a new, more dangerous war, the OSS believed, was just beginning: with the Red Hordes of the Soviet Union. It was time to learn what Ben Hood knew and make sure nobody else could learn it.

Hale, burdened only with a briefcase, walked uphill to State Bank of Concrete. Flags and bunting from the recent VJ Day celebration still hung from houses, and no service personnel were back home yet. Yet the sense of relief, after a bad Depression and worse war, seemed as palpable as the sweet smell of the surrounding forest. The bomb had ended the thing and ushered in a whole new world. There were even rumors of turning the OSS into some new kind of permanent intelligence outfit, he'd heard. The Russians were throwing their weight around just like the Nazis had, and America was going to have to respond.

Hale knew he might be wasting his time on Benjamin Hood. The guy was a crank, giving up a family fortune to live like a recluse on some stump ranch. Hood's trip back in '38 had cost the government next to nothing (it irked Hale that he'd never gotten much credit for yoking the playboy for all the heavy lifting) and nothing had come of the Nazi expedition, near as he could tell. It was as if Tibet had swallowed the whole lot. Hood's disappearance had been small brew in a world hurtling toward total war. So Hale hadn't thought much of it—he had a war to win!—but when the Japs threw in the towel after Nagasaki, the old mystery came back. He'd received an anonymous letter raising all kinds of interesting questions. Had Hood perished in central Asia? Or had he gone to ground like some crazy hillbilly, hiding out like some kind of goddamned draft dodger to let the others do the fighting for him?

More important, had the curator found something that could be important in the coming struggle? Was Hood trying to hide some terrible secret?

Terrible secrets were what Duncan Hale liked to find.

Picking up Hood's faded trail hadn't been easy. The American Museum of Natural History had no contact since '38. His family assumed him dead, and his inheritance had passed to his brothers. There'd been brief talk of giving Hood a posthumous medal, so the department could take credit for another secret mission . . . except no one was quite sure what the mission *was* or what it had accomplished. The Germans were no help either, their archives silent on Tibet except for some enigmatic hints from people like Goebbels. Himmler was dead, a suicide, after trying to sneak by the Allies in disguise. So was most of the SS. Ancient history.

Except Duncan Hale never forgot *anything*.

He tried military records first, then Social Security, and then voter registration and Census data. No Ben Hood. It finally occurred to him to try banking records. That was a needle in a haystack, except the FBI had required reporting of abnormally large deposits to keep tabs on spies during the war. Tucked in a card drawer from late 1938 was a deposit of $10,000, a tidy sum at the time. The depositor's name was Calloway, but there was a cross-reference noted to a Caucasian whose former address was Lhasa. On a hunch, he'd called up the bank.

The deposit had been made in another name: Benjamin Hood.

Bingo.

So now he'd come out to the moss-shrouded ass of the earth to find the happy hunter himself. Hood had gone from a corner office overlooking Central Park to a shack in the armpit of the Cascade Mountains. This when you had enough sitting in the bank to buy a nice house, and an inheritance back home worthy of a Rockefeller. It didn't make sense, and Duncan Hale didn't like things that didn't make sense.

He showed his credentials to a teller. "I need the address of one of your depositors."

The bank president, a fellow named Henderson, came out to confer. A visit from a G-man to Concrete was unusual indeed.

"This Hood, he live around here?" Hale asked.

"Upriver quite a few miles. Cascade River, I understand. We never see him."

"What do you mean you never see him? Isn't this his bank?"

"He's a hermit, except there's a woman living up there, too, and a child—none of it sanctified by marriage, I'm afraid. Maybe he doesn't want us judging him. In any event, he never comes downriver. We see Miss Calloway once in a while, shopping for groceries and supplies."

"And who is Miss Calloway?"

"His . . . housekeeper. Girlfriend. They have joint custody of the account."

"Have you *ever* seen Ben Hood?"

"Why no, I haven't. I'm sure my employees have. Is there something he's done?"

"Or not done. Look, if I go upriver, can I find him?"

"I'm sure you can. Everybody knows everybody up there. Just approach carefully. Upriver folk are possessive of their privacy, and some shoot first and ask later."

"I'll be careful." He thought. "This woman—she ever talk crazy?"

"What do you mean?"

"About treasure, or knowing something secret, or having to hide things from the world?"

"She doesn't talk at all. A real tight-lip for these parts. Good-looking dame, but nobody really knows her. You think she's some kind of Axis spy?"

He put his hands up, laughing. "Don't start *that* rumor. The war's over, buddy! No, no, not a spy. Just some anomalies on a tax form." He winked.

"*What* on a tax form?"

"Mistakes. And that's just between you and me." The gossip would be from one end of Concrete to the other by suppertime, he knew, which was just what he wanted. "Thanks for the help. Your government appreciates it."

"Well." Henderson puffed proudly. "Glad to serve."

Hale picked up his briefcase. "Just one more thing. You said there was a kid?"

"Yes, a girl by rumor. Daughter, I assume. She should be in school by now, but the district hasn't seen her."

"Ah. I'll ask about that, too. There are laws." He tipped his fedora. "Good day to you, Mr. Henderson."

"And good day to you."

Hale stepped outside, breathed in the clean air, and looked at the patriotic bunting. Concrete was probably a nice place. A decent place. It was too bad about the kid.

He walked to a garage where he'd been told he could rent a car, bought a county map, and asked some directions.

Then he slipped in the front seat, opened his suit jacket, and checked the load on his .32 Colt M1903 automatic. The OSS issue was light, deadly, and small enough that it was said gangster Bonnie Parker taped one to her thigh to break Clyde out of jail. Sweet little gun.

Time to tie up loose ends.

As Hale drove off, the gas station attendant looked again at the card given by an oddly pale stranger who'd shown up in town the day before, asking where a man might rent a car. The fellow didn't rent one, but the business card came wrapped in a one-hundred-dollar bill, a staggering sum. Now the attendant mouthed the number, picked up the phone, and cranked for the operator.

He was going to report who *did* rent a car.

41

The Kunlun Mountains, Tibet
September 19, Present Day

Nine days after leaving Lhasa, the trio of Americans stiffly got out of a Land Cruiser that had been transformed from white to brown from dust and mud. There'd been three flats and one broken water pump, all patched by Sam. Pavement had turned to dirt road, and dirt to rocky track. They jounced down jumbled dry streambeds and ground through the gears to creep up snaking passes. Rominy's heart almost stopped as they crept over a rope-and-wood suspension bridge hung across a precipitous canyon, water shining a thousand feet down. Had the Germans come this way? Later, the wind cut like a knife on one particularly high pass. There were still patches of dirty snow from the winter before, and the smell of new autumn storms in the air. Beyond were a vast basin, and then the white wall of the Kunlun. Now they parked directly below those remote and lofty mountains.

To their left ran a cold river, gray with glacial silt. They'd picked up its trace where it sank into the sands on the plain. As they drove toward its source the river became loud and vigorous, originating in a waterfall that plunged hundreds of feet before running white down a slope of shattered rock. The escarpment ahead was otherwise as sheer as a fortress wall, its black rock cliffs topped by slopes of ice and snow. They'd come to a dead end.

"This is where you want to be?" Sam asked.

Jake studied his GPS unit. "If the coordinates from the documents are correct, yes. Instruments weren't as good in those days, but Hood and Calloway had navigation skills."

Their guide turned and surveyed the landscape. Behind a pitiless plain, ahead precipitous mountains, chill gray sky, and lonely wind. "Scenic. If you like eastern Wyoming."

"What's beyond that waterfall?"

"Never been here, man. I'm feeling pretty cocky I got you here at all. This is pretty intense. It's not like we can call for pizza."

"No, Sam, we cannot." He took out the binoculars and studied the cliff. "Rominy, what did Hood's satchel say about the waterfall?"

"That there was one, low on the cliff, with a canyon above it. This looks different from the drawing, Jake. The falls seem much higher. I'm not sure we're at the right place."

"We'd better be in the right place." He studied the falls, as if willing them to look like he expected. "We've come ten thousand miles to be in the right place."

There was silence. Jake was the one who had used his GPS to direct them here.

"So," Sam finally asked, "we just going to hang out? Is this what you came for?"

"We could camp by the river," Rominy said.

"I came for the history of the Kurt Raeder expedition of 1938," Jake finally said. "We're going to climb that cliff and see what's on the other side."

"You don't mean *we* the literal way, right?" Sam said. "It's like the royal *we*, meaning you?"

"We've been sitting on our asses in that Land Cruiser for nine days. The exercise will do us good. I'll lead the way."

"Jake, I can't climb that," Rominy said.

"I think I see a way up. We'll fix some ropes."

"And just what's so fascinating on the other side?" Sam asked.

Jake considered the guide before answering, debating how much to confide. "Shambhala," he revealed. "If the stories are correct."

"Shambhala!" Sam groaned. "Come on, we're not here for some Shangri-la legend, are we? I could have talked you out of that one over beer in Lhasa."

"I'll tell you when I look over the top of that waterfall."

Sam shook his head. "Tourists."

Jake smiled. "Guides. You can't get decent help these days."

"Why don't I just wait with Rominy down here?"

"It's not safe to climb alone. Besides, I feel better having us all together. We're united on this. Right, Rominy?"

She frowned, looking up the falls. "I've never felt so far from everything. Sam, is there *anything* out here?"

"No. But I'm getting paid to humor your boyfriend. He'll see for himself, we'll come back down and console ourselves with Rice Krispies Treats and Bailey's. Sugar makes everything go down."

"Gear up, Mary Poppins," Jake said.

Once more, the ever-surprising Mr. Barrow seemed to have a good idea of what he was doing. They each took two coils of line, heavy but reassuring, and a hammer with some spikes Jake called pitons. "We'll string a rope across the worst pitches. It's mostly a scramble across rubble. Won't be too bad."

And it wasn't, at first. The three of them ascended alongside the roaring plunge of the river, staying just outside the mist that coated the rocks with frost. It was mostly like climbing a steep staircase. But eventually they came to sheer "pitches," or stretches of cliff where they couldn't boulder-hop their way. Jake went ahead, driving pitons and shouting down to Sam until a length of rope was secured. That was their handrail. With it, Rominy found the courage to climb higher. The last two weeks had carried her a long way from her confined existence as cubicle girl. They'd been camping in the Tibetan wilderness, fixing tires, pouring fuel out of jerry cans, and speculating under the stars. She made love to Jake in their tent. His anticipatory happiness calmed her, and his wacky historical and scientific passions were tolerable. He was very bright. She'd fallen in love with him, too, but hadn't confessed it yet.

Nor had they taken off the rings.

"Your boyfriend looks like he's done this before," Sam remarked as they waited for Jake to lead a pitch above.

"He's climbed in the Cascades back home," she said. "For a journalist, he's a jack-of-all-trades."

"All this for a story?"

"He thinks it could make his career."

"Looks like he's got a hell of an expense account."

"He found me an inheritance. I'm helping."

"Hmph." Sam looked skeptical. "How about you?"

"How about me?"

"What do you do when you're not retracing Nazi footsteps?"

"I'm a publicist. I spend my days promoting bug-laden software that will be obsolete six months after we sell it. I'm like Dilbert."

"Oh." He unwrapped a piece of gum. "Want some?"

"No, thanks."

He put it in his mouth to chew. "How'd you two meet?"

She pulled back her filthy hair. "He kidnapped me after my car blew up."

Mackenzie looked at her questioningly, like she was joking. "Oh . . . kay."

"It's a long story."

"I guess. You know this guy well?"

"Two weeks."

"And you come all the way to Tibet with him, wear a wedding ring, and pretend to be his wife?"

"Like I said, it's a long story."

"Don't you find his Nazi crap a little weird?"

"He just likes history." Mackenzie made her defensive.

"He talks about them like they were *normal* somehow. Like he could explain them. Who does that, man? I asked him what he wrote for the paper and he was real vague. He just seems a little . . . *off.* You know? You seen his stuff?"

She was annoyed. Sam Mackenzie had no idea what had been going on. "No."

"Meet his friends? Visit the paper?"

"Trust me, we haven't had time."

"But this guy's on the level, right?"

"Hasn't he paid you well so far?" Zing!

"Well, that's the thing. Most guys your age are backpackers, roaming Asia on the cheap. They're always trying to bid me down, or trying to write a check, or cursing at the cash machine at the Jokhang for not giving them what they want, because they don't really have it. And Jake pulls out all this cash." He shook his head. "I guess that's impressive that he got you to give it to him. But unusual, too, you know?"

She flushed. "Unexpected inheritance."

"But *he* spends it."

"*We* spend it."

"Okay. I mean I'm cool with it. I just . . ."

"Just what?"

"Want to make sure you're okay."

She spread her arms. "Other than being perched on a cliff in the middle of nowhere, I'm fine, see? Sorry, I just can't talk about everything. Don't worry, it's nothing illegal. No drugs. We're looking for my great-grandpa."

"And great-grandpa was a Nazi?"

"He was *fighting* the Nazis."

"Okay, that's cool."

But it wasn't, completely, and the look he gave bothered her because it reignited her own doubts. That bullet casing. The cell phone battery. But Jake had been kind to her a hundred times this trip. Gentle. Caring. Loving. Sexy. Able. Confident. It was like a check-off list from *Cosmo*.

So why hadn't she admitted she loved him?

Because he was guarded: he only revealed what he wanted to reveal. Because he was eccentric. Because, to be honest, sometimes he seemed too good to be true; guys weren't like that. Because he'd given her his charm, she sensed, but not his heart. And because if she were honest about her *own* heart, she was here for herself, not him. It was an adventure. She was curious. She wanted to do something, to *be* something, that wasn't just as add-along to some guy.

That wasn't the same as love.

Jake called down. "Ready!" And up they went again.

In all, it took three hours. At last they neared the brink of the falls, the last scramble the steepest. Jake impatiently disappeared over the brow of the cliff, and then Sam. Wearily, Rominy dragged herself over, too. Were they about to see the oddities depicted in the satchel of diagrams?

A cold wind cooled her sweat when she stood, blowing out at her from a broken canyon. Jake was staring as if hypnotized, his arms dangling, his shoulders sagged. Sam Mackenzie had already slumped to rest on a boulder, puffing.

Above them, a ravine continued to climb toward ice and clouds, but its edges were uneven and the rock a lighter color, as if great chunks had broken loose and tumbled down. Ahead, seen through the fractured gorge, was a bowl of bright mountains, shimmering with snow, a perfect stadium of peaks. And in the middle was . . .

A lake.

The water was slate gray and opaque. From it ran the river, twisting through a broken barrier of boulders before dipping over the falls. Rominy went to where Jake was standing. He was staring, shocked. Clearly, this wasn't what he expected to find.

"There's no Shambhala, Jake." She touched his shoulder. He twitched like a wary animal.

"They dammed the canyon," he whispered.

"Who dammed the canyon?"

"They made a lake. It flooded the valley. It flooded Shambhala."

"I don't see a dam."

"We just climbed up it. It's a rock dam, an earth-fill dam, not a concrete one. Look." He pointed up to the lighter-colored rock. "They blew out the canyon walls and it came down and plugged the river. Whatever was here is underwater."

It looked like other alpine lakes she'd seen in the Cascades and Olympics, but Rominy decided not to contradict him. If he wanted to believe some kind of lost utopia was under the water, fine with her. But if the coordinates were right, they weren't going to learn more about Benjamin Hood. And Jake didn't have his scoop.

Now they could go home.

To what? How much of a couple were they, now that the quest had ended?

"You mean this happened sometime after 1938?" she clarified.

"Or even *during* 1938. Maybe this is why Hood slunk home to America and hid. Maybe he spoiled what would have been the greatest find in archaeological history." The tone was bitter.

"You mean he was embarrassed by whatever happened here?"

"I *hope* he was embarrassed, if there was a Shambhala and he drowned it."

"Maybe you could come back with scuba gear."

"Maybe." He walked back to the brow of the cliff. To the south were the plains and mountains they'd already crossed, an immensity of emptiness. Far below, their parked Land Cruiser was a tiny toy. Vultures wheeled between them and that bottom.

"So it ain't here?" Mackenzie asked. *Told you so*, he thought to himself.

Jake ignored him, looking all about. He glanced at the lake but didn't seem inclined even to scramble the final distance to its shores.

Instead, he suddenly stiffened and pointed, bringing to Rominy's mind for a moment one of Delphina Clarkson's hunting hounds.

His head turned to them and he smiled. "Smoke."

42

The Nunnery of the Closed Door, Tibet
September 19, Present Day

The nunnery that Jake had spotted was a hunkered quadrangle built like an old Tibetan fort. A stone outer wall twenty feet high grew organically out of the rocks on a steep ridgetop that jutted like a tongue from the Kunlun Mountains. The wall undulated with the terrain to enclose a temple, sleeping cells, and kitchen. The wall and utility buildings were gray, while the rectangular, flat-roofed temple was the red ocher of the Potala Palace. The buildings turned inward from the world—all doors and windows opened onto the courtyard, not the harsh environment—but prayer flags rose gaily to the apex of a *darchen* like lines to a Maypole. Golden finials marked the temple's four corners.

It was from this refuge, so earth-toned that it was invisible from any distance, that smoke emanated.

"What the devil are Buddhists doing way out here, Sam?" Jake asked their guide.

"Contemplating the universe." He shrugged. "Usually the monasteries are near villages. I've never heard of this one."

"An unlikely location," Jake murmured. "Unless there *is* a Shambhala."

Getting to the nunnery was a tricky traverse, halfway down the rock dam they'd already climbed and then sideways to meet a goat track that led to the protruding ridge. A squall swept down from the mountains, first blowing gritty dust and then, when the sky darkened, rain mixed with snow. The dust and ice bits stung. The Americans, hoods up, looked like pilgrims themselves.

The gate, so old its wood seemed petrified, looked firm enough to withstand a battering ram. But it was the design upon them that startled Rominy. Strips of brass had been laid to make a pattern of interconnected squares, woven together so that each led to the other. It vaguely reminded Rominy of an Escher drawing of endless staircases leading up and down at the same time, an illusion that tricked the senses, but that's not why she found it arresting.

It was the same pattern etched onto the gold coins left in Benjamin Hood's safety deposit box.

"What does that symbol mean?" Rominy asked.

"That? Infinity," Sam said. "You see it everywhere in Tibet, just like you see swastikas at times. They'll take symbols like that and weave them into more complicated ones like a sun wheel."

Jake raised his eyebrows and gave her a glance. Rominy shivered in the damp.

Hood's souvenir gold coins weren't a clue to a North Cascades gold mine. They were a reminder of this nunnery. A sign they'd come to the right place.

The Americans were wondering how to contact the residents inside when the gate suddenly swung open of its own accord and scarlet-clad nuns beckoned them into the courtyard that promised shelter from the wind. A returning sun made the puddles on the cobblestones shine and steam.

The two young women who greeted the travelers were not at all surprised at their visit. From this aerie they could have seen the Land Cruiser's plume of dust for miles and followed the Americans' antlike assault up the rock dam. Yet so artfully was the nunnery situated that it was invisible from the base of the waterfall. It watched, without being seen.

The heavy gate swung shut behind them.

The nuns spoke and, as always, Rominy struggled even to pick out meaningful syllables. *Dga' bsu zhu sgo brgyab.*

"I think it was, 'Welcome to the Closed Door,'" Sam said.

"But they opened it."

"And closed it again," Jake said.

After the hike and rain, Rominy was trembling with cold. The nuns beckoned them onward to the temple. Inside, a single shaft of light shone down from a clerestory at the ceiling. The perimeter was shadowy, lit only by the flames that burned in lamps of yellow yak butter. The lamps weren't enough to make it really warm, but it was drier and warmer than outside. Rominy shivered and a young nun slid a red woolen cloak over her shoulders, which she gratefully wrapped around her. A huge, bronze-colored Buddha, the bright paints of its decoration faded by decades of time and lamp smoke, rose toward the clerestory, its flesh as round and robust as a planet. In front was an altar with seven sacred silver bowls of water and sculptures carved from butter, as transitory as life itself. To the side was a pillared seating area, the wooden benches softened by pillows. They were directed to sit.

"*Kha lan,*" Sam offered. *Thanks.*

Steaming cups were brought. Rominy sipped. It was milky broth, strange, but pleasantly hot and rich.

"Butter tea," Sam said. "Yak butter has the protein and fat to keep you going. Some people can't stand it, however."

Jake had put his aside.

"Anything warm is heavenly," Rominy said. "I'm so discouraged. We've come so far for nothing."

"Not necessarily," Jake said. "Why is this nunnery even here?"

"Yeah, maybe we came for this experience," said Sam. "These nuns are friendlier than Scientologists trolling for converts at a singles bar. We lucked out."

Their eyes adjusted to the gloom. Nuns were silently stitching and weaving. Great skeins of yarn—yak wool, she guessed—were heaped in corners. The colors were brilliant, and she wondered if the handiwork was sold in Lhasa to support the nunnery. She assumed they must have gardens or fields somewhere, but how did they get even the most basic tools to such a remote place? Were there no monks?

After tea, the day fading, the Americans were beckoned with gentle pantomime to rooms in the adjoining dormitory. Each cell had two cots, and Jake and Sam were given one room and Rominy another, the nuns making it plain they were expected to spend the night. Supper was barley cake *tsampa*s and dumpling *momo*s, and then *thugpa*, a noodle soup. The flavors were plain and pastelike to Western palates, but the trio ate greedily, the nuns pleased with their appetite. Everything was dim and medieval. There was no electricity, only butter lamps. When the Americans finished the nuns withdrew and they were left to sleep on cots of woven leather, the only mattress layers of thick woolen blankets. Rominy thought the strangeness would keep her awake.

The next thing she knew, it was morning.

They were given broad bowls of warm water to wash in, and then led outside to a courtyard bright with high-altitude sunshine. The snowy crowns of the Kunlun Mountains soared above the nunnery roof. Vultures, majestic from a distance, wheeled through the vault of heaven.

"Sky burial," Sam whispered as she watched them. "Traditional Tibetan practice is to dismember the dead and put them on a rack for the vultures to devour. It's considered divine recycling."

"It seems appropriate here," Rominy said. "Like letting them go to the sky through the birds. There's more sky here than in Seattle, Sam. Closer sky."

"You're beginning to see why I stayed."

She wondered if Jake minded that she was talking more to Sam. The guide's questions, while uncomfortable, had made her feel he cared. Her boyfriend didn't seem to notice. It would have been selfishly satisfying if he had, but Jake seemed a million miles away with his thoughts. He dreamed of lost cities.

A hooded woman, head bent, was cross-legged on the paving, and they were directed to sit on the stones before her. The Americans awkwardly crossed their legs, several nuns in a semicircle behind. Then the central figure lifted her head, hood falling away. Like the others, her skull was close-cropped, its iron-gray hinting at her age. Her face was lined but kindly, a regal grandmother's face, with the high cheekbones and deep-set eyes of her people.

"My name is Amrita," she said in accented but fluent English. "You have come many miles to the Closed Door."

"You speak our language?" Jake asked in surprise.

"We cared for an American generations ago and decided others might eventually be back. Your return has been foretold. The American taught us some of her tongue, and we're not entirely isolated. I was educated in Lhasa and Beijing."

"She? So it was Beth Calloway and not Benjamin Hood?" Rominy asked.

"Yes."

"But where was my great-grandfather?"

"Shambhala. We never met him."

This was disturbing news.

"Then Shambhala is really here?" Jake leaned forward.

"Where is *here*, Mr. Barrow? Yes, we looked at your identity while you were sleeping. Is paradise a place or a state of mind? Is the journey to reach it an outward one or inward?"

He sat back, disappointed. "I know you're on a spiritual journey, but we're on a physical one. Rominy's great-grandfather and, it appears, her great-grandmother, came here and saw *something*. We climbed to where we thought Shambhala might be and found only a lake. If it doesn't exist, so be it. But I want to know if it existed for *real*, not just in fable."

"Your definition of reality and mine are not the same." She looked at them closely, but not unkindly, in turn. "But I'll show you another door to satisfy your curiosity. The real Closed Door may or may not open. It may or may not give you what you need to find."

"Sometimes not finding is as important as finding," Rominy said. "You need things to end."

"Yes, beginning and endings. The Western goal, the Eastern illusion. Come."

They entered the temple again, butter lamps flickering, the air tanged with incense and smoke, the Buddha vast and hazy as a dream. Amrita led them around the statue. At the back of the temple was an ancient black iron door set in a wall of stone. It looked crudely hammered but immensely strong. From her cloak she took a ring of big, medieval-looking keys and inserted one in the lock. It wouldn't turn.

She addressed Jake. "This is the first Closed Door, Mr. Barrow. We never have occasion to open it, and so the lock is rusty. Do you have strong fingers?"

"Strong enough to get me this far." He wrenched, there was a grind and a clunk, and the metal door was pulled open, squealing on its hinges. Even though the temple itself was chilly, the air that wafted out at them was noticeably colder and moist. Their breath fogged.

"We've been the gatekeepers for two hundred generations. But what we guard is very different now. Do you have electric torches?"

"Yes."

"Then descend." She looked at Jake. "Be careful what you seek."

"I don't seek it for myself."

They stepped forward. On the other side of the door, stairs hewn out of mountain rock led downward in a spiral, like a castle tower. It was utterly dark below.

"I must close the door behind you to keep out the draft," Amrita said. "Knock when you wish to return." And with that the iron door swung shut, shutting with a booming clang. They jumped.

"Well, that's cozy," Sam muttered. "This feels like Frankenstein's castle, and she's Frau Blucher."

"You're a very skeptical guide, Sam," Jake said.

"Lapsed. Converts turned doubters are the worst. I came for enlightenment and got statuary and yak tea. I think I'm homesick."

"I'm paying you enough to get you home."

"And you hired me to take you as far from it as we can get."

"Well, I trust her," Rominy said.

"You trust everyone," said Sam.

They crept down, their flashlights providing a fan of light. In places they passed lovely carvings in the surrounding stone: a graceful script reminiscent of Tibetan—"It's not the same," Sam informed them—entwined with flowers, beasts, strange machines, and large-headed people in flowing robes. The bas-relief gave a three-dimensional quality so that the plants seemed to be blossoming from rock.

"These carvings weren't done by nuns," Jake said. "Shambhala is real."

"So who did do them?" Sam asked.

"Ancients or aliens who knew more than we do. Don't you think? I like the vines and trees. The Greeks believed we began as happy plants and devolved into our unhappy animal and human form, getting farther from the divine as we did so. The farther back you went, the better things were, they thought. The SS who came to Tibet thought that, too, that the distant past wasn't something we escaped but a paradise of adventure and power we'd lost."

"I don't know," Sam said. "An ancestral vegetable sounds even worse than an ancestral monkey."

"There's something peaceful in being a carrot," Rominy said.

"Not on a salad bar."

Then the walls would get plain again.

Suddenly one wall disappeared, and the Americans found themselves on an exposed stair at the side of a huge shaft a hundred feet across. It rose higher than their flashlight beams could probe. There were dark openings on the other side, and bats fluttered when Jake banged the edge of his flashlight on stone.

"Ventilation shaft," he guessed. "Bats means there has to be an opening above. This was for Shambhala, my friends."

"It's huge," said Rominy.

"Which means Shambhala was huge."

"I smell water," Sam said. "We're going to hit your lake, Barrow."

They carefully wound down the shaft, the staircase having no railing to keep them from falling. Then it wormed into the mountain again. A horizontal passageway ran on into darkness like the shaft of a mine. More stairs continued down.

"Down first," said Jake.

The stairs ended a hundred steps farther at water, dark and still. There was no landing. The steps just continued into the deep.

"It's the lake," Jake confirmed. "He drowned Shambhala."

"*Who* drowned it?" Rominy asked.

"Your great-grandpa."

"But why?"

He shook his head. "Who knows?"

"Look at the dark lines on the walls," Sam said. "You can see how the water rises and falls with the seasons."

Jake looked frustrated. "We need a submarine."

"Into *that*? Better you than me, buddy."

"This is as big as Machu Picchu or Angkor Wat. We'll do it eventually."

"Maybe Grandpa made the lake to bury whatever's down there," Rominy said. "Maybe it was something dangerous or evil."

"Or something invaluable." Jake sighed. "It's still a find. I've still got a hot news story. Benjamin Hood drowns a city. Is that why he became a hermit?"

"Maybe he tried to hide what he found," Rominy said.

They were quiet, the water opaque. Then Jake pointed back the way they'd come. "There's still that horizontal shaft. Last chance. Let's check that out."

They climbed back to the passageway and followed it. The shaft ended abruptly at a massive door.

Again, a riot of decoration, but this time cast instead of carved, as if the door were made of bronze. The material was dark and swallowed light, however, and was unlike anything they'd ever felt. It wasn't quite like stone, wood, metal, or plastic.

"Another dead end," Sam said.

Jake seemed transfixed. "Not necessarily. Doors open."

"There's no handle or keyhole," Rominy said.

Jake let his fingers trace the vines sculpted into the door. "Or it's a different kind of lock." He followed them down, a tangle of flowers, to a bas-relief of an anatomically correct carving of a heart. An artery was a tube with an opening like a flower, as thin as a fine vase but firm as steel.

"This is weird," Sam said, his palm to the door. "Do you feel that? This substance kind of tingles."

Rominy put her hand on the door. It seemed to vibrate in response, like a purring kitten. "It almost feels like it's alive," she agreed.

"Which raises the question of just what life is," Jake said. "At what point does matter, allied with energy, become life? Is energy itself life? Do you know our brain's chemistry throws off enough electricity to power a small lightbulb?"

"So talk to it, Barrow. Open, Sesame."

"Wait, I recognize these designs," Rominy said. "This door was drawn in the papers from Hood's satchel. Maybe *this* is the way into Shambhala. The Closed Door! Why would Benjamin Hood have drawn this?"

Jake nodded and pointed. "Blood lock," he said, pointing to the carving of a heart.

"Blood what?" asked Sam.

"According to my research, the Shambhala of legend devised a means by which doors could be opened only by a specified individual, who was identified by drops of his or her blood. The Germans who came in '38 brought a vial of blood with them for just that purpose. They didn't understand how such a thing could work, but today we know about DNA and how each of us has a unique genetic code. What's interesting is that access could thus become hereditary; a descendant's blood might contain the very same key." He looked at Rominy. "A great-granddaughter, perhaps." He slung off his pack and stooped to put it on the floor, groping inside. His tone had become businesslike. "Which explains, Rominy, why you're really here."

"What do you mean?"

He pulled out a knife and slid the blade clear from its hard scabbard. It was a wicked-looking, twin-edged weapon with an eagle on the handle and twin lightning bolts on the pommel. Some German words were etched onto the blade.

"What the fuck?" said Sam.

"I mean that I hope we found what we've been looking for after all." Jake looked up at the woman he said he loved with a face drained of all expression. "I'm afraid I need your blood."

43

Shambhala, Tibet
September 20, Present Day

"A re you *crazy?*" Rominy was looking at the blade
with wide eyes. It wasn't a hunting knife, it was a
dagger, the kind you used to kill people.

"Let's cool the jets, here, Barrow," Sam said, his
hands raised in alarm. "I think you're overdosing on
the exotic culture, man."

Jake's face was dead as a zombie, his tone clinical.
"And I think we've finally found what we hired you to
help us find, Sam." He used the other hand to pull a gun
from the backpack and Rominy gasped. "This is only a
.22, but I assure you that at this range I have the skill to
make it lethal. So you can stand in the corner there and
shut up, Mackenzie, or I can shut you up in my own efficient way." He had the remoteness of a lab technician.

Sam took a step back. "Just don't hurt the girl, bro."

"I'm not your brother. But she's the great-granddaughter we've been seeking."

"Why?" It was all Rominy could think to say. The blade looked as big as a sword.

"We won't know until we open it, will we? But someone very, very important thinks some *thing* that is very, very important was hidden here. Which is why I had to find and seduce *you*."

"You're going to cut her for a newspaper story, for crying out loud?"

"Are you both stupid enough to think I was really a journalist? I've never been in a newsroom in my life."

Rominy's mind was reeling, her eyes hypnotized by the bright dagger blade. Was everything a lie?

"If I'd allowed you a way to contact the *Seattle Times*, Rominy, you'd have learned in a minute they'd never heard of me," he said matter-of-factly.

"So you *did* take the battery from my cell phone."

"I used a magnet to disrupt it first, and removed the battery later. I've appreciated that you've given me the benefit of the doubt, since you've had quite legitimate suspicions. Fortunately, we've been in a bit of a hurry and you've been more resourceful at solving Hood's puzzles than I ever hoped. The Fourth Reich will acknowledge your contribution someday."

"The *Fourth* Reich?" Sam asked.

"Try, try again." Jake smiled at his little joke.

Their guide was struggling with which question to ask first. "How in hell did you get a pistol in Tibet?" he finally managed.

"By spending four thousand of my girlfriend's dollars. Outrageous markups in the Jokhang, but it's true, with cash enough, you can buy anything. The bullets cost ten dollars a piece. Can you believe that? Bandits."

"So think hard before you shoot one."

"I think very hard about everything I do." He was in a squat, gun in one hand, knife in the other. "Now, hold out your hand, Rominy. It's very sharp, so it really won't hurt."

"What is this really all about?" she asked, all certainty lost, all balance undone. Had it all been an act, even their lovemaking? Had she fallen for some lunatic Nazi? Who, then, was the skinhead in the Cascade Mountains? Once more, nothing seemed to make sense.

"Power." And before she could react he seized her wrist, jerked her to him, and sliced her palm with the SS dagger. Now she saw the words on the blade: *Meine Ehre Heist Treue.* It stung. Blood ran with alarming quickness from the wound. He stood and kissed her, quickly. "To make it all better." Then he matter-of-factly tucked the dagger in his belt and brought out a tin backpacking cup, catching the flow. She thought she might faint. When the cup was full, like thick burgundy, he brusquely shoved her backward toward Sam and set the cup aside. He reached inside the pack again and pulled out some bandages, throwing them at the guide. "Bind the wound, Mackenzie."

Then, picking up the pistol and keeping a wary eye on them, he went to the door, squatted again, and started pouring Rominy's blood into the carved artery of the heart.

"What are you doing, Barrow?" Sam asked.

"Watch and see. I don't know how much blood it will take, but we'll do it by the cup. Everything *is* alive, if you look at it the right way. Or rather, life itself is a kind of conceit, an illusion of energy, once you realize all is one."

A glow began to emanate from the rock. There was a clunk, a whir, and a line appeared to divide the solid slab. And then with a grind, it slowly slid apart.

There was a small chamber beyond, blank and featureless. It led nowhere.

"You cut Rominy to find a closet?" Sam asked.

Jake ignored him. Leaning against the back wall was a translucent staff. No light emanated from it but it was a beautifully sensual thing, smooth like colored glass, and its surface had subtle bas-relief of beasts and warriors.

"*Heil* Hitler," Jake whispered.

"Seriously, dude, this isn't cool. You need help, man."

"On the contrary, Mr. Mackenzie, I'm one of the few sane people on this planet."

"But you lied," Rominy said. "About everything."

"Not everything. I did save you from dying with your car. But I knew it was wired to explode. I did lie about who I am, but I didn't lie about who *you* are, and taught you more about yourself than you ever knew. I didn't tell you everything about what I was looking for, but I was absolutely sincere in bringing you to Tibet. I needed your DNA, Rominy, and you can feel satisfied you played a role in history."

"There were never any skinheads chasing us on the freeway, were there? You pretended, and shoved my head down, and fired that shot through the window yourself. With that pistol."

"Very good. I used a silencer. How did you know?"

"I found the bullet casing behind the seat."

"Ah. I looked for it several times."

"But you needed the safety deposit box. You needed me for that."

"That, and your blood. You *are* the correct descendant of the one who apparently sealed this chamber."

"You came for that rod like we talked about on the plane?"

"That rod, or staff, is a necessary first step in reconstituting Shambhala. As you've seen, the original city is quite wet, and even if we did have scuba equipment, I'm sure seventy years of immersion hasn't helped whatever machinery is down there. But science has advanced a great deal since 1938, and some of us are prepared to become Shambhalans ourselves. You have to understand that conventional history is a monstrous distortion of the evolutionary goals of National Socialism. Now we can finish what we started, and when we do, our species will realize its potential."

"Finish the Holocaust?" Sam asked.

"Finish purification, once we regain power. End global warming, stop population growth by the wrong people, and make room for the right. All it takes is organization, discipline, and will."

"Barrow, listen to yourself," Sam groaned. "Hitler couldn't do it with most of Europe under his boot. Germany's gone liberal. It's too late."

"On the contrary, it is finally time. The pair of you can take satisfaction in playing a role in the greatest experiment since the Manhattan Project."

"Jake, please," Rominy pleaded. "This makes no sense. If there was really Vril, wouldn't scientists have found it by now?"

"What's Vril?" Sam asked.

"This fantasy power source. He thinks Shambhala used it. But the city is gone, Jake. Drowned. Hitler lost the war. *Please* put the gun down."

"The resurrection will begin in the Camelot of the SS, my dear. Beyond that, I think the details are over your head. You already know more than is good for you, or rather me."

"So you're going to *kill* me?"

"There's one other thing I didn't lie about: I *was* falling in love with you, even as I used you. You're pretty, you're smart, and you're more than just a good lay."

She was shaking with fear and fury. "What a flatterer you are."

"I'm not comfortable shooting you. Instead, I'm going to have you step inside that chamber there."

"If you shut the door we'll suffocate," Sam said.

"Not if the nuns find you in time. So the answer to your question, Rominy, is no. I'm not a murderer."

But he *was* crazy. So Rominy lunged.

Her goal was the knife or gun, but her target was simply Jake Barrow, all the lies he'd told and all the manipulations he'd fostered. Her vision had gone red, furious at herself and furious at him, furious for letting herself stay off-balance while this maniac led her like a sheep. The fury consumed her; she didn't know anger and loathing could be so great. So she sprang with rage she didn't know she was capable of, and struck with explosive frustration. Jake pitched back in surprise, one hand on his knife and the other holding the gun, and they both went over, hitting the stone floor hard.

"Get him, Sam!" she screamed. She clawed at Jake's face.

Then the pistol went off, a pop, and she hesitated for just a fraction of a second.

The butt of the gun struck her temple, and her vision blurred.

Meanwhile, Sam Mackenzie was thrown back hard, grunting. "Jesus fuck! He shot me!" He sounded unbelieving.

Barrow twisted and threw Rominy off—he was strong as an animal—and leaped up to kick her in the stomach. She was gutted of wind.

"That was really stupid," he snarled. "Now you've killed your friend."

Curling in agony, she twisted to look. Sam had been shoved by the bullet against the back wall of the chamber and had slid down, his mouth gasping for air. The front of his shirt had a spreading red splotch. Her eyes blurred with tears, a torment of fury, pain, remorse, and helplessness.

Barrow lifted her like a sack of potatoes and pitched her into the little chamber against Sam, who yelped with pain. Then he grabbed the oddly translucent staff and stepped outside.

"Unfortunately for you, your blood doesn't open the chamber from the inside. There's no lock there." He clicked the staff against the edge of the portal and it began to slowly slide shut. He held the pistol on her. "I *do* care for you, Rominy—I've enjoyed our time together—so I really don't want to shoot you. I think this is better closure."

"Don't trap me here!" she screamed. "I'd rather die!"

"Too late."

The portal slammed shut.

They were locked in total blackness.

44

Shambhala, Tibet
September 20, Present Day

Jake Barrow trudged to the top of the stairs—he couldn't trot at this altitude—and pounded on the temple door to be let back into the nunnery. There was no latch on his side. He had enough C4 plastic explosive to blow his way out if necessary, and the pistol to cow the nuns, but the last thing he wanted was a running retreat from a mob of angry Buddhist women. A massacre would make it hard to escape Tibet. He had what he'd come for, and with Shambhala swamped there could be no more investigation until The Fellowship triumphed. Best now to slip quietly away to the Land Cruiser and head to Germany.

He waited impatiently for what seemed like an eon but was probably only a minute, and then there was a clank, a squeal, and the door creaked open. Even the dim light of the temple seemed bright after the gloom of the descending stairway.

"Mr. Barrow." Amrita bowed. "Did you find what you hoped?"

"I think so, but there's been an accident, sister." He was a good actor, and trusted that his face showed appropriate concern. "Rominy and Sam are trying to open some kind of door, but Sam's hurt. Rominy is looking after him while I fetch our first-aid kit from the Land Cruiser. Are there some young nuns you could send to help?"

Amrita's eyes fixed on the staff. "You found your desire."

"Yes. But Sam is more important."

"Perhaps we could use your new rod to help make a litter?"

"I'm afraid the ancient glass might break."

"Ah. You'll share your discovery with the Chinese authorities?"

"Of course." He smiled to mask his impatience. "Please, Sam is in pain. I've got to get some pills." These shaven-headed women were loopy as loons with religious mysticism and thwarted desire. It shouldn't be hard to lie his way past them.

But Amrita still blocked his way. "I see you're impatient, Mr. Barrow, but sometimes it's better to pause and meditate about your course."

"Not when a friend is injured."

She held his eye for a moment, his gaze sliding uncomfortably away, and then stood aside. "Of course. I'll take some acolytes and look to your companions while you hurry."

"Bless you. Good-bye." The ring holding the key to the iron door was hung nearby.

While Amrita called out for help he rounded the Buddha, feeling squeezed by its presence, its consciousness concentrated inside instead of out. No Nazi statue would ever pose in such a pensive, passive, decadent way. Then he hid in shadow. He needed as much time as possible.

Three other young nuns appeared with bandages, cloths, and what looked like their own herbal medicines. The nuns lit lamps small enough to carry by hand and, Amrita leading, disappeared down the winding stairs.

Jake slipped back, looked quickly about, and slammed the iron door shut, locking it with the ring of keys. These he pocketed. Then he hurried to his room, scooped up his backpack, and crossed the nunnery courtyard. A nun said something to him in Tibetan and he tensed, ready to draw and shoot her through the eye if he had to, the horror of it making the others hesitate. His hand curled on the grip. But while he didn't understand Tibetan, he did know one name.

"Amrita?" He held his other hand palm out in a gesture of confusion and nodded toward the gate.

The nun shook her head as if she didn't know.

He nodded as if searching and was past her, out the gate, and down the mountain, cold wind snapping at his clothes. He hurried to the plain where the Land Cruiser waited, keys still in the ignition. Even if they realized where Amrita was trapped, it would take them hours to pry that iron door back open.

He'd put the pieces in motion. And he hadn't killed anyone, he told himself, not yet. Even when surprised by Rominy's tackle, he had aimed very carefully.

Rominy's tomb was absolutely dark, absolutely hard, and absolutely silent, except for Sam's labored breathing. Terror was held at bay only by her mental paralysis; she was in shock at her own catastrophic misjudgment. Why had she followed *anyone* into the bowels of Tibet? Because of vanity, curiosity at her own heritage and importance, and belief that Jake Barrow had fallen hard for her. It had been the full-blown fairy tale, a kind of adventurous elopement complete with fake wedding ring.

What a fool she was.

The jewelry burned on her finger and she tugged it off, hurling it against the closed door.

It made a little clink as it fell.

She was going to suffocate and no one would even know where she died.

"Mu-thur-*fucker*!" Sam coughed, groaning. "I can't believe that lunatic shot me."

"It doesn't matter, Sam," Rominy said dully. "He locked us in. We're both going to die."

"It matters to *me*."

Of course. Her guide was *shot*, and she was just sitting here, feeling sorry for herself. Attention, Kmart shopper. There's a man bleeding to death right next to you.

"I'm sorry, I just feel so *dumb*. . . . Where are you hit, Sam? Can we stop the bleeding?"

He coughed again. "He hit me in the most vital part."

"Your heart?"

"My iPhone."

"What?"

"It was in my shirt pocket, under my jacket. The bastard just plugged two hundred dollars' worth of hardware, bruised a rib or two, and made me feel like I've been kicked by a mule."

"You mean the bullet didn't go in?"

"I can feel it squashed in the ruins. All my contacts were in there."

"You mean you're not dying?"

"You just said I *am* going to die."

"Well, yes, but from lack of oxygen or water, not bleeding. This is good news, isn't it?" It was odd how his survival cheered her.

"Good news *how*?"

"I don't want to suffocate alone."

He was dead silent for a moment. Then he barked a laugh, a gasping chuckle, and then coughed. "Ow! Jeez, that hurts. Oh, man, what a crazy chick you are. No wonder you wound up with losers like me and Jake Nazi. Geez, I'm glad to accommodate you, Rominy. That will be another three hundred dollars, please."

"Sam, I'm really, really sorry. I don't understand any of this. I wasn't with Jake on this at *all*. I mean, I was *with* him, but I thought he was a reporter and we were on this treasure hunt. I got . . . greedy, I think. I wanted to matter. And he babbled about atom smashers and funny little strings and it all seemed to make . . . sense. Until it didn't."

"I've heard of getting dumped, but man, that guy is *cold*. Why do women have such bad taste in men?"

"Because we hope." But what had she even been hoping for? Excitement. Purpose. Love. Oh, God, how she *ached*.

They were quiet for a moment. Then Sam spoke again. "So what's with the stick he grabbed? Is it a light saber, or what?"

"A magic wand, he called it. A wizard's staff. He thinks ancient people knew about particle physics and could do advanced science we'd think was magic."

"So now he's a sorcerer?"

"My guess is he's fetching for somebody else. If they really knew how such a thing works, why would they need an old one? I'll bet he's taking it somewhere to study. He wants to see if they have this power called Vril from Shambhala."

"Man, I must be one lousy guide. That's why I draw the lunatics."

"At least you try."

"That's supposed to make me feel better?"

"I think trying to do good counts. Trying to do bad, counts bad."

"I'm just doing this because I ran out of trekking money. College dropout, drifter, slacker. But I speak a little Tibetan and here I am. Locked in Shambhala's bowel."

They were quiet. "Should we stop talking to conserve oxygen?" Rominy finally asked.

"If we do that, I'll start to cry. No, better to curse that sonofabitch to the final breath. Maybe if we try hard enough, we can levitate our way out of here."

"If only that were true." But she decided to *try*, to not just wish but *pray*, to see if thoughts really could somehow affect the tons of rock hemming them in. So she concentrated, calling on the help of every Catholic saint she could remember, and Buddha to boot.

Nothing happened. It was as dark and confining as ever.

She could hear Sam wheezing like an old man.

She could feel the throb of her heart in her temples.

And then there was a clunk, a whir, and the door locking them in split in half and the soft, flickering light of carried butter lamps found its way inside. A miracle? Prayers answered? They blinked, from both the light and tears.

"Who's there?"

A tall, slender, robed woman was silhouetted in the doorway. "It's Amrita, Rominy. We came to let you out."

They stood, balancing against the wall and then stumbling into the arms of the nuns. Rominy was shaking with deliverance, her mind whirling. Sam's shirt was blotched with red.

"But how could you open it? He said it was a blood lock. He said it could only be opened with my blood." She lifted her crudely bandaged hand.

"Or the blood of your ancestors." Amrita smiled and lifted a vial. "Mr. Barrow never thought to ask if we'd kept something like this."

"But you've never used it?"

"We were told to wait, for you. Now that Mr. Barrow is gone, we've got a letter that's been waiting for you for a very long time."

"A letter?"

"I think it's time you finally got some answers."

45

Hood's Cabin, Cascade Mountains, United States
September 8, 1945

When Beth Calloway pulled into the weedy yard of her cabin hermitage, ten thousand miles from where the nightmare had begun, the gas gauge on the '29 Ford Woody was hovering on empty. The truck's panels were stained and mossy, its bed holding only her backpack. No matter. It was interesting what didn't matter when the end was finally near. They'd come sooner than she'd hoped, later than she'd feared. Once she read about the atomic bombings, she knew they'd want more magic. The world had gone nuts. She'd done her best, and now it was in God's hands.

Whatever God really was.

She eased herself out from behind the wheel and stood, her knees almost buckling. Duncan Hale had been quick and she'd been quicker, but the bastard had still put the bullet in her gut that changed everything. She'd wrapped a girdle of bandages around her waist and worn a pea jacket to hide the bleeding so her neighbor Margaret wouldn't be spooked any more than she already was . . . but Christ on a Crutch it hurt! Perversely, Beth smiled at the pain.

She'd known a man like Benjamin Hood was bad news.

And she'd still fly him anywhere, if she still had a plane.

Limping, she crossed the yard and stumped up onto the porch, wincing as she did so. She wished she still had the pistol, for comfort if nothing else, but she'd had to entrust it to Margaret to add to the other things in the safety deposit box. She couldn't fight anymore anyway.

"I'm moving, Gertie—moving back to Nebraska tonight," she lied to her friend. "You tell 'em you're just running an errand for me, and don't let 'em see the gun when you lock it in the bank." She'd rehearsed these instructions many times in her own head. "Then you get my kid down to Seattle and leave her with the Sisters until I can come back. That hundred dollars will more than cover it, I know."

"But why can't *you* do it, Beth?" Margaret had wailed. She wasn't the strongest of women, but there hadn't been time for a better choice. Margaret was just five miles down the road, and Beth dared not risk more time or blood loss. Poor little Sadie, short for Palisade, would likely wind up in an orphanage no matter who she picked, but that was a better chance for safety than she had here. It broke Beth's heart to hand her over, but it was a relief as well. Would it ever make a difference? That was in God's hand, too.

"And you mail that letter. That's the most important of all. You *mail* that. You hear?"

"I will, Beth." Her voice quavered. She was alarmed at the pallor of Calloway's complexion. What trouble had she brought here? Why this sudden run back to her family? She'd always been a little fascinated by Beth Calloway, but a little afraid, too. "When you going to come back for Sadie?"

"When I finish what I have to do."

But you didn't get back. Not from eternity.

Beth knew the end had finally come that morning, when Duncan Hale had driven up in the pale light of predawn. His hair was greasy from lack of washing, his face city-pale, and his suit looked about as appropriate as a hickory shirt and caulk boots on Wall Street. But he'd skipped up her deck slick as Eliot Ness, badge out and hand in one jacket pocket, the snout of his little pistol poking against the fabric like a tiny erection.

Girl's gun, that's what Beth had thought. She'd slipped Ben's heavy .45 automatic in her backpack before she opened the door.

Hale had been arrogant as snot, informing her that he was a by-god-genuine government G-man of some agency or other—who could tell which one, since Roosevelt and Truman had spawned all those bureaucracies?—and that he was looking for one Benjamin Grayson Hood, a special agent who'd gone missing for uh, seven years.

"You haven't found him in seven years, city boy?"

"I have now, sweetheart, haven't I? Or do you want to go to jail?"

She'd shrugged. "Sure, I can show you Ben. Or rather, what's left of him. But that's not what you really want, is it? Aren't you after what he *found*?"

"I'm after both. Benjamin Hood has a lot of questions to answer. It's a matter of national security, Miss Calloway. We live in a dangerous world. A very dangerous world. Hitler was bad, but Stalin is going to be worse. If there's something that might help America, Uncle Sam has a right to it."

"Does that include paying for that right?"

The G-man smirked. "Mr. Hood volunteered to bear most of the expense of his expedition himself. Nothing has changed that arrangement."

"He never paid *me*, you know. I flew him there."

"I can help you file the necessary paperwork for possible compensation." He glanced around. "We'll have to do it downriver. We'd need a typewriter."

"I got all day."

"You take me to Hood first."

She looked him up and down. "He's a bit reclusive. It's up a mountain and down a mine. No offense, but you aren't dressed to even trek across my yard."

"He lives in a mine?"

"It's safer that way."

Hale looked suspicious. "Is there a trail?"

"Miner's trail."

"Then don't worry how I'm dressed, Miss Calloway."

"How do you know I'm not a Mrs.?"

"I checked the records before I came. *All* the records."

She'd even fixed him breakfast before they went, thinking over what she had to do, and not liking the way he eyed Sadie so intently. She'd have run the child down to Gertie then, but she couldn't risk him knowing where the child was in case things didn't go as planned.

"Sadie, you stay in the cabin here and play while Mama goes up the mountain with this man. Understand?"

The girl nodded. The seven-year-old had been alone before and was precociously independent. "When will you be home?"

"By lunch, I hope. If I'm not, you fix yourself a peanut butter sandwich. Just stay here and don't open the door to anybody or anything. You want to be a cupcake for a black bear?" It was a running joke between them.

Sadie giggled. "No, Mama! Is the suit man a friend?"

"No, honey. Just a man."

She'd turned so Sadie couldn't see her cry. It spooked her, every time she looked into the child's eyes.

Then they drove down the brushy lane, Sadie at the window watching them go.

Hale was in shape, she'd give him that. He'd kept up with her brisk stride up the crude trail in country that stood on end. And even city boy Hale had marveled when they came over the rise and first saw Eldorado, wiping his face on his handkerchief as he viewed the glorious panorama of the North Cascades. Then they'd cut downhill on the eastern side, carefully working over to the mouth of the mine. It was halfway up the cliff face, with a bank of old tailings providing a crude ramp.

"What is this place?" he asked.

"Old gold mine. Probably didn't produce much more than cheap copper. Nobody's going to work it in today's economy, so it's a good hidey-hole."

Cautiously, he entered. "Hello?"

There was no answer.

He turned. "I'm warning you, Miss Calloway, my superiors know exactly where I am. If this is any kind of an ambush, the entire weight of the United States government will come down on you like a ton of bricks."

She looked around. "Yeah, I can see 'em."

He hesitated.

She smiled, an effort. "Go on, city boy. I'll show you what you came for."

They walked back into the shaft for a hundred yards. There was an oasis of light ahead, coming from some kind of hole above. Except for a couple of rusting tools and a pool of drip water under the vertical shaft, the mine was empty.

"Where's Hood?"

She gestured with her head. "There." A satchel dangled from one of the old mining timbers, wrapped tight in oilskins to keep out water and animals.

"Is this some kind of joke?"

"You ever wonder what we are, Mr. Hale?"

"What do you mean?"

"The meaning of life, and all that."

He grunted. "The meaning is to win instead of lose. We learned that in the war."

"The Tibetans believe it's divine *thinking* that created us. That when you kill something—kill *anything*—that thinks, you're killing something divine. Don't you wish the Nazis believed that before they started the last six years of insanity?"

"What's your point? Hood's dead?"

"If Benjamin was really just a *thought*, a divine thought, he's still a thought, I figure. I mean, if I write down his thoughts, write down what little I understand about what he *found*, then he's still here. There. In that satchel. That's all we remember, and if you can makes sense of it you're smarter than me. But it's all inside there: Shambhala."

"Then he *did* find it."

"He sure as hell found something."

"But he didn't come back?"

She pointed at the satchel. "I just told you he did."

The slightest glint of greed crossed his eyes. Then, his face more masklike, he took down the satchel and put its strap over his shoulder. "By the fact that Hood was on a government-sanctioned mission, this satchel is the rightful property of the U.S. government."

"An heir might dispute that."

"So sue me."

"Not me."

"That kid of yours?"

"I have to get back to Sadie."

"Your child should be downriver, enrolled in a proper school. She's going to grow up like an animal out here."

"I think I'll take your advice." Beth pointed to the mine entrance. "Lead on, Agent Hale."

"This is it? We're done?"

"Yeah. We're done."

He looked down the long, dark length of the mine and shook his head. "Ladies first."

It was an ambush all right, Hale thought, but not hers. Regrettable, but if Hood was dead it wasn't smart to leave Calloway alive either. Too much loose antigovernment crap about confiscatory federal agents. And she could still sell stories to the Commies. So as she started walking for the mine entrance, silhouetted against the circle of light, his hand felt for the little pistol to plug her. Loose end. First this pilot, then the little girl. He'd had to do much worse in the war.

But at a spot she'd picked, where just enough light came from the entrance to give her aim without being blinded, she suddenly stopped, unslung her knapsack, and knelt on one knee. "I need a drink of water," she said, reaching inside.

He watched her like a predator.

Her hand closed around the .45.

The bitch was trying something. He yanked out his pistol.

As he did so, she shot him through her knapsack, the bark of the report opening a neat little hole in the fabric. An instant later his own gun went off.

The reports boomed and echoed in the mine as one.

They both hit each other's stomachs.

Slow wounds, a terrible way to die.

Beth's caliber was heavier and Hale was kicked backward, grunting in surprise that the woman had beaten him. He fell on his back, his pistol flying wide before he could think to hold on to it. Damn.

She simply sat back, stunned that it had finally happened, and clenched her muscles against the pain. She hadn't expected it would hurt so much. It was hard to breathe. She imagined she could feel the bullet in there, eating, and a wash of nausea almost made her faint.

Steady, Beth. Not until you've taken care of Sadie.

Because it hasn't ended yet.

Wincing, she stood up, her gun out of the pack now and steady. Hale was lying on his back, his arms and legs making swimming motions as he tried to move. He was looking at her in fear.

She walked past him and scooped up his gun, pocketing it, and then quickly patted him down for another. He groaned as she pressed his sides. Then she stepped back.

"You don't deserve a finishing shot."

"Don't leave me," he begged.

She walked back to her pack. "You weren't going to let me live, were you, Hale? Because if there was anything really valuable in that satchel, anything really top secret, you couldn't risk having me run around with it in my head. You didn't even ask if I was a patriot, or if I'd help. Because you didn't want help. You wanted possession." She started to work, pulling sticks of dynamite out of her pack.

His mouth bubbled. "Hood?"

"The funny thing is that you got what you came for. Ben *is* in that bag, and all the strange and wondrous things you hoped for are in there, too. I've no doubt you'd find someone smart enough to figure them out. Maybe some of those Nazi scientists you boys have been capturing. So now we're both dying, and that's the best outcome of all. Because you know what, Mr. Hale? You don't really want to find Shambhala. You don't want to find what Ben found."

"Hood?" It was a gasp.

She unreeled fuse toward the mine entrance. "Goodbye, Duncan."

The explosion sent an arc of rock flying out toward Eldorado. As the fragments bounced and ricocheted off the talus slope below, there was a roar of collapse and a cloud of smoke and dust rolled out of the mine. Beth waited for the air to clear and then checked to make sure the cave was completely plugged. Yep. A solid wall of rock entombed Hale. Then she ripped off the bottom half of her shirt, bandaged herself as best she could, using the pain to keep her focus, and painfully climbed to the top of the cliff where the mine's vertical airshaft was. She'd prepared this cover long before. Wincing as she felt her gut leak into itself, she dragged the logs and brush over the hole and kicked on some dirt. Erosion and growth would seal the shaft for decades to come.

Agent Duncan Hale would bleed to death in the dark.

Then a stagger down to the cabin, forced smiles to a confused Sadie, and quick delivery to a frightened Margaret. The effort had just about killed her, but not quite.

Too bad, because what was coming up the road next *would* kill her. She'd die all right, but in the most horrible way possible, and not before she told them everything she knew.

One side would bring the other like flies to rot, she'd long figured.

So she lay on the bed, unarmed, dizzy, and resigned, curious about this other man to come. She prepared by putting on male boots and jacket, the latter with the fake credentials for Ben she'd had made in China and then used at the bank. It might help confuse things until the right descendant came along. The calendar pages were taped shut by the Tibetan stamp. She didn't think the county coroner would look too hard at a hermit's leavings. And after that? Would any of it ever matter?

She just had to hope the right blood lock heir would survive.

When dusk fell, headlights swung up the old access road: two or three vehicles, at least. Doors slammed and she heard the heavy tread of big men getting out.

She pulled off the rest of her bandage and peered at the puckered and swollen bullet hole, her stomach a mottle of purple and yellow bruising. Pain came in pulses. She didn't know you could hurt so much!

They were gathering outside. She could hear the muttered German.

So she plunged her forefinger into the bullet hole, screaming as she did so.

They froze, uncertain. Then there was a command, and they broke through the door.

Beth yanked her finger out. It was like taking a finger out of a dike. Blood spurted in a rush, a fountain of mortality, and her vision blurred.

As she faded into unconsciousness and death, she got a last glimpse of the man who'd first burst inside.

Oh, my God! He looked wild with disappointment.

And far, far worse than she did.

46

The Nunnery of the Closed Door, Tibet
September 20, Present Day

Since Sam wasn't critically hurt, the nuns didn't have to lug him. Wheezing and constantly cursing (until he remembered the company he was with, but then the soreness would make him forget again), he staggered step by step under his own power. He was bleeding, but the wound was a surface cut where the shattered iPhone had bruised and scraped his chest. Once at the iron door, Jake Barrow's theft of the keys delayed the party only fifteen minutes. After pounding, Amrita shouted directions to a spare set she kept hidden in her cell, and more nuns scurried to fetch them.

"It helps that Mr. Barrow has to think everyone else a fool," she told them. "If he didn't think that, his philosophy would collapse against commonsense reason."

When the Americans were released into the yellow glow of the nunnery temple, Rominy felt a rush of relief. Escape was like being raised from the dead. She knelt and touched her forehead to the base of the Buddha as the nuns looked on in sympathy. She could swear electricity coursed through her when she touched the relic, restoring her spirit and strength. Did God have many faces?

"Come on! Let's go after him," Sam said. He coughed and winced.

"How?" said Amrita. "He's taken your vehicle and by now is many miles from here. Which isn't such a bad place for him to be."

"But he'll get away!"

"Always you Americans are in such a hurry. You've just opened a secret that has been waiting for more than seventy years. No time has been lost. The world had to wait until this moment for the Closed Door to be relevant. And no time *will* be lost because you must first understand what it is you must do."

"Why is it relevant now?"

Rominy stood up from her prayer. "Because of atoms," she said.

Sam squinted. "Care to translate, Dharma?"

"Jake talked about how Shambhala may have had an ancient atom smasher. He thinks that staff is a wizard staff that can somehow play strings smaller than atoms. Scientists are learning new things that convinced Jake he can finally make the staff work. That's why he came after me now, after all this time. He thinks he can harness the new power source called Vril."

"This is the guy you picked as your boyfriend?"

"I didn't know this at first. And yes, I'll be kicking myself the rest of my life. Which might be a short life, if any more Nazis are around."

Sam nodded soberly. "How about it, Amrita? You spot anyone else skulking?"

She shook her head. "I suspect Mr. Barrow has not fully convinced his superiors, whoever they might be. They left him to succeed or fail on his own. Recovery of that staff may prove him to the others."

"And if anyone else had come with him, I wouldn't have trusted Jake," Rominy said. "Or at least I hope not."

"We can't catch that misguided man now," Amrita said. "So let's bind our wounds, give you butter tea, and let you sleep a little. Then, before you decide what to do next, I have something important to show you."

They met later in Amrita's cell. The floor was packed earth, the bed little more than a plank, and yet the nun seemed more content than any woman Rominy had ever met. What was the secret of satisfaction? Was letting go of desire liberation, or lobotomy?

"This letter was sent from America, sealed, and with instructions to give it only to the heir who could open the Closed Door," Amrita said. "That would be you, Rominy."

The envelope crackled with age, its airmail stamp and border dating from long, long ago. *To the Last Shambhalan*, it read. She shivered, Sam watching her closely. Then she opened it.

The writing was in English as she expected, the script a feminine hand similar to the other notes she'd retrieved. The paper was yellow and the ink slightly faded, but still quite legible. The penmanship was of a quality never taught anymore.

"Read it aloud, Rominy," Sam said. She did so.

Dear Descendant,

If you are reading this you've used the essence of your veins to open the last blood lock of the drowned city of Shambhala, or at least that is how I think of that odd, troubling place. My companion, who made more study than I ever will, doubts this is the Shambhala of legend at all; that it was a tragic experiment that delved too deep into the mysteries of creation and tapped what shouldn't be tapped. I don't know. Those of us who escaped did so in panic and confusion, and there was no time to really understand. If you've refound the door that we shut, it's possible you know far more than we do. Nonetheless, there may be some confusion. Let me share what I can.

In 1938, I was a pilot flying scouting and transport missions for the Chinese air force. At the order of Madame Chiang Kai-shek, I flew an American museum curator named Dr. Benjamin Hood from Hankow to Tibet. He was in pursuit of a German mission to that same mysterious nation. The Nazi goal was secret, and our own pursuit was secret as well. The world was slipping toward war, and great issues were at stake.

In due time, we were sent by the Reting Rinpoche to follow Germans led by a man named Kurt Raeder. The Nazis were going to the place in the Kunlun Mountains where you presumably are now. Hood parachuted into a remote valley that appeared to contain the ruins of Shambhala, the legendary city that was supposed to be a paradise and redeem the world. Instead, my companion related, they found a dead city full of bones, as if some terrible calamity had struck. I meanwhile landed my plane, made my way to this nearby nunnery, and convinced the nuns to show me a

*back way into the mountain and city. I found Ben,
but could not convince him to flee with us. He was
determined to stop Raeder. Shortly afterward,
huge explosions rocked the Kunlun Mountains and
a canyon caved in on itself, damming the city's
river. Shambhala, or whatever name it once really
went by, was flooded. Ben and Raeder were gone.*

This puzzled Rominy. Hadn't her great-grandfather
gone back to America? She looked at the envelope. It
was postmarked CONCRETE.

*I can't explain precisely what caused that
catastrophe, but I can explain a little of what
happened afterward. If you've come this far, on the
clues I left, you're worthy of your ancestors. But no
doubt you've wondered at your origins and how I
came—too briefly, I predict—to be a guardian.*

Guardian?

*Hood had saved a Tibetan nun named Keyuri Lin
from the Nazis. Keyuri was wounded in the
fighting, and after that terrible night in
Shambhala, neither Keyuri nor I was in a condition
to go anywhere. The nuns healed wounds both
physical and spiritual. And then came the*

pregnancy. We should have been grateful, but
instead were apprehensive. What if the Nazis came
back? We wrote down what we remembered, but it
was like reconstructing a dream. Keyuri was
crushed by the entire experience, and I feared for
her sanity. My duty was to return to the Chinese
front, but I dared not leave.

The birth was a difficult one and Keyuri
became even more depressed. Acquiescence and
acceptance had failed her, she said. Her Buddhist
faith had been shattered. I hoped the child would
give her hope, but the memories were too painful.
There were always fears the Germans were
coming; always rumors of the very worst things.

I think the force in Shambhala had made her go
mad. So a year after the discovery of the city, at a
time when Hitler was marching into Poland, I
decided during a sleepless night to ask her to come
home with me to America where we might seek a
cure.

But she wasn't in her cell, which was very
unusual.

It was a cold, windy night, the moon giving the
mountains a ghostly glow, and I was about to give
up and return to bed when I realized the baby was
missing as well.

Dread overwhelmed me.

I ran out the courtyard and up along the ridge crest, calling. I saw her at a cliff edge, silhouetted against the distant snow, and shouted.

She looked at me once, sadly, and then stepped.

I leaped and clutched as she was about to go over.

I couldn't save her, but I saved your ancestor. I was sprawled at the lip, my arms outstretched, the baby no bigger than a ball. And I watched Keyuri's robes flapping as she fell far, far away into a chasm, finally at peace.

When I stretched out my arms and rescued that bloodline, I made a choice. I could leave the artifact locked away forever as Keyuri urged, a forgotten power buried. Or I could preserve the chance it might someday be harnessed for good, but only by the right person. If you're reading this, you've followed clues I left behind. I hope you're that person.

Then it was time to go home to America.

As I write this, the United States has plunged into war. The stakes are enormous, and the effort vast. We are experiencing defeat after defeat, and the world grows ever darker. Because of this, whole armies would be traded for what we glimpsed at Shambhala. So if you find the staff we *hid, you must safeguard it. It must only be shared with the right people, at the right time, when we've gained wisdom to use it. If you lose it, you absolutely must get it back.*

Maybe our species is too young to cope with such responsibilities. Someday, millennia from now, when our wisdom has caught up with our ingenuity, maybe it will be time to finally go back to that lost, dark city. In the meantime, you've found all that is left.

To give you strength, remember that the baby's mother was a good person caught in a terrible time. I will do what little I can for the child, but sooner or later the men that dream of power may come looking for her, and me. If that happens, I will bury the secret until the right bloodline comes to set things right, and mail this letter.

That blood, dear reader, is you. May God protect you on your quest.

ELIZABETH CALLOWAY
April 17, 1942

It was postmarked September 10, 1945.

Rominy put the letter down. "I don't understand. Who exactly was this Keyuri Lin? And why does my great-grandmother talk as if she's already dead?" She read again. "*The baby's mother was a good one.*"

"Don't you get it, Rominy?" Sam asked gently.

"No, I don't get it."

Amrita took her hand and covered the young woman's. "Beth Calloway took your grandmother to America, as a baby, to raise her there, after leaving a vial of the child's blood here. But she was not the mother. Your ancestor, Rominy, is not American but Tibetan."

"*What?*"

Your great-grandmother is Keyuri Lin."

She was part Tibetan? Ben Hood had had sex with a Buddhist nun? When? How? She remembered what Jake had first told her: *You're not Rominy Pickett.* Well, that was the understatement of all time. Her previous life seemed light-years away.

"It wouldn't have been easy for a half-Asian baby in the '40s," Sam added. "West Coast Japanese were being locked up. Maybe that's one reason Calloway hid out in the sticks."

Rominy slowly nodded. How much Tibetan would she be now? One-eighth. "She wanted to save the baby but she didn't want to be found. To have the . . . blood lock be found." She turned to Amrita. "I thought they used a finger we found from my great-grandfather as the source of blood to lock the door. But they didn't, they used Keyuri."

The nun nodded. "And Keyuri, as she meditated here in the nunnery, decided the door should never be opened again. She and Miss Calloway disagreed on what they should do. That's why she took her baby to the cliff: to end the bloodline. The Nazis would have no more reason to come to Tibet."

"But Beth saved the child."

"And something of Benjamin Hood: the clues that brought you back here."

"And the nuns helped Beth."

"And the baby. It is not for us to take life, or alter destiny. And because of that you are alive, and you are here. Is that not curious? Who knows what fate intends?"

Rominy sat back worriedly. "And now Jake Barrow, if that's his real name, has the staff. Why did I ever go with him? And where will *he* go? And why did he want it so badly? It didn't look like it still worked."

"To recharge it, I'm guessing," said Sam. "For some reason the Nazis decided it was finally time to find the descendant and open the blood lock. So he hunted you down, lying all the way, to get you here in case they needed lots of blood."

"Sheep to slaughter," she murmured.

"Which means . . . ," Sam mused, "he's going to an atom smasher?"

"Maybe. Where do they have those, anyway?"

"Hell if I know. Geez, my chest hurts! No offense, Amrita, but I'm losing all serenity."

"You didn't have much to lose," Rominy said.

"It may help you that Jake, unwittingly, didn't take all his belongings with him," Amrita said. "In checking your identities, we removed an old baggage tag from a side pocket of his backpack. Before showing you too much, we wanted to know as much as possible about who you were. Here's the airport code."

They looked at it. "FRA."

"France?" guessed Rominy.

"Frankfurt," Sam said. "I flew through there to get here when I came to Tibet two years ago. It figures the dude goes to Germany. Maybe he's from there."

"He seemed pretty American to me."

"Where else would a Nazi go? Listen, during the war the Germans had guys posing as Americans. They misdirected our troops during the Battle of the Bulge. You're a victim of an impostor, Rominy. A secret agent."

"Whatever." She sighed. "But where in Germany? Wait . . . he mentioned a Vatican of the SS. He told me in the airport that there was a castle Himmler used."

"Do you remember where it was?"

"No. But if I saw the name again I'd recognize it. I bet we could look it up on the Web if we got to Germany."

"So how do we get to Germany?"

"There's something else he left, some money I took because I got tired of him doing all the spending." She felt more resolute. She'd been led since the explosion of her car. It was time she took charge of her own life and turned the tables. "I'll use it to go to Germany."

"*We'll* go to Germany," Mackenzie amended.

"Sam, this isn't your problem."

"After a bullet in my chest? And you've demonstrated you need adult supervision."

"Me! Has anyone accused you of being 'adult' your entire life?"

He smiled. "No, but I'd like to try. Besides, that bastard owes me an iPhone."

Rominy was actually relieved at the idea of company, since she had little idea of what to do next except look for this castle. Was all this *supposed* to happen? "Just don't lie to me, okay?"

"Promise," Sam said. "And we'd better start packing. He's got a long head start."

"Yes," she said, "but we've got one big advantage."

"What's that?"

"He thinks we're already dead."

47

Tibet to Germany
September–October, Present Day

The trek back to Lhasa was daunting, but there was peace in having to do little but walk a very long way. The nuns gave Rominy and Sam thick blankets, barley cakes, and yak butter, a gruesome but nutritious cuisine to keep them alive until they could find help and, eventually, Western food. They spent many miles discussing ideal pizza toppings.

Winter was fast approaching and traffic was infrequent even on the busiest highways, but eventually they'd encounter a vehicle when they returned to a road. In the meantime, the empty immensity was a recess from Nazis. Autumn's line of white kept creeping down the Kunlun range, but the cold north wind was at their backs and the only mystery was how to put one foot in front of the other. Despite a chest blackened with bruises, Sam took two thirds of the weight without complaint. He was big, strong, angry, and oddly serene about their immediate predicament. But then Tibet had been home to him for two years.

"It's not a question of *if* we'll get help, just when," he assured her. "I'd rather be lost in Tibet than Nevada. Less loopy."

They slept together, not for love but for warmth: it was too cold to take clothes off anyway. They had no fuel to make a fire, and no tent for shelter, so they'd find a wadi or outcrop and curl together behind the windbreak, burrowed beneath blankets. She knew he wasn't ignorant of the fact she was a woman—sometimes he moved restlessly as they nested, and at other times he looked at her with shy longing—but they were both filthy and cold, with no energy for sex and no reason yet for romantic affection. She appreciated him not talking about it. They huddled like fox kits, and when she woke up shivering he'd wrap her in his big arms and hug her until she stopped.

"Do you know all that I've got left of my old life?" she said one morning, after lying on her belly like an animal to drink from an icy pool.

"A Social Security number?"

She reached into a pocket inside her parka. "I took this from my great-grandfather's cabin. It's a Tibetan scarf he was given and somebody—Beth Calloway, I guess—wrote a code on it so we'd find an old mine. That's it. That's my ancestry. No journal, no satchel of maps, no car, no job."

"You told me you stashed some of the inheritance in a Seattle account."

"With no identification to get it."

"The less you have, the more it means."

"Give me a break."

When they recrossed the low saddle that had given them their first view of the Kunlun, an enveloping snow squall robbed her of any sense of direction. Sam had retained a compass in his pack, however, and followed a bearing as if he were at sea. "Always carry the ten essentials. Compass, margarita mix, dark chocolate." His skill was reassuring. Meanwhile, she'd been cold and hungry for so many days that discomfort had become the background buzz of existence. She knew she'd gone past the point of dieting to malnutrition, but the monotonous food did supply enough energy to keep her trudging. Her fantasies turned to yak burgers in the Shangri-la Hotel.

She didn't dwell on their mission. She dreaded having to confront the man she'd loved and now hated, Jake Barrow. She wanted to simply go home but couldn't. She wanted to give up but had to win. Courage, she'd decided, wasn't bestowed, it was chosen. Her ancestors had decided to be brave.

Now it was her turn.

"Do you believe in God, Sam?" she asked at one point as they trudged.

"God?" He paused, looking about. "Nope, don't see him. Santa Claus for grown-ups, Rominy."

"You're not spiritual anymore?"

"I'm not religious. There's a difference. Take Jesus, for example: a Xerox copy of gods who preceded. He was the son of a carpenter and virgin like Krishna, born on December twenty-fifth like Mithras, heralded by a star like Horus, walked on water like Buddha, healed like Pythagoras, raised people from the dead like Elisha, was executed on a tree like Adonis and Odin, and ascended into heaven like Hercules. The religious tradition is genuine, but to pretend he's the one and only, instead of the latest software update—no way."

"You're quite the theology student."

"You don't come to Tibet without wondering about things. I was a searcher, like everybody, but after a while I got bored with dogma. You know, the Buddhists don't have a lot to say about God or Creation at all. They stick to what they know, which is dealing with our fucked-up heads."

"But they talk about love and empathy. Wasn't that Jesus, too? Those nuns devote their lives to this cosmic . . . thing. This goodness, this grace, that unites all the great faiths. They see him, or it, or the Essence. They'd see God right now, right here, in this wilderness."

"I'm sorry, but that rock isn't God, not for me. And what Essence? Living in the Middle Ages at the edge of the world? Praying twenty million times a day? For more of the same in the next life? I've watched them for two years. It's an interesting show for tourists, but not to buy in to. I'm sorry, Rominy, but for those who find life pointless and death terrifying without religion, I just say maybe it *is* pointless and terrifying."

"Well, I've seen God," she said.

Now he stopped, hands on hips. "You have? And you didn't ask her for a ride?"

"Very funny. Remember when we climbed up the edge of the waterfall to the lake, saw the smoke from the nunnery, and started cutting along the mountain to get to it?"

"Yeah."

"It was so empty, so desolate, so lonely, that he, or she, filled it."

"Filled what?"

"Everything."

"If your dope was that good, I wish you'd shared it."

"It was a very odd feeling and it only lasted for a minute. As we worked our way toward the nunnery I suddenly felt completely at peace. As if I were exactly where I was supposed to be. And I felt *connected*. I felt connected to Jake, I felt connected to you, I felt connected to the river and the rock and the birds orbiting overhead, to the *universe*. I felt everything was one. And I thought, 'This must be what heaven is like.'"

He regarded her skeptically. "Brain chemicals. High altitude, sleep deprivation, faulty diet. You hallucinated, Rominy, like every prophet and guru who's gone into the desert and deliberately starved. You felt what you *wanted* to feel."

"But I didn't want it. In fact, for a few moments I didn't want *anything*."

He sighed. "Do you feel it now?"

"No."

"Will you concede it could all be a trick of the mind?"

"No."

"That maybe the Twelve Apostles were a bunch of potheads?"

"No. It was too real. It was so real that *that* was the reality, not"—she waved her hand at the landscape— "this. Not what I feel now. It's like I woke up, just for a second, and now I'm back asleep again, in this dream we call life."

"Wow. Whoa. Jake was just a snake, Rominy. There was no 'connection' to that Nazi-loving bastard."

"That's the weird part. He *is* a snake, but there *was* a connection. That if we could really see the essence that this staff is supposed to tap, that if we could lift the veil and get down to the fundamental that's behind everything, there was, *is*, a connection. It was spooky, wonderful, scary. The real Shambhala isn't lightning bolts, Sam, it's unity. That's what we lost. That's what we're looking for."

"I'm looking for a yak burger."

"Even Hitler, even though he was irretrievably lost."

"Rominy, come on. Now you're starting to sound like Jake Barrow. Is that what we're going to say to that bastard when we catch up to him? All is one, all is forgiven, now please give your stick back?"

"No. Just that he has no idea what he's really carrying. He was in a place to see, and stayed blind."

"And he locked us in a tomb. You pray, and I'll go in shooting."

It took them six days for the track to turn to a dirt road, and two more for the dirt to turn to gravel, and one more after that to reach pavement. They finally flagged down a farm truck and paid a few dollars to ride it back to the capital. Sam was apprehensive that Barrow might be laying a trap, but they saw no sign of him. So they had a blessed night in a hotel (separate rooms), a feast of the most American food they could shamelessly order, and then a flight (coach this time) to Delhi, Dubai, and Frankfurt. Sam retrieved his American passport; Rominy traveled as Lilith Anderson.

It was in Dubai during a three-hour layover that Sam wandered out of a magazine store with a *Herald Tribune.* "Look what I spotted."

It was an inside story, one column, from the Associated Press. "Collider to Attempt Full Power," the headline read.

"The European nuclear agency CERN will attempt soon to reach full power at its Large Hadron Collider near Geneva in hopes of testing theories about the origin of the Universe," the story began. *"By smashing subatomic particles at a velocity near the speed of light, scientists hope to answer such fundamental questions as why matter exists at all. The underground cyclotron, biggest in the world, is designed to reach proton beam energies of up to 7 trillion electron volts."*

"You think this has something to do with us?" Rominy asked.

"No, I think it has something to do with rat-bag Jake Barrow and why he played you when he did. This is an atom smasher, right? Going to full power? Can you say 'coincidence'?"

"Jake can't have anything to do with a huge super-collider. Can he?"

"Dollars to doughnuts says he does. How, I don't know. Is he an errand boy for some mad scientist? I just think it's too neat not to mean something."

"What about his SS Vatican, or whatever he called it?"

"We should start there, if we can find it. And warn this CERN outfit if we can get any evidence on the scum sucker." He stopped to listen for an announcement. "Come on, they're loading our plane."

Rominy's joy at being lifted from the twelfth century to the twenty-first in a matter of days faded when they broke through the clouds and saw the green platter of Germany.

Somewhere, they hoped, was the stolen staff. The problem would be if it came packaged with a packet of Nazis.

Sam persuaded her they needed to rent a BMW 3 Series Coupe. "If it was me it would be a Ford Fiesta," he admitted, "but we're secret agents now and have to keep up appearances. This is great, using your money. Maybe I *am* beginning to understand Jake Barrow."

"I've never been so popular with men," she said drily. "Don't worry, we've almost burned through my cash. After we save the world, I just hope we'll have enough left to buy a ticket home."

"You *are* home. All is one, remember? Cologne, Cleveland, Kathmandu . . ."

"I don't believe you're as cynical as you say. You don't live in Tibet for two years for nothing."

He laughed. "Check my bank account, Rominy. It *was* for nothing."

A Google search at the Frankfurt Airport Business Center swiftly identified the town of Wewelsburg as the site of "Himmler's Camelot," or the would-be spiritual home of the SS. There was nothing secret about it, thus making it seem an unlikely place to run Jake Barrow to ground. But it was only a hundred or so miles north of Frankfurt and they had no other clue. Sam threw himself into the task of driving with salacious joy, getting up to 80 mph on the autobahn and then throwing the sporty car into curves once they left the main highway. It reminded her of Jake's freeway "escape" in the pickup truck.

Sam had lost weight hiking from Shambhala and shaved in Lhasa, and he looked good without scraggle on his chin. With Jake she'd felt a tense electricity, but with Sam there was easygoing comfort. Not so much dependability as dogged loyalty, an instinct to look after her. He was, after all, a guide.

She'd catch him glancing at her at times.

"Do you think a lot about beer, breasts, and baseball?" Rominy asked once as he drove.

"*What?*"

"It's just something that Jake said. I'm wondering if all guys are alike."

"Oh. No way, man. Football is king."

She'd found, she supposed, a guy from the beer and chips aisle.

The shadow of war and Nazism seemed purged from Germany as they approached Wewelsburg. The landscape was fat, bucolic, satisfied. The villages were quaint. The cars were washed. The people looked prosperous. The politics were liberal. Hitler was dead history, wasn't he?

Sam pulled to the side when the castle came into view. It looked a little like a blunt-bowed ship perched on a low ridge that rose above the Alme Valley, its apex pointing north. A round, low-roofed tower was at the northern end. At the other two corners were smaller towers with dome roofs, like derbies.

Sam counted. "There's a good sixty windows just on the side we can see. For the home of the most sinister organization in world history, it doesn't look very scary."

"It's not a King Arthur castle. It's a Renaissance castle." Rominy was reading from notes they'd made in the airport. "Himmler wanted it to be more of a church, a pagan church, than a fortress. Or a meeting lodge for a new kind of Freemasonry. They had a world globe in there so big they couldn't bring it in the conventional way. They had to lift it through a window."

"The better to carve up the planet, my dear. Well, what's our plan? If Barrow sees us he's going to go ballistic, you know."

"There was a B and B about five klicks back. Let's check in there and go up to the castle after dark. We can sneak around when he can't see us."

"Great. Unarmed. Clueless. Unable to speak the language. I like the way you think, Tomb Raider."

"We need evidence for prosecution or to take to CERN. Jake tried to murder us, Sam. And we need to take him by surprise. Jake thinks we're dead, or that I'm a ninny waiting for him to tell me what to do. The best defense is a good offense. Let's start doing the unexpected."

"What evidence is there?"

"The staff. I want it back: it belonged to my great-grandparents. I'm going to find it and steal it. Then we go to the police."

"And tell them what?"

"That he tried to murder us in Tibet. That he stole from the nunnery."

"And how do we prove that, exactly?"

"The staff seemed made of something I've never seen before. We find that, and Jake's real identity. We show the bruises on your chest and the bullet in your iPhone. We even call the *Seattle Times* back home and get them to investigate this impostor."

"We sneak, we steal, we give a news tip, and we go to the cops. Golly. D-Day wasn't this carefully crafted."

She ignored the sarcasm, studying the castle like a besieging general. "Sam? You don't think the police could be in on this somehow, do you? You know, like neo-Nazis?"

He got serious. "Not in Germany. They're pretty paranoid about that stuff. And that was three generations back. I'm guessing Jake Barrow is on his own, except for a lunatic skinhead or two."

Rominy started. Had the bald man in the cabin window been working *with* Jake Barrow? Did he shoot his arrows to help them escape?

She realized how little she still knew about what was really going on.

48

Wewelsburg, Germany
October 2, Present Day

It was near midnight when they parked a quarter mile
from the castle and cautiously made their way through
the outskirts of Wewelsburg, their bags in the trunk in
case they had to suddenly flee. It was autumn, the days
shortening, the crops in, but even at that the town seemed
oddly quiet. Every curtain was drawn. They could see
the glow of lights and the flicker of television in a few
houses, but only occasionally did a car hiss down the village lanes. It was so quiet that the slam of a door could be
heard from a hundred yards away, and the bark of a dog
twice that. Their footsteps seemed loud, and Rominy had
a sense of being watched. Yet no one challenged them.

They studied the castle from the shadow of trees.
The building was entirely dark, shut for the night. A

ramp led across a ditch to the castle entrance, but the way was barricaded with lumber and tape, signs bearing international symbols for construction. Apparently off-season remodeling was going on. Looming above, the edifice seemed somber and sad, not a Camelot at all. Did the ghosts from old SS plots, seminars, initiation ceremonies, and Aryan weddings still linger here?

"Looks like a wild-goose chase," Sam murmured. "If the castle is closed, Barrow wouldn't come here, would he?"

"But where else would he go?" She was frustrated.

"We're not detectives, Rominy. We might have to hire one, or find some officials who'd believe our story and do the detective work themselves. Jake might not even be in Germany. We need Interpol, not our instincts."

"But we don't even have proof Jake Barrow exists, or whatever his real name is."

"Maybe if we told our story, the Chinese police would verify it for Interpol by interviewing the nuns."

"I'm not going to sic Communist Chinese cops on a Buddhist nunnery."

He looked back at the quiet village. It looked Disney clean, like everything in this model railroad of a country. "What then?"

"I don't know. Let's look around a little more."

"We can't even get in the place."

"There's a dry moat on this side. I think that sign in German says it leads to a tower. Let's try that. Maybe we can peek in some windows."

"You got balls, girl."

"I just don't want to waste my plane ticket. And I'm angry for letting life happen to me, instead of me happening *it*."

"Happening it?"

"You know what I mean. Come on, you're the one who lost his iPhone to that maniac."

Skirting the barricades, they made their way down into a grassy moat. A three-quarter moon floated above and gave enough light to mark their way through the mown trench. Down there the castle seemed even higher and darker, a cliff like the cliff that had barred their way to Shambhala. There were actually no windows at moat level to peer into, and Rominy was almost pleased. She'd be glad to get away from this creepy castle, but she had to do *something*. Her best, and then go home.

The moat led them north to the big, flat-roofed tower. The ditch ended where the castle ridge dropped toward the valley below, since no barrier was needed on that steep side. A few farm lights glittered on the plain beyond. They backed away from the tower and looked up, its crenellations picked out by the moon. Nothing . . .

Except *that.*

"Did you see it?" Rominy whispered.

"What?"

"A candle. It moved. Someone's inside." She shivered from both excitement and dread.

"This isn't one of your wacky 'I see God' moments, is it?"

"No, there was a light, I swear it." She pointed. "It was up where the main floor of the tower would be."

"A janitor with a flashlight."

"Or someone sneaking around inside."

"In that case, let's call the cops."

"We can't. It might just be a janitor with a flashlight."

"Rominy . . ."

"Look, there are some stairs leading down from the base of the tower into a well with a basement door. Maybe we can get in there."

"You're going to break into a Nazi castle in the middle of Germany? And *then* make our case to the police?"

"We need *proof.*" She sounded a lot braver than she felt. "It probably is just a janitor."

"I'm not even getting paid anymore."

"I let you rent the BMW. Or should I go by myself?"

"No, you need adult supervision. Lacking that, you get me."

They descended the stairwell to a wooden door with an old-fashioned iron handle and latch. "How are your lock-picking skills?" Sam whispered.

She grasped the latch. It lifted. "Perfect. It's unlocked."

He put his hand on her arm. "That's not necessarily a good sign."

"Sam, we have to peek. We don't know what else to do."

"Vin Diesel and Schwarzenegger would go in shooting."

"Come *on*."

It was pitch-black inside. They shuffled into the basement of the tower carefully, wary of unseen steps. Then they halted. Only the palest radiance came from the open door they'd crept through. They could see nothing.

"Light the candle," she whispered.

They'd found one in the bed-and-breakfast they'd checked into, provided either as insurance against power outages or to let guests cast a romantic mood. Now Sam pulled it out and used the hostel's matches to light it. The sudden illumination threw back the shadows and revealed a round, stark, gloomy room.

It was the basement of the tower. The roof was a stone dome.

"Oh my God, look at that!" Rominy hissed.

At the dome's apex was a stone swastika, each arm extended with additional turns. Despite countless war movies it looked, in its geometric intricacy, oddly compelling.

"I've seen that kind in Tibet," Sam muttered. "Sometimes it's called a sun wheel."

Their feet were at the edge of a sunken circle in the room, like a shallow pool. Directly below the swastika was a circle within this circle, a depression that sank a few inches deeper. Its purpose was unclear.

Arranged around the room were twelve squat round stone pedestals, like the bases of pillars. Placed on each one was a bronze sculpture.

"The signs of the zodiac," Rominy said. "What could this be for?"

"Pagan cosmology," said Sam. "Twelve is an ancient sacred number, like seven. The ancients believed the gods were aligned with the planets, and the Web site said Himmler planned an observatory here. Maybe the Nazis came down here to cast the future."

"Must have been disheartening if it worked."

"Maybe they still come down. The sculptures look bright and new, and they're not all aligned evenly, like someone just set them up."

"Very perceptive, Mr. Mackenzie!" a new voice said.

The door through which they'd entered closed with a boom, and they whirled. There was a figure in the shadows.

"It's actually Valhalla," a woman's voice said with a crisp German accent. A flashlight blazed, freezing them like deer in its beam. "A Hall of the Dead." The woman shining the light was standing next to the door, wearing a business suit and pumps and holding a wicked-looking assault rifle. "There are tours that explain all this when the castle is open. Which it is not."

"The door was unlocked," Sam tried.

"Convenient, don't you think?" The light danced on them, making sure they had no weapons.

"You know Jake Barrow?" Rominy asked, her voice trembling despite her best effort to be brave. Why not get to the point?

"Silly girl. Of course I do."

The woman came closer, the beam lowering so they could see.

And Rominy almost fainted.

Her hair was coiffed, her teeth were perfect, her makeup carefully applied, and her look a generation younger. But holding the gun was Delphina Clarkson, Rominy's backwoods neighbor from the Cascade Mountains.

49

Wewelsburg, Germany
October 2, Present Day

H immler built it as a hall for the dead of the SS elite," Clarkson said, letting the beam bounce around the chamber for a moment. "What the pedestals were designed for isn't entirely clear. Statues? Urns? The twelve comes of course from the twelve signs of the zodiac, so we decorate accordingly when we meet."

"Nazis *decorate*?" Sam asked.

"She isn't a Nazi, she's my neighbor. Aren't you?" But why was Delphina dressed up and talking with a German accent? Why was she *here*?

"And you're supposed to be dead, Rominy. Aren't you?" Her smile was sly.

"You look different." She sounded one step behind again, naive and dimwitted, which was precisely what she didn't want to be.

"No, Rominy, it was Mrs. Clarkson who looked different. I usually look exactly like this."

The perfection of the disguise, the Tar Heel accent, the language, the age . . . was stupefying. Was *anyone* who they said they were?

"The castle entrance is closed for construction," Sam said.

"It is closed for *us*," Clarkson corrected. "Remodeling is a cover. This is a special time, and we wanted a special place, with special privacy, with special uninvited guests. We watched you approach."

"Who's 'us'?" Sam asked.

She motioned with the wicked-looking weapon. "Upstairs."

It was an order. They passed through an interior doorway with a gate of iron bars and ascended to the room above the crypt. This was circular, too, with twelve pillars and twelve arches at its periphery, and a round medieval-style chandelier overhead with twelve bulbs. The lights weren't lit, and the only dim illumination came from a couple of desk lamps sitting on the floor against the walls. Whoever was here did not seem anxious to advertise their presence to the village outside. On the marble floor beneath the chandelier was another design that played off the wheeling swastika. Rominy had a jolt of recognition.

"It's the sun wheel you saw on my shoulder," said a voice from the shadows. And out stepped Jake Barrow, or the man who'd claimed to be Jake. He was dressed in a black business suit with white shirt and silk tie of maroon, like a politician or CEO. The tie's subtle pattern was runic lightning bolts. Jake's left wrist glinted with an expensive gold watch. And his right held an automatic pistol, black and deadly, its dark mouth aimed waist high. There were, Rominy decided, entirely too many guns in the world.

"Thought we'd catch you in storm trooper drag, Barrow," Sam said.

"And I thought you might try to improve on slacker-slob apparel should you ever make it to Europe, but apparently not," Jake responded. "The clean chin is a start, however. Trying to impress Rominy, Sam?"

"Just airport security."

"We of The Fellowship don't wear the clothes of three generations ago. National Socialism is about ideas, not uniforms."

"Yeah, genocide. Conquest. Looting. Book burning. And attempted murder of a woman you claimed you loved."

"Not murder, but simply a delay so we had time to prepare things. I'd no doubt the nuns would get you out sooner or later, no doubt that you'd follow me here. I deliberately aimed for your mobile phone so you'd survive to help deliver her. I deliberately gave Rominy clues. So welcome, we've been impatiently expecting you, and now the final act in our little play can finally begin."

"Play?" Rominy asked.

"Surely Ursula Kalb's performance as an American hick deserves an Academy Award." Jake gestured toward the woman she thought of as Delphina.

"So it was all a charade? The skinhead, too?"

"Fashionably bald." And the man Rominy had seen at the cabin window, the one who'd killed the poor hounds, emerged from behind another pillar. His Mohawk stripe was gone and he was completely shaven. "Otto Nietzel, at your service." He, too, had a suit and narrow black tie, but his feet were armored with high-top black military boots. Tie or no tie, he still looked like a thug. "I'm real, not a charade."

"You butchered those dogs?"

"Put them to use. You fled with Jakob as intended."

She looked from one to another. "My car explosion was your doing?" she finally asked Jake.

"I'm afraid so. More effective than an opening line in a single's bar."

"Was *anything* real?"

"As I said in Tibet, you, to start. I'm glad your hand appears to be healing. The mystery was real. We couldn't get access to the safety deposit box short of robbery, which would bring in the FBI. We didn't know if there was anything useful in it but had to look. We knew nothing about the mine or satchel. The physics we discussed on the plane is real. Your ingenuity was real, and your body was real."

"Is your scar real? Flipping your bike?"

He fingered his chin. "A Jew fought back."

She shuddered. She'd had sex with this manipulative monster.

"Ursula did use the hounds to track us and rescue us at the Eldorado mine," he went on, "after I sent a signal from an EPIRB rescue beacon I'd hidden in my pack. The toughs at the airport were an American bodyguard for me, should you panic and run for a cop. The inheritance was a stroke of luck. You've contributed to a noble cause."

"Is there a real Delphina Clarkson?"

"There was. She has, alas, passed away."

"You *murdered* her?"

"We solved a problem. She was . . . recalcitrant."

"Oh, my God." Rominy felt sick. The poor woman would never have been harmed if Rominy hadn't drawn these lunatics into her life. It just got worse and worse.

"I'm not real," Jake said amiably. "I'm not a reporter, not an American, and not very fond of wine. My German name is Jakob."

"At least your English is impressive," Sam said sourly.

"I studied at Columbia and Yale. Laughably liberal, decadently idealistic."

"Obviously you flunked."

At that Frau Kalb rammed the muzzle of her M3 assault rifle into the guide's kidneys. Sam gasped and fell to his knees.

Otto grinned at the blow.

Rominy's heart was hammering. Please don't be a hero, Sam.

He struggled to talk. "Brave move, Ursula, just like your mass-murdering master. Uncle Adolf never won a battle when he couldn't land a sucker punch."

Otto's expression darkened and he strode quickly across the room's circle, the steel at the tip of his boots ringing on the marble. "You want to fight, American?" He grabbed Mackenzie's ears and brought up his knee, slamming it into Sam's face. Blood spurted. Sam fell sideways and Nietzel kicked viciously, a hard boot to the groin. The victim curled like a slug that's been salted. The Nazi kicked him again, in the side. Sam went white.

"Enough." It was Jake, or Jakob. "You'll have opportunity to play with him later, Otto."

The skinhead spat and stepped back.

Rominy was trembling. She hated violence and these people were bullies, killers, and liars. And now she had some answers, at least, to who they were and what they'd done. Which meant they were planning to kill her, too, didn't it? Or were they? She was tensed for a blow herself, but none came. For some reason they were leaving her alone. It didn't make sense. "Why did you even let us come here?" She hated the way her voice broke.

"It's obvious, isn't it?" A new voice sounded, low and sonorous, and when this figure stepped from behind a pillar the other Germans unconsciously straightened. More people emerged as well, men and women, all dressed as high-ranking professionals. Conspiracy with style. But this figure alone advanced across the room's circle, walking erect and gracefully over the inlaid sun wheel.

"You've been chosen, Rominy," the man said. "That's why Jakob here didn't simply kill you in America and take your blood to Tibet. He didn't kidnap you, either. We've been testing you, to see if you meet our criteria as a Chosen One. It's not that different from the hunt for the next Dalai Lama, really."

"Jacob?" Sam wheezed. "The Jew who wrestled an angel and was renamed Israel? Have your friends checked your bloodline, Jake?"

"Shut up, or Otto will kick you again," Jake—or Jakob—warned. "No one here is interested in your muddle of religious tripe."

"Sam, don't provoke them," Rominy added. She turned to their leader. "You murdered my mother and grandmother, too?"

"Your mother and grandmother had to be disposed of because the time of discovery was not yet ripe and we didn't want to risk them falling into American hands," the new man said smoothly, ignoring the others. "We waited for the next heir before extermination. You're fortunate in being alive at a pivotal time. Science has saved you."

"You mean physics."

"Particle accelerators," Jake said. "Atom smashers."

"You're going to try to revive the Vril in that staff. You're going to use the big supercollider near Geneva and make a weapon that can kill more people."

"Very good," the older man said calmly.

There was something wrong with this new individual who was clearly their leader, Rominy thought. He was still in shadow so she couldn't pin it down, but there was an odd, mechanical manner in his movements and a sickly paleness in his face.

"So if physics hadn't advanced, I'd be dead, too."

"Yes. That's why it was best you grow up not knowing too much. It made you safer. It made you happier."

Her mind was struggling to absorb just how thoroughly she'd been duped. They'd all been duped, for decades. "What happened to my great-grandfather?"

"He never left Tibet."

"Then who lived and died in the cabin?"

"I'll explain all that on our journey, but first let me introduce myself." He moved into the light and held out a hand in a leather glove. Involuntarily, she stepped back. His skin wasn't just pale, it was partly translucent, hinting at the muscle structure beneath, like the rubber of a yellow balloon stretched over someone who had been skinned. His eyes were bloodshot and feverish, his hair iron gray, and his frame thin, cadaverous, like an ascetic prophet or concentration camp victim. He looked gaunt, fanatic, ethereal. What was wrong with him?

"Hello, Rominy." He smiled, his teeth dull and worn. "You are witness to a miracle. I'm Kurt Raeder. I'm the man who slew your great-grandfather, and I've been waiting for this moment for more than seventy years."

50

Wewelsburg, Germany
October 3, Present Day

Rominy and Sam were marched down stairs even deeper than the tower crypt to the *Hexenkeller*, the witches' cellar, and shoved inside a whitewashed stone cell by Otto. The room was barren and cold.

"You'll be leaving in the morning," the skinhead Nazi said to Rominy. "See that you get some rest."

"What about Sam?" Her friend was leaning painfully against one wall.

"We don't need him anymore." A two-inch-thick heavy oak door slammed shut. They heard a bar drop over it.

The only ventilation was a tiny grilled window in the thick castle wall, too high to reach and too narrow to crawl through. There were two mattresses on the floor with woolen military blankets.

Sam sat down heavily on one, groaning. It crackled. "Straw. Welcome to the Middle Ages." There was a single lightbulb in a protective cage high overhead and no switch they could see to turn it off. A bucket was apparently supposed to serve as a toilet. There was no water and no privacy. "I'll never complain about Motel Six again."

Rominy kneeled by him. "Are you all right, Sam?"

"No, I'm not all right, Rominy. I've been shot in the chest, forced to walk out of the wilderness, and clubbed in the kidneys. And don't get me started about the leg room and in-flight meal on the airline."

"I'm a disaster for everyone who comes into contact with me. Poor Mrs. Clarkson."

"Mrs. Clarkson apparently never came into contact with you at all. Don't blame yourself for what these lunatic murderers have been up to. We're victims of madmen, led by a guy who looks like he climbed out of a coffin. If a bat flies through that little window, I'm giving up." He shifted and groaned.

"That *couldn't* be Kurt Raeder. He'd be over a hundred years old."

"Doesn't look a day over ninety-nine."

"Did something happen to make him live this long?"

"Who knows? These may just be inmates from the local asylum. Next up will be a guy with a Charlie Chaplin mustache giving a Hitler salute, and another with a bicorne hat and his hand tucked into his waist-coat. At least we were right about the atom smasher. They've been waiting for it to go to full power."

"How are they going to make use of it? It's a big international science project."

"I have a feeling these Nazis aren't going to ask permission." He looked at the door. "And apparently we don't get a vote. So what now?"

She sat next to him, having no idea. But the worst choice would be surrender. "I think we'd better starting acting and not reacting. I think we'd better make some plans."

The cell light never went out, and they dozed as best they could on the thin, scratchy mattresses. There was no heat, and the temperature hovered somewhere between barely tolerable and freezing. Rominy crawled to Sam's mattress and curled inside him as she'd done in the wilderness of Tibet. There was a comfort to it more profound than anything she'd felt with Jake. Sam put his arm around her and actually managed to doze while she thought fretfully. He groaned sometimes in his sleep.

So the thinnest light from a gray dawn was just penetrating their distant window when he abruptly sat up.

"What is it?" she whispered.

"I hurt."

"Sam, I'm sorry."

"That's okay. It woke me up enough to think. Rominy, they're going to take you somewhere, maybe the collider—I don't know why—and kill me. It's the only thing that makes sense. So the only thing that makes sense to *me* is to get clear of these thugs and come after you. So that's what I have to do."

"Just save yourself." Her tone was hopeless.

"No, that's what people like this count on—their enemies just trying to save themselves, and being picked off one by one. Do you know what a fascist is?"

"Like a Nazi. Extreme right-wing."

"The term came from Mussolini in Italy. And he got it from the Romans. In ceremonies, Roman leaders would carry a bundle of sticks called fasces. It symbolized the strength that comes from sticking together. Any one of the sticks could be broken, but if bundled in a bunch they were unbreakable. The Gauls or the Germans might have the biggest warriors, but when they ran into the bundled power of a Roman legion, pow! The barbarians lost. Mussolini liked this idea and called his followers fascists."

How do guys carry so much trivia around? "So?"

"So we've got to become fascists, too. Work together." He rubbed his hands. "I'm going to save you, Rominy."

"That's very sweet, but you're not a Roman."

"Doesn't matter. I've got a crush on you."

"Sam . . ." She didn't want to start something she'd quickly lose.

"You can't help it. You're cute. It's just biology, forget about it. But I've got an idea for a weapon and an idea of where you're going: that atom smasher. When you get there, you've got to figure out some way to let me know exactly where you are."

"And then what?"

His smile was a tight white line in the gloom. "We avenge your family."

Ursula Kalb came for Rominy soon after dawn, dressed in a business suit and stylish pumps. She looked like a corporate vice president. "Come. The construction workers will arrive soon and we must be out of here by then. Their boss is a believer and gives us good cover, but not all his men know about us."

Rominy remained sitting on the mattress. "I'm not going without Sam."

"That is not your choice."

"Then I'm not going."

Kalb struck like a snake. The woman stepped forward and jerked Rominy up with surprising strength and slapped her, shockingly hard and blindingly fast, once, twice, across the face. The blows knocked her head sideways and her eyes spurted tears. "You think I am a patient person, like our *Führer*, Kurt Raeder? You come or I sic a *real* dog on you, not those mutts you saw in America. Come!"

"Leave her alone!"

The German dragged Rominy to the door. "Otto is coming for *you*," she said to Sam.

The guide was rubbing his lower back and eyeing Frau Kalb with malice, but the German kept Rominy between her and Mackenzie, her nose wrinkled as she held the young woman. "Little pig. A shower first and then we go."

"Sam!" Her hands were outstretched but he hung back.

"Good-bye, Rominy." He said it with resignation, the farewell of a doomed man. They had rehearsed this.

"Wait!" She tried to yank away from Kalb but the woman's grip held her like a manacle.

"Remember what I told you," Sam said flatly.

"Please don't hurt him!" And then they were out of the cell and the door slammed shut.

For half an hour Sam heard little. Then there was the faint sound of doors slamming, a car starting, and tires crunching on gravel. Quiet. He was thirsty and hungry, but he was betting they wouldn't just leave him to rot. Otto would want to have some fun. He stretched and loosened, trying to get ready. He trembled from anticipation. Fear was good. Fear made him ready.

He heard the faint sound of electric saws and pounding hammers. The construction crew had arrived. Finally there was the tread of boots coming down the stairs outside and then the scrape of the bar being lifted. The door opened to reveal Otto, not in a suit this time but in loose combat pants tucked into his army boots. He wore a black turtleneck and bomber jacket.

"Now we play, yes?" He smirked.

"You're a skinhead goon, Otto. Don't you need to wait until my back is turned?"

The Nazi shook his head. "I don't think so. Not for you. You look like a pussy man. You know that word? Look, I have no weapon. Bare hands, like you. Maybe you can teach me a lesson. I've been a very bad boy." The skinhead took a step in and closed the door. "So the workers aren't disturbed, yes?"

Sam braced, balling his hands and putting them up. "I'm a lover, not a fighter."

Otto sneered. "You sleep with your woman?"

"No."

"I will rape her when this is over, I think. Maybe she will be a screamer." His own hands went up, opened,

to chop. "But I can make the girls promise not to tell."
He smiled evilly, imagining it. Then he weaved slightly
like a boxer, as he advanced into the cell.

Sam swallowed, his eyes flickering with fear, his
voice quavering with false bravado. "Where did it go
wrong, Otto? Bad parents? Wrong crowd? Bullied at
school?"

"I just like to hurt things." The German jabbed.

Sam ducked to one side, but the punch was just a
feint. Otto's boot swung up, a wicked arc that swung
across the cell and kicked the American in the side.
Mackenzie gave a bark of pain and went over, landing
on his mattress. "Ow!" he cried. He groaned, holding
himself. "Oh, fuck!"

"Get up. I want to kick you again."

Sam crawled toward a corner of the cell, gasping.
"Leave me alone!"

So the German came after him, grasping his shirt to
haul him upright. "No. I think we play some more."

Sam raised his hands to cover his face, fists clenched.
He was sobbing. Otto felt revulsion. The American was
a woman! The German spat at him, to try to get a reaction. Sam just cringed. It was like beating dead meat.

Mackenzie reached to clutch at his captor. "Please,
please . . ."

This was so pathetic, it wasn't even fun.

Otto decided he would bounce Sam's head against the stonework. He would bounce it and bounce it, and count how many times it took to crack.

And then the German felt the most excruciating pain of his life. Sam's fist suddenly slapped the side of the Nazi's head and it was as if someone had inserted a hot needle into his ear. Something sharp and wicked rammed, piercing the ear canal and driving deep into his skull. My God, he could feel it sliding in like the mandible of an insect, as if burrowing from one side of his head to the other! The agony was electric, unbelievable, explosive. What had the bastard done? Did he have a knife or pick?

The German opened his mouth to scream.

Then Sam's other fist plunged something into his right eye.

It pierced through Otto's eyeball. The pain was like fire. Blood spurted from his socket. He was paralyzed with horror, too shocked for a moment to react.

The delay was catastrophic.

Because then the other eye was blinded by another excruciating splinter and Otto exploded backward, launching himself off his unexpected tormentor and crashing back against the door of the cell. He clawed at his face, shrieking, boots scrabbling. There were sticks in his eyes! He was blind! Where had the American gotten them? His back arched in agony. He slid to the floor.

A boot came down on the Nazi's nose and it broke, exploding, and then on his teeth. They cracked. Otto couldn't react, his muscles wouldn't obey, because the pain was like an electrocution. He was accustomed to hurting, not being hurt. Then he dimly felt hands clawing at his turtleneck, hauling the collar down. And something very thin and very sharp sliced deep, very deep, into his neck. His jugular geysered.

When he opened his mouth to scream no sound came out.

Sam sat back, wheezing. He was sprayed with blood. Otto's corpse was frozen in a spasm of pain, back arched, boots twitching, crimson spurting from his neck until it stopped like a depleted gusher. Oh, Lord. He'd just killed a man, and in the most brutal way possible. He hadn't been sure it would work. The anger had been easy to summon, but to actually *do* it!

He surveyed his handiwork. His makeshift weapons jutted from ear, eyes, and throat. Fasces.

Sam knew it was unlikely he could beat Otto in a fistfight. He was already half-crippled from the earlier beating and had no martial arts training. So he'd pondered some advantage or weapon he could obtain. Then the word *fascist* had popped into his head and he'd remembered where it came from.

What did he have to work with in this bare cell?

Straw. The only thing they had in their lousy mattress.

It was stiff and prickly but weak, if each stalk was taken alone. But a bundle, carefully shaped like a sharpened pencil and reinforced with more straw wrapped around its shaft, became a crude stiletto if rammed into something vulnerable. Sam had fashioned four of them, each with the strength of a quill, and practiced hiding them in his fists and sleeves. Then he'd pondered how he could get Otto close enough to use them.

By playing coward.

Now the arrogant skinhead was dead. And the weird thing was, it didn't feel completely horrible. It felt *good*.

Shakily, Sam stood. He felt like he'd just been pummeled in a football game, but he was breathing and Otto wasn't. He spat at the man for good measure. Rape Rominy? I don't think so, Nazi shit.

Shuddering with release, he cracked open the door. What if more of them were out there?

Then you're already dead, Sam, no different from five minutes ago. One step at a time, man.

But the hall was empty. He stepped out. Otto had left a pistol, a menacing black one, on a bench. Probably to make things "fair." How thoughtful, skinhead. Above, he could hear the bang and clump of the construction workers.

Which meant there must be vehicles out there.

Sam crept up the stairs and turned to the gate that led to the crypt. Then across the basement room and out the rear door to the dry moat. If anyone saw him he'd look like some lunatic jihadist with his blood and pistol, but, no, it was still very early and the worker guys were all inside.

A plumbing van had keys.

So he drove carefully through the village, parked the vehicle behind a shed, and retrieved his BMW. He popped the trunk. Their belongings were still inside, including passports and Rominy's remaining cash. Slowly, not wanting any attention from police, he drove out of Wewelsburg.

In a stand of trees by the river he stopped to wash, rinsing his clothes as best he could and putting them back on wet. He'd crank up the Beamer heater. He had a little cash, a pistol, and their hunch about where Kurt Raeder and Jake Barrow, or Jakob, were going. He had a young woman who didn't deserve any of this. And he had, just maybe, a world to save.

Sam Mackenzie, necessary. Who woulda thunk it?

51

Wewelsburg, Germany
October 3, Present Day

Rominy had been given a shower, coffee, and a German pastry by a stone-faced Ursula Kalb, plus a reassuring smile that was not at all reassuring by the ghostly-looking Kurt Raeder. Then she was shoved into the backseat of a big black German Mercedes, solid as a tank and smelling of money. Apparently being a Nazi fanatic paid very well. Rominy had never been in a Mercedes before, and this one had leather seats, an engine that purred like a puma, and wood trim as shiny as a violin. She felt intimidated.

They drove south very fast, the tires taking curves in the bucolic German countryside as if they were on a train track.

"What's going to happen to Sam?" she asked Raeder.

He was sitting next to her in the backseat, with Jake in the front passenger seat as Ursula drove. Raeder was looking straight ahead. Without turning, he said, "Do you know that I've been waiting for this moment since 1938?"

"If you hurt Sam, I won't help you."

"Sam is on his way to a plane back to the United States. Don't worry about Sam."

She hoped that was true but didn't think so. Had this man killed her parents and grandmother, too? Was he really more than a century old?

"I can't believe you're Kurt Raeder. He must have been born near 1900. You look weird, but not like you're one hundred and ten or something."

"I'll take that as a compliment."

"And I don't believe your liar Jakob up there intended us to escape from Tibet. He boasted that there was no way to unlock the door when he sealed us in."

"And there wasn't, from inside."

She wanted to provoke some reaction beyond smug superiority. "We're going to an atom smasher, aren't we?"

"We are going, Rominy, to the Large Hadron Collider operated by CERN, the European Organization for Nuclear Research. It operates a seventeen-mile circular tunnel capable of accelerating subatomic particles to 99.999999991 percent of the speed of light." He clicked off every decimal as if taking credit for it. "Nothing like this has been achieved since the days of Shambhala. For me, it's a homecoming. It's a return to what I found in Tibet."

"Why me?"

"That will become clear in due course. In the meantime, I think I'll tell you a story. You asked last night about the body found in a cabin in America's Cascade Mountains. Do you want to know whose body that was?"

"Yes."

"It was Elizabeth Calloway, an aviatrix who flew Benjamin Hood from China to Tibet. Jakob tells me you've heard of her."

"I thought she was my great-grandmother. But I learned in Tibet my great-grandmother was actually a nun named Keyuri Lin. She killed herself and almost killed her baby, my grandmother."

"Ah. Keyuri is a sad story."

"But Jake told me the body was my great-grandfather, Benjamin Hood."

"Jakob told you a lot of things to make happen what is necessary to happen. But now that you're with us, Rominy, much more can be explained. We can share the truth, so you come to trust me. I want to tell you what happened by telling you about me: what I was, and what I am."

"How can you *be* Kurt Raeder?"

"Because I was . . . *changed*. Yes, I am more than one hundred years old, even though I have the body of a much younger man." He glanced at her skepticism. "All right, just *younger*. I can only assume that such transfiguration was for a purpose, a higher purpose. Dreams that were ashes in 1945 are about to be revived."

"Of Nazi conquest?"

"Of human transformation."

She put her hands to her temples. "I wish I was home."

"You *are* home. Hear me out."

Jake turned in the front seat. "We *do* care about you, Rominy." He sounded like an insurance salesman betting she wouldn't die to collect.

She stuck her tongue out at him and he flushed.

"In 1938," Raeder began, "I led a scientific expedition to Tibet. We'd heard legends of an ancient lost kingdom called Shambhala, and National Socialism took the initiative to investigate. Keyuri was a scholar who had studied old records. She agreed to act as our guide. Working together, we found a hidden valley and an underground city."

"Where we found the lake."

"Correct. Unfortunately, just as we were beginning our research, we were interrupted by Benjamin Hood, who came in shooting. He literally destroyed what would have been the greatest archaeological discovery of all time. Keyuri managed to escape with the staff that Jakob has since recovered for us, but my companions were all killed. And as Hood attacked he set off explosions that wrecked the valley."

"You're the victim here," she said drily.

"No, we both wanted to possess Shambhala, but I hoped its secrets would yield a higher purpose, not some cheap exhibit in a dusty New York museum. Hood would have bottled Shambhala, but I wanted to harness it. In any event, there was a machine we believe was related to today's colliders. It shattered and threw out a blinding light. And that's the last thing I remember."

"None of which would have happened if you hadn't led Nazis to Shambhala."

"I awoke thrown on the side of a mountain, my body in a state I'd never felt before. You're familiar with the process of photosynthesis, by which plants absorb and use the sun's energy? I felt I was absorbing energy, too, but from a new and wondrous source. It's not just that my flesh tingled, it felt like I was aware of every cell, every capillary, ever corpuscle. I saw the world I was familiar with, and at the same time a different world of shimmering force fields. A veil had been lifted. The blind had been given sight. It's impossible to accurately describe, but if you think of the aurora borealis, or the galactic clouds of gas photographed by the Hubble Space Telescope, you have some idea of the beauty of what's all around us, all the time, that we're ignorant of. I thought I'd died and become a ghost."

"And in a way, you had," said Jake.

"Yes. I *was* still alive, and hungry, and susceptible to heat and cold and all our other environmental burdens, but I'd somehow been infused with new dimensions of power as well. I was enormously confused, of course, but over the decades I've come to suspect I'd broken into a part of our universe we can't yet perceive. We Nazis called it Vril. Modern physicists talk of dark energy and dark matter. We can't *see* it, but we can see its effects on the universe we *do* see. It helps hold galaxies together, and accelerates the expansion of the cosmos. It's rather like a child recognizing the reality of air, or watching a bending tree from inside a house and realizing it's windy outside."

"Kurt had become a Shambhalan," Jake said. "A new man, like the superman dreamed of by German theorists. The next step in evolution."

"The master race," Rominy said.

"That term has been besmirched by history, but yes," said Raeder. "Hominids became human. Neanderthals gave way to *Homo sapiens*. Are humans never to evolve again? Or is there a higher destiny? We'd no time to determine where Shambhala came from. Was it simply an act of early human genius that somehow ran afoul of some calamity? Was it a work by space visitors who subsequently left? Was it the product of early gods from other dimensions, whom we've squeezed out in our narrow perception of existence? I've considered all these things. What if satyrs and dryads and Minotaurs were once real?"

"What if whatever the Shambhalans found killed them?" Rominy asked. "The notes we found talked of bones."

Raeder shrugged. "Or transformed them, transfigured them, for escape and elevation? If not for Hood, we might have answered such things. Instead I've been wandering for decades, waiting for our own science to catch up to that of the Shambhalans. I've become a very patient man."

"Why did my great-grandfather die and you didn't?"

"I wasn't at all sure he *did* die. I awoke to total disorientation. I was no longer at Shambhala. I'd been displaced, like a subatomic particle, to a spot some distance away. It was as if the entire experience had been a dream, or Shambhala had vanished. I wouldn't learn about the nunnery and Beth Calloway until much later. I wouldn't hear rumors that the staff Hood stole had survived until much later, when gold and terror persuaded some fallen nuns. I wouldn't learn about the lake until Jakob here returned from Tibet. So I set off on foot, weary but buoyed by this curious new energy. Knowing the British would likely try to capture and torture me for what I knew, I made my way west through the Hindu Kush, begging, working, and stealing. I survived blizzards and bandits in Afghanistan. I was briefly enslaved in Kandahar. I finally came to Persia. There I contacted German embassy personnel and was eventually flown to Berlin. By then, alas, the war had started and travel back to Tibet became impossible. I'd been exiled like Adam and Eve from Eden."

"You're not Adam, and that's no Eden."

He paid her no mind.

"No one knew what to make of me. My appearance had changed, not as drastically as you see now, but people responded to me as an oddity, a freak: the Yellow Ghost. I seemed infused with light, and babbling nonsense. My superiors kept me out of the way in obscure research work. Then came Barbarossa." He paused.

"What's that?" Rominy finally asked. She'd heard the name but had no idea what it meant.

"The code word for the invasion of the Soviet Union in 1941. Barbarossa was a medieval German hero, a Crusader king, and the world assumed the code word was simply taken from history. A few of us knew better. It was the blood of Frederick Barbarossa that won us admittance to Shambhala, and I was determined to return. It was the one thing that could win the war. Barbarossa was not just to conquer Russia. It was to reopen the way to Tibet."

"But you didn't conquer it."

"No." Raeder looked sad, lost in memory. "I accompanied the panzers driving toward the Caucasus but we were turned back, and then trapped at Stalingrad. I was captured when Paulus surrendered, and transported east to a Soviet prison camp. Yet Shambhala was as far away as ever. I had unusual powers—I could see what other men can't, and sometimes disable men with my will—but my capability wasn't mastered or consistent. I couldn't walk through the Soviet Union to Tibet. Instead I took an opportunity to escape and head northeast into the Siberian wilderness toward its junction with Alaska. I waited until autumn knocked down the blackflies and froze the worst of the mud and then raced the onset of winter. The natives recognized me as something strange, and gave me a skin boat to get rid of me. I paddled across the Bering Sea and made my way to Alaska, pretending to be a wrecked merchant seaman suffering from amnesia. Eventually I reached Seattle, was given the necessary American papers I claimed I'd lost, and took the train to New York. I wanted to track down Benjamin Hood. But at the Museum of American History I was told he'd never returned from Tibet. Even more mysteriously, his office papers had been shipped, at the request of the United States government, to a federal agent named Duncan Hale. And there the trail ended. I had no way to effectively hunt for Hood in a foreign country. As a German national I was wary of approaching Hale and being arrested as a spy. By now it was 1945 and clear that the end was near. Finally the *Führer* died and the Mongol hordes seized Berlin. Everything we'd dreamed of had crumbled."

"Except for killing millions of innocent people."

Raeder looked disapproving. "Then came news of the atomic bombing of Hiroshima and Nagasaki— far more indiscriminate than anything Germany had done—and inspiration came. Here was terrifying new atomic energy that would change the course of power politics. What if there was another, rival energy? What if there was Vril? I wrote Hale an anonymous letter, explaining that the American naturalist Benjamin Hood had found just such a power and was in hiding somewhere in the United States. Why look for my rival when your government would do it for me? I didn't have to follow Hood, I only had to follow Hale. Which I did. Much to my surprise, he traveled to Seattle, the very city I'd used to enter the United States. And then north to the area where you and Jakob visited the cabin. I bribed people to alert me where Hale might be going."

A practical consideration had occurred to Rominy. "Didn't you have to work? How did you get the time and money to do all this?"

"There was still a network of Nazi sympathizers in the United States. The FBI thought they'd caught all our agents, but they hadn't. I looked up members of the old German-American Bund and was eventually put into contact. I had a team following Hale."

"To Concrete and Cascade River?"

"Yes. Our plan was for Hale to confront Hood, have him seize whatever the zoologist had or knew, and then ambush them both in the cabin. It was too late for Hitler, but if we could return to Germany with a secret as potent as the atomic bomb, a secret revival could begin."

"The Fourth Reich," said Jake. "Purer and better than the Third."

"Hitler made mistakes," Raeder conceded.

"Which this time we'll avoid," Jake amended.

"Unfortunately," Raeder went on, "it was at the cabin that the real mystery began. We didn't find Hood, we found Beth Calloway, dead of a gunshot wound. Nor could we find Duncan Hale."

"Until Jake and I found his corpse in that mine."

"My guess is there was some kind of showdown between Hale and Beth," Jake said. "Gunshots, a mine cave-in . . . we won't ever have the whole story, but in 1945 the secret seemed lost."

"And moot," Raeder said. "Shambhala was closed off, and the staff I'd had was shattered in the explosions. The legend was lost. And yet I couldn't let it go. I snuck back into Tibet in the turbulent 1950s and heard rumors that a surviving relic had been locked away by Keyuri Lin, who was gone. There were also stories of a child, taken to America. I began to put two and two together. I guessed there was another blood lock, meaning the only one who could open it was the missing child, your half-Tibetan grandmother. But even if we found a surviving staff, what would we do with it? The machine to energize it had been destroyed. So I decided to wait."

"Immortality gives you patience," said Jake.

"You're *immortal?*" Rominy asked Raeder.

Raeder's smile was stretched, like rubber, over those worn teeth. "Unfortunately not. Just *extended*. Vril does not end the aging process, as we hoped, but it *has* prolonged it by halting the natural aging process in the telomeres of my cells. We have a fuse that burns down, but in my case the fuse got snuffed. I get sick, I feel pain, but I persist. Which meant that no one followed the progress of subatomic physics more avidly than I. This, I realized, was the answer. So I began to recruit promising young scientists and encouraged them to enter the field. We are a fraternity within a scientific fraternity, with political goals as well as scientific ones."

"To bring back Nazi barbarism."

"To resurrect the Aryan and with it a new Germany, a Germany of the kind envisioned by National Socialism but better, firmer, truer. Pure, evolved, cleansed, the leader of mankind. A race as superior to the rest of our species as *Homo sapiens* were to Neanderthals. It will start with Vril, Rominy, this secret energy I was the first to find. With Vril, and with you."

"I'm not cooperating with any of this!"

"You have the right blood, Rominy. We're going to expose you to this new light, this new science, and turn you, with me, into the first Shambhalans."

582 • WILLIAM DIETRICH

52

Large Hadron Collider, Geneva, Switzerland
October 4, Present Day

Between Lake Geneva and the Jura Mountains, a platter of farm and industrial land hides the largest supercollider on earth. It is built in a tunnel seventeen miles in circumference and more than 300 feet underground, split into eight arcs and interrupted by four gigantic detectors the size of dam powerhouses. These trace the invisibly small particle collisions that the device creates.

The CERN collider consumes enough electricity to power the homes of Geneva, Switzerland. It creates vacuums that in total equal in size the nave of a great cathedral. It uses liquid helium to cool its superconducting magnets that bend and accelerate the beams to nearly absolute zero. The machine's goal is to re-create on the tiniest scale the extremes of temperature and energy at the Big Bang and thus give a peek at the origin of the universe. Its particle beam is so sensitive that the tidal pull of the moon must be taken into effect when it whirls around its gigantic racetrack.

Kurt Raeder was determined to put this achievement to his own use.

Physicists had made careful calculations to reassure the public that the Large Hadron Collider would not create earth-swallowing black holes or theorized "strange" subatomic quarks, called strangelets, that might detonate with matter. What they'd not calculated was that the vast energies the machine focuses could be used to reconstitute the lost technology of Shambhala.

Instead, a cabal of neo-Nazi physicists secretly had.

"Our Fellowship has been waiting for a long time, Rominy," Raeder lectured as the Mercedes hummed along the lakeside boulevard in Geneva, headed toward the CERN complex west of the city. Night had fallen, and lights glinted in the lake. "Waiting for science to catch up. Waiting for the blood heir we needed, which was you. And waiting for generations of our ideological followers to graduate with physics degrees and infiltrate the subatomic fraternity. Yes, we have allies! Not just scientists but guards, administrators, public relations personnel, science writers, mechanics, custodians, and suppliers. For half a century I've been constructing a web of loyalists, a mafia if you will, who have been working toward this day. The Large Hadron Collider itself has been a project twenty years in the making."

"You're claiming that *Nazis* built the supercollider?"

"No. A few who helped are National Socialists or, in more contemporary terms, conservative visionaries. And our broader Fellowship plans to use it, to borrow it. Our members extend to the very highest ranks of government and finance. Think about it: Why are the world's organizations spending more than six billion dollars to slap protons together? Six thousand *million* dollars? They raised this for a science project? Yes, many of those involved naively believe the supercollider is for pure science. In their ignorance they are our most valuable allies. The American physicist Leon Lederman used the term *God Particle* to explain the search for the Higgs boson, a property that could explain why matter exists at all. Scientists are very clever, and they have succeeded in capturing the public's imagination."

"But you're smarter than all of them," Rominy said sarcastically.

He smiled. "But *governments* and *business* want more out of this underground cathedral we've constructed. They want power for their investment. And so we promised; if they built it we would deliver magic of a kind never seen before, and turn the balance of power on its head. Northern Europe will regain its rightful role as ruler of the world. Those bureaucrats who have backed construction and development think the secret benefits will be shared, yielding discovery that will remake economies and technology. They envision an era of unparalleled prosperity. But those closest to me know that the mysteries of Shambhala must *not* be shared, that democracy is a Jewish idea that poisons society, and that these discoveries are by rightful bloodline the inheritance of the Aryan, governed by National Socialism, and will be used to establish our reign on earth. If you want to call that Nazism, so be it."

He was obviously mad, but that didn't mean a cabal of madmen couldn't wreak havoc. Hadn't that been the cause of World War II? And out of it had come the atom bomb. And now this?

"But you needed the staff hidden in Shambhala," she clarified. "This machine wasn't enough."

He looked at the window at the dark lake. "Yes. We don't really understand how the staff worked, or how to duplicate it. But if it can be made to work now, we can begin to study and replicate. Eventually we'll have legions of staff-wielding Aryans, imposing their will by the force of their thought. They will strum the consciousness that undergirds the universe. We'll play the cosmic music and reconfigure the world."

"What did you mean about us becoming the first Shambhalans?"

"That you will be envied by every woman in the world. What we are about, as I explained, is human evolution. We can't go on as advanced apes armed with atomic bombs and spewing a million tons of carbon a day. We have to evolve, to reach a higher plane. We need to reproduce selectively to accelerate mankind's biologic destiny. So we've been searching for candidates."

They sped on a boulevard. She saw an airport, hotels, office buildings, and the cozy rectangles of lighted apartment windows, a world of normality that seemed impossibly far away. What quiet domestic life was plodding along there, a pot of tea, a TV show, a book, and the silken warmth of a cat on someone's lap? Children in their beds. A glass of wine with a loved one. All light-years away.

She'd already tried the handle of the Mercedes. Useless, like the handle of Jake Barrow's truck. Hadn't her mother told her never to get in a car with strangers?

How was she going to stop this if Sam didn't come?

Then they were approaching a sculptured sphere, lit by floodlights, that rose above a lawn like a representation of . . . what? The earth? The atom? The cosmos? It was rust red. Dried-blood red.

"What the hell does that *mean*?" she pressed. "Reproduce selectively?"

"That will be explained at the moment of transfiguration. Ah, here we are."

They were pulling into a parking lot at a complex of large, mostly windowless, blandly boxed research buildings of the kind stamped out all over the world, like pieces of a game of Risk. There was a word on one: *Atlas*. Hadn't he held up the cosmos?

"Will you give me your hands please?"

"My hands?"

"Just lift them up."

Hesitantly she did so, keeping balled in her fist something she'd held tightly as a teddy bear since Wewelsburg. Raeder smoothly reached out and snapped handcuffs on her wrists. "Just so you won't hurt anything, or yourself. Routine precaution." Then the sedan doors opened and strong, military hands pulled her out into the chilly air.

Someone snapped something on her ankle.

"A tracking device," Jake said. "Please don't try to run. We have dogs and Tasers."

Yep, that's quite the boyfriend you picked, Rominy.

She'd felt this way only one time before, on a gurney wheeling down a sterile hospital hallway for removal of her appendix, lights passing overhead like flickering suns, doors hissing open and shutting behind her like portals to hell. She'd been ten, and terribly frightened. Now she felt numbing dread, as she realized that the last weeks had been a long, sickening plummet into an abyss.

"Six billion dollars to find a particle? Absurd," Raeder said as they walked toward the building. "But six billion dollars to *manipulate* those particles, and with them the world itself? *That's* a bargain. Six billion dollars of taxpayer money to seize power for yourself? To rule? To monopolize? To become unbelievably rich by reducing lesser races to slavery, their natural state? That's why so many were persuaded to help us. Some with doubts were bribed. Others blackmailed. Any would-be heroes suffered untimely accidents. We've been very thorough."

They stopped at a door. Green-uniformed guards with black berets and belts weighted with equipment were clustered there. One of them stepped forward. "We can only guarantee control of the sector until the morning shift, *Reichsführer*," he said, addressing Raeder. "Rennsler is still in the dark, but when he comes to work he'll mobilize the rest of security against us. After that, it will be on the news and everything will come crashing down."

The German nodded. "If our calculations are correct, the remaining night will be time enough. Once we demonstrate the staff, they'll give us time to complete our mission. Key government officials will stand with us. And if not, they cannot stand against us, once we have Vril."

The man gave a stiff-armed salute. "Fellowship!"

"Fellowship." They passed inside. As they did, Rominy let the thing she'd held in her hands fall, kicking it against a drainpipe.

A million-to-one shot. But when there was no hope, those were good odds.

The next door was stronger, and here waited a cluster of men who looked like academics. One had the proverbial white jacket, but the others were casual in khakis or jeans. They looked nervous, but none showed any surprise at her handcuffs. White-jacket greeted Raeder and then stepped to a keypad next to the door and typed in a code. Then he put his eye to a small eyepiece above it.

"Retinal scan," Jake said to Rominy, standing close like he was still her freaking boyfriend. Maybe he thought he still would be, once the master race had established control. She looked away and tried to psychically relay waves of revulsion at him, but if he detected her contempt, he gave no sign.

The door opened and they entered a shaft landing. Stairs led downward into gloom. Next to it was an elevator shaft. Elevator doors opened and a dozen packed in, Rominy squeezed by aspiring Nazi lunatics, her handcuffed hands held humiliatingly in front of her. Men glanced at her curiously and she wanted to spit in their face. Should she make a scene? But what could she do? She was utterly alone, at the spire of a scientific cathedral buried in the bowels of the earth.

The elevator disgorged them just one floor down. Another door, and another retinal scan, and then they passed into a control room, banks of computers and video screens taking up an otherwise bland, off-white windowless space. Industrial carpet, mesh office chairs, laminate counters. The screens showed columns of numbers, graphs, and video camera scenes of tunnels and huge machines. She assumed the videos were showing parts of the supercollider. It looked as colorful as a Tinker Toy.

Then she started. Three bodies lay facedown on the floor against one wall, with a cowl of blood around their heads and neat round holes in the backs of their skulls.

"It was easier to dispose of them than try to persuade them," the security chief said.

Raeder nodded. "There's no turning back. We'll put up a plaque. Sacrifices to human evolution."

The scientists who had ridden the elevator with them scattered to the screens. Now there was a faint whine as something was started up. A faint odor of oil and ozone. "It will take about an hour to regain full power," one of the men said.

"Time enough to get the girl into position. Jakob? Rominy? Follow me."

She hesitated, wondering where best to make a stand, but then the big cop guy stepped menacingly toward her. So she reluctantly followed, but took a moment to turn and stick her tongue out at the security chief, too.

He took it in, his expression not changing.

Not a good sign.

On they marched, meek little Rominy like a little lamb to the slaughter, software cubicle-ista to her newest duty, proud feminist a dutiful two steps behind.

She began trying to guess how to blow things up.

She didn't even have chewing gum.

Down an elevator again, much farther this time, dropping three hundred feet into the bedrock of the Swiss-French border. They came out into the nave of this colossal church of physics.

An enormous room, four or five stories high, and atop it a shaft the size of a missile silo that clawed toward the surface like the spout hole of a whale. To look at the origin of the sky, the physicists had delved underground like Tolkien's cursed dwarves. But what a wonderland they'd created. The chamber was lined with tiers of catwalks like the balconies of an opera house, plus pipes, ducts, great metal troughs crammed with cables, cranes, stairs, ladders, columns, beams, grids, tanks, levers, air conditioners, hatches . . . it was a cornucopia of technology. And the colors! They were taken from a crayon set. Red, green, blue, and yellow, bright as Legos, and then spotless stainless, shiny copper, burnished bronze, reflective blacks, all glinting at each other like a hall of mirrors. How had they ever conjured such magnificent complexity? It was like the riot of color she'd seen in the temples of Lhasa. It was not just science, it was art, not just instrument but beauty. It hummed and buzzed and clicked and crackled like a child's toy and had the smell of a place entirely unnatural: concrete, paint, oil, grease, rubber, and plastic. The particle detector was scrupulously clean, absolutely sterile, and yet as sensory as a field of wildflowers. Fluorescent light cast everything in a cold, metallic glow.

It was another secret city, like Shambhala.

And somehow Kurt Raeder had penetrated this, to corrupt it. To re-create his lost ruin.

Another scientist saluted them. My God, how many physicists had signed on for this craziness? But then Raeder, if it was really Raeder, had been building toward this moment for seventy years. An incongruous thought occurred.

"Did you ever open a bank account?"

He turned. "What?"

"When you got back from Tibet. With compound interest, you might be a rich man by now if you've really lived all those years. Hood did that, or Beth Calloway. I inherited."

He wasn't sure if she was joking and for the first time looked off-balance. "I've spent ever pfennig, every moment, every drop of sweat and blood on this dream."

"Too bad. You could have retired by now and left us all alone."

Jakob, or Jake, pushed her from behind. "Pay no attention to her, Kurt. She's an idiot who will completely waste your time."

"*I* wasted *your* time?" But then she felt the press of a gun barrel in the small of her back.

"Shut up and do as you're told," her ex-lover said.

They walked a balcony, heels drumming on textured metal, walking into the technology like sperm penetrating the gigantic egg of this vast, bulky machine. Centenarian Raeder obscenely spry like an animated cadaver, Jake/Jakob robotic, Rominy mournful. If the cathedral nave was complicated, this tighter area deeper into the machine works was incomprehensible. There were steel panels, copper conduits, and brightly colored pistons, bobbins, and spools. She was making the words up because she had no idea what she was looking at. The riotous assemblage of finely machined parts reminded her of pictures of rocket engines and submarines. The barrel-shaped *thing* was as big as the cross section of a small ship. On its face, triangular pie-piece panels, each the size of an apartment, radiated out like the petals of a flower. The stamen in the middle was a narrow pipe that jutted out and ran toward a tunnel beyond.

"It reminds me of a sun wheel," Jake said. "All worship, rightfully so, goes back to the sun. All life originates there."

They came to a smaller gallery leading to the jutting pipe. There was an arched ceiling twenty feet overhead, with a tracked crane spanning the gallery's width. An orange-colored hook to hoist things dangled from it. Cables and chains dropped down to a narrow pipe, little bigger than a household waterline, which ran from the center of the vast machine. This extended to a much larger pipe, the size of a sewer line with the diameter of a manhole. The big pipe was painted blue and extended into a tunnel as far as she could see.

It was like being inside a giant mechanical cocoon. A section of the silvery smaller pipe had been removed and technicians were bolting a new apparatus in its place. This new piece was about the size of a submarine torpedo and consisted of a cylindrical bundle of rods. There was space between each rod, connected with colored wires. Inside was a clear Plexiglas tube.

The bundle reminded her of the fasces that Sam had talked about.

She hoped his scheme had worked, but she suspected Otto had killed her friend by now. The sadness added to her feeling of hopelessness.

Then she noticed that there was another rod, a staff, lying horizontally in the midst of this new device. Its ends lined up with the narrow pipe.

It was the amber-colored staff Jake had stolen from the chamber below the nunnery at the edge of Shambhala. It was Kurt Raeder's magic wand, the wizard's staff, the gun of Vril. My God. They were going to recharge it.

"Hurry, before the radiation levels climb too high," Raeder told the technicians.

They nodded. "We have our REM badges. But you can hear the machine accelerating." And indeed the background whine was rising. There was a deeper rumble, too, of huge generators and pumps, the lungs of the whale.

Radiation? Her heart began to hammer.

"Rominy, we're at the end of our journey and I can't follow you any longer," said Jake. "Not yet." He was still pointing a pistol at her. It looked like the kind the Germans used in the old World War II movies. What were they called?

A Luger.

At least he wasn't hanging around to have some kind of weird SS sex. With Raeder talking about spawning a new master race, she'd worried she was supposed to get it on with her kidnapper. But then that couldn't be true, could it? She was part Asian, thanks to Great-grandma Keyuri, and mongrel American to boot.

So just what *was* she doing here?

The technicians twisted a few final bolts and stood. "That's it. Really just a harness to hold the staff in place. The rest is up to the accelerator itself."

"You may watch from the control room," Raeder said. "Jakob, you'd better remove her handcuffs."

"What if she panics?"

"There's nowhere for her to go. I'm worried that with the electromagnetic energies involved, that much metal might trigger something we haven't planned for. Take the tracking device, too. I don't want the large amounts of electricity involved arcing into her body."

"Maybe I should stay with you, Kurt."

"It's too much of a gamble to risk both of us on Vril's first manifestation," Raeder replied. "I've staked my life on this, but if it doesn't work as expected, I want you to survive to carry on. Rominy must be the seed carrier."

"The *what* carrier?" she protested.

Kurt turned to her as Jake removed the cuffs and stooped to take off the ankle bracelet. "Of the next evolution. You're going to experience the fundamental energies of the universe as I have, Rominy. It will stun you, and frighten you, but it's quite survivable, as you can see by looking at me. You will be transfigured, transformed. It will feel good when it's over. You'll absorb dark energy like a plant. You'll have a longevity that the ones left behind will long for. And then you're going to carry my first child. You are going to be as revered as the Virgin Mary." He smiled, plasticky lips stretched over worn teeth, eyes sunken, skin like wax.

She looked at him with horror. "And stay a virgin, right?"

"We all know you're no virgin and no, I'm not a god to inseminate you with my spirit. I'm afraid we'll do it the old-fashioned way."

"Are you joking?" Not with Barrow, but with *him*?

"It's a necessary step for the future the *Führer* dreamed of."

"You want me to have *sex* with you? My God, you're a hundred and ten, a hundred and twenty years old!"

"Which doesn't matter. You'll see."

"It's just sex, Rominy," Jake added. "Don't put so much meaning into it."

"It sure as hell had no meaning to *you*, did it?"

He shrugged. "I enjoyed it well enough."

"God, why don't you just shoot me?"

"I'm afraid that isn't part of the plan," Jake said. "You're to be infused with the light as Kurt was at Shambhala, and then bred. No different than on the farm."

"No! This is crazy! Look at him, he's hideous! And I'm no Aryan!" She was desperate. "You said yourself I'm part Tibetan and who knows what else. I'm the wrong blood! You've got the wrong woman!"

"No we don't," Raeder said calmly.

"How do you *know* that?"

"Because Jakob did all the DNA tests back in the United States. You're precisely who we thought you are."

She was sweating. The younger man had stood closer, and she longingly eyed his pistol. But then he gave it to Raeder and backed away.

"I'll wait in the control room," he said. "Himmler's dream, Kurt."

The older man nodded. "Himmler's dream." He watched Barrow retreat. She heard the click of a door closing. "Now you learn who you really are."

"Who?" she asked. "Who am I, Raeder?"

"You're my descendant, Rominy."

Now there was a roaring in her ears. "What?"

"Benjamin Hood wasn't your great-grandfather. I was."

She looked at him in horror.

"I possessed Keyuri Lin on the way to Shambhala. She insisted on sex with Hood, but it was *my* child she had in the nunnery. That's why she tried to kill it. But Fate intervened, in the person of Beth Calloway. It was *my* DNA that Jakob brought to have tested in the United States with yours to prove the match to the bankers, not that from Hood's finger. But you and I *are* separated by enough generations. And now we, you and I, are going to have a child—a super-child, a master child—together."

His eyes were bright, his skin cracked, his grin a death's-head grimace. "One of the powers of Vril is that my sexual appetite hasn't slackened, it's increased." He took a small leather folder from the breast pocket of his suit. "So have my *tastes*." He flipped it open.

It held an array of bright, shiny surgical instruments, things to cut and pinch.

The whine of the machine climbed to a shriek, matching her scream.

53

Large Hadron Collider, Geneva, Switzerland
October 4, Present Day

S am had gotten the Beamer up to 200 kilometers an hour, which he calculated was somewhere north of 125 mph, faster than he'd ever driven. It was gray German autumn, the autobahn his crowded racetrack, and he'd weaved past speeding trucks as if they were standing still. The astonishing thing was that occasionally an Audi or Lotus kept pace with him. What a crazy country. He was gambling where they'd taken Rominy and hoped he got there before the Nazis found skewered Otto back in Wewelsburg, or the German police came after him with too many questions. It was dark by the time he got to Switzerland and Geneva, where he promptly got lost because he was too hurried to ask directions. *That's dude thinking, dude.* He finally got

straight—everybody seemed to speak some English—
and now it was the middle of the night as he drove more
cautiously toward CERN headquarters. He was looking for something out of the ordinary and hoped to find
Rominy in the middle of it.

There was a weird globe thingy that looked like sal-
vage from a world's fair, and a sprawl of office buildings in generic business-park blah. Roads, parking
lots, museum signs, the whole nine yards. So he was
at one point in a seventeen-mile underground loop he
couldn't even see . . .

How was he ever going to find Rominy?

And then there was a cluster of cars and men and
bobbing flashlights by some boxy building that looked
about as elegant as an airplane hangar. So what was a
cluster of men who looked like they were carrying assault rifles doing in the middle of the night in a science
park?

He slowed. Had Rominy left a sign as he'd asked?

And then he saw it, a scrap that would be taken for
insignificant garbage at any other time. It was the white
of a *khata* scarf, the scrap Beth Calloway had used in a
Cascades cabin to write a code in invisible ink.

Rominy had dropped it.

Bingo. "Mackenzie, you're not such a bad guide
after all," he murmured.

Yep, why were the world's top physicists hanging out in a parking lot in the wee hours of the morning unless they were up to some Nazi-no-good? So all he had to do was . . .

What? He had Otto's gun but it was twenty to one, at least. How many skinhead sympathizers were there in the world, anyway? What he really needed was a bazooka, or a battery of Hawk missiles, or the ability to call in an airstrike, but he'd left his Pentagon calling card at home. While the Good Ol' USA would have had a neon reader board thirty feet high screaming "Guns!" and a cash register line of stubble-head goobers who looked like they shouldn't be licensed to handle screwdrivers, everything in Europe was very low-key pacifist and urban cool. Where did you get your hands on an RPG launcher when you needed one? Especially on a continent where every town looked as dandy as Disneyland?

He had to get inside and poke around for Rominy. Which meant getting in the door, which meant distracting the Nazi goons, which meant . . .

He let his car cruise by the cluster of crazies. They eyed him like an L.A. street gang but didn't budge. Then buildings shielded him from view, and he looked around.

Which *meant* driving full-tilt into something that said *Verboten* and was decorated with skull and crossbones. Like those tanks behind a cyclone fence next to what looked to be some kind of laboratory.

"Double bingo."

He needed noise. There couldn't be *that* many people who'd signed on with that lunatic Raeder, which meant the more folks Sam could pull into ground zero, the more likely someone in authority would start asking the bad guys some awkward questions. And if Otto's murderous intentions were any indication, Sam Mackenzie needed to hurry.

Plan One: suicide charge into a tank farm and hope the airbag worked and he was conscious enough to crawl out before he fried.

Bad plan.

So how about Plan Two? He parked in the shadows and popped the BMW's trunk. He took his backpack, stuffed Rominy's passport and cash with his own belongings, and slung it on his back. There was an emergency kit inside with road flares. There was also a doughnut spare tire, just the size for what he had in mind.

He drove the BMW to within a hundred yards of the cluster of tanks, aimed the wheels, and used the jumper cables in the rental trunk to clamp the steering wheel to the passenger door handle. That would keep his new robot car on course, he hoped. The Beamer was still rumbling, unaware of its impending sacrifice. Parking brake *on*. He cradled the spare tire, took it to the front seat, and leaned in.

"The rental company is going to be very, very pissed," he whispered to himself.

He jammed the spare forward under the dash on top of the gas pedal, where it stuck, snug as a cork.

The engine screamed. Parking brake *off.* And as Sam sprang backward, the car howled, that beautiful Bavarian whine, and shot forward.

It was his very own cruise missile. The Beamer accelerated like a drag racer, tires smoking, and hit freeway speeds at the collision point. There was tragic beauty in how it ran straight and true. The coupe smashed through the fence and plowed into the tanks, knocking them sideways. The bang of the collision echoed in the peaceful night air, and he could see the white of the Beamer's airbags deployed as a building alarm began to sound. There was a gush, and the air smelled like propane.

The car's front end had accordioned, steam erupting, but nothing else had happened yet. Sam ran as close as he dared, snapped a highway flare to light it, and threw. Then he dashed away.

Night flashed into day. A fireball erupted skyward, pieces of tank and car arcing outward like meteors.

Then another explosion, and another. He could feel the heat and punches of air.

Wow, better than the Fourth of July.

Sam ducked into the shadows. The swarm of men outside the hangarlike building had broken and were running toward the fire he'd set, shouting in German and French and waving guns.

In the distance he could hear sirens. The concussions from the explosions had set off car alarms.

"Well, it's a start."

He glanced about and spied a utility pipe grating. Lifting it, he saw metal rungs. He jammed the pack behind them for temporary safekeeping. Then he trotted in the shadows toward his goal.

"I'm coming, Rominy."

There was still a sprawl of cars and vans around the entrance but most of the Nazi goons, if that's what they were, had been drawn off to investigate. Two remained at the door, holding wicked-looking rifles. Sam didn't hesitate; if he did, his nerve would fail him. He knew something awful was about to happen to the young woman he'd come to like so much. Sam had Otto's automatic tucked in the small of his back and a second or two of surprise. He walked forward like he belonged. The men raised their guns.

"Raeder?" Sam demanded.

They hesitated, one giving a nod inside and then thinking better of it.

Triple bingo.

The Nazi bastard was here all right, which meant Sam's spectacular arson and Wewelsburg killing just might be justifiable to the authorities, in the unlikely event slacker Mackenzie survived this night. He strode for the door, trying to look as important as the VIPs waved through the velvet rope at a nightclub, rather than the cheap Third World tourist guide he was. Attitude, man.

The goons hesitated, and Sam guessed these weren't hired paramilitary but just weekend Nazis told to keep watch while the big dogs worked inside. They shouted some German crap.

"Stoppen. Wer sind sie?"

So he pulled the pistol and shot one of them in the leg. Necessity made you one motherfucker of invention, didn't it? The man yelped in surprise and fell, writhing. Before the other could lift his assault rifle Sam was on top of him, his barrel pressed against the man's left eye. "Droppen, you Nazi dick. I'm tired of this shit." As the man's gun fell he shoved him through the door, slamming and locking it behind them. "*Schnell, schnell*," he ordered, pushing the man down a short corridor. "Yeah, I've seen the war movies."

A fusillade of shots stuttered through the door he'd just locked. The wounded man didn't care for being wounded, apparently, and was venting his frustration. The bullet holes popped through the metal like expressions of surprise.

That was okay. The noise would bring more police.

There was another door with a keypad next to it. "Open it!"

His prisoner shook his head, his courage back after the surprise attack.

So Sam shot him in the foot.

He yelled and hopped, Sam grabbing his shoulder and pistol-whipping his face. "Open it!" he screamed. He shook his gun. "Or I kill you! *Verstehen?*" Yeah, he understood.

Shaking, the guard tapped some numbers. Nothing happened.

Sam lifted his pistol to the man's temple. "One."

The man was sweating, but frozen.

"Two . . ." Surely this bastard knew how to count to three in English? "Three is the last word you're going to hear, Fritz." Nothing. "Thre . . ." He tightened on the trigger.

The guard lurched forward, blood gushing from his foot, mouth bruised, and put his eye up against some kind of reader. Now there were shouts outside and more shots. With a bang, the outer lock disintegrated. Damn. The Nazi rescue posse had arrived. They'd probably gotten tired of watching his car burn.

But now the door Sam needed to get through was opening.

He brought down his pistol as heavily as he could on the guard's head, and with a crack the sentry went down. Then the American stepped through and the door slid shut. As he did so he could see men bursting through the outer entrance and spying him. They raised their guns.

Sam's door hissed to a close just as another volley of bullets hit it. None penetrated.

"Good Swiss engineering." Sam shot a keypad on his side, hoping that would disable the opening mechanism, and looked around. There was an elevator—a box to be trapped in, he feared—and flights of stairs.

Sam started down the stairs.

54

Large Hadron Collider, Geneva, Switzerland
October 4, Present Day

Y ou're too young to fully understand the intellectual
marathon I required to get to this point," Raeder
said to Rominy. He regarded her with disappointment.
"You're shaking."

"Please don't hurt me."

"I'm going to *pleasure* you. You'll see. Pain is
exquisite."

What could she use as a weapon? Everything was
bolted, wired, fused. There were danger signs and
voltage warnings.

"When we found Shambhala," Raeder went on, "it
had a machine much like this one, but we were like
cavemen contemplating a computer. We had no idea,
really, what it was for, except that it seemed capable

of energizing quite marvelous staffs. Then a blizzard of inventions. Radar. Television. Atomic bombs. Microwave ovens. Laser disks. And more than these toys, this incredible creation story being spun out by physicists. A big bang. A divorce between energy and matter. Thirteen billion years of galactic evolution. And even a microscopic wonderland of particles too tiny to ever see, which didn't even seem to follow the laws of nature. Or rather, we had the laws all wrong at the most fundamental level. Moreover, new kinds of energy and matter we can't even detect that nonetheless dominate the universe. I began to understand what had infused and powered me, and had infused and powered Shambhala. The legends of the Vril Society were based on truth! So I began to seek out key young physicists who wanted to do more than just watch protons collide. Men and women with ambition. Vision. A sense of history."

"German scientists."

"Some, but not all."

"People of ruthless greed."

"The ideals of National Socialism have universal appeal."

"Nobody told you that you look embalmed?"

Some color actually came into his cheeks. "Invigorated, given my age. Potent, as you'll see."

She closed her eyes. "That's the *last* thing I want to see."

"Eventually I realized that Shambhala had been a supercollider. We began to theorize the staff's properties. We didn't have one to study, and no technology to make it, but bright young men could calculate a molecular structure that might carry messages from the string realm and its curled dimensions to our own. Eventually we realized that the energy levels achieved by the Large Hadron Collider at CERN might be enough, if properly diverted, to activate a dark energy flow, if it ran at full power. What we needed was an actual staff, and to get that we needed an actual heir. And if you helped us, how to reward you? By making you mother of the new master race."

"I don't want to be the mother of your damn race! Your stupid lectures are *not* seductive!"

The whine was growing louder. "It's destiny, Rominy. Accept your fate. We're locked together by blood." He raised his pistol to aim at her face, his arm rock steady. "There will be a flash of illuminating light such as you've never felt before, and it will irradiate every cell in your body. Do not fear. It will only purify, not kill."

"Will it hurt?" Her voice broke, and she was struggling not to cry.

"Yes."

Lights flickered. The sound of the machines kept rising, like a building hurricane. Inside its fascist cage, the staff of Shambhala began to glow.

"I fell unconscious when it happened to me," he added.

She glanced wildly about for some way to fight back. All she saw was a web of pipes and power cables, a hive of bus bars, and warning signs in English, French, and German. If she grabbed the wrong thing she would die.

But was that so bad, given the alternative?

Then, over the shrill sound of the accelerator, there was a more guttural rattling.

She looked up. The crane had moved to a point directly above them. And now, from the shadows, a great black chain that had been suspended like the cord of a swag lamp swung down with its heavy yellow hook. It was arcing toward them, a thousand pounds in weight, as powerful as a scythe.

Riding it was a wild-eyed tour guide. "Rominy, get out of the way!"

Sam! He was aiming a pistol.

Raeder shouted in rage and aimed his own gun.

Rominy leaped and bit his hand.

He howled, both men shooting as Sam swept down like some demented Tarzan, bullets ricocheting like popcorn.

Rominy bit harder. Raeder, snarling, hurled her aside, his strength immense, inhuman. She skidded on the slick floor.

But the chain, which had been suspended above, cut down through the tunnel air with the power of a wrecking ball, clearing the cement floor by inches. With a tremendous clang it smashed into the side of the metal cage where the Shambhala staff glowed and knocked the whole apparatus askew. Sam went flying toward the piping on the far wall and hit the cables. There was a crack like thunder and a flash as blinding as the sun. Then all light winked out.

With a groan, the whine of the accelerator began to drop, its power short-circuited. They'd blown the mother of all fuses, apparently.

And, much to her amazement, Rominy was still alive.

Red emergency lighting came on. Sam lay like a dead man, clothes smoking, obviously electrocuted. The great chain and hook had come to rest against the pipe it had ruptured. The break sizzled, and a fog was filling the room. The Klaxons of alarms were going off, and she thought she could hear distant shooting.

Where was Raeder?

She got to her hands and knees. She was shaking, whether from fear or adrenaline she wasn't sure. Probably both. She crawled to Sam and bent to his lips.

The wispiest of breaths. Barely, he was alive.

Rominy looked around. Two pistols lay on the floor. And half falling out of its bent cradle and still glowing faintly was the crystalline staff.

She could smell burning rubber and plastic.

Then a figure staggered out of the smoke and mist. It was Kurt.

Now he looked every bit his hundred and ten years, gaunt, lined, exhausted, furious. He lurched toward her like a broken monster, eyes filled with disbelief.

"He displaced the magnets," the German croaked. "Proton beam. It went out of alignment. Seven trillion volts."

She didn't understand what he meant. But then she saw his head droop toward his torso. His shirt had been sliced open and there was a thin black line etched halfway across his chest. Even as he stared, it began to bleed the thinnest of sheets.

"The idiot cut me in two." Then Raeder collapsed.

Now Rominy could hear explosions in the rooms above, shouts, doors slamming. It sounded like a battle. She had to hide! She no longer knew whom to trust, except Sam, who had somehow miraculously escaped Wewelsburg only to fry here! Should she stay with him? Take a gun?

Then she saw motion at the far end of the balcony they'd used to get to this chamber. She recognized the silhouette with sick dread. It was Jake.

A voice came into her head, a presence she'd never felt before. *Take the staff.* She flushed and felt renewed from a burst of energy. And knew, instantly, that she'd heard the voice of Benjamin Hood.

She looked around. Was he here?

Nothing. But his spirit? That was present. *Take the staff.*

She hesitated only a moment. Then she seized the crystalline rod, stood, and began a stumbling run into the tunnel where the big blue pipe ran. The rod vibrated slightly, making her palm tingle. Jake must not get his hands on the staff, not when it might have absorbed the necessary energy. So she fled in the only direction she could, straight down an apparently endless tunnel. She didn't know where else to go. She began running faster as the shock wore off, carrying the ancient artifact. The tunnel gently curved, she realized, just as Jake had said it would. How long had he said the tube was? Seventeen miles?

She had to be marathon girl.

But there was no end, really. She could run and run, and just get back to where she started, again and again. With Nazis after her. Now she did begin to sob.

"Rominy!" It was Jake's shout, far behind.

And then she saw a bicycle.

55

Large Hadron Collider, Geneva, Switzerland
October 4, Present Day

For the first time Rominy felt hope. Bicycles must be how the collider staff got from detector to detector. She was pedaling madly down the endless tunnel, the Shambhala staff jutting forward from her grip like a knight's lance. It glowed. All she had to find was some exit from which she could escape and hide in the woods. She had no idea what was happening elsewhere in the giant machine, but it was a battle she wanted no part of. She'd done enough.

Kurt Raeder was finally dead.

Jake hadn't fired at her. She'd heard him running, shouting, but not shooting. Was there a glimmer of feeling there? Or was it too dangerous down here to shoot? In any event, there was only one bike. Now she pedaled madly away in the red glow of emergency lighting, lungs heaving, terrified and exultant, leaving him behind.

Where was everybody? Why was she the only one down here?

Then she remembered Raeder had said something about radiation, and Barrow had prudently retreated.

Was the radiation gone, now that the power had blacked out?

Or was she irreversibly poisoning herself?

I just have to live long enough to hide, Rominy thought. She'd sneak through the woods like an animal, not chancing a meeting with anyone, afraid of her own shadow, staff in hand. Then, if she could find Lake Geneva, she'd hurl the cursed thing into the deepest part and let it sink like Excalibur, drowned like the rest of Shambhala.

Then she could finally grieve, for an identity and a past in tatters.

The tunnel debouched into another large machine like the one where she'd descended, another temple of physics painted in brilliant colors. She considered ascending to the surface there. But it seemed too close to the battle behind her, and too close to Jake Barrow. Balconies led her past it and onward to the tunnel on its far side. Particle detectors seemed to be spaced every few miles. She'd try the next one.

It felt good just to pedal and flee.

The tunnel was lit the color of hell, Klaxons blaring in the distance, pipes extending to infinity. She'd entered the mythical underworld.

Mile followed mile.

She was gasping now, as weary and sore as she'd ever been, and her bicycle slowed. Surely Jake was far behind. The opposite side of the ring would be, what, nine miles away? Less as the crow flies, but any farther would just bring her around and closer to the Nazis again. Could she guess how far that was? As she rode she noticed that blue lights in red boxes gave a flash as she passed them, and they seemed spaced about every half mile. Say eight miles . . . how many had flashed? Ten, perhaps, or five miles. When she got anywhere close to sixteen and there was a way up, she'd try that.

And after Lake Geneva? She had no money, no passport, no clothes, and no friends. Sam was probably dying. The police, perhaps. But who knew how many millions of dollars of damage she and Sam had caused or deaths they'd initiated? Would the authorities be in on the conspiracy, too? Yet prison, if it came to that, seemed a snug refuge right now. Or would they just take her into a courtyard and shoot her, like in the movies?

Or put her in a cell with Nazis?

Another blue flash.

It came on only when she whizzed by.

Was her passage triggering the lights? She looked down. The bicycle had a small metal box attached with two screws to its frame. It was blinking, too.

Like a beacon. An airplane transponder. An ankle bracelet.

Oh, no.

The blue lights were tracking her.

Up on the surface, Kurt Raeder's Mercedes screeched to a halt at the Compact Muon Solenoid detector, at the far side of the collider ring. Ursula Kalb had driven like a madwoman to let Jakob get ahead of Rominy and descend to cut the American off. Now he leaped from the passenger seat and leaned in for final instructions.

"Our second *Führer* is dead, but the staff has been energized. We're going to have to start over, Ursula, but we'll be able to demonstrate its potential for key allies. We'll have more powerful backers than ever."

"If you can get the staff from the girl." Even from here they could hear sirens. The burning propane tanks threw lurid light into the sky. Police lights blinked from the Atlas complex and they could hear the rattle of gunfire. The Nazi plan had turned into a disaster, but she didn't say that. Her life, her love, had turned into disaster, too, but she didn't say that, either.

"The cause is not lost," Jakob said. "Trust me, Rominy still has feelings for the man she knows as Jake. I'll persuade her. I'll subdue her. And when I come back to the surface with the staff we'll go into hiding to reorganize."

"You must kill the American girl."

"No. She's still a breeder."

Kalb looked out the windshield with gloom.

"Wait for me. I won't be long."

"If you are, I *won't* wait."

"Understood. If I don't return . . ."

Ursula nodded. "I have the cyanide."

She watched him jog toward the CMS detector building. As he entered to take the elevator underground, a helicopter roared over the Mercedes, stabbing the grounds with a searchlight.

Ursula Kalb looked up. Kurt had moved too fast, with insufficient preparation, and had refused to listen to her caution. The staff's recovery had excited him too much. She admired his keenness, but it had eroded his discipline. The night was another Stalingrad. Now, catastrophically, her lover was gone. So as soon as the door closed behind the young believer, she lowered the window and pitched out the poison pills and her Fellowship identification. She didn't want to have to answer awkward questions if stopped.

Yes, they would start again. But not with a damned American girl bred to Kurt Raeder.

Ursula didn't think Jakob would emerge. Police were converging. So she put the car in gear and began driving, at the exact speed limit, away from the collider. She had prepared a safe house on the Amalfi coast and by dawn she could be in Italy. She touched the leather. It was a very fine Mercedes.

But Ursula Kalb did not intend to leave Geneva just yet. There was a blood debt to be answered.

Rominy realized the Nazis knew where she was.

She slowed the bicycle, wondering what to do. And then, as she coasted toward the next junction point, someone was standing in her way. The figure was still but alert, poised, like a gunfighter. She felt sick, stupid, trapped.

It was Jake. Somehow he'd gotten ahead of her.

Her concentration lost, her bike wheel wobbled. It glanced off the pipe in the narrow walkway and suddenly she lost control. Her tire hit a flange and she cartwheeled over the handlebars, landing hard and skinning her knees.

Just like in the Safeway parking lot.

The staff clattered down next to her.

Wincing, she boosted herself up on her arms, glaring ahead at Jake. This was the bastard who'd arranged to have her MINI Cooper, thirty-nine payments still outstanding, blown into scrap metal. Who'd lied to her, imprisoned her, handcuffed her, and seduced her with his remorseless cunning. And now he was smiling in triumph.

"It's over, Rominy," he called. "My men are behind you, too. You can't escape, because we still need that shaft. This isn't what we wanted to happen for you or Kurt. But now we're left to carry on the quest. You and me."

"For the master race."

"For world harmony, with all pollutants finally eradicated." He aimed a pistol at her. "I'd hoped you'd be our queen by now."

"You are *so* sick."

He shook his head. "Idealistic. Give me the shaft." He stayed a cautious thirty feet away, the automatic pointed. "I *will* shoot you if I have to."

"You think you can hide from the police after this fiasco?"

"Rominy, we *are* the police."

She rocked back on her heels and painfully stood up. "At least I don't have to be raped by my great-grandfather."

"Yes, we'll have to find another Adam and Eve. The shaft, please."

She picked it up. The material was smooth and warm, a cross between plastic and carbon fiber, and she wondered what it was made of. It tingled when she touched it, vibrating slightly, and the glow it gave off was weirdly beautiful, even hypnotic. "I was really falling in love with you, Jake."

He nodded. "It was for your own good."

Just beyond him, near where the tunnel joined the next connector point and detector, there was a small blue tank. Hoses led to a white pipe that ran next to the tunnel's large blue pipe, and more pipes connected the two. Couplings were white with frost. Something very cold was in there. Lettering on the tank said HE.

He? Who? But no, what did that mean? Something tickled from chemistry course work with the periodic table. Rominy retained more science than this man gave her credit for, and she longed for something terrible to match her own coldness.

Liquid helium, she recalled, was very, very cold.

She pointed the staff at Jake Barrow.

"Careful with that!" Jake warned. "Don't make me shoot you." She realized he was nervous. She finally had a weapon. Had it received enough charge from the . . . what had Raeder called it? A proton beam? She took courage from Jake's fright.

"Don't make me shoot *you*. Put your pistol down, Jake."

"Rominy, we don't have time for this."

"Let's take time with the authorities. Your police and mine. Let's talk this out in an interrogation room somewhere."

"I know you're rattled. It's understandable. But what you're holding is very, very dangerous. Please lower the tip before you hurt yourself."

"If you lower the gun, Jake."

He hesitated, thinking. "How can I trust you?"

She gasped. "How can *you* trust *me*?"

He lowered his pistol barrel slightly. "Okay, I'm moving my aim. You do the same. We need to talk, Rominy. Talk and think about the future."

She began aiming the shaft to one side. "Keep your gun down, Jake. I'm very jumpy."

"Me, too. Don't point that rod at me."

"It's aimed at the wall." Aimed at that tank that said HE. How did her weapon work? How *could* it work? There was no trigger, no switch.

"We're pioneers of science," Jake said. "Right here. Right now."

How she longed that the Vril staff *would* zap that creepy bastard! So she poured all of her hatred of Jake Barrow into the core of her being, infusing her very soul, and let it pour down her arm and into her hand, and from her hand to the shaft. She *wished*, with her consciousness, for it to destroy that helium tank.

"It's not too late for you and me to make utopia," Jake tried.

Suddenly she experienced unity, but not the warm feeling of brotherhood she'd experienced on a Kunlun mountain. This was a link to something vastly darker and frighteningly powerful, terrifying and wonderful, a momentary glimpse of a universe of strange matter and different energies that had always been invisible. Rominy *saw*.

"It's not too late to join us. Join *me*."

And with that something leaped with her thoughts to the helium tank, like a subatomic particle jumping from one point to another with no intervening travel.

There was an explosion, a corona of sparks, and electricity arced into a mini-sun that dazzled her. The tank blew apart.

Air flashed into snow.

The staff hurt! It kicked her hand and arm so hard that she lost her grip and flew backward. As if with a mind of its own, the staff recoiled in the other direction, toward Barrow and the haze rushing from the pipes. Rominy fell to the floor and skidded, simultaneously fearing his gun, the sparks, the cold, and the vast energies she'd glimpsed. She watched, horrified, as the staff came near him. But, no, he'd been paralyzed by the burst of helium as the liquid flashed to gas, and obscured by the bits of ice suddenly filling the wickedly frigid air, every droplet of water vapor in the tunnel having instantly turned to ice. Liquid helium with a temperature at nearly absolute zero erupted from the broken tank and turned to a fog that rolled along the ceiling.

Rominy crawled in terror, trying to hold her breath. The cold punched her, puffing past, so empty that her lungs ached. But at floor level she could gasp a feeble breath. She looked back to watch as the shaft fell through the fog of expanding helium.

Thirty feet away, Jake was looking at her in disbelief. The helium had displaced the oxygen in the air and all he could suck into his lungs was frigid gas. There was nothing he could breathe. His eyes were wide and desperate. His hands had hooked into claws, instantly frostbitten. His joints had gone rigid.

His lungs flash froze and cracked.

It was as if he'd become a statue, a man turned to stone.

And then the staff of Shambhala, its light gone now since Rominy's explosive thought, fell through the freezing fog and turned brittle. When it hit the concrete floor, it shattered.

The rod disintegrated into a thousand pieces of dusty glass.

Jake toppled, his eyes wide and sorrowful.

And the mist swirled on, snow falling, walls coated with frost. Rominy was covered with rime, too. She slithered on her belly to get away.

There was a box ahead with an oxygen mask.

More alarms were going off, and there were shouts. Then she reached, grabbed rubber, and pulled it to her face. She shuddered from the icy envelopment.

And blacked out.

56

Geneva, Switzerland
October 17, Present Day

The Cantonal Hospital of the University of Geneva kept Rominy and Sam apart for two weeks. She healed from cold burns and bruises, and he battled for his life. Tests were run, questions asked. Police, American embassy personnel, officials from CERN, and physicists all interviewed her, some coaxing, some cruel, some sympathetic, and all suspicious. The neo-Nazis had apparently died or disappeared. So, officials asked, what were they after? Why had they taken over a particle accelerator? *How* had they taken over?

Rominy put the same questions back to her interrogators.

She trusted no one anymore. *We are the police.* She told the authorities that she and Sam were dumb tourists who'd stumbled onto a group of fanatics at Wewelsburg Castle while trying to poke about the SS shrine after hours. It had been a foolish lark that resulted in being taken hostage. Sam had gotten away and helped rescue her. There hadn't been time to call the police, so he'd heroically started a fire and nearly died fighting her captor.

"And how did you and Mr. Mackenzie meet, miss?"

"In Tibet. He was a guide. We hit it off."

"Chinese records show you had permits to go toward the Kunlun Mountains. That's a very unusual destination at the beginning of autumn."

"It was silly. We never got there."

"But you were with another gentleman, a Mr. Barrow? Traveling under a false passport as Mr. and Mrs. Anderson?"

"He was in a hurry to get to China. Jake and I broke up."

"And what became of Mr. Barrow?"

"I have no idea."

"And you turned to Mr. Mackenzie?"

"As a friend. The Tibetan tourist season was ending. We decided Europe would be restful." She laughed, and then coughed. The damage to her lungs would heal with time, doctors said.

"Was Sam Mackenzie your lover?"

"That's a rather personal question, isn't it?"

"He seemed unusually motivated to rescue you."

"We rescued each other."

"We're just trying to understand, Ms. Pickett."

"Am I under arrest or something?"

"No."

"Then I think I'll keep my love life to myself."

Once she'd woken in the hospital she realized no one would tell her the entirety of what had happened at the supercollider or who the conspirators were. They didn't want the world to know Nazis had invaded a scientific temple. They didn't want to reveal—or perhaps they didn't know—what The Fellowship was after.

So she began to piece together where she was and what had happened from memory, comments from her interrogators, and snippets of news, while guarding what she remembered like a Chinese gold coin. How could she be certain what side anybody was on?

There was another reason for being coy: she was tired of this madness and simply wanted to disappear, as Beth Calloway had disappeared three generations before. The helium breach? No idea how it occurred. The frozen corpse? No idea who the victim was; she'd been fleeing the chaos when a man appeared and an explosion occurred. The oddly aged old man cut almost in two by a beam of subatomic protons before the collider shut down? Another Nazi nut, she guessed. He'd certainly looked *strange*.

Her own presence at CERN?

"They said I'd be a bargaining chip in case they got cornered. I don't remember much else. I was terrified and confused." That was true enough.

"You have a nasty scar on the palm of your hand."

"A pocket-knife accident. We were camping in Tibet."

And the glassy staff fragments on the tunnel floor? Intriguingly, no one mentioned them. She didn't either. But she wondered if somewhere, somehow, laboratory tests were being done.

Or if some janitor had swept them into a dustbin, sending the secret texture of the universe to a landfill.

Would authorities eventually find the same old records on her family that Jake Barrow had? Would somebody, someday, come after her again?

Would she live in fear the rest of her life?

Rominy had seen a brief press report in the *International Herald Tribune*.

GENEVA—Attempts by the European Nuclear Agency, or CERN, to reach full-power operation of its Large Hadron Collider (LHC) here were dealt a serious setback Tuesday when an electrical arc from a faulty bus bar broke a tank of liquid helium.

The accident killed eleven CERN employees and will likely shut down the facility for months, if not longer.

"Repairs could take a full year," said Franklin Rutherford, the American operations manager for the international consortium operating the machine. "The damage is quite extensive and we want to make sure we identify the causes so there won't be a repeat of this terrible industrial tragedy. As you can imagine, it's been quite stressful for all of us at CERN."

A faulty connection in superconducting magnets caused a similar delay at the LHC in late 2008.

Asked if there was a fundamental design flaw in the supercollider, Rutherford replied, "I think we've just had a run of bad luck. These are very complex machines, and every collider has start-up pains."

Witnesses said there was a surface explosion at the LHC and even reports of gunfire, but Rutherford said laymen had mistaken "an auto accident and a mechanical issue for something more dramatic. I'm afraid we've just had a problem with our plumbing. After a thorough safety review, we still expect to reach our goal of 7 trillion electron volts sometime next year."

The 27-kilometer supercollider, largest in the world, uses such energies to break apart subatomic particles. Scientists hope to learn the answers to such fundamental questions as how the universe was created and why matter exists at all.

The story suited Rominy. The last thing she wanted was a press conference or paparazzi. She was alive and Sam was supposedly alive, and Jake and Raeder were dead. That was science miracle enough.

The neo-Nazis had disappeared like helium mist. For the first few nights she had nightmares of them peering in her hospital window, like the skinhead Otto Nietzel. But no, not a whisper, not an arrest, not a threat. No story of a dead skinhead at Wewelsburg Castle. Even the police seemed reluctant to probe too deeply into the disruption.

We are *the police.*

When she asked to see Sam, they put her off. "When he's better, we will discuss a visit," doctors told her.

And, "Before we can release *you*, we need more tests."

They took blood samples several times. Her arms and fingers ached from the punctures.

There was an unsettling blankness about some of the physicians who looked at her, seeing her without seeing her. She was an isolated specimen: a private room, a door that automatically locked with its latch on the corridor side, and no word from America. There was no telephone. Television was set to a single French entertainment channel she asked be shut off.

Surely she wasn't a prisoner. Was she? "Where are my clothes?"

"We have them in storage."

"Where's the locker?"

"In a safe place."

"Did you find my money or passport?"

"Your hospital bills are being covered. Rest, please."

From her bed she could look out at autumn leaves blowing down from Geneva's trees, with the gray lake beyond. She waited for release, but none came. She waited for information, but that didn't come either.

"Rest, rest. Tomorrow, we take more blood."

She felt groggy. Were they drugging her?

Why was she always waiting for someone else to act? She waited for Sam.

"He is recuperating."

One of the nurses carried a smartphone in her white coat pocket, pink as lipstick. Rominy finally complained of fever, the woman leaned in to take her temperature, and the phone slipped into Rominy's slyly reaching hand, slick and palm-sized. She tucked it under a blanket.

The nurse read the digital readout, touched Rominy's forehead, and grunted. "No fever." She peered at her ward suspiciously, as if impatient with malingerers.

Rominy shrugged. "Some aspirin, s'il vous plaît?"

"*Oui.*" The reply was grumpy. The nurse strode off, rubber soles squeaking.

The hospital was listed on the nurse's "favorites" list on the cell phone. Rominy dialed, asked for the nurses' station, and began, "Do you speak English?"

"*Oui.* Yes."

"Melissa Jenkins here, from the American embassy. I have some papers for patient Sam Mackenzie but he's not on the floor where I thought. Young American?"

"A minute." Rustle of papers. "Five-one-seven. Is not correct?"

"Ah, I had it wrong. *Merci.*" She hung up and deleted the record of the call.

The nurse came back with aspirin. "Have you seen my cell phone?"

Rominy shook her head. "Did it fall out?"

The nurse found the device under a stainless trolley. While she bent to retrieve it, Rominy tore several pages from her lab-slip tablet. The nurse straightened to glare at her patient, but the American was innocently taking aspirin. When the woman pocketed her phone and went out, Rominy jumped from the bed and caught the door just before it closed. She inserted the paper she'd stolen in the jamb, preventing the latch from locking.

Later that night, hospital sounds a murmur, machines beeping, she slid out of bed, opened the door, checked that no one was watching, slipped into the corridor, and padded furtively down the hallway, her gown held tight around her. Peeking in rooms, she found a deserted nurses' changing station and pilfered a uniform, bundling her hospital gown with its clipped identity tag under her arm.

After killing her former lover with liquid helium, confiscating clothes seemed a minor sin.

She changed into the white belted dress in a restroom stall, ascended an elevator, and took a man's clothes from a drugged and sleeping patient, lifting them from his closet. Those would be for Sam.

Then she set out to find Mackenzie. Maybe it was time for *her* to rescue *him*.

57

Geneva, Switzerland
October 18, Present Day

Sam was still bedridden but awake at two A.M., leaner and better-looking for it. His face had matured in a way that flattered him. He looked at her with surprised delight when she slipped in.

"Rominy! Didn't have the sense to ditch me, girl?" He was propped up on pillows, watching all-night French TV with the sound off.

"Don't you sleep?"

"That's all I've done for two weeks."

She glanced at the television. "How can you tell what's going on?"

"I just wait for the ads. They're sexier than ours."

"So you *are* feeling better."

"Oh yeah. I couldn't feel any worse, not after getting a jolt that's the equivalent of grasping a power line." Then he squinted at her nurse's garb. "What the hell?"

She put her fingers to her lips. "I'm getting us out of here."

"Why?"

"I'm tired of being poked. I don't trust them."

He grasped her hand, tight as a knot. "Me neither. They ask a million questions and don't answer a one."

"Are you well enough to move?"

"Healthier than Kurt Raeder."

"You got him, Sam, when you broke that pipe."

"I'm told the proton beam is directed by magnets. When I knocked some askew, the beam went wide just long enough to slice the bastard. It was like a microscopic knife cutting through his chest. His heart exploded."

"The beam only persisted one second before a circuit blew."

"Best second of my life."

"Do you feel guilty?"

"Are you kidding? The guy lived way past a hundred. I should be so lucky."

She shook her head. "Did you know Raeder was planning to have sex with me?"

"You're joking."

"He also told me DNA proved I'm his great-granddaughter."

"What!"

"He raped Keyuri way back in 1938. It wasn't Hood. It was Raeder who made the baby."

"Oh, Rominy. Man, I'm sorry. This is sick. Those guys were animals. And Jake, what a dirtbag. We're not all like that, trust me."

She sat on his bed. "I know guys aren't all like that, Sam. But I don't think my grocery aisle method works very well."

"Your what?"

"I'll explain someday. I just wish it hadn't gone so far with Jake."

"I heard you ended *that* relationship rather emphatically as well."

"Yes." She looked sad. "I don't regret it . . . but it's not easy to kill someone, Sam."

"Just remember, it would have been easy for *him* to kill *you*."

She nodded, but she wondered if that was true. She hoped not, even after all that had happened. Emotions don't conveniently evaporate, they just burn holes and leave scars.

He raised an eyebrow. "Well, are *we* still friends?"

"Sam, you almost died saving my life."

"I just half saved it. You finished off Barrow."

"And the staff shattered. Odd that no one mentions it."

"Not odd. Predictable. You can bet there's a lot they're not telling us, just like we're not telling them. You don't take over a seventeen-mile doughnut without a lot of inside help. You don't get away with having nothing in the media unless the big dogs have all pledged not to bark. Can you spell 'conspiracy'?"

"They don't believe me any more than I believe them."

"Then that's it." He took her other hand. "Over. *Fini*. Kaput. We beat the bad guys, Rominy, at least the ones we could identify. End of story, for us. The cops say they can't find *any* surviving neo-Nazis. Yeah, right. The physicists claim everyone on their team is clean. It's like the whole thing never happened."

"Almost." She looked away from him, staring at nothing. "I had to play-act to find you. I broke out of my room. Snuck through corridors. Are we prisoners?"

"Let's find out."

"What if Nazis are still out there?"

"There's no magic staff. There's no Shambhala, unless we spill the beans and somebody drains that lake. No Vril, unless scientists rediscover it on their own. No more blood locks, unless there's one nobody told us about. Nobody needs us anymore. This is where we live happily after. Right?"

"I hope."

He looked at her worriedly. "What's bugging you, girl? I want to go home with you, and maybe finish my degree."

She knew he wanted to be more than just friends someday after all they'd gone through together. And so she shivered, remembering the tender touch of Jake Barrow. And the warning of Delphina Clarkson, or was it Ursula Kalb? *Stay away from men, that's my advice.*

No woman's body had been reported among the casualties.

So Rominy was taking relationship advice from a Nazi now?

"I hope we really can get away, Sam. Stolen clothes, no passports, no money."

"Trust your tourist guide. It just so happens I stashed our spare clothes, papers, and cash in a cubbyhole. If we can sneak out to the collider site before dawn, we can retrieve enough stuff from a manhole to keep going. We'll look for a red-eye to America, with cheap seats and cranky stews."

She smiled. Hope came from action. "Will it work?"

"If we hurry."

And then came a rap on the door. "Herr Mackenzie? Medication time."

"Ah, crap," he muttered. "Now? I'm already dopier than a big league ballplayer."

"She'll report me!" Rominy hissed.

He pointed. "Get under the bed."

She slid under on slick linoleum, feeling absurd, and peered out as a German-speaking nurse entered. There was a clack of heels, not rubber soles. No blaze of room light. Just a click, like a door locking. Footsteps to the window to close the blinds. A blue plastic bucket set on the floor.

Rominy listened to them talk.

"I'm not scheduled for medication, nurse."

"I heard talking. You alone, Herr Mackenzie?"

"You heard the TV."

"I help you sleep, I think."

"I sleep too much already."

"Doctor orders."

Her voice was oddly muffled. Rominy felt trapped.

"What's the bucket for?" Sam asked. "And why the face mask?"

"I have cold. Here, antiseptic cloth."

"It stinks. Hey!" He jerked.

"Relax, no? Take away pain."

Sam thrashed, then slowly stilled. Silence. The nurse seemed to be waiting, bent over the bed. No one else had entered the room. What was going on? If Rominy revealed herself, there'd be an uproar. She'd just have to wait it out. Of all the bad luck.

Or was it bad luck? Why had this nurse come in the middle of the night, right after Rominy had entered Sam's room for the first time in two weeks? Had this medical worker been *waiting* for Rominy to come? The American had finally left the protection of her own locked room. Slipped through the hospital without escort. Not encountered another soul. Had someone followed? And locked her in here? Closing the blinds, leaving the lights dim?

The silent TV strobed with dim light.

Rominy peered out. An IV pole being wheeled to Sam's bed. Mackenzie had gone silent, which was hardly characteristic. Was he drugged?

"It's all about blood," the nurse murmured. A loop of plastic tubing drooped.

Twisting, Rominy looked out at the nurse's ankles.

She was wearing low leather pumps.

The American's heart began hammering. Liquid began pattering into the plastic bucket. She twisted to see. Now the tube was red.

"We keep, just in case," the nurse murmured.

Keep it for what? Lost cities and secret doors? Something was terribly wrong. Could she bolt for the door? She shifted to crawl out from the far side of the bed.

And suddenly a grip as hard as Prussian iron seized Rominy's ankle and she was jerked out from under

Sam's mattress like a rag doll, spinning on the floor. The strength and violence of it was shocking, yet sickeningly familiar. A woman in a nurse's dress similar to Rominy's clamped the ankle of the American like a vise, eyes malevolent, mouth covered by a gauze mask.

"You think I let you go, little mouse?" the nurse said. "I listened to your breathing like a cat."

The woman had a cloth in her hand that smelled of some kind of ether or chloroform. Rominy twisted and kicked, flopping like a fish.

"I have been waiting. Waiting for reunion." It was the voice of Delphina Clarkson, or rather Ursula Kalb. "You think you can have your blood if we can't, American witch?"

For one terrible moment, Rominy felt paralyzed. Fear froze her. Panic turned her mind blank. Then that voice again, that ghost she'd heard at the supercollider. *So what have you learned?*

Fight!

Rominy lashed out with her other leg and struck the side of the woman's knee. Kalb shrieked as the leg bent and then toppled, cursing in German. The Nazi scrabbled toward her, mask askew, and tried to get a cloth to Rominy's face. The American pivoted on the floor like a demented break-dancer, kicking and punching. She hit the blue pail and it went over, spilling blood that made a crimson fan across the linoleum. Ursula fumbled under her jacket and brought out a gun with a sausage-fat silencer. "Stay still!" she hissed. "Or I shoot!"

Rominy seized the base of the IV pole and hurled it at their tormentor. On the bed one of Sam's arms jerked as an IV needle pulled out, the needle and its medical tape writhing at the end of its tubing. There was an arc of blood spatter across the walls of the room, while the crimson on the floor spread like an oil slick. A *phhttt* as a silenced bullet went by, whapping into a wall, but the distraction of the fallen pole had worked to make the Nazi miss. Kalb reared up on one leg to take better aim. Rominy flung the bucket at her and lunged.

The German shrieked as she was peppered with droplets of Sam's blood, slapping the bucket away. "Filth!" she roared.

Then Rominy dove into her as the German fired again, the bullet shredding air next to the American's ear. Ursula fell hard, grunting, her gauze mask ripped away. They rolled in the blood, the German's eyes wide with terror and hatred. A trolley and a chair crashed. They lurched upright, clawing, and wrestled against the window and its blinds. Then they slipped in blood and went down again with grunts.

"You killed my lover!" Ursula screamed.

My God, which one? Jake, or the hideous Kurt Raeder?

"He wanted your genes! Now I kill *you*!"

They were fighting for the gun. Another shot, somewhere into the ceiling. Would anyone ever come? Or had hospital personnel agreed to leave the corridor outside Sam's room empty while The Fellowship struck back? How deep was the conspiracy?

The German woman was immensely strong. She was twisting her gun wrist out of Rominy's grasp, getting ready for a final shot.

"So we'll get your blood *this* way! I'll drain you into that pail!"

Rominy's other hand was scrabbling. It closed on a cloth and she realized it must be the anesthetic. She swung and slapped it over Ursula's mouth.

The German writhed like a snake as Rominy clamped her nose. More shots thudded into the wallboard, each puncture puffing a geyser of powder. Ursula kicked, her yells muffled. The women twisted across the floor in demented embrace, soaked and straining.

Finally, the pistol fell with a thud. Kalb's movements slowed, becoming feeble. Then, she stilled completely.

The monster was unconscious.

Rominy shakily stood, leaving the cloth over the German's mouth. She scooped up the pistol, trembling but efficient, functioning now with grim determination. The pistol was an automatic with trigger, hammer, and a safety, she saw. Should she shoot? A quick execution of an impostor and murderess?

No. There was more fitting revenge.

Rominy tucked the weapon in the white belt of her bloody uniform. Who knew when some skinheads might burst through the door? She wouldn't hesitate to fire if they did. Her days of being squeamish about firearms were over.

"This ends, *now*."

She went to Sam. His arm was bleeding where the IV draining his blood had been, but he was still breathing, thank God. When would the ether wear off?

She found some gauze from the toppled trolley and bandaged his arm. Then, straining, Rominy pulled and yanked Sam to the edge of the bed. She dragged Kalb's unconscious body and heaved her up beside him, making an unholy couple.

"It's just for a minute, Sam," she whispered.

She took a breath. Then, groaning as she bent, she picked up the IV stand and wheeled it to the bed. She wasn't sure how to find a vein, so just started jabbing in Kalb's wrist, waiting after each stab for blood to come out. When the flow started, she inserted the tubing and let it empty into the blue bucket. The receptacle began to fill with plasma, dark and thick.

"Why wouldn't you leave me alone?"

Rominy found a bottle of anesthesia that Kalb had brought and, shielding her own face with a towel, renewed the cloth. Then she put it back on the German's mouth, the mere fumes making her dizzy.

The German grimaced and breathed them in.

Shuddering from adrenaline, Rominy staggered to the door, unlocked it, and peered out into the corridor. It was still deserted. Staff had been ordered to stay away. She wiped her feet on the towel she'd used to shield her face from the ether and slipped out, pistol in hand.

No one. She found a gurney and wheeled it back, awkwardly rolling Sam onto the bed. He muttered, which she took to be a good sign. Then she unclipped her hospital identification bracelet and taped it back together on Ursula's wrist, and fastened her hospital gown tag to the Nazi's collar. It was time to disappear.

"Rominy Pickett, rest in peace." It might buy them a little time.

The woman's complexion had gone chalk white, her eyes staring. Was she breathing? Rominy bent close, holding her breath against the anesthetic.

No.

She felt only cold relief.

The last dribbles of blood were pooling in the plastic pail. What kind of hideous mind would still want Rominy's blood, after all the catastrophes it had caused?

She spread the towel out by the door so it would soak up any carnage on the gurney wheels. Sam's hospital room looked like a slaughterhouse, the floor smeared scarlet, bullet holes in walls and ceiling, furniture toppled, blinds askew.

Then she pushed Sam into the hallway and let the door close behind her. It clicked, lock fastening. She threw a sheet over her guide to hide his identity and wheeled toward the elevator. At a desk she saw a lab coat draped on the back of a chair and put it over her own bloody clothes, sticky and stiff. She still had the male street clothes for Mackenzie, and they'd fetch replacements at his "cubbyhole" at the super-collider.

He was moaning, waking up. The elevator gonged and she pushed him in, selecting a button for the basement. She pulled the pistol out and set it on the gurney near Sam's head, in case someone tried to stop them. "Wake up, Mackenzie!" Her voice was sharp. She slapped him, hard.

He blinked. "Rominy?"

At every floor she expected the elevator to stop, and was prepared to use the gun to bluff if she needed to. But instead the conveyance sank smoothly to the basement. A blank corridor, rumbling generators, a sign with a symbol for cars. She pushed ahead, went through double doors, spied a ramp, and with a running start pushed Sam up into a courtyard where a few privileged autos were parked. The air was sharp and tangy after the hospital stink, washed clean of all corruption.

She was trembling with excitement and exhaustion. No strangers would ever take blood from her again.

Sam hoisted his head woozily. "Where are we, girl?"

"Out. Can you sit?"

"Maybe. I feel light-headed."

"We had to leave a lot of you behind."

He sat up, swaying. "What happened?"

She glanced up and around, most windows dark, an archway leading to the world beyond. "We chose to be brave, I guess." She thrust the stolen clothes at him. "Put some pants on, Sam Mackenzie. We're going home."

Acknowledgments

This novel draws from a large number of written sources. Those interested in the historical background of an actual 1938 Nazi expedition to Tibet might enjoy *Himmler's Crusade* by Christopher Hale, first published in the United Kingdom in 2003. It was an insightful resource for my fiction. An edited photographic account is *Tibet in 1938–1939* by Isrun Englehardt. The novel that inspired later Nazi theorists was *Vril, The Power of the Coming Race*, written by Sir Edward Bulwer-Lytton in 1871. I also drew on a large number of popular science books describing string theory and its overarching M-theory about the makeup of the universe.

When visiting Tibet I benefited from the insights of Tibetan guide Ugyen Kyab and traveling companions

Marc Stoelinga of the Netherlands and Johan Willemse and Sherine Geusens of Belgium. The Buddhist nunnery at Sakya offered shelter from a Himalayan storm and gave new direction to my imagination.

Special thanks goes to Katie Yurkewicz, a physicist with Fermilab stationed at the CERN Large Hadron Collider in Geneva, for documents, photographs, and patient exploration of ways to dispatch the bad guys. She gets credit for anything that is right; the deliberate fictions are my own.

And once again I'm indebted to the astute advice of HarperCollins publisher Jonathan Burnham, editor Rakesh Satyal, copy editor Muriel Jorgensen, designer Renato Stanisic, publicist Heather Drucker, my agent Andrew Stuart, and first reader Holly, my wife. While I played with superstrings, they coached me to strike the right chord.

HARPER LUXE

THE NEW LUXURY IN READING

We hope you enjoyed reading
our new, comfortable print size and found it
an experience you would like to repeat.

Well — you're in luck!

HarperLuxe offers the finest in fiction and
nonfiction books in this same larger print size and
paperback format. Light and easy to read, HarperLuxe
paperbacks are for book lovers who want to see
what they are reading without the strain.

For a full listing of titles and
new releases to come, please visit our website:

www.HarperLuxe.com